DEATH FROM THE FOURTH DIMENSION

The "Gizmo"—the secret device that instantly transported men and objects to and from any point in the Universe—dropped the six killers into Seaton's dining room. Their guns blasted once—and before they could fire again, all were dead, as the lightning-fast reflexes of the *Skylark's* crew went into lethal action.

The attack had failed—but the wail of warning sirens filled the ship! Weapons of undreamed-of power were hitting the *Skylark*—and the defense screens could hold out for only seconds more!

Novels of science-fiction

by

"DOC" SMITH

●

SKYLARK DUQUESNE

E. E. "DOC" SMITH

PYRAMID BOOKS NEW YORK

SKYLARK DUQUESNE

A PYRAMID BOOK
Published by arrangement with Jeannie M. Smith

Pyramid edition published November, 1966

Copyright 1965 by Galaxy Publications Corporation, for **Worlds of Science Fiction**

Printed in the United States of America

PYRAMID BOOKS are published by Pyramid Publications, Inc.
444 Madison Avenue, New York, New York 10022, U.S.A.

TABLE OF CONTENTS

1 · S.O.S.

APPEARANCES are deceiving. A polished chunk of metal that shines like a Christmas-tree ornament may hold—and release—energy to destroy a city. A seed is quite another order of being to the murderous majesty of a toppling tree. A match flame can become a holocaust.

And the chain of events that can unseat the rulers of galaxies can begin in a cozy living room, before a hearth. . . .

Outwardly, the comfortable (if somewhat splendidly furnished) living room of the home of the Richard Ballinger Seatons of Earth presented a peaceful scene. Peaceful? It was sheerly pastoral! Seaton and Dorothy, his spectacularly auburn-haired wife, sat on a davenport, holding hands. A fire of pine logs burned slowly, crackling occasionally and sending sparks against the fine bronze screen of the fireplace. Richard Ballinger Seaton Junior lay on the rug, trying doggedly, silently, and manfully, if unsuccessfully, to wriggle toward those entrancing flames.

Inwardly, however, it was very much otherwise. Dorothy's normally pleasant—as well as beautiful—face wore a veritable scowl.

The dinner they had just eaten had been over two hours late; wherefore not one single item of it had been fit to feed to a pig. Furthermore, and worse, Dick was not relaxed and was not paying any attention to her at all. He was still wound up tight; was still concentrating on the multitude of messages driving into his brain through the button in his left ear—messages of such urgency of drive that she herself could actually read them, even though she was wearing no apparatus whatever.

She reached up, twitched the button out of his ear, and tossed it onto a table. "Will you please lay off of that stuff for a minute, Dick?" she demanded. "I'm fed up to the eyeballs with this business of you killing yourself with all time work and no time sleep. You *never* had any such horrible

7

black circles under your eyes before and you're getting positively *scrawny*. You've got to quit it. Can't you let somebody else carry some of the load? Delegate some authority?"

"I'm delegating all I possibly can already, Red-Top." Seaton absently rubbed his ear. Until Dorothy had flipped it away, the button had been carrying to him a transcription of the taped reports of more than one hundred Planetary Observers from the planet of Norlamin, each with the IQ of an Einstein and the sagacity of an owl. The last report had had to do with plentiful supplies of X metal that had been turned up on a planet of Omicron Eridani, and the decision to dispatch a fleet of cargo-carrying ships to fetch them away.

But he admitted grudgingly to himself that that particular decision had already been made. His wife was a nearer problem. Paying full attention to her now, he put his arm around her and squeezed.

"Converting a whole planet practically all at once to use fourth-, fifth-, and sixth-order stuff is a job of work, believe me. It's all so new and so tough that not too many people can handle any part of it. It takes brains. And what makes it extra tough is that altogether too many people who are smart enough to learn it are crooks. Shysters—hoodlers—sticky-fingers generally. But I think we're just about over the hump. I wouldn't wonder if these Norlaminian 'Observers'—snoopers, really—from the Country of Youth will turn out to be the answer to prayer."

"They'd better," she said, darkly. "At least, *something* had better."

"Besides, if you think I look like the wrath of God, take a good look at Mart sometime. He's having more grief than I am."

"I already have; he looks like a refugee from a concentration camp. Peggy was screaming about it this morning, and we're both going to just simply . . ."

What the girls intended to do was not revealed, for at that moment there appeared in the air before them the projected simulacra of eight green-skinned, more-or-less-human men; the men with whom they had worked so long; the ablest thinkers of the Central System.

There was majestic Fodan, the Chief of the Five of Norlamin; there was white-bearded Orlon, the First of Astronomy; Rovol, the First of Rays; Astron, the First of Energy; Drasnik, the First of Psychology; Satrazon and

Caslor, the Firsts of Chemistry and of Mechanism, respectively; and—in some ways not the least—there was that powerhouse of thought, Sacner Carfon the two thousand three hundred forty-sixth: the hairless, almost porpoise-like Chief of the Council of the watery planet Dasor. They were not present in the flesh. But their energy projections were as seemingly solid as Seaton's own tall, lean body.

"We come, Overlord of the System, upon a matter of—" the Chief of the Five began.

"*Don't* call me 'Overlord'. Please." Seaton broke in, with grim foreboding in his eyes, while Dorothy stiffened rigidly in the circle of his arms. Both knew that those masters of thought could scarcely be prevailed upon to leave their own worlds even via projection. For all eight of them to come *this* far—almost halfway across the galaxy!—meant that something was very wrong indeed.

"I've told you a dozen times, not only I ain't no Overlord but I don't want to be and won't be. I *don't* like to play God—I simply have not got what it takes."

" 'Coordinator', then, which is of course a far better term for all except the more primitive races," Fodan went imperturbably on. "We have told you, youth, not a dozen times, but once, which should have been sufficient, that your young and vigorous race possesses qualities that our immensely older peoples no longer have. You, as the ablest individual of your race, are uniquely qualified to serve total civilization. Thus, whenever your services become necessary, you will so serve. Your services have again become necessary. Orlon, in whose province the matter primarily lies, will explain."

Seaton nodded to himself. It was going to be bad, all right, he thought as the First of Astronomy took over.

"You, friend Richard, with some help from us, succeeded in encapsulating a group of malignant immaterial entities, including the disembodied personality of your fellow-scientist Doctor Marc C. DuQuesne, in a stasis of time. This capsule, within which no time whatever could or can elapse, was launched into space with a linear acceleration of approximately three times ten to the twelfth centimeters per second squared. It was designed and powered to travel at that acceleration for something over one hundred thousand million Tellurian years; at the end of which time it was to have been rotated through the fourth dimension into an unknown and unknowable location in normal three-dimensional space."

"That's right," Seaton said. "And it will. It'll do just exactly that. Those pure-intellectual louses are gone for good; and so is Blackie DuQuesne."

"You err, youth," corrected the Norlaminian. "You did not allow us time sufficient to consider and to evaluate all the many factors involved. Rigid analysis and extended computation show that the probability approaches unity that the capsule of stasis will, almost certainly within one Tellurian year of its launching and highly probably in much less time, encounter celestial matter of sufficient density to volatilize its uranium power bars. This event will of course allow the stasis of time to collapse and the imprisoned immaterial entities will be liberated; in precisely the same condition as in the instant of their encapsulation."

Dorothy Seaton gasped. Even her husband showed that he was shaken. DuQuesne and the Immortals free? But—

"But it *can't!*" he fairly yelled the protest. "It'll dodge— it's built to dodge anything that dense!"

"At ordinary—or even extraordinary—velocities, yes," the ancient sage agreed, unmoved. "Its speed of reaction is great, yes; a rather small fraction of a trillionth of a second. That interval of time, however, while small, is very large indeed relative to zero. Compute for yourself, please, what distance that capsule will in theory traverse during that space of time at the end of only one third of one of your years."

Seaton strode across the room and uncovered a machine that resembled somewhat a small, unpretentious desk calculator.* He picked up a helmet and thought into it briefly; then stared appalled at the figure that appeared on a tape.

"My—aunt's—cat's—kitten's—pants—buttons," he said, slowly. "It'd've been smarter, maybe, to've put 'em in orbit around a planetless sun. . . . And I don't suppose there's a Chinaman's chance of catching 'em again that same way."

"No. Those minds are competent," agreed the Norlaminian. "Only one point is clear. You must again activate the *Skylark of Valeron* and again wear its sixth-order controller, since we know of no other entity who either can wear

_____

* Dorothy Seaton was highly averse to having the appearance of her living room ruined by office equipment. Seaton, however, was living and working under such high tension that he had to have almost instant access to the *Valeron's* Brain, at any time of the day or night or wherever he might be. Hence this compromise—inconspicuous machines, each direct-connected to the cubic mile of ultra-miniaturization that was the Brain. E. E. S.

it or should. We eight are here to confer and, on the basis of the few data now available, to plan."

Seaton scowled in concentration for two long minutes.

It was a measure of the strain that had been working on him that it took that long. As he had said, he was no God, and didn't want to be. He had not gone looking for either conquest or glory. One thing at a time . . . but that "one thing" had successively led him across a galaxy, into another dimension, through many a hard and desperate fight against some of the most keen-honed killers of a universe.

His gray eyes hardened. Of all those killers, it was Blackie DuQuesne who posed the greatest threat—to civilization, to Seaton himself, and above all to his wife, Dorothy. DuQuesne at large was deadly.

"All right," he snapped at last. "If that's all that's in the wood, I suppose that's the way it'll have to be carved."

The Norlaminian merely nodded. He, at least, had had no doubts of how Seaton would react to the challenge. Typically, once Seaton had decided speed became of the essence. "We'll start moving now," he barked. "The parameters give us up to a year—*maybe*—but from this minute we act as though DuQuesne and the Intellectuals are back in circulation *right now*. So if one of you—Rovol?—will put beams on Mart and Peg and project them over here, we'll get right at it."

And Dorothy, her face turning so white that a line of freckles stood boldly out across the bridge of her nose, picked the baby up and clasped him fiercely, protectively to her breast.

M. Reynolds ("Martin" or "Mart") Crane was tall, slender, imperturbable; his black-haired, ivory-skinned wife Margaret was tall and whistle stacked—she and Dorothy were just about of a size and a shape. In a second or two their full working projections appeared, standing in the middle of the room facing the Seatons—projections so exactly true to life and so solid-seeming as to give no indication whatever that they were not composed of fabric and of flesh and bone and blood.

Seaton stood up and half-bowed to Margaret, but wasted no time in getting down to business. "Hi, Peg—Mart. He briefed you?"

"Up to the moment, yes," Crane replied.

"You know, then, that some time in the indeterminate but not too distant future all hell is going to be out for noon. Any way I scan it, it looks to me as though, more or less shortly, we're going to be *spurlos versenkt*—sunk without a trace."

"You err, youth." Drasnik, the First of Psychology of Norlamin, spoke quite sharply, for him. "Your thinking is loose, turbid, confused; inexcusably superficial; completely . . ."

"But you know what their top man said!" Seaton snapped. "The one they called 'One'—and he wasn't kidding, either, believe me!"

"I do, youth. I know more than that, since they visited us long since. They were not exactly 'kidding' you, perhaps, but your several various interpretations of One's actual words and actions were inconsistent with any and every aspect of the truth. Those words and actions were in all probability designed to elicit such responses and reactions as would enable him to analyze and classify your race. Having done so, the probability approaches unity that you will not again encounter him or any of his group."

"My—God!" Dorothy, drawing a tremendously deep breath, put Dick the Small back down on the rug and left him to his own devices. "That makes sense . . . I was scared simply witless."

"Maybe," Seaton admitted, "as far as One and the rest of his original gang are concerned. But there's still DuQuesne. And if Blackie DuQuesne, even as an immaterial pattern of pure sixth-order force, thinks that way about me I'm a Digger Indian."

"Ah, yes; DuQuesne. One question, please, to clarify my thinking. Can you, do you think, even with the fullest use of all the resources of your *Skylark of Valeron*, release the intact mind from any body?"

"Of course I . . . oh, I see what you mean. Just a minute; I think probably I can find out from here." He went over to his calculator-like instrument, put on a helmet, and stood motionless for a couple of minutes while the great brain of the machine made its computation. Then, wearing a sheepish grin:

"A flat bust. I not only couldn't, I didn't," he reported. cheerfully. "So One not only did the business, but he was good enough to make me *know* that I was doing it. What an operator!" He sobered, thought intensely, then went on, "So they sucked us in. Played with us."

"You are now beginning to think clearly, youth," Drasnik said. "We come now, then, to lesser probabilities. DuQuesne's mind, of itself, is a mind of power."

"You can broadcast *that* to the all-attentive universe," Seaton said. "Question: how much stuff has he got now? We know he's got the fifth order down solid. Incarnate, he didn't know any more than that. *However*, mind is a pattern of sixth-order force. Knowing what we went through to get the sixth, and that we haven't got it all yet by seven thousand rows of Christmas trees, the first sub-quesion asks itself: Can a free mind analyze itself completely enough to work out and to handle the entire order of force in which it lies?

"We may assume, I think, that One *could* have given DuQuesne full knowledge of the sixth if he felt like it. The second sub-question, then, is; did he? If those questions aren't enough to start with I can think of plenty more."

"They are enough, youth," Fodan said. "You have pointed out the crux. We will now discuss the matter. Since this first phase lies largely in your province, Drasnik, you will now take over."

The discussion mounted, and grew, and went on and on. Silently Dorothy slipped away, and the projection of force that was Margaret Crane followed her into the kitchen.

There was no need for Dorothy to prepare coffee and sandwiches for her husband, not by hand; one thought into a controller would have produced any desired amount of any desired comestibles. But she wanted something to do. Both girls knew from experience that a conference of this sort might go on for hours; and Dorothy knew that with food placed before him, Seaton would eat; without it, he would never notice the lack.

She did not, of course, prepare anything for the others. They were not there. Their bodies were at varying distances—a few miles for Crane and his wife, an unthinkable number of parsecs for the Norlaminians and Sacner Carfon. The distance between Earth and the Green System was so unthinkably vast that there was no point in trying to express it in numbers of miles, or even parsecs. The central green sun of the cluster that held Norlamin, Osnome and Dasor was visible from Earth, all right—in Earth's hugest optical telescopes, as a tiny, 20th-magnitude point—but the light that reached Earth had been on its way for tens of thousand of years before Seaton's ancestors had turned from hunting to agriculture, had taken off their crude skins and begun to build houses, cities, machines and, ultimately, spaceships.

To all of this Dorothy and Peggy Crane were no strangers; they had been themselves in such projections countless times. If they were more than usually silent, it was not because of the astonishing quality of the meeting that was taking place in the Seatons' living room, but because of the subject of that meeting. Both Dorothy and Peg knew Marc DuQuesne well. Both of them had experienced his cold, impersonal deadliness.

Neither wanted to come close to it again.

Back in the living room, Seaton was saying: "If One gave DuQuesne all of the sixth-order force patterns, he can be anywhere and can do practically anything. So he probably didn't. On the other hand if One didn't give him any of it DuQuesne couldn't get back here in forty lifetimes. So he probably gave him some of it. The drive and the projector, at least. Maybe as much as we have, to equalize us. Maybe One figured he owed the ape that much. Whatever the truth may be, we've got to assume that DuQuesne knows as much as we do about sixth-order forces." He paused, then corrected himself. "If we're smart we'll assume that he knows *more* than we do. So we'll have to find somebody else who knows more than we do to learn from. Question— how do we go about doing that? Not by just wandering around the galaxy at random, looking; that's one certain damn sure thing."

"It is indeed," the moderator agreed. "Sacner Carfon, you have, I think, a contribution to make at this point?"

"I have?" The Dasorian was surprised at first, but caught on quickly. "Oh—perhaps I have, at that. By using Seaton's power and that of the Brain on the Fodan-Carfon band of the sixth, it will undoubtedly be possible to broadcast a thought that would affect selected mentalities wherever situate in any galaxy of this universe."

"But listen!" protested Seaton. "We don't want to *advertise* how dumb we are all over space!"

"Of course not. The thought would be very carefully built and highly selective. It would tell who we are, what we have done, and what we intend and hope to do. It would state our abilities and—by inference, and only to those we seek—our lacks; and would invite all qualified persons and entities to get in touch with us."

Seaton looked abstracted for a moment. He was thinking. The notion of sending out a beacon of thought was probably a good one—*had* to be a good one—after all, the Norlaminians and Sacner Carfon knew what they were doing. Yet he could see complications. The Fodan-Carfon band of the sixth order was still very new and very experimental. "Can you make it selective?" he demanded. "I don't mind telling our prospective friends we need help—I don't want to holler it to our enemies."

The Dasorian's deep voice chuckled. "It can not be made selective," he said. "The message would of necessity be on such a carrier as to be receivable by any intelligent brain. Yet it can be hedged about with such safeguards, limitations and compulsions that no one could or would pay attention to it except those who possess at least some ability, overt or latent, to handle the Fodan-Carfon band."

Seaton whistled through his teeth. "Wow! And just how are you going to clamp on such controls as *those*? I don't see how anything but magic—sheer, unadulterated, pure black magic!—could swing that load."

"Precisely. Or, rather, imprecisely. It is unfortunate that your term 'magic' is so inexcusably loose and carries so many and so deplorable connotations and implications. Shall we design and build the thought we wish to send out?"

The thought was designed and was built; and was launched into space with the inconceivable, the utterly immeasurable velocity of its order of being.

A red-haired stripper called Madlyn Mannis, strutting her stuff in Tampa in Peninsula Florida, felt it and almost got it; but, not being very strongly psychic, shrugged it off and went on about the business of removing the last sequin-bedecked trifle of her costume. And, as close to the dancer as plenteous baksheesh could arrange for, a husky, good-looking young petrochemical engineer named Charles K. van der Gleiss felt a thrill like nothing he had ever felt before—but ascribed it, naturally enough, to the fact that this was the first time he had ever seen Madlyn Mannis dance. And in Washington, D.C. one Doctor Stephanie de Marigny, a nuclear physicist, pricked up her ears, tightened the muscles of her scalp, and tried for two full minutes to think of something she *ought* to think of but couldn't.

Out past the Green System the message sped, and past the dust and the incandescent gas that had once been the noisome planet of the Fenachrone. Past worlds where amphibians roared and bellowed; past planets of methane ice where crystalline life brooded sluggishly on its destiny.

In the same infinitesimal instant it reached and passed the Rim Worlds of our galaxy; touching many minds but really affecting none. Farther and farther out, with no decrease whatever in speed, it flew; past the inconceivably tiny, inconceivably fast-moving point that housed the seven greatest, most fearsome minds that the Macrocosmic All had ever spawned—minds that, knowing all about that thought already, ignored it completely.

Immensely farther out, it flashed through the galaxy in which was the solar system of Ray-See-Nee—where, for the first time, it made solid contact with a mind in a body human to the limit of classification. Kay-Lee Barlo, confidential secretary of Department Head Bay-Lay Boyn, stiffened so suddenly that she stuttered into her microphone and had to erase three words from a tape—and in that same instant her mother at home went into deep trance.

And still farther out, in a galaxy lying almost on the universe's Arbitrary Rim, in the Realm of the Llurdi, the message found a much larger group of receivers. While none of the practically enslaved Jelmi could do much of anything about that weirdly peculiar and inexplicably guarded thought, many of them were very much interested in it; particularly Valkyrie-like Sennlloy, a native of the planet Allondax and the master biologist of all known space; ancient Tammon, the greatest genius of the entire Jelman race; and newlyweds Mergon and Luloy, the Mallidaxian savants.

None of the monstrous Llurdi—not even their most monstrous "director", Klazmon the Fifteenth—being monstrous—could receive the message in any part. And how well that was! For if those tremendously able aliens could have received that message, could have understood it and acted upon it, how vastly different the history of all humanity would have been!

2 • LLURDI AND JELMI

THE distance from Earth to the Realm of the Llurdi is such that it is worth while to take a moment to locate it in space. It has been known for a long time that solar systems occur in lenticular aggregations galled galaxies; each galaxy consisting of one or more thousands of millions of solar systems. And for almost as long a time, since no definite or systematic arrangement of the galaxies could be demonstrated, the terms "Universe" and "Cosmic All" were interchangeable; each meaning the absolute totality of all matter and all space in existence anywhere and everywhere.

There had been speculations, of course, that galaxies were arranged in lenticular universes incomprehensibly vast in size, so that the term "Cosmic All" should be reserved for a plurality of universes and a hyper-space of more than three spatial dimensions.

Seaton and Crane in the *Skylark of Valeron* proved that our galaxy, the Milky Way, lies in a lenticular universe by charting every galaxy in that universe. And they suggested to the various learned societies that the two celestial aggregates should be named, respectively, the First Galaxy and the First Universe.

Many millions of parsecs distant from Tellus and its First Galaxy, then, out near the Arbitrary Rim of the First Universe, there lay the Realm of the Llurdi. This Realm, which had existed for over seventy thousand Tellurian years, was made up of four hundred eighty-two planets in exactly half that many solar systems.

Two planets in each populated system were necessary because the population of the Realm was composed of two entirely different forms of highly intelligent life. Of these two races the Jelmi—the subject race, living practically in vassalage—were strictly human beings and lived on strictly Tellus-type worlds.

The master race, the Llurdi, had originated upon the harsh and hostile planet Llurdiax—Llurdiaxorb Five—with its distant, wan, almost-never-seen sun and its incessant gales of frigid, ice-laden, ammonia- and methane-impregnated, forty-pounds-to-the-square-inch air. Like mankind, they wore clothing against the rigors of their environment. Unlike mankind, however, they wore clothes only for protection, and only when protection was actually necessary. Nor was Llurdiax harsh or forbidding—to them.

It was the best of all possible worlds. They would not colonize any planet that was not as nearly as possible like the mother world of their race.

Llurdi, although they are erect, bifurcate, bi-laterally symmetrical, bi-sexual, mammalian, and have a large crania and six-digited hands each having two opposed thumbs, are not humanoids. Nor, despite their tremendous, insensitive, unfreezable wings, are they either birds or bats. Nor flying cats, although they have huge, vertically-slitted eyes and needle-sharp canine teeth that protrude well below and above their upper and lower lips. Also, they have immensely strong and highly versatile tails; but there is nothing simian about them or in their ancestry.

The Realm was not exactly an empire. Nor was Llanzlan Klazmon the Fifteenth exactly an emperor. The title "Llanzlan" translates, as nearly as possible, into "Director"; and that was what Klazmon regarded himself as being.

It is true that what he said, went; and that if he didn't like any existing law he expunged it from all existence. But that was exactly the way things should be. How else could optimum conditions be achieved and maintained in an ever-expanding, ever-changing, ever-rising economy? He ruled, he said and thoroughly believed, with complete reason and perfect fairness and strictly in accordance with the findings of the universe's largest and most competent computers as to what was for the best good of all.

Wherefore everyone who did not agree with him was—automatically, obviously, and unquestionably—wrong.

Llurdias, the capital city of the world Llurdiax and of the Realm, had a population of just over ten million and covered more than nine hundred square miles of ground. At its geometrical center towered the mile-square, half-mile-high office-residence-palace (the Llurdian word "llanzlan-ate" has no Tellurian equivalent) of Llanzlan Klazmon the Fifteenth of the Realm of the Llurdi. And in that building's fifth sub-basement, in Hall Prime of Computation, Klazmon and his Board of Advisors were hard at work.

That vast room, the first receptor of all the reports of the Realm, was three-quarters full of receivers, recorders, analyzers—bewilderingly complex instrumentation of all kinds. From most of these devices tapes were issuing—tapes that, en route to semi-permanent storage, were being monitored by specialists in the hundreds of different fields of the Llurdan-Jelmi economy.

Klazmon the Fifteenth and his Board, seated at a long conference table in hard-upholstered "chairs" shaped to fit the Llurdan anatomy, were paying no attention to routine affairs.

"I have called this meeting," the ruler said, "to decide what can be done to alleviate an intolerable situation. As you all know, we live in what could be called symbiosis with the Jelmi; who are so unstable, so illogical, so bird-brained generally that they would destroy themselves in a century were it not for our gentle but firm insistence that they conduct themselves in all matters for their own best good. This very instability of their illogical minds, however, enables them to arrive occasionally at valid conclusions from insufficient data; a thing that no logical mind can do. These conclusions—they are intuitions, really—account for practically all the advancement we Llurdi have made and explain why we have put up with the Jelmi—yes, cherished them—so long."

He paused, contemplating the justice of the arrangement he had just described. It did not occur to him that it could in any way be described as "wrong."

He went on: "What most of you do not know is that intuitions of any large worth have become less and less frequent, decade by decade, over the last few centuries. It was twelve years ago that the Jelm Jarxon elucidated the 'Jarxon' band of the sixth order, and no worth-while intuition has been achieved since that time. Beeloy, has your more rigorous analysis revealed any new fact of interest?"

A young female stood up, preened the short fur back of her left ear with the tip of her tail, and said, "No, sir. Logic can not be applied to illogic. Statistical analysis is still the only possible tool and it cannot be made to apply to the point in question, since it is incapable of certainty and since the genius-type mind occurs in only one out of thousands of millions of Jelmi. I found a very high probability, however—point nine nine nine plus—that the techniques set up by our ancestors are wrong. In breeding for contentment by destroying the discontented we are very probably breeding out the very characteristics we wish to encourage."

"Thank you, Beeloy. That finding was not unanticipated. Kalton, your report on Project University, please."

"Yes, sir." An old male, so old that his fur was almost white, stood up. "Four hundred males and the same number of females, the most intelligent and most capable Jelmi alive, were selected and were brought here to the Llanzlanate. They were put into quarters that were Jelm-type in every respect, even to gravity. They were given every inducement and every facility to work-study and to breed.

"First, as to work-study. They have done practically nothing except waste time. They seem to devote their every effort to what they call 'escape' by means of already-well-known constructions of the fifth and sixth orders—all of which are of course promptly negated. See for yourselves what these insanely illogical malcontents are doing and know for yourselves that, in its present form, Project University is a failure as far as producing intuitions is concerned."

Kalton picked up a fist-sized instrument between the thumbs of his left hand and a tri-di "tank" appeared on the table's top, in plain sight of every member of the Board. Then, as he began to finger controls, a three-dimensional scene in true color appeared in the tank; a smoothly-flowing, ever-shifting scene that moved from room to room and from place to place as the point of view traversed the vast volume of the prison.

It did not look like a prison. The apartments, of which there were as many as the Jelmi wanted, were furnished as luxuriously as the various occupants desired; with furniture and equipment every item of which had been selected by each occupant himself or herself. There were wonderful rugs and hangings; masterpieces of painting and of sculpture; triumphs of design in fireplaces and tables and chairs and couches. Each room or suite could be set up for individual control of gravity, temperature, pressure, and humidity. Any imaginable item of food or drink was available on fifteen seconds' notice at any hour of the day or night.

In the magnificent laboratories every known or conceivable piece of apparatus could be had for the asking; the memory banks of the library would furnish in seconds any item of information that had been stored in any one of them during all seventy thousand years of the Realm's existence.

And there were fully-equipped game and exercise rooms, ranging in size from tiny card-rooms up to a full-sized football field, to suit every Jelman need or desire for play or for exercise.

But not one of the hundreds of Jelmi observed—each one a perfect specimen physically, as was plainly revealed by the complete absence of clothing—appreciated any one of these advantages! Most of the laboratories were vacant and dark. The few scientists who were apparently at work were not doing anything that made sense. The library was not in use at all; the Jelmi who were reading anything were reading works of purely Jelman authorship—mostly love stories, murder mysteries, and science fiction. Many Jelmi seemed to be busy but their activities were as pointless as cutting out paper dolls.

"The pale, frail, practically hairless, repulsive, incomplete, illogical, and insane animals refuse steadfastly to cooperate with us on any level."

Any Earthman so frustrated would have snarled the sentence, but the Llurd merely stated it as a fact. "You can all see for yourselves that as far as productive work is . . . but hold!"

The viewpoint stopped moving and focussed sharply on a young man and a young woman who, bending over a table, were working on two lengths of smooth yellow material that looked something like varnished cambric. "Mergon and Luloy of planet Mallidax," Kalton said into the microphone. "What are you doing? Why are you so far away from your own laboratories?"

Mergon straightened up and glared at what he thought was the point of origin of the voice. "If it's any of your business, funnyface, which it isn't," he said savagely, "I'm building a shortlong whatsit, and Luloy has nothing to do with it. When I get it done I'm personally going to tear your left leg off and beat you to death with the bloody end of it."

"You see?" Kalton dispassionately addressed the other members of the Board. "That reaction is typical."

He manipulated controls and both Jelmi leaped to their feet, with all four hands pressed to their buttocks. The fact that Luloy was a woman—scarcely more than a girl, in fact—was of no consequence at all to Kalton. Even Llurdan sex meant very little to the Llurdi. Jelman sex meant nothing whatever.

"Nerve-whip," Kalton explained to his fellows. He dropped his controller into his lap and the tri-di tank vanished. "Nothing serious—only sightly painful and producing only a little ecchymosis and extravasation. Neither of those two beasts, however, will be at all comfortable until they get back where they belong. Now, to continue my report:

"So much for failure to work-study. Failure-refusal to breed, while not possible of such simple and easy demonstration, is no less actual, effective, and determined. A purely emotional, non-logical, and ridiculous factor they call 'love' seems to be involved, as does their incomprehensibly exaggerated, inexplicable craving for 'liberty' or 'freedom'."

The Llanzlan said thoughtfully, "But surely, unwillingness to breed cannot possibly affect the results of artificial insemination?"

"It seems to, sir. Definitely. There is some non-physical and non-logical, but nevertheless powerful, operator involved. My assistants and I have not been able to develop any techniques that result in any except the most ephemeral pregnancies."

"You apparently wish to comment, Velloy?" Klazmon asked.

"I certainly do!" a middle-aged female snapped, giving one tautly-outstretched wing a resounding whack with her tail. "Of course they haven't! As Prime Sociologist I said five years ago and I repeat now that no mind of the quality of those of the Jelmi here in the llanzlanate can be coerced by any such gross physical means. Kalton talks of them and thinks of them as animals—meaning lower animals. I said five years ago and still say that they are not. Their minds, while unstable and completely illogical and in many instances unsane to the point of insanity, are nevertheless minds of tremendous power. I told this Board five years ago that the only way to make that project work—to cause selected Jelmi to produce either ideas or young or both—was to give the selectees a perfect illusion of complete freedom, and I recommended that course of action. Since I could not prove my statement mathematically, my recommendation was rejected. While I still cannot prove that statement, it is still my considered opinion that it is true; and I now repeat both statement and recommendation. I will keep on repeating them at every opportunity as long as this Board wastes time by not accepting them. I remind you that you have already wasted—lost—over five years."

"Your statement becomes more probable year by year," the Llanzlan admitted. "Kalton, have you anything more to say?"

"Very little. Only that, since Project University has admittedly failed, we should of course adopt—"

Kalton was silenced in mid-sentence by a terrific explosion, which was followed by a rumbling crash as half of one wall of the Hall collapsed inward.

A volume of Jelman air rushed in, enveloping a purposeful company of Jelmi in yellow coveralls and wearing gasmasks. Some of these invaders were shooting pistols; some were using or throwing knives; but all were covering and protecting eight Jelmi who were launching bombs at one great installation of sixth-order gear—the computer complex that was the very nerve center of the entire Realm.

For the Jelmi—who, as has been said, were human to the last decimal of classification—had been working on fifth- and sixth-order devices purely as a blind; their real effort had been on first-order effects so old that their use had been all but forgotten.

The Jelman plan was simple: Thirty men and thirty women would destroy the central complex of the computer system of the entire Realm. Then, if possible, the survivors of the sixty would join their fellows in taking over an already-selected Llurdan scout cruiser and taking off at max.

It was quite probable that many or even most of the attacking sixty would die. It was distinctly possible that they all would. All sixty, however, were perfectly willing to trade their lives for that particular bank of sixth-order apparatus, in order that seven hundred forty other Jelmi could escape from Llurdiax and, before control could be re-established, be beyond their masters' reach.

Theoretically, the first phase of the operation should have been successful; the Realm's nerve center should have been blown to unrecognizable bits. The Jelmi knew exactly what they were going to do, exactly how they were going to do it, and exactly how long it would take. They knew that they would have the advantage of complete surprise. There would be, they were sure, half a second or so of the paralysis of shock, followed by at least one second of utter confusion; which would give them plenty of time.

They were sure it would be as though, during a full-formal session of the Supreme Court, a gang of hoodlums should blast down a wall and come leaping into the courtroom with Tommy-guns ablaze and with long knives flying and stabbing and slashing. Grave, stately, and thoughtful, the justices could not possibly react fast enough to save their lives or their records or whatever else it was that the gangsters were after.

The Jelmi, however, had never seen any Llurd in emergency action; did not know or suspect how nearly instantaneous the Llurdan speed of reaction was; did not realize that a perfectly logical mind can not be surprised by any happening, however unusual or however outrageous.

Thus:

Yelling, shooting, throwing, stabbing, slashing, the men

and women of the Jelmi rushed into battle; to be met—
with no paralysis and no confusion and no loss of time
whatever—by buffeting wings, flailing tails, tearing teeth,
and hard, highly skilled hands and fists and feet.

Many machine operators, as agile in the air as bats, met
the bombs in midair and hurled them out into and along
the corridor through the already-breached wall, where they
exploded harmlessly. Harmlessly, that is, except for a con-
siderable increase in the relatively unimportant structural
damage already wrought.

Two knives were buried to their hilts in the huge flying
muscles of the Llanzlan's chest. His left wing hung useless,
its bones shattered by bullets. So did his right arm. Nevertheless, he made it at speed to his console—and the battle
was over.

Beams of force lashed out, immobilizing the human
beings where they stood. Curtains of force closed in, pressing the Jelmi together into a tightly packed group. An im-
permeable membrane of force confined all the Jelman air
and whatever Llurdan atmosphere had been mixed with it.

The Llanzlan, after glancing at his own wounds and at
the corps of surgeons already ministering to his more
seriously wounded fellows, resumed his place at the conference table.

He said, "This meeting will resume. The places of those
department heads who died will be taken by their first
assistants. All department heads are hereby directed to
listen, to note, and to act. Since Project University has
failed, it is to be closed out immediately. All Jelmi—I perceive that none of those present is dead, or even seriously
wounded—will be put aboard the ship in which they intended to leave Llurdiax. They will be given all the supplies, apparatus, and equipment that they care to requisition
and will be allowed to take off for any destination they
please."

He glanced at the captured Jelmi, imprisoned in their
force-bubble of atmosphere. To them it reeked of methane
and halogens, but they stood proudly and coldly listening
to what he said.

He dismissed them from his mind and said. "A recess
will now be taken so that those of us who are wounded
may have our wounds dressed. After that we will consider
in detail means of inducing the Jelmi to resume the production of breakthroughs in science."

3 • FREE (?)

SOME hours later, far out in deep space, the ex-Llurdan scout cruiser—now named the *Mallidax*, after the most populous Jelman planet of the Realm—bored savagely through the ether. Its crew of late revolutionaries, still dazed by the fact that they were still alive, recuperated in their various ways.

In one of the larger, more luxurious cabins Luloy of Mallidax lay prone on a three-quarter-size-bed, sobbing convulsively, uncontrollably. Her left eye was swollen shut. The left side of her face and most of her naked body bore livid black and blue bruises—bruises so brutally severe that the marks of Kalton's sense-whip punishment, incurred earlier for insubordination, were almost invisible. A dozen bandages showed white against the bronzed skin of her neck and shoulders and torso and arms and legs.

"Oh, snap out of it, Lu, *please!*" Mergon ordered, almost brusquely. He was a burly youth with crew-cut straw-colored hair; and he, too, showed plenty of evidence of having been to the wars. He had even more bruises and bandages than she did. "Don't claim that you wanted to be a martyr any more than I did. And they can engrave it on a platinum plaque that I'm damned glad to get out of that fracas alive."

Stopping her crying by main strength, the girl hauled herself up into a half-sitting position and glared at the man out of her one good eye.

"You . . . you clod!" she stormed. "It isn't that at all! And you know it as well as I do. It's just that we . . . they . . . he . . . not a single *one* of them so much as . . . why, we might just as well have been merely that many mosquitoes—midges—worse, exactly that many perfectly innocuous saprophytic bacilli."

"Exactly," he agreed, sourly, and her glare changed to a look almost of surprise. "That's precisely what we were. It's humiliating, yes. It's devastating and it's frustrating. We tried to hit the Llurdi where it hurt, and they ignored us. Agreed. I don't like it a bit better than you do; but caterwauling and being sorry for yourself isn't going to help matters a—"

"*Caterwauling!* Being *sorry* for myself! If *that's* what you think, you can . . ."

"Stop it, Lu!" he broke in sharply, "before I have to spank your fanny to a rosy blister!"

She threw up her head in defiance; then what was almost a smile began to quirk at the corners of her battered mouth. "You can't, Merg," she said, much more quietly than she had said anything so far. "Look—it's all red, green, blue, yellow, and black already. That last panel I bounced off of was no pillow, friend."

"Llenderllon's favor, sweetheart!" Bending over, he kissed her gingerly, then drew a deep breath of relief. "You scared me like I don't know when I've been scared before," he admitted. "We need you too much—and I love you too much—to have you go off the deep end now. Especially now, when for the first time in our lives we're in position to do something."

"Such as what?" Luloy's tone was more lifeless than skeptical. "How many of our whole race are worth saving, do you think? How many Jelmi of all our worlds can be made to believe that their present way of life is anything short of perfection?"

"Very few, probably," Mergon conceded. "As of now. But—"

He paused, looking around their surroundings. The spaceship, which had once been one of the Llurdi's best, might have a few surprises for them. It was a matter for debate whether the Llurdi might not have put concealed spy devices in the rooms. On balance, however, Mergon thought not. The Llurdi operated on grander scales than that.

He said, "Luloy, listen. We tried to fight our way to freedom by attacking the Llurdi right where it hurts, in center of their power. We lost the battle. But we have what we were fighting for, don't we? Why do you think they let us go, perfectly free?"

Luloy's eye brightened a little, but not too much. "That's plain enough. Since they couldn't make us produce either new theories or children in captivity, they're giving us what they *say* is complete freedom, so that we'll produce both. How stupid do they think we are? How stupid can they get? If we could have wrecked their long eyes, yes, we could have got away clean to a planet in some other galaxy, 'way out of their range; but now? If I know anything at all, it's that they'll hold a tracer beam—so weak as to be practically indetectable, of course—on us forever."

"I think you're right," Mergon said, and paused. Luloy looked at him questioningly and he went on, "I'm sure you are, but I don't think it's us they are aiming at. They're probably taking the long view—betting that, with a life-long illusion of freedom, we'll have children of our own free will."

Luloy nodded thoughtfully. "And we would," she said, definitely. "All of us would. For, after all, if we on this ship all die childless what chance is there that any other Jelmi will try it again for thousands of years? And our children would have a chance, even if we never have another."

"True. But on the other hand, how many generations will it take for things now known to be facts to degenerate into myths? To be discredited completely, in spite of the solidest records we can make as to the truth and the danger?"

Luloy started to gnaw her lip, but winced sharply and stopped the motion. "I see what you mean. Inevitable. But you don't seem very downcast about it, so you have an idea. Tell me, quick!"

"Yes, but I'm just hatching it; I haven't mentioned it even to Tammon yet, so I don't know whether it will work or not. At present a sixth-order breakthrough can't be hidden from even a very loose surveillance. Right?"

By now Luloy's aches and pains were forgotten. Eyes bright, she nodded. "You're so right. Do *you* think one can be? Possibly? How?"

"By finding a solar system somewhere whose inhabitants know so much more than we do that the emanations of their sixth-order installations continuously or regularly at work will mask those of any full-scale tests we want to make. There *must* be some such race, somewhere in this universe. The Llurdi charted this universe long ago—they call it U-Prime—and I requisitioned copies of all the tapes. Second: the Llurdi are all strictly logical. Right?"

"That's right," the girl agreed. "Strictly. Insanely, almost, you might say."

"So my idea is to do something as illogical as possible. They think we'll head for a new planet of our own; either in this galaxy or one not too far away. So we won't. We'll drive at absolute max for the center of the universe, with the most sensitive feelers we have full out for very strong sixth-order emanations. En route, we'll use every iota of brain-power aboard this heap in developing some new band of the sixth, being mighty careful to use so little power that the ship's emanations will mask it. Having found the hiding-place we want, we'll tear into developing and building something, not only that the Llurdi haven't got, but a thing that by use of which we can bust Llanzlan Klazmon the Fifteenth loose from his wings and tail—and through which he can't fight back. So, being absolutely—stupidly—logical about everything, what would His Supreme Omnipotence do about it?"

Luloy thought in silence for a few seconds, then tried unsuccessfully to whistle through battered, swollen lips. "Oh, boy!" she exclaimed, delightedly. "Slug him with a thing like that—demonstrate superiority—and the battle is over. He'll concede us everything we want, full equality, independence, you name it, without a fight—without even an argument!"

Grinning, Mergon caught her arm and led her out of the room. Throughout the great hulk of the Llurd spaceship the other battered Jelmi veterans were beginning to stir. To each of them, Mergon explained his plan and from each came the same response. "Oh, boy!"

They began at once setting up their work plans.

The first project was to find—somewhere!—a planet generating sufficient sixth-order forces to screen what they were going to do. In the great vastnesses of the Over-Universe there were many such planets. They could have chosen that which was inhabited by Norlaminian or Dasorian peoples. They could have chosen one of a score which were comparatively nearby. They, in fact, ultimately chose and set course for the third planet of a comparatively small G-type star known to its people as Tellus, or Earth.

They could have given many reasons why this particular planet had been selected.

None of these reasons would have included the receipt of the brief pulse of telepathic communication which none of them, any longer, consciously remembered.

And back on Llurdiax the Llanzlan followed the progress of the fleeing ship of Jelm rebels with calm perception.

His great bat wings were already mending, even as the scars of the late assault on his headquarters were already nearly repaired by a host of servo-mechanisms. Deaf to the noise and commotion of the repairs, heedless of the healing wounds which any human would have devoted a month in bed to curing, the Llanzlan once again summoned his department heads and issued his pronouncement:

"War, being purely destructive, is a product of unsanity. The Jelmi are, however, unsane; many of them are insane. Thus, if allowed to do so, they commit warfare at unpredictable times and for incomprehensible, indefensible, and/or whimsical reasons. Nevertheless, since the techniques we have been employing have been proven ineffective and therefore wrong, they will now be changed. During the tenure of this directive no more Jelmi will be executed or castrated: in fact, a certain amount of unsane thinking will not merely be tolerated but encouraged, even though it lead to the unsanity termed 'war'. It should not, however, be permitted to exceed that quantity of 'war' which would result in the destruction of, let us say, three of their own planets.

"This course will entail a risk that we, as the 'oppressors' of the Jelmi, will be attacked by them. The magnitude of this risk—the probability of such an attack—cannot be calculated with the data now available. Also, these data are rendered even less meaningful by the complete unpredictability of the actions of the group of Jelmi released from study here.

"It is therefore directed that all necessary steps be taken particularly in fifth and sixth-order devices, that no even theoretically possible attack on this planet will succeed.

"This meeting will now adjourn."

It did; and within fifteen minutes heavy construction began—construction that was to go on at a pace and on a scale and with an intensity of drive theretofore unknown throughout the Realm's long history. Whole worldlets were destroyed, scavenged for their minerals, their ores smelted in giant atomic space-borne foundries and cast and shaped into complex machines of offense and defense. Delicate networks of radiation surrounded every Jelm and Llurd world, ready to detect, trace, report and home on any artifact whatsoever which might approach them. Weapons capable of blasting moons out of orbit slipped into position in great latticework spheres of defensive emplacements.

The Llurdi were preparing for anything.

Llurdan computations were never wrong. Computers, however, even Llurdan computers, are not really smart—they can't really think. Unlike the human brain, they can not arrive at valid conclusions from insufficient data. In fact, they don't even try to. They stop working and say—

in words or by printing or typing or by flashing a light or by ringing a bell—"DATA INSUFFICIENT": and then continue to do nothing until they are fed additional information.

Thus, while the Llanzlan and his mathematicians and logicians fed enough data into their machines to obtain valid conclusions, there were many facts that no Llurd then knew. And thus those conclusions, while valid, were woefully incomplete; they did not cover all of actuality by far.

For, in actuality, there had already begun a chain of events that was to render those mighty fortresses precisely as efficacious against one certain type of attack as that many cubic miles of sheerest vacuum.

4 • LLURDI AND FENACHRONE

THE type of attack which was about to challenge the Llurdi was from a source no civilized human would have believed still existed.

If Richard Seaton, laboring at Earth's own defenses uncountable parsecs away, had been told of it, he would flatly have declared the story a lie. He ought to know, he would have said. That particular danger to the harmony of the worlds had long since been destroyed . . . and he was the man who had destroyed it!

When the noisome planet of the Fenachrone was destroyed it was taken for granted that Ravindau and his faction of the Party of Postponement of Universal Conquest, who had fled from the planet just before its destruction, were the last surviving members of their monstrous race. When they in turn were destroyed it was assumed that no Fenachrone remained alive.

That assumption was wrong. There was another faction of the Party of Postponement much larger than Ravindau's, much more secretive, and much better organized.

Its leader, one Sleemet, while an extremely able scientist, had taken lifelong pains that neither his name nor his ability should become known to any except a select few. He was as patriotic as was any other member of his race; he believed as implicitly as did any other that the Fenachrone should and one day would rule not only this one universe, but the entire Cosmic All. However, he believed, and as firmly, that The Day should not be set until the probability of success of the project should begin to approach unity as a limit.

According to Sleemet's exceedingly rigorous analysis, the time at which success would become virtually certain would not arrive for at least three hundred Fenachronian years.

From the day of Fenor's accession to the throne Sleemet had been grimly certain that this Emperor Fenor—headstrong, basically ignorant, and inordinately prideful even for an absolute monarch of the Fenachrone—would set The Day during his own reign; centuries before its proper time.

Therefore, for over fifty years, Sleemet had been preparing for exactly the eventuality that came about, and:

Therefore, after listening to only a few phrases of the ultimatum given to Emperor Fenor by Sacner Carfon of Dasor, speaking for the Overlord Seaton and his Forces of Universal Peace, Sleemet sent out his signal and:

Therefore, even before Ravindau's forces began to board their single vessel Sleemet's fleet of seventeen superdreadnoughts was out in deep space, blasting at full-emergency fifth-order cosmic-energy drive away from the planet so surely doomed.

Surely doomed? Yes. Knowing vastly more about the sixth order than did any other of his race, he was the only one of his race who knew anything about the Overlord of the Central System; of who and what that Overlord was and of what that Overlord had done. He, Sleemet, did not want any part of Richard Ballinger Seaton. Not then or ever.

Curse Fenor's abysmal stupidity! Since a whole new Fenachrone planet would now have to be developed, the Conquest could not be begun for *more* than three hundred years!

While Sleemet knew much more about the sixth order than Ravindau did, he did not have the sixth-order drive and it took him and his scientists and engineers several months to develop and to perfect it. Thus their fleet was still inside the First Galaxy when they finally changed drives and began really to travel—on a course that, since it was laid out to reach the most distant galaxies of the First Universe, would of necessity lie within two and a quarter hundreds of thousands of light-years of the galaxy in which the Realm of the Llurdi lay.

As has been intimated, the Llurdi were literal folk. When any llanzlan issued a directive he meant it literally, and it was always as literally carried out.

Thus, when Llanzlan Klazmon ordered the construction of an installation of such a nature that "no even theoretically possible attack on this planet will succeed" he meant precisely that—and that was precisely what was built. Nor, since the Llurdi had full command of the fourth and fifth orders, and some sixth-order apparatus as well, was the task overlong in the doing.

The entire one-hundred-six-mile circumference of Llurdias and a wide annulus outside the city proper were filled with tremendous fortresses; each of which was armed and powered against any contingency to which Computer Prime —almost half a cubic mile of miniaturization packed with the accumulated knowledges and happenings of some seventy thousand years—could assign a probability greater than point zero zero zero one.

Each of those fortresses covered five acres of ground; was low and flat. Each was built of super-hard, super-tough, super-refractory synthetic. Each had twenty-seven high-rising, lightning-rodlike spikes of the same material. Fortress-shell and spikes through closely spaced cast-in tubes; and the entire periphery of each fortress, as well as dozens of interior relief-points, went deep into constantly water-soaked, heavily salted ground. Each fortress sprouted scores of antennae—parabolic, box, flat, and straight—and scores of heavily insulated projectors of shapes to be defined only by a professional mathematician of solid geometry.

And *how* the Llurdan detectors could now cover space! The Jelm Mergon, long before his abortive attempt to break jail, had developed a miniaturized monitor station that could detect, amplify, and retransmit on an aimed tight beam any fifth- or sixth-order signal from and to a distance of many kiloparsecs.

Hundreds of these "mergons" were already out in deep space. Now mergons were being manufactured in lots of a thousand, and in their thousands they were being hurled outward from Llurdiax, to cover—by relays *en cascade*— not only the Llurdan galaxy and a great deal of intergalactic space, but also a good big chunk of inter-universal space as well.

The Fenachrone fleet bored on through inter-galactic

space at its distance-devouring sixth-order pace. Its fourth-, fifth-, and sixth-order detector webs fanned out far—"far" in the astronomical sense of the word—ahead of it. They were set to detect, not only the most tenuous cloud of gas, but also any manifestation whatever upon any of the known bands of any of those orders. Similar detectors reached out to an equal distance above and below and to the left of and to the right of the line of flight; so that the entire forward hemisphere was on continuous web of ultra-tenuous but ultra-sensitive detection.

And, as that fleet approached a galaxy lying well to "starboard"—the term was still in use aboard ship except for matters of record, since the direction of action of artificial gravity, whatever its actual direction, was always "down"—two sets of detectors tripped at once.

The squat and monstrous officer on watch reported this happening instantly, of course, to Sleemet himself; and of course Sleemet himself went instantly into action. He energized his flagship's immense fifth-order projector.

Those detections could have only one meaning. There was at least one solar system in that galaxy peopled by entities advanced enough to work with forces of at least the fifth order. They should be destroyed—that is, he corrected himself warily, unless they were allied with or belonged to that never-to-be-sufficiently-damned Overlord of the Central System of the First Galaxy . . . But no, at this immense distance the probability of that was vanishingly small.

They might, however, have weapons of the sixth. The fact that there were no such devices in operation at the moment did not preclude that possibility.

Very unlike the late unlamented Fenor he, First Scientist Sleemet, was not stupidly and arrogantly sure that the Fenachrone were in fact the ablest, most intelligent, and most powerful race of beings in existence. He would investigate, of course. But he would do it cautiously.

The working projections of the Fenachrone were tight patterns of force mounted on tight beams. Thus, until they began to perform exterior work, they were virtually indetectable except by direct interception and hard-driven specific taps. Sleemet knew this to be a fact; whether the projection was on, above, or below the target planet's surface and even though that planet was so far away that it would take light hundreds of centuries to make the one-way trip.

The emanations of his vessels' sixth-order cosmic-energy

drive, however, were very distinctly something else. They could not be damped out or masked and they could be detected very easily by whoever or whatever it was that was out there . . . Yes, an exploration would not change matters at all . . .

As a matter of fact, the Fenachrone Fleet's emanations had been detected a full two seconds since.

A far-outpost mergon had picked it up and passed it along to a second, which in turn had relayed it inward to its Number Three, which finally had delivered it to Computer Prime on incredibly distant Llurdiax.

There, in Hall Prime of Computation, a section supervisor had flicked the switch that had transferred the unusual bit of information to his immediate superior, Head Supervisor Klarton—who had at sight of it gone into a tizzy (for a Llurd) of worrying his left ear with the tip of his tail. He stared at the motionless bit of tape as though it were very apt indeed to bite him in the eye.

What to do? Should he disturb the llanzlan with this or not?

This was a nose-twitching borderline case if there ever was one. If he didn't, and it turned out to be something important, he'd get his tail singed—he'd be reduced to section supervisor. But if he did, and it didn't, he'd get exactly the same treatment . . . However, the thing, whatever it might be, was so *terrifically* far away . . .

Yes, that was it! The smart thing to do would be to watch it for a few seconds—determine exact distance, direction of flight, velocity, and so forth—before reporting to the Big Boss. That would protect him either way.

Wherefore Sleemet had time to launch an analsynth projection along the indicated line.

He found a solar system containing two highly industrialized planets; one of which was cool, the other cold. One was peopled by those never-to-be-sufficiently-damned human beings; the other by a race of creatures even more monstrous and therefore even less entitled to exist.

He studied those planets and their inhabitants quickly but thoroughly, and the more he studied them the more derisive and contemptuous he became. They had no warships, no fortresses either above or below ground, no missiles, even! Their every effort and all their energies were devoted to affairs of *peace!*

Therefore, every detail having been recorded, including the gibberish being broadcast and tightbeamed by various communications satellites, Sleemet pulled in his analsynth and sent out a full working projection.

He had already located great stores of prepared power-uranium bars and blocks on both planets. Careless of detection now and working at his usual fantastic speed and with his usual perfect control, he built in seconds six termendous pyramids upon each of the two doomed worlds—pyramids of now one-hundred-percent-convertible superatomic explosive. He assembled twenty-four exceedingly complex, carefully aimed forces and put them on trip. Then, glaring balefully into an almost opaque visiplate, he reached out without looking and rammed a plunger home—and in an instant those two distant planets became two tremendous fireballs of hellishly intolerable, mostly invisible, energies.

And almost eight thousand million highly intelligent creatures—eating, sleeping, loving, fighting, reading, thinking, working, playing—died in that utterly cataclysmic rending of two entire worlds.

Practically all of them died not knowing even that they had been hurt. A few—a *very* few—watch officers in interplanetary spaceships observed one or the other of those frightful catastrophes in time to have an instant's warning of what was coming; but only three such officers, it became known later, had enough time to throw on their faster-than-light drives and thus outrun the ravening front of annihilation.

Cosmically, however, the thing didn't amount to much. Its duration was very short indeed. While a little of each planet's substance was volatilized, practically all of it was scarcely more than melted. When equilibrium was restored they did not shine like little suns. They scarcely glowed.

Hands quietly poised, Sleemet again paused in thought.

The fact that he had murdered almost eight billion people did not bother him at all. In fact, he did not think of the action at all, as murder or as killing or as anything else. If he had, the thought would have been the Fenachrone equivalent of "pesticide." All space comprising the Cosmic All and every planet therein should and would belong to the Master Race; no competing race had any right whatever to live.

Should he, or should he not, explore the lines of those communications beams and destroy the other planets of this group? He should not, he decided. He would have to slow down, perhaps even change course; and it was quite possible that he was still within range of the sixth-order stuff of that self-styled Overlord. Besides, this group of queerly mixed entities would keep. After he had found a really distant Fenatype planet and had developed it, he would come back here and finish this minor chore.

But very shortly after making this decision Sleemet was given cause to know starkly that he had not investigated this civilization thoroughly enough by far; for his vessel was being assailed by forces of such incredible magnitude that his instantaneously reactive outer screen was already radiating in the high violet!

And, before he could do much more than put a hand to his construction panel, that outer screen began to show black spots of failure!

In Hall of Prime Computation, on Llurdiax, one entire panel of instrumentation went suddenly dead. The supervisor of that section flicked two testing switches, then scanned the last couple of inches of each of two tapes. Then he paused, for a moment stunned: knocked completely out of any Llurd's calm poise. Then, licking his lips, he spoke; apparently to empty air:

"Llanzlan Klazmon, sir, Blaydaxorb Three and Blaydaxorb Five stopped reporting, simultaneously, eleven seconds ago. Orbiting pyrometers of both planets reported thermonuclear temperatures at the end-points of their respective transmissions. End of report, sir."

The supervisor did not elaborate.

While he was appalled and terribly shocked—he had never imagined such disasters possible—it was not his job to comment or to deduce or to theorize. His business—his *only* business—was to report to a higher echelon the pertinent facts of any and all unusual events or conditions; the height of the echelon to which he reported being directly proportional to the unusualness and/or magnitude of the event or condition.

Since this event was unprecedented and of very great magnitude indeed, his report went straight to the top—thus overtaking and passing the report of Head Supervisor Klarton, which was not yet ready for delivery.

Having reported the pertinent facts to the proper echelon, the section supervisor went calmly, almost unconcernedly, back to his job of supervising his section. He paid no more attention to the incident even when the llanzlan—fully recovered now from his wounds—who had been asleep in his penthouse apartment came into the Hall from the down-flyway. (Everyone rode a force-beam up, but came down on his own wings.)

While Klazmon was not hurrying any more than usual, his usual technique was to drop a full half mile with folded wings before beginning to put on his brakes. Hence his tremendous wings and stabilizing surfaces sent blasts of cold, dense air throughout the whole end of the Hall as he slowed down for a high-G landing in his seat at his master-control console. Fingers, thumbs, and tail-tip flashed over the banked and tiered keyboards of that console; and, all around the periphery of Llurdias, that miles-wide girdle of mighty fortresses came instantly to life.

A multi-layered umbrella of full-coverage screens flashed into being over the whole city and Klazmon, engineering his fifth-order projector, sent his simulacrum of pure force out to see what had happened in or to the solar system of Blaydaxorb.

He was now, to all intents and purposes, in two places at once.

He could see, hear, feel, taste, and smell exactly as well with one self as with the other. He was, however, thoroughly accustomed to the peculiar sensations of having a complete personality; he could block out at will any perceptions of either self. And his immaterial self had two tremendous advantages over his material one. It could traverse incredibly immense distances in no measurable time; and, no matter where it went or what it encountered, his physical self would remain entirely unaffected.

In a mere flick of time, then, Klazmon was in the solar system of Blaydaxorb. The sun itself was unchanged, but in orbits three and five, where the two inhabited planets had been, there were two still-wildly-disturbed masses of liquids and gases.

He threw out a light, fast detector web, which located the marauding Fenachrone fleet in less than a second. Then, returning most of his attention to his console, he assembled seventeen exceedingly complex forces and hurled them, one at each vessel of the invading fleet.

Actually, Klazmon was little if any more affected than was Sleemet the Fenachrone about either that utterly frightful loss of life as such or the loss of those two planets as such. The Realm was big enough so that the total destruction of those two planets—of *any* two planets except of course Llurdiax itself—was unimportant to the economy of the Realm as a whole. No; what burned the llanzlan up—

made it mandatory that that fleet and the entire race whose people manned it should, after thorough study, be wiped completely out—was the brazenness, the uncivilized and illogical savagery, the incredible effrontery of this completely intolerable insult to the realm of the Llurdi and to imperial Klazmon its llanzlan.

Klazmon knew of only one race who made a habit of performing such atrocities; such wanton, illogical, insane offenses against all sense and all reason: those chlorine-breathing, amoeboid monstrosities inhabiting Galaxy DW-427-LU. Those creatures, however, as far as any Llurd had ever learned, had always confined their activities to their own galaxy. If, Klazmon thought grimly to himself, those insanely murderous amoeboids had decided to extend their operations into the Galaxy of the Llurdi, they would find such extension a very expensive one indeed.

Wherefore, hunched now over a black-filtered visiplate, with slitted eyes narrow and cat-whiskers stiffly outthrust; with both hands manipulating high-ratio vernier knobs in infinitesimal arcs; Klazmon shoveled on the coal.

5 • COMBAT!

As has been said, the Llurdi were a literal folk. Klazmon's directive had specified ". . . that no even theoretically possible attack on this planet will succeed."

Hence that was precisely what had been built. No conceivable force or combination of forces, however applied and even at pointblank range, could crack Llurdiax's utterly impenetrable shields.

Nor was that all; for Llurdan engineers, as well as Llurdan philosophers, were thoroughly familiar with the concept that "The best defense is a powerful offense." Wherefore Llurdiax's offensive projectors were designed to smash down any theoretically possible threat originating anywhere within a distance that light would require one and three-quarters millions of Tellurian years to traverse.

Under the thrustings and the stabbings, the twistings and the tearings, the wrenchings and the bludgeonings of those frightful fields of force, seventeen sets of Fenachrone defensive screens—outer, intermediate, and inner—went successively upward through the visible spectrum, through the ultra-violet, and into the black of failure; baring the individual vessel's last lines of defense, the wall-shields themselves.

Then Klazmon increased the power, gouging and raving at those ultra-stubborn defenses until those defenses were just barely holding; at which point he relaxed a little, read his verniers, leaned back in his bucket seat, and took stock.

The marauding spaceships were tremendous things; cigar-shaped; flying in hollow-globe formation with one vessel—the flagship, of course—at the exact center; spaced so closely that their screens had overlapped—overlapped in such fashion that unless and until that shell of force was broken no attack could be made upon that central ship.

So far, so good. With the overwhelming superiority of ultimate-planetary over any at-all-probable mobile installations he, Llanzlan Klazmon the Fifteenth, had smashed that shell completely. He could, he was sure, destroy all those vessels as completely.

But it would not do at all to destroy even one of them without examining both it and its crew. Klazmon *had* to know the who and the what and the wherefore and the how and the why. Therefore, leaving all of his attacking beams exactly as they were, Klazmon assembled another gigantic beam—the entire output of one Llurdiaxian fortress—and hurled it against the tail-section of the flagship.

Wall-shield and tail-section vanished in a few mano-seconds of time; and not only the tail-section, but also a few hundreds of yards of the flagship's prodigious length as well, became a furiously raging fireball; a sphere of violence incredible.

Klazmon drove his projection forward then, through the now unresisting steel wall and into the control room; where it was met by blasts of force from the hand-weapons of the Fenachrone officers.

This demonstration, however, lasted for only a second or two. Then those officers, knowing what it was that was standing there so unconcernedly, abandoned their physical assault and attacked the invading projection with the full power of the huge, black, flame-shot wells of hypnotic force that were their eyes. When the mental attack also failed they merely stood there; glaring a hatred that was actually tangible.

Klazmon immobilized each one of the officers individually with pencils of force and began to study them intensively. While much shorter and thicker and wider and immensely stronger than the Jelmi of the Realm, they were definitely Jelmoid in every important respect . . . yes, the two races had certainly had a common ancestry, and not too far back. Also, their thinking and conduct were precisely as was to be expected of any Jelman or Jelmoid race that had been allowed to develop in its unsane and illogical way for many thousands of years without the many benefits of Llurdan control!

They would of course have thought-exchange gear; any race of their evident advancement must have . . . ah, yes; over there.

Now—which of these wights would be the admiral? That one wearing the multiplex scanner would be the pilot; that one facing the banks of dials and gages would be the prime engineer; those six panels *had* to be battle panels, so those six monsters had to be gunnery officers . . . ah!

That one there—off by himself; seated (in spite of the fact that with their short, blocky legs no Fenachrone had any need, ever, to sit) at a desk that was practically a throne; facing no gadgetry and wearing consciously an aura of power and authority—that one would be the one Klazmon wanted.

Klazmon's projection flashed up to the motionlessly straining admiral. The helmets of the "mechanical educator" snapped onto the Llurd's quietly studious head and onto the head with the contemptuously sneering face—the head of First Scientist Fleet Admiral Sleemet of the Fenachrone.

That face, however, lost its sneer instantly, for Sleemet—even more overweeningly and brutally and vaingloriously prideful now than were the lower echelons of his race—had never imagined the possibility of the existence of such a mind as this monstrous invader had.

Klazmon's mind, the product of seventy thousand years of coldly logical evolution, tore ruthlessly into the mind of the Fenachrone. It bored into and twisted at that straining mind's hard-held blocks; it battered and shattered them; it knocked them down flat.

Then Klazmon, omnivorous scholar that he was, set about transferring to his own brain practically everything that the Fenachrone had ever learned. Klazmon learned, as Richard Seaton had learned previously, that all Fenachrone have authority and responsibility were meticulous record-keepers. He learned what had happened to the civilization of the Fenachrone and to its world, and who had done it and how; he learned that each and every captain knew exactly the same and had exactly the same records as did First Scientist Fleet Admiral Sleemet himself; he learned that each vessel, alone by itself, was thoroughly capable of re-creating the entire Fenachrone civilization and culture.

A few of the many other thousands of things that Klazmon learned were: That there were many Jelman and Jelmoid—human and humanoid, that is—races living in what they called the First Galaxy. That all these races were alike in destructiveness, belligerence to the point of war-lust, savagery, implacability, vengefulness, intolerance, and frightfulness generally. Not one of them (by Klazmon's light!) had any redeeming features or qualities whatever. That all these races must be destroyed if any worthwhile civilization were ever to thrive and spread.

There was no word in any language of the Realm of the Llurdi corresponding even remotely to "genocide." If there had been, Klazmon would have regarded it an an etymological curiosity. All those surviving Fenachrone would have to die: no such race as that had any right whatever to live.

Before being destroyed, however, they would have to be studied with Llurdan thoroughness; and any and all worthwhile ideas and devices and other artifacts should be and would be incorporated into the Llurdan-Jelman way of life.

One vessel would be enough, however, to preserve temporarily for the purpose of study. In fact, what was left of the flagship would be enough.

The now-vanished tail-section had contained nothing new to Llurdan science, the encyclopedic records were intact, and the flagship's personnel—males and females, adults and adolescents and children and babies—were alive and well.

Wherefore sixteen sets of multiplex projectors doubled their drain of power from Llurdias' mighty defensive girdle, and all the Fenachrone aboard sixteen superdreadnoughts died in situ, wherever they happened to be, as those sixteen vessels became tiny sunlets.

And the llanzlan issued orders:

1) The bulk of the Fenachrone flagship was to be brought in to the llanzlanate at full sixth-order drive.

2) A test section of the llanzlanate was to be converted at once to a completely authentic Fenachrone environment.

3) Every possible precaution was to be taken that no Fenachrone suffered any ill effects on the way, during transfer to their new quarters, or while in their new quarters.

Dropping the Fenachrone flagship and its personnel from his mind, Klazmon immersed himself in thought.

He had learned much. There was much more of menace than he had supposed, in many galaxies other than Galaxy DW-427-LU . . . especially that so-called First Galaxy . . . and particularly the Green System or Central System of that galaxy? The green-skinned Norlaminians—how of them? And how of that system's overlord, Seaton of Tellus? That one was, very evidently, a Jelm . . . and, even after making all due allowance for Sleemet's bias, he was of a completely uncontrolled and therefore extremely dangerous type.

And as, evidently, his was a mind of exceeding power, he could very well be a very dangerous and quite immediate threat.

The mergons must be wider-spread even than originally planned and they must be on the lookout for this Overlord Seaton. In fact, he might be worth interviewing personally. It might be well worth while, some of these years, to take some time off and go to that distant galaxy, purposely to make that Jelm Seaton's acquaintance . . .

Shrugging his shoulders and shaking both wings, Klazmon cut off his projection and called another meeting of his Board of Advisors.

He briefed them on what had happened; then went on:

"We must protect all our planets in the same way and to the same extent that this planet Llurdiax is protected now: a course of action now necessary because of these many Jelman and Jelmoid races that have been developing for untold millenia in their unsane and illogical ways, with no semblance of or attempt at either guidance or control. for untold millennia in their unsane and illogical ways, with be desroyed before it or they can do us any harm.

"Third: the manufacture and distribution of mergons will continue indefinitely at the present rate.

"Fourth: No chance or casual vessel or fleet traversing any part of the vast volume of space to be covered by our mergons is to be destroyed, or even hailed, until I myself decide what action, if any, is to be taken."

So saying, the Llanzlan Klazmon dismissed his advisors.

His great wings fanned idly as he contemplated what he had done. He was well pleased with it. He had, he reflected, scratching his head contentedly with the tip of his tail, provided for every possible contingency. Whatever this Jelm, or Jelmlike creature, named Seaton might be or do, he would pose no real threat to the llanzlanate.

Of that Klazmon was one hundred per cent sure . . .

And wrong!

6 • OF DISEMBODIED INTELLIGENCES

WE have now seen how the ripple of thought that began with the conference between Seaton and his advisors from the Green System had spread throughout all of recorded space, and how it had affected the lives and destinies of countless millions of persons who had never heard of him.

Yet a few threads remain to be drawn into our net. And one of these threads represents the strangest entities Seaton had encountered, ever . . . as well as the most deadly.

To understand what these entities are like, it is necessary to look back to their beginnings.

These are most remote, both in space and in time. In a solar system so distant from that of Sol as to be forever unknowable to anyone of Earth, and at a time an inconceivably vast number of millennia in the past, there once existed a lusty and fertile Tellus-type planet named Marghol. Over the usual millions of years mankind evolved on Marghol and thrived as usual. And finally, also as usual and according to the scheduled fate of all created material things, the planet Marghol grew old.

Whether or not a Tellus-type planet ordinarily becomes unfit to support human life before its sun goes nova is not surely known. Nor does it matter very much; for, long before either event occurs, the human race involved has developed a faster-than-light drive and has at its disposal dozens or hundreds of Earth-like planets upon which even subhuman life has not yet developed. The planet Marghol, however, while following the usual pattern in general, developed a specific thing that was, as far as is known, unique throughout all the reaches of total space and throughout all time up to the present.

On Marghol, during many, many millions of years of its prime, there had continued to exist a small, tightly-inbred, self-perpetuating cult of thinkers—of men and women who devoted their every effort and their total power to thought.

They themselves did not know what freak of mind or quirk of physical environment made the ultimate outcome possible; but after those many millions of years, during which the perpetually inbreeding group grew stronger and stronger mentally and weaker and weaker physically, the seven survivors of the group succeeded finally in liberating their minds—minds perfectly intact and perfectly functioning—from the gross and perishable flesh of their physical bodies.

Then, able to travel at the unmeasurable speed of thought and with all future time in which to work, they set out to learn everything there was to know. They would learn, they declared, not only all about space and time and zero and infinity and animals and people and life and death, but also everything else comprising or having anything to do with the totality of existence that is the Cosmic All.

This quest for knowledge has been going on, through universe after universe and through dimension after dimension, for a stretch of time that, given as a number in Tellurian years, would be a number utterly incomprehensible to the human mind. For—what perceptible or tangible difference is there, to the human mind, between a googol-plex of seconds and the same number of centuries? And, since these free minds ordinarily kept track of time only by the life-cycles of suns, the period of time during which they had already traveled and studied could have been either shorter or longer than either of the two exact figures mentioned.

Seven free minds had left the planet Marghol. They called themselves, in lieu of names, "One" to "Seven" in order of their liberation.

For a brief time—a mere cosmic eye-wink; a few hundreds of millions of years—there had been eight, since One had consented to dematerialize one applicant for immortality. The applicant Eight, however, sick and tired of eternal life, had committed suicide by smashing his sixth-order being out of existence against Richard Seaton's sixth-order screens.

Now those seven free minds, accompanied by the free mind of Immortality Candidate Doctor Marc C. DuQuesne, were flying through ultra-deep space in a time-stasis capsule. This capsule, as has been said, was designed and powered to travel almost to infinity in both space and time. But, as the Norlaminians pointed out to Seaton, his basic assumptions were invalid.

Nothing happened, however, for week after week. Then, so immensely far out in intergalactic space that even the vast bulk of a galaxy lying there would have been invisible even to Palomar's "Long Eye," the hurtling capsule struck a cloud of hydrogen gas.

That gas was, by Earthly standards, a hard vacuum; but the capsule's velocity by that time was so immensely great that that cloud might just as well have been a mountain of solid rock. The capsule's directors tried, with all their prodigious might and speed, to avoid the obstruction, but even with fullest power they did not have time enough.

Eight multi-ton power-bars of activated uranium flared practically instantaneously into ragingly incandescent gas; into molecular, atomic, and subatomic vapor and debris. A fireball brighter than a sun glared briefly; then nothing whatever was visible where that massive structure had been.

And out of that sheer emptiness came a cold, clear thought: the thought of Doctor Marc C. DuQuesne.

"One, are you familiar enough with this region of space to estimate at all closely how long we were in that stasis of time and where we now are with reference to the First Galaxy?"

Freemind One did not exactly answer the question. "What matters it?" he asked. If the thought of an immortal and already incredibly old and incredibly knowledgeful mind can be said to show surprise, that thought did. "It should be clear, even to you of infinitesimally short life, that any length of time expressible in any finite number of definite time periods is actually but a moment. Also, the Cosmic All is vast indeed; larger by many orders of magnitude than any that the boldest of your thinkers has as yet dared to imagine.

"Whether or not space is infinite I do not know. Whether or not my life span will be infinite I do not know. I do not as yet completely understand infinity. I do know, however, that both infinite time and infinite space are requisite for the acquisition of infinite knowledge, which is my goal; wherefore I am well content. You have no valid reason whatever for wishing to return to your Earth. Instead, you should be as eager as I am to explore and to study the as yet unknown."

"I have unfinished business there." DuQuesne's thought was icy cold. "I'm going back there whether you do or not."

"To kill beings who have at best but an instant to live? To rule an ultra-microscopic speck of cosmic dust? A speck whose fleeting existence is of but infinitesimal importance to the Great Scheme of Things? Are you still infantile enough, despite your recent transformation, to regard as valid such indefensible reasons as those?"

"They're valid enough to me. And you'd have to go back, too, I should think. Or isn't it still true that science demands the dematerialization of the whole *Skylark* party?"

"Truth is variable," One said. "Thus, while certain of our remarks were not true in the smaller aspect, each of them was designed to elicit a larger truth. They aided in the initiation of chains of events by observation of which I will be able to fit many more constituent parts of this you call the First Universe precisely into place in the Great Scheme.

"Now as to you, DuQuesne. The probability was small that you were sufficiently advanced to become a worthy member of our group; but I decided to give you your chance and permitted Richard Seaton to do what he did. As a matter of fact I, not Seaton, did it. You have failed; and I now know that no member of your race can ever become a true Scholar. In a very few millions of your years you would not be thinking of knowledge at all, but merely of self-destruction. I erred, one-tenth of a cycle since, in admitting Freemind Eight to our study group; an entity who was then at approximately the same stage of development as you now are. I will not repeat that error. You will be rematerialized and will be allowed to do whatever you please."

The mind of DuQuesne almost gasped.

"Out here? Even if you re-create my ship I'd never get back!"

"You should and will have precisely the same chance as before of living out your normal instant of life in normal fashion. To that end I will construct for you a vessel that will be the replica of your former one except in that it will have a sixth-order drive—what your fellow-human Seaton called the 'Cosmic Energy' drive—so that you will be able to make the journey in comparatively few of your days. I will instruct you in this drive and in certain other matters that will be required to implement what I have said. I will set your vessel's controls upon your home galaxy at the correct acceleration.

"I compute . . . I construct."

And faster by far than even an electronic eye could follow, a pattern of incredibly complex stresses formed in the empty other.

Elemental particles, combining instantaneously, built practically instantaneously upward through electrons and protons and atoms and molecules beams and weaponry up to a million tons or more of perfectly-operating super-dreadnought—and at the same time built the vastly more complex structure of the two hundred pounds or so of meat and so forth that were to enclothe Freemind DuQuesne—and did the whole job in much less time than the blink of an eye.

". . . I instruct . . . It is done," and all seven freeminds vanished.

And DuQuesne, seated at a thoroughly familar control-board and feeling normal gravity on the seat of his pants, stared at that board's instruments, for a moment stunned.

According to those instruments the ship was actually travelling at an acceleration of one hundred twenty-seven lights; its internal gravity was actually nine hundred eighty-one point zero six centimeters per second squared.

He stared around the entire room, examining minutely each familiar object. Activating a visiplate, he scanned the immense skyrover, inside and out, from stem to stern: finding that it was in fact, except for the stated improvements, an exact duplicate of the mighty ship of war he had formerly owned: which, he still thought, had been one of the most powerful battleships ever built by man.

Then, and only then, did he examine the hands resting, quiescent but instantly ready, upon the board's flat, bare table. They were big tanned, powerful hands; with long, strong, tapering, highly competent fingers. They were his hands—his own hands in every particular, clear down to the tiny scar on the side of his left index finger; where, years before, a bit of flying glass from an exploding flask had left its mark.

Shaking his head, he got up and went to his private cabin, where he strode up to a full-length mirror.

The man who stared back at him out of it was tall and powerfully built; with thick, slightly wavy hair of an intense, glossy black. The eyes, only a trifle lighter in shade, were surmounted by heavy black eyebrows growing together above his finely-chiseled aquiline beak of a nose. His saturnine face, while actually tanned, looked almost pale because of the blackness of the heavy beard always showing through, even after the closest possible shave.

"He *could* rematerialize me perfectly—and did," he said aloud to himself, "and the whole ship—exactly!"

Scowling in concentration, he went into his bathroom and stepped upon the platform of his weight-and-height Fairbanks. Six feet and seven-eighths of an inch. Precisely right. Two hundred two and three-quarters pounds. Ditto.

He examined the various items of equipment and of every-day use. There was his cutthroat razor, Osnomian-made of arenak—vastly sharper than any Earthly razor could possibly be honed and so incredibly hard that it could shave generation after generation of men with no loss whatever of edge.

Comb, brush, toothbrush, lotion—inside the drawers and out—every item was exactly as he had left it . . . clear down to the correctly-printed, peculiarly-distorted tubes of tooth-paste and of shaving cream; each of which, when he picked it up, fitted perfectly into the grip of his left hand.

"I'll . . . be . . . totally . . . damned," DuQuesne said then, aloud.

7 • DU QUESNE AND KLAZMON

THE *Skylark of Valeron* swung in orbit around the sun of Earth. She was much more of worldlet than a spaceship, being a perfect sphere over a thousand kilometers in diameter. She *had* to be big. She had to house, among other things, the one-thousand-kilometers-diameter graduated circles of declination and of right ascension required to chart the thousands of millions of galaxies making up any given universe of the Cosmic All.

She was for the most part cold and dark. Even the master-control helmets, sprouting masses and mazes of thigh-thick bundles of hair-thin silver wire, hung inactivated in the neutral gray, featureless master-control room. The giant computer, however—the cubic mile of ultra-miniaturization that everyone called the "Brain"—was still in operation; and in the worldlet's miles-wide chart-room, called the "tank," there still glowed the enormous lenticular aggregation of points of light that was the chart of the First Universe—each tiny pool of light representing a galaxy composed of thousands of millions of solar systems.

A precisely coded thought impinged upon a receptor.

A relay clicked, whereupon a neighboring instrument, noting the passage of current through its vitals, went busily but silently to work, and an entire panel of instrumentation came to life.

Switch after switch snapped home. Field after field of time-stasis collapsed. The planetoid's artificial sun resumed its shining; breezes began again to stir the leaves of trees and of shrubbery; insects resumed their flitting from bloom to once-more-scented bloom. Worms resumed their gnawings and borings beneath the green velvet carpets that were the lawns. Brooks began again to flow; gurglingly. Birds took up their caroling and chirping and twittering precisely where they had left off so long before; and three houses— there was a house now for Shiro and his bride of a month —became comfortably warm and softly, invitingly livable.

All that activity meant, of course, that the Seaton-Crane party would soon be coming aboard.

They were in fact already on the way, in *Skylark Two;* the forty-foot globe which, made originally of Osnomian arenak and the only spaceship they owned, had been "flashed over" into ultra-refractory inoson and now served as Captain's gig, pinnace, dinghy, lifeboat, landing craft, and so forth—whatever any of the party wanted her to do. There were many other craft aboard the *Skylark of Valeron,* of course, of various shapes and sizes; but *Two* had always been the Seatons' favorite "small boat."

As *Two* approached the *Valeron,* directly in line with one of her huge main ports, Seaton slowed down to a dawdling crawl—a mere handful of miles per second—and thought into a helmet already on his head; and the massive gates of locks—of a miles-long succession of locks through the immensely thick skin of the planetoid—opened in front of flying *Two* and closed behind her. Clearing the last gate, Seaton put on a gee and a half of deceleration and brought the little flying sphere down to a soft and easy landing in her berth in the back yard of the Seatons' house.

Eight people disembarked; five of whom were the three Seatons and Martin and Margaret Crane. (Infant Lucile Crane rode joyously on her mother's left hip.) Seventh was short, chunky, lightning-fast Shiro, whose place in these *Skylark* annals has not been small. Originally Crane's "man," he had long since become Crane's firm friend; and he was now as much of a Skylarker as was any of the others.

Eighth was Lotus Blossom, Shiro's small, finely wrought, San Francisco-born and western-dressed bride, whom the others had met only that morning, just before leaving Earth. She looked like a living doll—but appearances can be *so* deceiving! She was in fact one of the most proficient female experts in unarmed combat then alive.

"Our house first, please, all of you," Dorothy said. "We'll eat before we do one single solitary thing else. I could eat that fabled missionary from the plains of Timbuctoo."

Margaret laughed. "Hat and gown and hymnbook too," she finished. "Me, too, Dick."

"Okay by me; I could toy with a couple of morsels myself," Seaton said, and pencils of force wafted the eight into the roomy kitchen of the house that was in almost every detail an exact duplicate of the Seatons' home on Earth. "You're the chief kitchen mechanic, Red-Top; strut your stuff."

Dorothy looked at and thought into the controller—she no longer had to wear any of the limited-control headsets to operate them—and a damask-clothed table, set for six, laden with a wide variety of food and equipped with six carved oak chairs and two high-chairs, came instantly into being in the middle of the room.

The Nisei girl jumped violently; then smiled apologetically. "Shiro *told* me about such things, but . . . well, maybe I'll get used to them sometimes I hope."

"Sure you will, Lotus," Seaton assured her. "It's pretty weird at first, but you get used to it fast."

"I sincerely hope so," Lotus said, and eyed the six dinner places dubiously. She had thought that she was thoroughly American, but she wasn't quite. Traditions are strong. With an IQ that a Heidelberg student might envy, part of the crew of the most powerful vehicle man had ever seen, fully educated and trained . . . it was evident that Shiro's dainty little bride was more than a little doubtful about sitting at that table.

Until Dorothy took her by the hand and sat her down. "This is where I like my friends to sit," she announced. "Where I can see them."

A flush dyed the porcelain-like perfection of Lotus's skin. "I thank you, Mrs.—"

"Friends, remember?" Seaton broke in. "Call her Dot. Now let's eat!"

Whereafter, they worked.

It may be wondered, among those historians not familiar with the saga of the Skylarks, why so much consternation and trouble should come from so small an event as the probabilistic speculation of a single Norlaminian sage that one mere human body, lately cast into the energy forms of the disembodied intelligences, might soon return into the universe in a viable form.

Such historians do not, of course, know Blackie DuQuesne.

While Seaton, Crane and the others were eating their meal, across distances to be measured in gigaparsecs, countless millions of persons were in one way or another busy at work on projects central to their own central concern. Seaton and Crane were not idle. They were waiting for further information . . . and at the same time, refurbishing the inner man with food, with rest and with pleasant company; but an hour later, after dinner, after the table and its appurtenances had vanished and the three couples were seated in the living room, more or less facing the fire, Seaton stoked up his battered black briar and Crane lighted one of his specially made cigarettes.

"Well?" Seaton demanded then. "Have you thunk up anything you think is worth two tinker's whoops in Hades?"

Crane smiled ruefully. "Not more than one, I'd say—if that many. Let's consider that thought or message that Carfon is sending out. It will be received, he says, only by persons or entities who not only know more than we do about one or more specific things, but also are friendly enough to be willing to share their knowledge with us. And to make the matter murkier, we have no idea either of what it is that we lack or what it, whatever it is, is supposed to be able to do. Therefore Point One would be: how are they going to get in touch with us? By what you called magic?"

Seaton did not answer at first, then only nodded. "Magic" was still a much less than real concept to him. He said, "If you say so—but remember the Peruvian Indian medicine-men and the cinchona bark that just happened to be full of quinine. So, whatever you want to call it—magic or extra-sensory perception or an unknown band of the sixth or what-have-you—I'll bet my last shirt it'll be *bio*. And who-ever pitches it at us will be good enough at it to *know* that they can hit us with it, so all we have to do about that is wait for it to happen. However, what I'm mostly interested in right now is nothing that far out, but what we *know* that a reincarnated Blackie DuQuesne could and probably would do."

"Such as?"

"The first thing he'll do, for all the tea in China, will be to design and set up some gadget or gizmo or technique to kill me with. Certainly me, and probably you, and quite possibly all of us."

Dorothy and Margaret both gasped; but Crane nodded and said, "Check. I check you to your proverbial nineteen decimals. Also, and quite possibly along with that opera-tion, an all-out attempt to reconquer Earth. He wouldn't set out to destroy Earth, at this time, at least . . . would he, do you think?"

Seaton thought for seconds, then said, "My best guess would be no. He wants to boss it, not wipe it out. How-ever, there are a few other things that might come . . ."

"Wait up, presh!" Dorothy snapped. "Those two will hold us for a while; especially the first one. I wish to go on record at this point to the effect that I want my husband *alive*, not dead."

Seaton grinned. "You and me both, pet," he said. "I'm in favor of it. Definitely. However, as long as I stay inside the *Valeron* here he doesn't stand the chance of a snow-flake in you-know-where of getting at me . . ."

How wrong Seaton was!

". . . so the second point is the one that's really of over-riding importance. The rub is that we can't make even a wild guess at when he's going to get loose . . . He *could* be building his ship right now . . . so, Engineer Martin Crane, what's your thought as to defending Earth; as adequately as possible but in the shortest possible time?"

Crane inhaled—slowly—a deep lungful of smoke, ex-haled it even more slowly, and stubbed out the butt. "That's a tall order, Dick," he said, finally, "but I don't think it's hopeless. Since we know DuQuesne's exact line of departure, we know at least approximately the line of his return. As a first-approximation idea we should, I think, cover that line thoroughly with hair-triggered automation. We should occupy the fourth and the fifth completely; thus taking care of everything we *know* that he knows . . . but as for the sixth . . ." Crane paused in thought.

"Yeah," Seaton agreed. "That sixth order's an entirely different breed of cats. It's a pistol—a question with a capital Q. About all we can do on it, I'd say, is cover everything we know of it and then set up supersensitive analsynths coupled to all the automatic constructors and such-like gizmos we can dream up—with as big a gaggle of ground-and-lofty dreamers as we can round up. The Norlaminians, certainly; and Sacner Carfon for sure. If what he and Drasnik pulled off wasn't magic it certainly was a remarkably reasonable facsimile thereof. All six of us, of course, and . . ."

"But what can you possibly want of us?" Shiro asked, and Dorothy said, "That goes double for Peggy and me, Dick. Of what good could we two possibly be, thinking about such stuff as that?"

Seaton flushed. " 'Scuse, please; my error. I switched thinking without announcing the switch. I do know, though, that our minds all work differently—especially Shiro's and double-especially Lotus's—and that when you don't have the faintest glimmering of what you're getting into you don't know what you're going to have to have to cope with it." He grinned.

"If you can untangle that, I mean," he said.

"I think so," said Crane, unruffled; he had had long practice in following Seaton's lightning leaps past syntax. "And you think that this will enable us to deal with DuQuesne?"

"It'll have to," Seaton said positively. "One thing we know, *something* has to. He's not going to send us a polite message asking to be friends—he's going to hit with all he's got. So," he finished, "let's hop to it. The Norlaminian observers' reports are piling up on the tapes right now. And we'd all better keep our eyes peeled—as well as all the rest of our senses and instruments!—for Doctor Marc C. Blackie DuQuesne!"

And DuQuesne, so immensely far out in intergalactic space, at control board and computer, explored for ten solid hours the vastnesses of his new knowledge.

Then he donned a thought-helmet and thought himself up a snack; after eating which—scarcely tasting any part of it—he put in another ten solid hours of work. Then, leaning back in his form-fitting seat, he immersed himself in thought—and, being corporeal, no longer a pattern of pure force, went sound asleep.

He woke up a couple of hours later; stiff, groggy, and ravenous. He thought himself up a supper of steak and mushrooms, hashed browns, spinach, coffee, and apple pie a la mode. He ate it—with zest, this time—then sought his long-overdue bed.

In the morning, after a shower and a snave and a breakfast of crisp bacon and over-easy eggs, toast and butter and marmalade, and four cups of strong, black coffee, he sat down at his board and again went deep into thought. This time, he thought in words and sentences, the better to nail down his conclusions.

"One said I'd have precisely the same chance as before of living out my normal lifetime. Before what? Before the dematerialization or before Seaton got all that extra stuff? Since he gave me sixth order drive, offense, defense, and communications, he could have—probably did—put me on a basis of equality with Seaton as of now. Would he have given me any more than that?"

DuQuesne paused and worked for ten busy minutes at computer and control board again. What he learned was in the form of curves and quantities, not words; he did not attempt to speak them aloud, but sat staring into space.

Then, satisfied that the probabilities were adequate to base a plan on, he spoke out loud again: "No. Why should he give me everything that Seaton's got? He didn't owe me anything." To Blackie DuQuesne that was not a rueful complaint but a statement of fact. He went on. "Assume we both now have a relatively small part of the spectrum of the sixth-order forces, if I keep using this drive—Ouch! What the living *hell* was *that?*"

DuQuesne leaped to his feet. "That" had been a sixth-order probe, at the touch of which his vessel's every course of defensive screen had flared into action.

DuQuesne was not shaken, no. But he was surprised, and he didn't like to be surprised. There should have been no probes out here!

The probe had been cut off almost instantaneously; but "almost" instantaneously is not quite zero time, and sixth-order forces operate at the speed of thought. Hence, in that not-quite-zero instant of time during which the intruding mind had been in contact with his own, DuQuesne learned a little. The creature was undoubtedly highly intelligent—and, as undoubtedly, unhuman to the point of monstrosity . . . and DuQuesne had no doubt whatever in his own mind that the alien would think the same of any Tellurian.

DuQuesne studied his board and saw, much to his surprise, that only one instrument showed any drain at all above maintenance level, and that one was a *milli*ammeter —the needle of which was steady on the scale at a reading of one point three seven *mils!* He was not being attacked at all—merely being observed—and by an observation system that was using practically no power at all!

Donning a helmet, so as to be able himself to operate at the speed of thought, DuQuesne began—very skittishly and very gingerly indeed—to soften down his spheres and zones and shells and solid fields of defensive force. He softened and softened them down; down to the point at which a working projection could come through and work.

And a working projection came through.

No one of Marc C. DuQuesne's acquaintances, friend or enemy, had ever said that he was any part of either a weakling or a coward. The consensus was that he was harder than the ultra-refractory hubs of hell itself. Nevertheless, when the simulacrum of Llanzlan Klazmon the Fifteenth of the Realm of the Llurdi came up to within three feet of him and waggled one gnarled forefinger at the helmets of a mechanical educator, even DuQuesne's burly spirit began to quail a little—but he was strong enough and hard enough not let any sign show.

With every mind-block he owned set hard, DuQuesne donned a headset and handed its mate to his visitor. He engaged that monstrous alien mind to mind. Then, releasing his blocks, he sent the Llurdi a hard, cold, sharp, diamond-clear—and lying!—thought:

"Yes? Who are you, pray, and what, to obtrude your uninvited presence upon me, Foalang Kassi a' Doompf, the Highest Imperial of the Drailsen Quadrant?"

This approach was, of course, the natural one for DuQuesne to make; he did not believe in giving away truth when lies might be so much cheaper—and less dangerous. It was equally of course the worst possible approach to Klazmon: reenforcing as it did every unfavorable idea the Llurd had already formed from his lightning-fast preliminary once-over-lightly of the man and of the man's tremendous spaceship.

Klazmon did not think back at DuQuesne directly. Instead, he thought to himself and, as DuQuesne knew, for the record; thoughts that the Earthman could read like print.

To the Llurd, DuQuesne was a peculiarly and repulsively obnoxious monstrosity. Physically a Jelm, he belonged to a race of Jelmi that had never been subjected to any kind of logical, sensible, or even intelligent control.

Klazmon then thought at DuQuesne; comparing him with Mergon and Luloy on the one hand and with Sleemet of the Fenachrone on the other—and deciding that all three races were basically the same. The Llurd showed neither hatred nor detestation; he was merely contemptuous, intolerant, and utterly logical. "Like the few remaining Fenachrone and the rebel faction of our own Jelmi and the people you think of as the Chlorans, your race is, definitely, surplus population; a nuisance that must be and shall be abated. Where—" Klazmon suddenly drove a thought— "is the Drailsen Quadrant?"

DuQuesne, however, was not to be caught napping. His blocks held. "You'll never know," he sneered. "Any task-force of yours that ever comes anywhere near us will not last long enough to energize a sixth-order communicator."

"That's an idle boast," Klazmon stated thoughtfully. "It is true that you and your vessel are far out of range of any possible Llurdiaxian attacking beam. Even this projection of me is being relayed through four mergons. Nevertheless we can and we will find you easily when this becomes desirable. This point will be reached as soon as we have computed the most logical course to take in exterminating all such surplus races as yours."

And Klazmon's projection vanished; and the helmet he had been wearing fell toward the floor.

DuQuesne was shocked as he had never been shocked before; and when he learned from his analsynths just what the range of *one* of those incredible "mergons" was, he was starkly appalled.

One thing was crystal-clear: He was up against some truly first-class opposition here. And it had just stated, calmly and definitely, that its intention was to exterminate him, Blackie DuQuesne.

The master of lies had learned to assess the value of a truth very precisely. He knew this one to be 22-karat, crystal-clear, pure quill. Whereupon Blackie DuQuesne turned to some very intensive thought indeed, compared with which his previous efforts might have been no more than a summer afternoon's reverie.

We know now, of course, that Blackie DuQuesne lacked major elements of information, and that his constructions could not therefore be complete. They lacked Norlaminian rigor, or the total visualization of his late companions, the disembodied intellectuals. And they lacked information.

DuQuesne knew nothing of Mergon and Luloy, now inward bound on Earth in a hideout orbit. He could not guess how his late visitor had ever heard of the Fenachrone. Nor knew he anything of that strange band of the sixth order to which Seaton referred, with more than half a worried frown, as "magic." In short, DuQuesne was attempting to reach the greatest conclusion of his life through less than perfect means, with only fragmentary facts to go on.

Nevertheless, Blackie C. DuQuesne, as Seaton was wont to declare, was no slouch at figuring; and so he did in time come to a plan which was perhaps the most brilliant—and also was perhaps the most witless!—of his career.

Lips curled into something much more sneer than grin, DuQuesne sat down at his construction board. He had come to the conclusion that what he needed was help, and he knew exactly where to go to get it. His ship wasn't big enough by far to hold a sixth-order projection across any important distance . . . but he could build, in less than an hour, a sixth-order broadcaster. It wouldn't be selective. It would be enormously wasteful of power. But it would carry a signal across half a universe.

Whereupon, in less than an hour, a signal began to pour out, into and through space:

"DuQuesne calling Seaton! Reply on tight beam of the sixth. DuQuesne calling Seaton! Reply on tight beam of the sixth. DuQuesne calling Seaton . . ."

8 • INDUSTRIAL REVOLUTION

WHEN Seaton and Crane had begun to supply the Earth with ridiculously cheap power, they had expected an economic boom and a significant improvement in the standard of living. Neither of them had any idea, however, of the effect upon the world's economy that their space-flights would have; but many tycoons of industry did.

They were shrewd operators, those tycoons. As one man they licked their chops at the idea of interstellar passages made in days. They gloated over thoughts of the multifold increase in productive capacity that would have to be made so soon; as soon as commerce was opened up with dozens and then with hundreds of Tellus-type worlds, inhabited by human beings as human as those of Earth. And when they envisioned hundreds and hundreds of uninhabited Tellus-type worlds, each begging to be grabbed and exploited by whoever got to it first with enough stuff to hold it and to develop it . . . they positively drooled.

These men did not think of money as money, but as their most effective and most important tool: a tool to be used as knowledgeably as the old-time lumberjack used his axe.

Thus, Earth was going through convulsions of change more revolutionary by far than any it had experienced throughout all previous history. All those pressures building up at once had blown the lid completely off. Seaton and Crane and their associates had been working fifteen hours a day for months training people in previously unimagined skills; trying to keep the literally exploding economy from degenerating into complete chaos.

They could not have done it alone, of course. In fact, it was all that a thousand Norlaminian "Observers" could do to keep the situation even approximately in hand. And even the Congress—*mirabile dictu!*—welcomed those aliens with open arms; for it was so hopelessly deadlocked in trying to work out any workable or enforceable laws that it was accomplishing nothing at all.

All steel mills were working at one hundred ten per cent of capacity. So were almost all other kinds of plants. Machine tools were in such demand that no estimated time of delivery could be obtained. Arenak, dagal, and inoson, those wonder-materials of the construction industry, would be in general supply some day; but that day would not be allowed to come until the changeover could be made without disrupting the entire economy. Inoson especially was confined to the spaceship builders; and, while every pretense was being made that production was being increased as fast as possible, the demand for spaceships was so insatiable that every hulk that could leave atmosphere was out in deep space.

Multi-billion-dollar corporations were springing up all over Earth. Each sought out and began to develop a Tellus-type planet of its own, to bring up as a civilized planet or merely to exploit as it saw fit. Each was clamoring for—and using every possible artifice of persuasion, lobbying, horse-trading, and out-and-out bribery and corruption to obtain—spaceships, personnel, machinery light and heavy, office equipment, and supplies. All the employables of Earth, and many theretofore considered unemployable, were at work.

Earth was a celestial madhouse . . .

It is no wonder, then, that Seaton and Crane were haggard and worn when they had to turn their jobs over to two upper-bracket Norlaminians and leave Earth.

Their situation thereafter was not much better.

The first steps were easy—anyway, the decisions involved were easy; the actual work involved was roughly equivalent to the energy budget of several Sol-type suns. It is an enormous project to set up a line of defense hundreds of thousands of miles long; especially when the setters-up do not know exactly what to expect in the way of attack. They knew, in fact, only one thing: that the Norlaminians had made a probabilistic statement that Marc C. DuQuesne was likely to be present among them before long.

That was excuse, reason and compulsion enough to demand the largest and most protracted effort they could make. The mere preliminaries involved laying out axes of action that embraced many solar systems, locating and developing sources of materials and energies that were enough to smother a hundred suns. As that work began to shape up, Seaton and Crane came face to face with the secondary line of problems . . . and at that point Seaton suddenly smote himself on the forehead and cried: "Dunark!"

Crane looked up. "Dunark? Why, yes, Dick. Quite right. Not only is he probably the universe's greatest strategist, but he knows the enemy almost as well as you and I do."

"And besides," Seaton added, "he doesn't think like us. Not at all. And that's what we want; so I'll call him now and we'll compute a rendezvous."

Wherefore, a few days later, Dunark's Osnomian cruiser matched velocities with the hurtling worldlet and began to negotiate its locks. Seaton shoved up the *Valeron's* air-pressure, cut down its gravity, and reached for the master thermostat.

"Not too hot, Dick," Dorothy said. "Light gravity is all right, but make them wear some clothes any time they're outside their special quarters. I simply *won't* run around naked in my own house. And I won't have them doing it, either."

Seaton laughed. "The usual eighty-three degrees and twenty-five per cent humidity. They'll wear clothes, all right. She'll be tickled to death to wear that fur coat you gave her—she doesn't get a chance to, very often—and we can stand it easily enough," and the four Tellurians went out to the dock to greet their green-skinned friends of old: Crown Prince Dunark and Crown Princess Sitar of Osnome, one of the planets of the enormous central sun of the Central System.

Warlike, bloodthirsty, supremely able Dunark; and Sitar, his lovely, vivacious—and equally warlike—wife. He was wearing ski-pants (Osnome's temperature, at every point on its surface and during every minute of every day of the year, is one hundred degrees Fahrenheit), a heavy sweater, wool socks, and fur-lined moccasins. She wore a sweater and slacks under her usual fantastic array of Osnomian jewelry; and over it, as Seaton had predicted, the full-length mink coat. Each was wearing only one Osnomian machine-pistol instead of the arsenal that had been their customary garb such a short time before.

The three men greeted each other warmly and executed a six-hand handshake; the while the two white women and the green one went into an arms-wrapped group; each talking two hundred words to the minute.

A couple of days later, the Norlaminian task-force arrived and a council of war was held that lasted for one full working day. Then, the defense planned in length and in depth, construction began. Seaton and Crane sat in the two master-control helmets of the Brain. Rovol worked with the brain of the Norlaminian spaceship. Dozens of other operators, men and women, worked at and with other, less powerful devices.

On the surface of a nearby planet, ten thousand square miles of land were leveled and paved to form the Area of Work. Stacks and piles and rows and assortments of hundreds of kinds of structural members appeared as though by magic. Gigantic beams of force, made visible by a thin and dusty pseudo-mist, flashed here and there; seizing this member and that and these and them and those and joining them together with fantastic speed to form enormous towers and platforms and telescope-like things and dirigible tubes and projectors.

Some of these projectors took containers of pure force out to white dwarf stars after neutronium. Others took faidons—those indestructible jewels that are the *sine qua non* of higher-order operation—out to the cores of stars to be worked into lenses of various shapes and sizes. Out into the environment of scores of millions of degrees of temperature and of scores of millions of tons per square inch of pressure that is the only environment in which the faidon can be worked by any force known to the science of man.

The base-line, which was to be built of enormous, absolutely rigid beams of force, could not be of planetary, or even of orbital dimensions. It had to extend, a precisely measured length, from the core of a star to that of another, having as nearly as possible the same proper motion, over a hundred parsecs away. Thus it took over a week to build and to calibrate that base-line; but, once that was done, the work went fast.

The most probable lines of approach were blocked by fourth-, fifth-, and sixth-order installations of tremendous range and of planetary power; less probable ones by defenses of somewhat lesser might; supersensitive detector webs fanned out everywhere. And this work, which would have required years a short time before, was only a matter of a couple of weeks for the gigantic constructor-projectors now filling the entire Area of Work.

When everything that anyone could think of doing had been done, Seaton lit his pipe, jammed both hands into his pockets, and turned to his wife. "Well, we've got it made—now what are we going to do with it? Sit on our hands until Blackie DuQuesne trips a trigger or some Good Samaritan answers our call? I'd give three nickels to know whether he's loose yet or not, and if he is loose, just where he is at this moment."

"I'd raise you a dime," she said; and then, since Dorothy Seaton concealed an extremely useful brain under her red curls, she added slowly, "And maybe . . . you know what the Norlaminians deduced: that, upon liberation, he'd be rematerialized? That he'd have a very good spaceship. That, before attacking us, he would recruit personnel, both men and women, both from need of their help and from loneliness . . . wait up—*loneliness!* Who—a girl, probably—would he get loneliest for?"

Seaton snapped his fingers. "I can make an awfully good guess. Hunkie de Marigny."

"Hunkie de Who? Oh, I remember. That big moose with the black hair and the shape."

Seaton laughed. "Funny, isn't it, that such an accurate description can be so misleading? But my guess is, if he's back she knows it . . . I think it'd be smart to flip myself over to the Bureau and see what I can find out. Want to come along?"

"Uh-uh; she isn't my dish of tea."

Seaton projected his solid-seeming simulacrum of pure force to distant Tellus, to Washington, and to the sidewalk in front of the Bureau. He mounted the steps, entered the building, said "Hi, Gorgeous" to the shapely blonde receptionist, and took an elevator to the sixteenth floor; where he paused briefly in thought.

He hadn't better see Hunkie first, or only; Ferdinand Scott, the world's worst gossip, would talk about it, and Hunkie would draw her own conclusions. He'd pull Scotty's teeth first.

Wherefore he turned into the laboratory beside the one that once had been his own. "Hi, Scotty," he said, holding out his hand, "Don't tell me they've actually got you *working* for a change."

Scott, a chunky youth with straw-colored hair that needed cutting, jumped off of his stool and shook hands vigorously. "Hi, Dickie, old top! Alla time work. 'Slavey' Scott; that's me. But boy oh boy, *did* I goof on that 'Nobody Holme' bit! You and that bottle of waste solution, that you stirred the whole world up with like goulash! Why can't anything like that ever happen to me? But I s'pose I'd've blown the whole world to hellangone up instead of just putting it into the God-awful shape it's in now, like you and Blackie DuQuesne did. *Wow*, what a mess!"

"Yeah. Speaking of DuQuesne—seen him lately?"

"Not since the big bust. The Norlaminians probably know all about him."

"They don't. I asked. They lost him."

"Well, you might ask Hunkie de Marigny. She'll know if anybody does."

"Oh—she still here?"

"Yeah. Most of us are, and will be."

Seaton chatted for another minute, then, "Take it easy, guy," he said; and went up the corridor to Room 1631. The door was wide open, so he went in without knocking.

"Park it. Be with you in a moment," a smooth contralto voice said, and Seaton sat down on a chair near the door.

The woman—Doctor Stephanie de Marigny, nuclear physicist and good at her trade—kept both eyes fastened on a four-needle meter about eighteen inches in front of her nose. Her well-kept hands and red-nailed fingers, working blind with the sure precision of those of a world-champion typist, opened and closed switches, moved sliders and levers, and manipulated a dozen or so vernier knobs in tiny arcs.

There was nothing to show any uninformed observer what she was doing. Whatever it was that she was working on could have been behind that instrument-filled panel—or down in some sub-basement—or at the Proving Grounds down the Potomac—or a million miles or parsecs out in space. Whatever it was or wherever, as she worked the four needles of the master-meter closer and closer together as each needle approached the center-zero mark of the meter's scale—

Until finally the four hair-thin flat needles were exactly in line with each other and with the hair-thin zero mark. Whereupon four heavy plungers drove home and every light on the panel flashed green and went out.

"On the button," she said then, aloud. She rose to her feet, stretched as gracefully and luxuriously and unselfconsciously as does a cat, and turned toward her visitor.

"Hi, Hunkie," Seaton said. "Can you spare me a minute?"

"Nice to see you again, Dick." She came toward him, hand outstretched. "I could probably be talked into making it two minutes."

The word "big," while true, was both inadequate and misleading. Stephanie de Marigny was tall—five feet ten in her nylons—and looked even taller because of her three-inch heels, her erect posture, and because of the mass of jet-black hair piled high on her head.

Her breasts jutted; her abdomen was flat and hard; her wide, flat hips flared out from a startlingly narrow waist; and her legs would have made any professional glamour-photographer drool. And her face, if not as beautiful as her body, was fully as striking. Her unplucked eyebrows, as black as her hair, were too long and too thick and too bushy and grew too nearly together above a nose that was as much of a beak as DuQuesne's own. The lashes over her deep brown eyes were simply incredible. Her cheekbones were too large and too prominent. Her fire-engine-red mouth was too big. Her square chin and her hard, clean line of jaw were too outstanding; demanded too much notice. Her warm, friendly, dimple-displaying smile, however, revealed the charm that was actually hers.

Seaton said, "As always, you're really a treat for the optic nerve."

She ignored the compliment. "You aren't; you look like a catastrophe looking for a place to happen. You ought to take better care of yourself, Dick. Get some sleep once in a while."

"I'm going to, as soon as I can. But what I came in for —have you heard anything of Blackie lately?"

"No. Not since he got delusions of grandeur. Why? Should I have?"

"Not that I know of. I just thought maybe you two had enough of a thing on so you'd keep in touch."

"Uh-uh. I ran around with him a little, is all. Nothing serious. Of all the men I know who understand and appreciate good music, he's the youngest, the best-looking, and the most fun. Also the biggest. I can wear high heels and not tower over him, which I can't do with most men . . ." She paused, nibbling at her lower lip, then went on, "My best guess is that he's out on one of the new planets somewhere, making several hundred thousand tax-free dollars per year. That's what I'm going to be doing as soon as I finish Observers' School here."

"You're the gal who can do it, too. Luck, Hunkie."

"Same to you, Dick. Drop in again, any time you're around."

And aboard the *Skylark of Valeron,* Seaton turned to Dorothy with a scowl. "Nobody's seen him or heard anything of him, so he probably isn't loose yet. I *hate* this waiting. Confound it, I wish the big black ape would get loose and start something!"

Although Seaton did not know it, DuQuesne had, and was about to.

It happened that night, after Seaton had gone to bed.

The message came in loud and clear on Seaton's private all-hours receiver, monitored and directed by the unsleeping Brain:

". . . Seaton reply on tight beam of the sixth stop DuQuesne calling Seaton reply on tight beam of the sixth stop DuQuesne calling . . ."

Coming instantly awake at the sound of his name, Seaton kicked off the covers, thought a light on, and, setting hands and feet, made a gymnast's twisting, turning leap over Dorothy without touching her. There was plenty of room on his own side of the bed, but the direct route was quicker. He landed on his feet, took two quick steps, and slapped the remote-control helmet on his head.

"Trace this call. Hit its source with a tight beam of the sixth," he thought into the helmet; then took it off and said aloud, "You're coming in loud and clear. What gives?"

"Loud and clear here. All hell's out for noon. I just met the damndest alien any science-fiction fan ever imagined— teeth, wings, tail—the works. Klazmon by name; boss of two hundred forty-one planets full of monsters just like him. He's decided that all humanity everywhere should be liquidated; and it looks as though he may have enough stuff to do just that."

Dorothy had sat up in bed, sleepily. She made a gorgeously beautiful picture, Seaton thought; wearing a wisp of practically nothing and her hair a tousled auburn riot. As the sense of DuQuesne's words struck home, however, a look of horror spread over her face and she started to say something; but Seaton touched his lips with a forefinger and she, wide awake now, nodded.

"Nice summary, DuQuesne," Seaton said then. "Now break it down into smaller pieces, huh?" and DuQuesne went on to give a verbatim report of his interview with Llanzlan Klazmon of the Realm of the Llurdi.

"So much for facts," DuQuesne said. "Now for inferences and deductions. You know how, when you're thinking with anyone, other information, more or less relevant and more or less clear, comes along? A sort of side-band effect?"

"Yeah, always. I can see how you picked up the business

about the stranger ships that way. But how sure are you that those seventeen ships were *Fenachrone?*"

"Positive. That thought was *clear*. And for that matter, there must be others running around loose somewhere. How possible is it, do you think, to wipe out completely a race that has had spaceships as long as they have?"

"Could be," agreed Seaton. "And this ape Klazmon figured it that we were the same race, basically, both mentally—savage, egocentric, homicidal—and physically. How could he arrive at any such bobbled-up, cockeyed conclusions as that?"

"For him, easily enough. Klazmon is just about as much like us as we are like those X-planet cockroaches. Imagine a man-sized bat, with a super-able tail, cat's eyes and teeth, humanoid arms and hands, a breastbone like the prow of a battleship, pectoral muscles the size of forty-pound hams, and—"

"Wait up a sec—this size thing. His projection?"

"That's right. Six feet tall. He wasn't the type to shrink or expand it."

"I'll buy that. And strictly logical—with their own idea of what logic is."

"Check. According to which logic we're surplus population and are to be done away with. So I decided to warn you as to what the human race is up against and to suggest a meeting with you that we *know* can't be listened in on. Check?"

"Definitely. We'll lock our sixths on and instruct our computers to compute and effect rendezvous at null relative velocity in minimum time. Can do?"

"Can do—am doing," DuQuesne said; and Seaton, donning his helmet, perceived that the only fifth- or sixth-order stuff anywhere near the *Skylark of Valeron*—except what she was putting out herself, of course—was the thin, tight beam that was the base-line.

Seaton thought into his helmet for a few seconds; then, discarding it, he went around the bed, got into it on his own side, and started to kiss Dorothy a second good night.

"But, Dick," she protested. "That DuQuesne! Do you think it's safe to let him come actually aboard?"

"Yes. Not only safe, but necessary—we don't want to be blabbing that kind of stuff all over a billion parsecs of space. And safe because I still say we're better than he is at anything he want to start, for fun, money, chalk, or marbles. So good night again, ace of my bosom."

"Hadn't you better notify somebody else first? Especially the Norlaminians?"

"You said it, presh; I sure should." Seaton put on his helmet; and it was a long time before either of the Seatons got back to sleep. Long for Dorothy, heroically keeping eyes closed and breathing regularly so that her husband would not know how shaken and terrified she really was; long for Seaton himself, who lay hour upon endless hour, hands linked behind his head, gray eyes staring fiercely up into the darkness.

It had been a long time since Richard Ballinger Seaton and Marc C. DuQuesne had locked horns last. This galaxy —this cluster—this whole First Universe was not large enough for the two of them. When they met again one of them would dispose of the other.

It was as simple as that. Yet Seaton had accepted a call for help. The whole enormous complex of defenses that he had labored so hard and long to erect again DuQuesne would now be diverted to another, perhaps even a greater, threat to the safety of civilization. It was right and proper that this should be so.

But Seaton knew that whatever the best interests of civilization in this matter, there could and would never be any greater personal threat to himself than was incarnate in the cold, hard, transcendentally logical person of Blackie DuQuesne.

9 · AMONG THE JELMI

AND half a universe away other events were moving to fruition.

As has been said, the eight hundred Jelmi aboard the ship that had once been a Llurdan cruiser were the selected pick of the teeming billions of their race inhabiting two hundred forty-one planets. The younger ones had been selected for brains, ability, and physical perfection; the older ones for a hundred years or more of outstanding scientific achievement. And of the older group, Tammon stood out head and shoulders above all the rest. He was the Einstein of his race.

He looked a vigorous, bushily gray-haired sixty; but was in fact two hundred eleven Mallidaxian years old.

Tammon was poring over a computed graph, measuring its various characteristics with vernier calipers, a filar microscope, and an integrating planimeter, when Mergon and Luloy came swinging hand in hand into his laboratory. Both were now fully recovered from the wounds they had suffered in that hand-to-hand battle with the Llurdi on now-far-distant Llurdiax. Muscles moved smoothly under the unblemished bronze of Mergon's skin; Luloy's swirling shoulder-length mop of gleaming chestnut hair was a turbulent glory.

"Hail, Tamm," the two said in unison, and Mergon went on: "Have you unscrewed the inscrutability of that anomalous peak yet?"

Tammon picked up another chart and scowled at a sharp spike going up almost to the top of the scale. "This? I'm not exactly sure yet, but I may have. At least, by recomputing with an entirely new and more-than-somewhat weird set of determinors, I got this," and he ran his fingertip along the smooth curve on the chart he had been studying.

Mergon whistled through his teeth and Luloy, after staring for a moment said, "Wonderful! Expound, oh sage, and elucidate."

"It had to have at least one component in the sixth, on the level of thought, but no known determinors would affect it. Therefore I applied the mathematics of symbolic logic to a wide variety of hunches, dreams, I've-been-here-or-done-this-befores, premonitions, intuitions . . ."

"Llenderllon's eyeballs!" Luloy broke in. "So *that* was what you ran us all through the wringer for, a while back."

"Precisely. Using these new determinors in various configurations—dictated not by mathematical reasoning, but by luck and by hunch and by perseverance—I finally obtained a set of uniquely manipulable determinants that yielded this final smooth curve, the exactly fitting equation of which reduces beautifully to . . ."

"Hold it, Tamm," Mergon said, "you're losing me," and Luloy added,

"You lost *me* long ago. What does it *mean?*"

"It will take years to explore its ramifications, but one

fact is clear: the fourth dimension of space does actually exist. Therefore the conclusion seems inescapable that . . ."

"Stop it!" Luloy snapped. "This is terribly dangerous stuff to be talking about. That terrific kind of a breakthrough is just *exactly* what Klazmon—the beast!—has been after for years. And you know very well that we're not really free; that he has us under constant surveillance."

"But by detector only," Mergon said. "A full working projection at this distance? Uh-uh. It might be smart, though, to be a little on the careful side, at that."

named the *Mallidax* and converted into a Jelman worldlet,

Days lengthened into weeks. The ex-Llurdan cruiser, re-still hurtled along a right-line course toward the center of the First Universe, at a positive-and-negative acceleration that would keep her—just barely!—safe against collision with intergalactic clouds of gas or dust.

The objective of their flight was a small sun, among whose quite undistinguished family of planets were a moderate-sized oxygen-bearing world and its rather large, but otherwise uninteresting companion moon.

Tammon, hot on the trail of his breakthrough in science, kept his First Assistant Mergon busy fourteen or sixteen hours per day designing and building—and sometimes inventing—new and extremely special gear; and Mergon in turn drove Luloy, his wife and Girl Friday, as hard as he drove himself.

Tammon, half the time, wore armor and billion-volt gloves against the terribly lethal forces he was tossing so nonchalantly from point to point. Mergon, only slightly less powerfully insulated, had to keep his variable-density goggles practically opaque against the eye-tearing frequencies of his welding arcs. And even Luloy, much as she detested the feel of clothing against her skin, was as armored and as insulated as was either of the men as she tested and checked and double-checked and operated, with heavily gloved flying fingers, the maze of unguarded controls that was her constructor station.

And all the other Jelmi were working just as hard; even —or especially?—Master Biologist Sennlloy: who, with her long, thick braids of Norse-goddess hair piled high on her head and held in place by a platinum-filigree net, was delving deeper and ever deeper into the mystery of life.

Any research man worth his salt must not be the type to give up: he must be able to keep on butting his head against a stone wall indefinitely without hoisting the white flag. Thus, Tammon developed theory after theory after theory for, and Mergon and Luloy built model after model after model of, mechanisms to transport material objects from one place to another in normal space by moving them *through* the fourth dimension—and model after model after model failed to work.

They failed unfailingly. Unanimously. Wherefore Mergon had run somewhat low on enthusiasm when he and Luloy carried the forty-ninth model of the series into Tammon's laboratory to be put to the test. While the old savant hooked the device up into a breadboard layout of gadgetry some fifteen feet long, Mergon somewhat boredly picked up an empty steel box, dropped six large ball-bearings into it, closed and hasped its cover, grasped it firmly in his left hand, and placed an empty steel bowl on the bench.

"Now," Tammon said, and flipped a switch—and six heavy steel balls clanged into the bowl out of nowhere.

"Huh?" Mergon's left hand had jumped upward of its own accord; and, fumbling in his haste, he opened the box in that hand and stared, jaw actually agape, at its empty interior.

"Llenderllon's eyeballs!" Luloy shrieked. *"This* one works!"

"It does indeed," a technician agreed, and turned anxiously to Tammon. "But sir, doesn't that fact put us into a highly dangerous position? Even though Klazmon can't operate a full working projection at this distance, he undoubtedly has had all his analytical detectors out all this time and this successful demonstration must have tripped at least some of them."

"Not a chance," Mergon said. "He'll *never* find these bands—it'd be exactly like trying to analyze a pattern of fifth- or sixth-order force with a visible-light spectroscope."

"It probably would be, at that," the technician agreed, and Luloy said, "But what I've been wondering about all along is, what *good* is it? What's it *for?* Except robbing a bank or something, maybe."

"It reduces theory to practice," Tammon told her. "It gives us priceless data, by the application of which to already-known concepts we will be able to build mechanisms and devices to perform operations hitherto deemed impossible. Operations unthought-of, in fact."

"Maybe we should be pretty careful about it, though, at that," Mergon said. "To do very much real development work, we'll have to be using a lot of fairly unusual sixth-order stuff that he can detect and analyze. That will make him wonder what we're up to and he won't stop at wondering. He'll take steps."

"Big steps," Luloy agreed.

Tammon nodded. "That is true . . . and we must land somewhere to do any worthwhile development work, since this ship is not large enough to house the projectors we will have to have. Also, we are short of certain necessities for such work, notably neutronium and faidons . . . and the projectors of these ultra-bands will have to be of tremendous power, range, and scope . . . you are right. We must find a solar system emanating sixth-order energies. Enough of them, if possible, to mask completely our own unavoidable emanations. We now have enough new data so that we can increase tremendously the range, delicacy, and accuracy of our own detectors. See to it, Mergon, and find a good landing place."

"Yes, *sir!"* and Mergon went, with enthusiasm again soaring high, to work.

Rebuilding and re-powering their detector systems did not take very long; but finding the kind of landing place they needed proved to be something entirely else.

They had more or less assumed that many galaxies would show as much sixth-order activity as did their own, but that assumption was wrong. In three weeks they found only three galaxies showing any at all; and not one of the three was emanating as much sixth-order stuff as their own small vessel was putting out.

After another week or so, however, the savant on watch asked Mergon to come to his station. "There's something tremendous up ahead and off to starboard, Merg. That spot there." He pointed. "It's been there for almost half an hour and it hasn't increased by a thousandth of what I expected it to. I would have said that at that distance nothing could possibly register that high."

"Did you check your circuits?" Mergon asked.

"Of course; everything's on the green."

"Main Control!" Mergon snapped into a microphone. "Mergon speaking. Flip one eighty immediately. Decel max."

"Flip one eighty," the speaker said, and the vessel turned rapidly end for end. ". . . ON the mark and decelerating at max."

Mergon whirled around and sprinted for Tammon's laboratory. He yanked the door and reported, concluding,

"It's apparently emanating thousands of times as much as our whole galaxy does, so we'd better sneak up on it with care."

"Can we stop in time or will we have to overshoot and come back to it from the other side? That may affect course, you know."

Mergon hadn't thought of that point, but he soon found out. They couldn't stop quite in time, but the overshoot would be a matter of less than a day.

"See to it, Mergon," Tammon said, and resumed his interrupted studies.

The approach was made. Surprise turned to consternation when it was learned that practically all of that emanation was coming from one planet instead of a thousand; but since that condition was even better than any that had been hoped for, they shielded everything that could be shielded and sneaked up on that extraordinary world—the third planet of a Type G sun. It had an unusually large satellite . . . and ideal location for their proposed operation . . . there were two small clusters of dome-shaped structures . . . abandoned . . . quite recently . . . with advanced technology all such things and procedures would of course be abandoned . . . and there were bits and pieces of what looked like wreckage.

Seaton—who had not yet seen at close up any part of the moon!—would have recognized at a glance the American and the Russian Lunar outposts, and also what was left of Ranger Seven and of several other American and Russian moon-rockets.

As a matter of fact, the Jelmi could deduce, within fairly narrow limits, what had happened on Earth's moon.

But all they cared about was that, since the moon was not inhabited at that time, they would probably not attract undue attention if they landed on it and, thoroughly and properly screened, went to work. And Klazmon could not possibly detect them there.

Luna's mountains are high and steep. Therefore, after the *Mallidax* had come easily to ground at the foot of one such mountain, it took only a day for the *Mallidan's* mighty construction-projectors to hollow out and finish off a sub-Lunar base in that mountain's depths.

And next day, early, work was begun upon the tremendous new superdreadnought of the void that was going to be named the *Mallidaxian*.

10 • JELMI ON THE MOON

Miss Madlyn Mannis—nee Gretchen Schneider—stood in the shade of a huge beach umbrella (perish forbid that any single square inch of that petal-smooth, creamily flawless epidermis should be exposed to Florida's fervent sun!) on Clearwater Beach. She was digging first one set of red-nailed toes and then the other, into the soft white sand, and was gazing pensively out over the wavelets of the Gulf.

She was a tall girl, and beautifully built, with artistically waved artistically red hair; and every motion she made was made with the lithe grace of the highly trained professional dancer that she in fact was. She was one of the best exotic dancers in the business. As a matter of box-office fact, she was actually almost as good as she thought she was.

She was wearing the skimpiest neo-bikini ever seen on Clearwater Beach and was paying no attention whatever, either to the outraged glares of all the other women in sight or to the distinctly unoutraged glances of the well built, deeply tanned, and highly appreciative young man who was standing some twenty feet away.

She was wondering, however, and quite intensely, about the guy. He'd been following her around for a couple of weeks. Or had he? She'd seen him somewhere every day—but he couldn't *possibly* have followed her here. Not only she hadn't known she was coming here until just before she started, but she had come by speedboat and had found him on the beach when she arrived!

And the man was wondering, too. He knew that he hadn't been following her. Without hiring an eye, he wouldn't know how to. And the idea that Madlyn Mannis would be following *him* around was ridiculous—it *really* stunk. But how many times in a row could heads turn up by pure chance alone?

He didn't dare move any closer, but he kept on looking and he kept on wondering. Would she slug him or just slap him or maybe even accept it, he wondered, if he should offer to buy *the* Miss Mannis a drink . . .

Miss Mannis was also being studied, much more intensively and from much closer viewpoints, by two Jelmi in an immense new spaceship, the *Mallidaxian,* on the moon; and the more they studied the Mannis costume the more baffled they became.

As had been said, the Jelmi had had to build this immense new spaceship because the comparatively tiny *Mallidax,* in which they had escaped from the Realm of the Llurdi, had proved too small by far to house the outsized gear necessary for accurately controlled intergalactic work of any kind. The *Mallidaxian,* however—built as she was of inoson and sister-ship as she was to the largest, heaviest, and most powerful space-sluggers of the Realm— was not only big enough to carry any instrumentation known to the science of the age, but also powerful enough to cope with any foreseeable development or contingency.

The Jelman sub-Lunar base had been dismantled and collapsed. Its every distinguishing feature had been reduced to moon-dust. The *Mallidaxian's* slimly powerful length now extended for a distance of two and one half miles from the mountain's foot out into the level-floored crater: in less than an hour she would take off for Mallidax, the home world of Tammon, Mergon, Luloy, and several other top-bracket Jelmi of the fugitive eight hundred.

The vessel's officers and crew were giving their instruments and mechanisms one last pre-flight check. Tammon was still studying the offensive and defensive capabilities of Cape Kennedy; Mergon and Luloy—among others—had been studying the human beings of this hitherto unknown world. Everyone aboard, of course, had long since mastered the principal languages of Earth.

That Madlyn Mannis should have been selected for observation was not very astonishing. Some thousands of Earthmen—and Earthwomen, Earthchildren, even Earthdogs and cats—had been. There was that about Madlyn Mannis, however, and to a lesser degree about the male with whom she seemed in some way associated, that seemed to deserve special study. For one thing, the Jelmi had been totally unable to deduce any shred of evidence that might indicate her profession—not so surprising, since the work of a stripper must seem pure fantasy to a world which habitually wears no clothes at all! Madlyn, although used to being talked about, would have been quite astonished to learn how interestedly she was being discussed on the far side of the moon.

"Oh, let's bring her up here, Merg," Luloy said in disgust. "I want to talk to her—find out what this idiocy *means*. We'd better bring that fellow along, too: she'd probably be scared out of her wits—if any—alone."

"Check," Mergon said, and the two Tellurians appeared, standing close together, in the middle of the room.

The girl screamed once; then, her eyes caught by the awesome moonscape so starkly visible through the transparent wall, she froze and stared in terror. Then, finding that she was not being hurt, she fought her terror down. She took one fleeting glance at Mergon, blushed to the waist, and concentrated on Luloy. "Why, you must . . . you *do* go naked!" she gasped. *"All* the time! How utterly, *utterly* shameless!"

"Shameless?" Luloy wrinkled her nose in perplexity. "That's what I want to talk to you about, this 'shame' concept. I can't understand it and its dictionary definition is senseless to the point of unsanity. I never heard of a concept before that so utterly lacked sense, reason, and logic. What significant difference can there *possibly* be between nakedness and one ribbon and two bits of gauze? And why in the name of All-Seeing Llenderllon wear any clothing at all when you don't have to? Against cold or thorns or whatever? And especially when you swim? And you take *off* your clothes too . . ."

"I do no such thing!" The dancer drew herself up haughtily. "I am an artiste. An exotic dancer's disrobing is a fine art, and I am Madlyn Mannis, *the* exotic dancer."

"Be that as it may, just answer one question and we'll put you back where you were, on the beach. What *possible* logical, reasonable, or even comprehensible relationship can there be between clothing and sex?"

While the girl was groping for an answer, the man took one step forward and said, "She can't answer that question. Neither can I, fully, but I can state as a fact that such a relationship is a fact of our lives; of the lives of all the peoples—even the least civilized peoples—of our world. It's an inbred, ages-old, world-wide sexual taboo. Based, possibly or even probably, upon the idea 'out of sight, out of mind'. "

"A *sexual* taboo?" Luloy shook her head in complete bafflement. "Why, I never heard of anything so completely idiotic in my whole life! Will you wear these thought-caps with me for a moment, please, so that we may explore this weird concept in depth?"

The girl flinched away from the helmet at first, but the man reached out for his, saying, "I've always claimed to have an open mind, but *this* I've got to see."

Since complete non-comprehension of motivation on one side met fundamental ignorance on the other, however, thoughts were no more illuminating than words had been.

"Neither she nor I know enough about the basics of that branch of anthropology," the man said, handing the helmet back to Luloy. "You'd better get a book. *Mores and Customs of Tellus,* by David Lisser, in five volumes, is the most complete work I know of. You can find it in any big bookstore. It's expensive, though—it costs seventy-five dollars."

"Oh? And we haven't any American money and we don't steal . . . but I've noticed that highly refractive bits of crystalline carbon of certain shades of color are of value here."

Turning her back on the two Tellurians, Luloy went to the laboratory bench, opened a drawer, glanced into it, and shook her head. She picked up a helmet, thought into it, and there appeared upon the palm of her hand a perfectly cut, perfectly polished, blue-white diamond half the size of an egg.

She turned back toward the two and held out her hand so that the man could inspect the gem, saying, "I have not given any attention at all to your monetary system, but this should be worth enough, I think, to leave in the place of the book of five volumes. Or should it be bigger?"

Close up, the man goggled at blue-white fire. "*Bigger!* Than *that* rock? *Lady!* Are you *kidding?* If that thing will stand inspection it'll buy you a *library,* buildings and all!"

"That's all I wanted to know. Thank you." Luloy turned to Mergon. "They don't know any more than . . ."

"Just a minute, please," the man broke in. "If diamonds don't mean any more than that to you, why wouldn't it be a good idea for you to make her some? To alleviate the shock she has just had? Not as big, of course; none bigger than the end of my thumb."

Luloy nodded. "I know. Various sizes, for full-formal array. She's just about my size, so eleven of your quarts will do it."

"My God, no. . . ." Madlyn began, but the man took smoothly over.

"Not quite, Miss Luloy. Our ladies don't decorate their formals as lavishly as you apparently do. One quart, or maybe a quart and a half, will do very nicely."

"Very well," Luloy looked directly at the man. "But you won't want to be lugging them around with you all the rest of the day—they're heavy—so I'll put them in the right-hand top drawer of the bureau in your bedroom. Good-by," and Mergon's hands began to move toward his controls.

"Wait a minute!" the man exclaimed. "You *can't* just dump us back where we were without a word of explanation! While spaceships aren't my specialty—I'm a petro-chemical engineer tee eight—I've never imagined anything as big as this vessel actually flying, and I'm just about as much interested in that as I am in the way we got here—which *has* to be fourth-dimensional translation; it *can't* be anything else. So if everything isn't top secret, how about showing us around a little?"

"The fourth-dimension device is top secret; so much so that only three or four of us know anything about it. You may study anything else you please. Bearing in mind that we have only a few seconds over three of your minutes left, where would you like to begin?"

"The engines first, please, and the drives."

"And you, Miss Mannis? Arts? Crafts? Sciences? There is no dancing going on at the moment."

The dancer's right hand flashed out, seized her fellow Earthman's forearm and clung to it. "Wherever *he* goes I go along!" she said, very positively.

Since neither of the two Earthpeople had even been projected before, they were both very much surprised at how much can be learned via projection, and in how short a time. They saw tremendous receptors and generators and propulsors; they saw the massed and banked and tiered keyboards and instrumentation of the control stations; they saw how the incredibly huge vessel's inoson structural members were trussed and latticed and braced and buttressed to make it possible for such a titanic structure to fly.

Since everything aboard the original Jelman vessel had been moved aboard this vastly larger one before the original had been reduced to moon-dust, the dancer and her companion also saw beautiful, splendid, and magnificent—if peculiarly unearthly—paintings and statues and tapestries and rugs. They heard music, ranging from vast orchestral recordings down to the squeakings and tootlings of beginners learning to play musical instruments unknown to the humanity of Earth.

And above all they saw people. Hundreds and hundreds

of people; each one completely naked and each one of a physical perfection almost never to be found on Earth.

At time zero minus twenty seconds Mergon cut off the projectors and the Earthman looked at Luloy.

She not only had swapped the diamond for the five-volume set of books; she had already read over a hundred pages of Volume One. She was flipping pages almost as fast as her thumb and forefinger could move, and she was absorbing the full content of the work at the rate of one glance per page.

"You people seem to be as human as we are," Madlyn said, worriedly, "but outside of that you're nothing like us at all in any way. *Where* did you come from anyway?"

"I can't tell you," Mergon said, flatly. "Not that I don't want to, I can't. We're what you call human, yes; but our world Mallidax is a myriad of galaxies away from here—so far away that the distance is completely incomprehensible to the mind. Good-by."

And Madlyn Mannis found herself—with no lapse of time and with no sensation whatever of motion—standing in her former tracks under the big umbrella on the beach. The only difference was that she was now standing still instead of digging her toes into the sand.

She looked at her fellow moon-traveler. He, too, was standing in the same place as before, but he now looked as though he had been struck by lightning. She swallowed twice, then said, "Well, I'm awfully glad I wasn't alone when *that* hap . . ." she broke off abruptly, licked her lips, and went on in a strangely altered tone, "Or am I nuttier than a fruit-cake? *Vas* you dere, Shar-lee?"

"I vas dere, Madlyn." He walked toward her. He was trying to grin, but was not having much success with it. "And my name *is* Charley—Charles K. van der Gleiss."

"My God! That makes it even worse—or does it?"

"I don't see how anything could; very well or very much . . . but I need a drink. How about you?"

"*Brother! Do* I! But we'll have to dress. You can't get anything on the beach here that's strong enough to cope with anything like *that!*"

"I know. City owned. Teetotal. I'll see you out in front in a couple of minutes. In a taxi."

"Make it five minutes, or maybe a bit more. And if you run out on me, Charles K. van der Gleiss, I'll . . . I'll hunt you up and kill you absolutely dead, so help me!"

"Okay, I'll wait, but make it snappy. I need that drink."

She had snatched up her robe and had taken off across the sand like a startled doe; her reply came back over one shoulder. *"You* need a drink? Oh, *brother!"*

11 • BLOTTO

THE world had come a long way from the insular, mud-bound globe of rock and sea of the 1950s and 1970s; Seaton and Crane had seen to that. Norlaminian observers were a familiar sight to most humans—if not in person, then surely through the medium of TV or tapefax. A thousand worlds had been photographed by Tellurian cameramen and reporters; the stories of the Osnomians, the Fenachrone, the Valeronians, even the Chlorans and the other weirdly non-human races of the outer void were a matter of public record.

Nevertheless, it is a far different thing from knowing that other races exist to find yourself a guest of one of them, a quarter of a million miles from home; wherefore Madlyn and Charley's expressed intentions took immediate and tangible form.

Madlyn Mannis and Charles K. van der Gleiss were facing each other across a small table in a curtained booth; a table upon which a waiter was placing a pint of bonded hundred-proof bourbon and the various items properly accessory thereto. As soon as the curtain fell into place behind the departing waiter the girl seized the bottle, raised it to her mouth, and belted down a good two fingers—as much as she could force down before her coughing, choking, and strangling made her stop.

"Hey! Take it easy!" the man protested, taking the bottle from her hand and putting it gently down on the table. "You're not used to guzzling it like *that;* that's for plain damn sure."

She gulped and coughed a few times; wiped her streaming eyes. "I'll tell the world I'm not; two little ones is always my limit, ordinarily. But I *needed* that jolt, Charley, to keep from flipping my lid completely. Don't you need one, too?"

"I certainly do. A triple, at least, with a couple of snowflakes of ice and about five drops of water." He built the drink substantially as specified, took it down in three swallows, and drew a profoundly deep breath. "You heard me tell them I'm a petrochemical engineer, tee eight. So maybe that didn't hit me *quite* as hard as it did you, but bottled courage helps, believe me." He mixed another drink—a single—and cocked an eyebrow at the girl. "What'll you have as a chaser for that God-awful belt?"

"A scant jigger—three-quarters, about—in a water glass," she said, promptly. "Two ice-cubes and fill it up with ice-water." He mixed the drink and she took a sip. "Thanks, Charley. This is *much* better for *drinking* purposes. Now maybe I can talk about what happened without blowing my top. I was going to wonder why we've been running into each other all the time lately, but that doesn't amount to *anything* compared to . . . I actually thought . . . in fact, I know very well . . . we *were* on . . . weren't we? Both of us?"

"We were both on the moon," he said flatly. "To make things worse, we were inside a spaceship that I still don't believe can be built. Those are *facts.*"

"Uh-uh; that's what I mean. Positively *nobody* ever went to the moon or anywhere else off-Earth without being *in* something, and we didn't have even the famous paddle. And posi-*damn*-tively nobody—but *nobody!*—ever got into and out of a tightly closed, vacuum-tight spaceship without anybody opening any doors or ports or anything. How do you play them tunes on your piccolo, friend?"

"I don't; and the ship itself was almost as bad. Not only was it impossibly big; it was full of stuff that makes the equipment of the *General Hoyt S. Vandenberg* look like picks and shovels." She raised an eyebrow questioningly and he went on, "One of the missile-tracking vessels—the hairiest hunks of electronic gadgetry ever built by man. What it all adds up to is a race of people somewhere who know as much more than even the Norlaminians do as we do than grasshoppers. So I think we had better report to the cops."

"The *cops!*" she spat the word out like an oath. "Me? Madlyn Mannis? Squeal to the fuzz? When a great big gorilla slugs me in the brisket and heists fifteen grands' worth of diamonds off of me and I don't get . . ."

She broke off suddenly. Both had avoided mentioning the diamonds, but now the word was accidentally out. She shook her head vigorously, then said, "Uh-uh. They aren't there. Who ever heard of diamonds by the quart? Anyway, even if that Luloy could have done it and did, I'll bet they evaporated or something."

"Or they'll turn out to be glass," he agreed. "No use looking, hardly, I don't think. Even if they are there and are real, you couldn't sell 'em without telling where they came from—and you can't do that."

"I couldn't? Don't be naive, Charley. Nobody ever asks me where I got any diamonds I sell—I'd slap his silly face off. I can peddle your half, too, at almost wholesale. Not all at once, of course, but a few at a time, here and there."

"Half, Uh-uh," he objected. "I was acting as your agent on that deal. Ten per cent."

"Half," she insisted; then grinned suddenly. "But why argue about half of nothing? To get back onto the subject of cops—the lugs!—they brushed my report off as a stripper's publicity gag and I didn't get even one line in the papers. And if I report *this* weirdie they'll give me a one-way, most-direct-route ticket to the nearest funny-farm."

"You've got a point there." He glowered at his drink. "I can see us babbling about instantaneous translation through the fourth dimension and an impossible spaceship on the moon manned by people exactly like us—except that the men all look like Green Bay Packers and all the girls without exception are stacked like . . . like . . ." Words failed him.

Madlyn nodded thoughtfully. "Uh-huh," she agreed. "They were certainly stacked. That Luloy . . . that biologist Sennlloy, who was studying all those worms and mice and things . . . all of 'em. And they swap hundred-carat perfect blue-white diamonds for books."

"Yeah. We start babbling that kind of stuff and we wind up in wrap-arounds."

"You said it. But we've got to do *something!*"

"Well, we can report to an Observer—"

"I've got a better idea. Let's tie one really on."

Neither of them remembered very much of what happned after that, but at about three o'clock the following afternoon Charley van der Gleiss struggled upward through a million miles of foul-tasting molasses to consciousness. He was lying on the couch in his living room; fully dressed, even to his shoes. He worked himself up, very carefully, to a sitting position and shook his head as carefully. It didn't *quite* explode. Good—he'd probably live.

Walking as though on eggs, he made cautious way to the bedroom. She was lying, also fully dressed, on his bed. On the coverlet. As he sat gingerly down on the side of the bed she opened one eye, then the other, put both hands to her head, and groaned; her features twisting in agony. "Stop shaking me, you . . . *please*," she begged. "Oh, my poor head! It's coming clear off . . . right at the neck . . ."

Then, becoming a little more conscious, she went on, "It didn't go back into the woodwork, Charley, did it? I'll see that horrible moonscape and that naked Luloy as long as I live."

"And I'll see that nightmare of a spaceship. While you're taking the first shot at the bathroom I'll have 'em send up a gallon of black coffee, a couple of quarts of orange juice, and whatever the pill-roller downstairs says is good for what ails us. In the meantime, would you like a hair of the dog?"

"My God, no!" She shuddered visibly. "I never got drunk in my life before—I have to keep in shape, you know—and if I live through this I swear I'll never take another drink as long as I live!"

When they began to feel better Madlyn said, "Why don't you peek into that drawer, Charley? There just *might* be something in it."

He did, and there was, and he gave her the honor of lifting the soft plastic bag out of the drawer.

"My God!" she gasped. "There's four or five *pounds* of them!" She opened the bag with trembling fingers and stood entranced for half a minute, then took out a few of the gems and examined them minutely.

"Charley," she said then, "if I know anything about diamonds—and I admit that I know a lot—these are not only real, but the finest things I have ever seen. I'm almost afraid to try to sell even the littlest ones. Men just simply don't give girls rocks like that. I'm not even sure that there are very many others like those around. If any."

"Well, we would probably have had to talk to an Observer anyway, and this makes it a forced putt. Let's go, Maddy."

"In *this* wreckage?" Expression highly scornful, she waved a hand at her rumpled and wrinkled green afternoon gown. "Are you completely out of your mind?"

"Oh, that's easy. I'll shave and put on a clean shirt and an intelligent look and then we'll skip over to your place for you to slick up and *then* we'll go down to the Observer's office. Say, have you got a safe-deposit box?"

"No, but don't worry about that for a while, my friend. We haven't got 'em past the Observer yet!"

An hour later, looking and feeling almost human again, the two were ushered into the Observer's heavily screened private office. They told him, as nearly as they could remember, every detail of everything that had happened.

He listened attentively. He had been among the Tellurians only a few short months; in the cautious thoughtful way of Norlaminians, he was far from ready to claim that he understood them. These two in particular seemed quite non-scientific and un-logical in their attitudes . . . and yet, he thought, and yet there was that about them which seemed to deserve a hearing. So he heard. Then he put on a headset and saw. Visually he investigated the far side of the moon; then, frowning slightly, he increased his power to microscopic magnification and re-examined half a dozen tiny areas. He then conferred briefly with Rovol of Rays on distant Norlamin, who in turn called Seaton into a long-distance three-way.

"No doubt whatever about it," Seaton said. "If they hadn't been hiding from somebody or something they wouldn't have ground up that many thousands of tons of inoson into moon-dust—that's a project, you know—and I don't need to tell you that inoson does *not* occur in nature. Yes, we definitely need to know more about this one. Coming in!"

Seaton's projection appeared in the Observer's office and, after being introduced, handed thought-helmets to Madlyn and Charley. "Put these on, please, and go over the whole thing again, in as fine detail as you possibly can. It's not that we doubt any of your statements; it's just that we want to record and to study very carefully all the side-bands of thought that can be made to appear."

The two went over their stories again; this time being interrupted, every other second or two, by either Seaton or the Observer with sharply pertinent questions or suggestions. When, finally, both had been wrung completely dry, the Observer took off his helmet and said:

"Although much of this material is not for public dissemination, I will tell you enough to relieve your minds of stress; especially since you have already seen some of it and

I know that neither of you will talk." Being a very young Norlaminian, just graduated from the Country of Youth, he smiled at this, and the two smiled—somewhat wryly—back.

"Wait a minute," Seaton said. "I'm not sure we want their minds relieved of too much stress. They both ring bells—loud ones. I'd swear I know you both from somewhere, except I know darn well I've never met either of you before . . . it's a cinch *nobody* could ever forget meeting Madlyn Mannis . . ." He paused, then snapped a finger sharply. "Idiot! Of course! Where were you, both of you, at hours twenty-three forty fifty-nine on the eighteenth?"

"Huh? What is this, a gag?" van der Gleiss demanded.

"Anything else but, believe me," Seaton assured him. "Madlyn?"

"One minute of midnight? That would be the finale of my first show . . . Oh-oh! Was the eighteenth a Friday?"

"Yes."

"That's it!" The girl was visibly excited now. "Something *did* happen. Don't ask me what—all I know is I was just finishing my routine, and I got this feeling—this feeling of *importance* about something. Why, you were in it!" She stared at Seaton's projection incredulously. "Yes! But—you were different somehow. I don't know how. Like a—like a reflection of you, or a bad photograph . . ."

Through his headset Seaton thought a quick, private three-way conference with Rovol and the Norlaminian on Earth: "—clearly refers to our beacon message—" "—yes, but holy cats, Rovol, what's this about a 'reflection'?—" "—conceivably some sort of triggered response from another race—"

It took less than a second, then Seaton continued with the girl and her companion, who were unaware that any interchange had taken place.

"The 'something important' you're talking about, Madlyn, was a message that we broadcast. You might call it an SOS; we were looking for a response from some other race or civilization with a little more on the ball than we have. We've been hoping for an answer; it's just possible that, through you, we've got one. What was that 'reflection' like?"

"I'd call it a psychic pull," said Madlyn promptly. "And now that you mention it, I felt it with these Jelmi too. And—" Her eyes widened, and she turned to stare at Charley.

Seaton snapped his fingers. "Look, Madlyn. Can you

take time off to spend with us? I don't know what you've got into—but I want you nearby if you get into it again!"

"Why, certainly, Mr. Seaton. I mean—Doctor Seaton. I'll call Moe—that's my agent—and cancel Vegas, and—"

"Thanks," grinned Seaton. "You won't lose anything by it."

"I'm sure I won't, judging by . . . but oh, yes, *how* about those diamonds—*if* they are?"

"Oh, they are," the Norlaminian assured her, "and they're of course yours. Would you like to have me sell them for you?"

She glanced questioningly at van der Gleiss, who nodded and gave the jewels to the Observer. Then, "We'd like that very much, sir," Madlyn said, "and thanks a lot."

"Okay," Seaton said then. "Now, how about you, Charley. What kind of a jolt did you get at one minute of twelve that Friday night?"

"Well, it was the first time I caught Madlyn's act, and I admit it's a sockeroo. She has the wallop of a piledriver, no question of that. But if you mean spirit-message flapdoodle or psychic poppycock, nothing. I'm not psychic myself—not a trace—and nobody can sell me that anybody else is, either. That stuff is purely the bunk—it's strictly for the birds."

"It isn't either, Mister Charles K. van der Gleiss!" Madlyn exclaimed. "And you are too psychic—very strongly so! How else would we be stumbling over each other everywhere we go? And how else would I possibly get drunk with you?" She spread her hands out in appeal to the Observer. *"Isn't* he psychic?"

"My opinion is that he is unusually sensitive to certain forces, yes," the Norlaminian said. "Think carefully, youth. Wasn't there something more than the mental or esthetic appreciation of, and the physical-sexual thrill at, the work of a superb exotic dancer?"

"Of course there was!" the man snapped. "But . . . but . . . oh, I don't know. Now that Madlyn mentions it, there *was* a sort of a feeling of a message. But I haven't got even the *foggiest* idea of what the goddam thing was!"

"And that," Seaton said, "is about the best definition of it I've ever heard. We haven't either."

12 · DU QUESNE AND THE JELMI

DuQuesne, who had not seen enough of the *Skylark of Valeron* to realize that it was an intergalactic spacecraft, had supposed that Seaton and his party were still aboard *Skylark Three,* which was of the same size and power as DuQuesne's own ship, the *Capital D.* Therefore, when it became clear just what it was with which the *Capital D* was making rendezvous, to say that DuQuesne was surprised is putting it very mildly indeed.

He had supposed that his vessel was one of the three most powerful superdreadnoughts of space ever built—but *this!* This thing was not a spaceship at all! In every important respect it was a world. It was big enough to mount and to power offensive and defensive armament of full planetary capability . . . and if he knew Seaton and Crane half as well as he thought he did, that monstrosity could volatilize a world as easily as it could light a firecracker.

He was second. Again. And such an insignificantly poor second as to be completely out of the competition.

Something would have to be done about this intolerable situation . . . and finding out what could be done about it would take precedence over everything else until he did find out.

He scowled in thought. That worldlet of a spaceship changed everything—radically. He'd been going to let eager-beaver Seaton grab the ball and run with it while he, DuQuesne, went on about his own business. But now— could he take the risk? Ten to one—or a hundred to one? —he couldn't touch that planetoid's safety screens with anything he had. But it was worth his while to try . . .

Energizing the lightest possible fifth- and sixth-order webs, he reached out with his utmost delicacy of touch to feel out the huge globe's equipment; to find out exactly what it had.

He found out exactly nothing; and in zero time. At the first, almost imperceptible touch of DuQuesne's web the mighty planetoid's every defense flared instantaneously into being.

DuQuesne cut his webbing, the defenses vanished, and Seaton said, "No peeking, DuQuesne. Come inside and you can look around all you please, but from outside it can't be done."

"I see it can't. How do I get inside?"

"One of your shuttles or small boats. Go neutral as soon as you clear your outer skin and I'll bring you in."

"I'll do that,"—and as DuQuesne in one of his vessel's lifeboats traversed the long series of locks through the worldlet's tremendously thick shell he kept on wrestling with his problem.

No, the idea of letting Seaton be the Big Solo Hero was out like the well-known light. Seaton and his whole party would have to die. And the sooner the better.

He'd known it all along, really; his thinking had slipped, back there, for sure. With *that* fireball of a ship—flying base, rather—by the time Seaton got the job done he would be so big that nothing could ever cut him down to size. For that matter, was there anything that could be done about Seaton and his planetoid, even at the size they already were? There was no vulnerability apparent . . . on the outside, at least. But there *had* to be something; some chink or opening; all he had to do was think of it—like the time he and "Baby Doll" Loring had taken over a fully-manned superdreadnought of the Fenachrone.

The smart thing to do, the best thing for Marc C. DuQuesne, would be to join Seaton and work hand in glove with him—for a while. Until he had a bigger, more powerful worldlet than Seaton did and knew more than all the Skylarkers put together. Then blow the *Skylark of Valeron* and everyone and everything in it into impalpable dust and go on about his own business; letting Civilization worry about itself.

To get away with that, he might have to give his word to act as one of the party, as before.

He never had broken his word . . . so he wouldn't give it, this time, unless he had to . . . but if he had to? If it came to a choice—breaking his word or being Emperor Marc the First of a galaxy, founder of a dynasty the like of which no civilization had ever seen before?

Whatever happened, come hell or high water, Seaton and his crew must and would die. He, DuQuesne, must and would come out on top!

As soon as DuQuesne's lifeboat was inside the enormous hollow globe that was the *Skylark of Valeron,* Seaton brought it to a gentle landing in a dock behind his own home and walked out to the dock with a thought-helmet on his head and its mate in his hand.

DuQuesne opened his lifeboat's locks and Seaton joined him in the tiny craft's main compartment.

Face to face, neither man spoke in greeting or offered to shake hands; both knew that there was nothing of friendship between them or ever would be. Nor did DuQuesne wonder why Seaton was meeting him thus: outside and alone. He knew exactly what the women, especially Margaret, thought of him; but such trifles had no effect whatever upon the essence of Marc C. DuQuesne.

Seaton handed DuQuesne the spare headset. DuQuesne put it on and Seaton said in thought, "This, you'll notice, is no ordinary mechanical educator; not by seven thousand rows of Christmas trees. I suppose you know you're in the *Skylark of Valeron.* Study it, and take your time. I'll give you her prints before you go—if we're going to have to be allies again you ought to have something better than your *Capital D* to work with."

Seaton thought that this surprise might make DuQuesne's guard slip for an instant, but it didn't. DuQuesne studied the worldlet intensively for over an hour, then took off his headset and said:

"Nice job, Seaton. Beautiful; especially that tank-chart of the First Universe and that super-computer brain—some parts of which, I see, this headset enables me to operate. The rest of it, I suppose, is keyed to and in sync with your own mind? No others mind apply?"

"That's right. So, with the prints, you'll have everything you need, I think. But before you go into detail, I may know a thing that you don't and that many have a lot of bearing, one place or another. Have you ever heard of any way of getting into or through the fourth dimension except by rotation?"

"No. Not even in theory. How sure are you that there is or can be any other way of doing it?"

"Positive. One that not even the Norlaminians know anything about," and Seaton gave DuQuesne the full picture and the full story and all the side-bands of thought of everything that had happened to Madlyn Mannis and Charles van der Gleiss.

At the sight of Mergon and Luloy—two of the three

Jelmi whom the monstrous alien Klazmon had been comparing with the Fenachrone and with the chlorine-breathing amoeboid Chlorans and with DuQuesne himself—it took every iota of DuQuesne's iron control to make no sign of the astounding burst of interest he felt; for in one blinding flash of revealment his entire course of action became pellucidly clear. He knew exactly where and what Galaxy DW-427-LU was. He knew how to get Seaton headed toward that galaxy. He knew how to kill Seaton and all his crew and take over the *Skylark of Valeron. And, best of all, he knew how to cover his tracks!*

Completely unsuspicious of any of these thoughts, Seaton went on, "Now we're ready, I think, for the fine details of what you found out."

After giving a precisely detailed report that lasted for twenty minutes, DuQuesne said, "Now as to location. I have a cylindrical chart—a plug-chart, you might call it—of all the galaxies lying close to the line between the point in space where your stasis-capsule whiffed out and the First Galaxy. Those four reels there." He pointed. "But I have no idea whatever as to where that plug lies in the universe—its universal coordinates. But since you know where you are and I know how I got here, it can be computed—in time."

"In practically nothing flat," Seaton said. "As fast as you can run your tapes through your scanner there." Seaton put his headset back on; DuQuesne followed suit. "They don't even have to be in order. When the end of the last tape clears the scanner your plug will be in our tank."

And it was: a long, narrow cylinder of yellowish-green haze.

"Nice; very nice indeed." DuQuesne paid tribute to performance. "I started my trip right there." He marked the spot with a tiny purple light. It was a weird sensation, this; working, with that gigantic brain, in that super-gigantic tank-chart, with only a headset and at a distance of miles!

"With my artificial gravity set to exact universal north as straight up," DuQuesne went on, "I moved along a course as close as possible to the axis of that cylinder to this point here." The purple point extended itself into a long line of purple light and stopped. "Klazmon's tight beam hit me at that point there, coming in from eighty-seven point four one eight degrees starboard and three point nine two six degrees universal south."

DuQuesne's mind, terrifically hard held for that particular statement, revealed not the faintest side-band or other indication of what a monstrous lie that was. The figures themselves were very nearly right; but the fact that the beam had actually come in from the port and the north made a tremendous difference. The purple line darted off at almost a right angle to itself and DuQuesne went on without a break:

"You'll note that there are two galaxies on that line; one about half way out to the rim of the universe—" this galaxy actually was, in Klazmon's nomenclature, Galaxy DW-427-LU—"the other one clear out; right on the rim itself. Under those conditions no reliable estimate of distance was possible, but if we assume that Klazmon's power is of the same order of magnitude as ours it would have to be the first one. However, I'm making no attempt to defend that assumption."

"Sure not; but it's safe enough, I'd say, for a first approximation. So, making that assumption, that galaxy is where the Realm of the Llurdi is—where the Llurdi and the Jelmi are. Where the folks that built that big battle-wagon on the moon came from."

"While the data do not prove it, by any means, that would be my best-educated guess. But my next one—that that's where they're going back to—isn't based on anything anywhere near that solid. Side-bands only, and not too many or too strong."

"Yeah, I got some, too. But you're having first cut at this; go ahead," Seaton said.

"Okay. First, you have to dig up some kind of an answer to the question of why those Jelmi came such an ungodly long distance away from home to do what was, after all, a small job of work. We know that they didn't do it just for fun. We know that the whole race of Jelmi is oppressed; we know that those eight hundred rebelled. We're fairly sure that Earth alone is, right now, putting out more sixth-order emanation than all the rest of the First Universe put together.

"Okay. There were some indications that Tammon worked out the theory of that fourth-dimensional gizmo quite a while back; but they had to come this tremendous distance to find enough high-order emanation to mask their research and development work from His Nibs Llanzlan Klazmon the Fifteenth.

"Now. My argument gets pretty tenuous at this point, but isn't it a fairly safe bet that, having reduced the theory of said gizmo to practice and having built a ship big enough to handle it like toothpicks, they'd beat it right back home as fast as they could leg it, knock the living hell out of the Llurdi—they could, you know, like shooting fish in a well —and issue a star-spangled Declaration of Independence? It does to me."

"Check. While I didn't get there by exactly the same route you did, I arrived at the same destination. So it's not only got to be investigated; it's got to be Number One on the agenda. Question; who operates? Your baby or mine?"

"You know the answer to that. I'll have other fish to fry; quite possibly until after you have the Jelman angle solved."

"My thought exactly." Seaton assumed that DuQuesne's first, most urgent job would be to build a worldlet of his own; DuQuesne did not correct this thought. Seaton went on, "The other question, then, is—do we join forces again, or work independently . . . or maybe table the question temporarily, until you get yourself organized and we will have made at least a stab at evaluating what this Llurdan menace actually amounts to?"

"The last . . . I think." DuQuesne scowled in thought, then his face cleared; but at no time was there the slightest seepage of side-bands to the effect that he, DuQuesne, would see to it that Seaton would be dead long before that. Or that he, DuQuesne, did not give a tinker's damn whether anything was ever done about the Llurdan menace or not.

The two men discussed less important details for perhaps ten minutes longer; then DuQuesne took his leave. And, out in deep space again, with his mighty *Capital D* again boring a hole through the protesting ether, DuQuesne allowed himself a contemptuous and highly satisfactory sneer.

Back in their own living room, Seaton asked his wife, "Dottie, did you smell anything the least bit fishy about that?"

"Not a thing, Dick. I gave it everything I had, and everything about it rang as true as a silver bell. Did you detect anything?"

"Not a thing—curse it! Even helmet to helmet—as deep as I could go without putting the screws on and blowing everything higher than up—it was flawless. But you've got to remember the guy's case-hardened and diamond finished . . . But you've also got to remember that I came to exactly the same conclusions he did—and completely independently."

"So every indication is that he *is* acting decently. He's been known to, you know."

"Yeah. It's possible." Seaton did not sound at all sold on the possibility. "But I wouldn't trust that big black ape as far as I could drop-kick him. . . . I'd like awfully well to know whether he's pitching us a curve or not . . . and if he is, what the barb-tailed devil it can possibly be . . . so what we'll have to do, pet, is keep our eyes peeled and look a little bit out *all* the time."

And, still scowling and still scanning and re-scanning every tiniest bit of data for flaws, Seaton set course for Galaxy DW-427-LU, having every reason to believe it the galaxy in which the Realm of the Llurdi lay. Also, although he did not mention this fact even to Dorothy, that course "felt right" to some deeply buried, unknown, and impossible sense in which he did not, could not, and would not believe.

For Seaton did not know that Galaxy DW-427-LU was in fact going to be highly important to him in a way that he could not foresee; if he had known, would not have believed; if he had believed, would not have understood.

For at that moment in time, not even Richard Ballinger Seaton knew what forces he had unleashed with his "cosmic beacon."

13 • DU QUESNE AND SENNLLOY

IN the eyes of Blackie DuQuesne, Seaton was forever and helplessly trapped in the philosophy of the "good guy." It was difficult for DuQuesne to comprehend why a mind of as high an order of excellence as Seaton's—fully the equal of DuQuesne's own in many respects, as DuQuesne himself was prepared to concede—should subscribe to the philosophy of lending a helping hand, accepting the defeat of an enemy without rancor, refraining from personal aggrandizement when the way was so easily and temptingly clear to take over the best part of a universe.

Nevertheless, DuQuesne knew that these traits were part

of Seaton's makeup. He had counted on them. He had not been disappointed. It would have been child's play for Seaton to have tricked and destroyed him as he entered that monster spaceship Seaton had somehow acquired. Instead of that, Seaton had made him a free gift of its equal!

That, however, was not good enough for Blackie Du-Quesne. Seeing how far Seaton had progressed had changed things. He could not accept the status of co-belligerent. He had to be the victor.

And the one portentous hint he had gleaned from Seaton of the existence of a true fourth-dimensional system could be the tool that would make him the victor; wherefore he set out at once to get it.

Since he had misdireced Seaton as to the vector of the course of the Jelmi, sending him off on what, DuQuesne congratulated himself, was the wildest of wild-goose chases, DuQuesne need only proceed in the right direction and somehow—anyhow; DuQuesne was superbly confident that he would find a means—get from them the secret of what he needed to know. His vessel had power to spare. Therefore he cut in everything his mighty drives could take, computed a tremendous asymptotic curve into the line that the Jelmi must have taken, and took out after the intergalactic flyer that had left Earth's moon such a short time before.

DuQuesne was aware that force would be an improbably successful means of getting what he wanted. Guile was equally satisfactory. Accordingly he took off his clothes and examined himself, front and back and sides, in a full-length mirror.

He would do, he concluded. There would be nothing about his physical person which would cause him any trouble in his dealings with the Jelmi. Since he always took his sun-lamp treatments in the raw, his color gradation was right. He was too dark for a typical Caucasian Tellurian; but that was all right—he wasn't going to be a Tellurian. He would, he decided, be a native of some planet whose people went naked . . . the planet Xylmny, in a galaxy 'way out on the Rim somewhere . . . yes, he had self-control enough not to give himself away.

But his cabin wouldn't stand inspection on a usually naked basis, nor would any other private room of the ship. All had closets designed unmistakeably for clothing and it wasn't worth while to rebuild them.

Okay, he'd be a researcher who had visited dozens of planets, and *everybody* had to wear some kind of clothing or trappings at some time or other. Protectively at least. And probably for formality or for decoration.

Wherefore DuQuesne, with a helmet on his head and a half-smile, half-sneer on his face, let his imagination run riot in filling closet after closet with the utilitarian and the decorative garmenture of world after purely imaginative world. Then, after transferring his own Tellurian clothing to an empty closet, he devoted a couple of hours to designing and constructing the apparel of his equally imaginary native world Xylmny.

In due time a call came in from the spaceship up ahead. "You who are following us from the direction of the world Tellus: do you speak English?"

"Yes."

"Why are you following us, Tellurian?"

"I am not a Tellurian. I am from the planet Xylmny; which, while very similar to Tellus, lies in a distant galaxy." He told the caller, as well as he could in words, where Xylmny was. "I am a Seeker, Sevance by name. I have visited many planets very similar to yours and to Tellus and to my own in my Seeking. Tellus itself had nothing worthy of my time, but I learned there that you have a certain knowledge as yet unknown to me; that of operating through the fourth dimension of space instantaneously, without becoming lost hopelessly therein, as is practically always the case when rotation is employed. Therefore I of course followed you."

"Naturally. I would have done the same. I am Savant Tammon of the planet Mallidax—Llurdiaxorb Three— which is our destination. You, then, have had one or more successes in rotation? Our rotational tests all failed."

"We had only one success. As a Seeker I will be glad to give you the specifications of the structures, computers, and forces required for any possibility of success—which is very slight at best."

"This meeting is fortunate indeed. Have I your permission to come aboard your vessel, as such time as we approach each other nearly enough to make the fourth-dimensional transfer feasible?"

"You certainly may, sir. I'll be very glad indeed to greet you in the flesh. And until that hour, Savant Tammon, so long and thanks."

Since Mergon braked the *Mallidaxian* down hard to help make the approach, and since the two vessels did not have to be close together even in astronomical terms, it was not long until Tammon stood facing DuQuesne in the *Capital D's* control room.

The aged savant inhaled deeply, flexed his knees, and said, "As I expected, our environments are very similar. We greet new friends with a four-hand clasp. Is that form satisfactory?"

"Perfectly; it's very much like our own," DuQuesne said; and four hands clasped briefly.

"Would you like to come aboard our vessel now?" Tammon asked.

"The sooner the better," and they were both in Tammon's laboratory, where Mergon and Luloy looked DuQuesne over with interest.

"Seeker Sevance," Tammon said then, "these are Savant Mergon, my first assistant, and Savant Luloy, his . . . well, 'wife' would be, I think, the closest possible English equivalent. You three are to become friends."

The hand-clasp was six-fold this time, and the two Jelmi said in unison. "I'm happy that we are to become friends."

"May our friendship ripen and deepen," DuQuesne improvised the formula and bowed over the cluster of hands.

"But Seeker," Luloy said, as the cluster fell apart, "must all Seekers do their Seeking alone? I'd go stark raving mad if I had to be alone as long as you must have been."

"True Seekers, yes. While it is true that any normal man misses the companionship of his kind, especially that of the opposite sex—" DuQuesne gave Luloy a cool, contained smile as his glance traversed her superb figure—"even such a master of concentration as a true Seeker must be can concentrate better, more productively, when absolutely alone."

Tammon nodded thoughtfully. "That may well be true. Perhaps I shall try it myself. Now—we have some little time before dinner. Is there any other matter you would like to discuss?"

For that question DuQuesne was well prepared. A Seeker, after all, needs something to be Sought; and as he did not want to appear exclusively interested in something which even the unsuspicious Jelmi would be aware was a weapon of war, he had selected another subject about which to inquire. So he said at once:

"A minor one, yes. While I am scarcely even a tyro in biology, I have pondered the matter of many hundreds—probably many millions—of apparently identical and quite possibly inter-fertile human races spaced so immensely far apart in space that any possibility of a common ancestry is precluded."

"Ah!" Tammon's eyes lit up. "One of my favorite subjects; one upon which I have done much work. We Jelmi and the Tellurians are very far apart indeed in space, yet cross-breeding is successful. *In vitro*, that is, and as far as I could carry the experiment. I can not synthesize a living placenta. No *in vitro* trial was made, since we of course could not abduct a Tellurian woman and not one of our young women cared to bear a child fathered by any Tellurian male we saw."

"From what I saw there I don't blame them," agreed DuQuesne. It was only the truth of his feelings about Tellurians—with one important exception. "But doesn't your success *in vitro* necessitate a common ancestry?"

"In a sense, yes; but not in the ordinary sense. It goes back to the unthinkably remote origin of all life. You can, I suppose, synthesize any non-living substance you please? Perfectly, down to what is apparently its ultimately fine structure?"

"I see what you mean." DuQuesne, who had never thought really deeply about that fact, was hit hard. "Steak, for instance. Perfect in every respect except in that it never has been alive. No. We can synthesize DNA-RNA complexes, the building blocks of life, but they are not alive and we can not bring them to life. And, conversely, we cannot dematerialize living flesh."

"Precisely. Life may be an extra-dimensional attribute. Its basis may lie in some order deeper than any now known. Whatever the truth may be, it seems to be known at present only to the omnipotence Who we of Mallidax call Llenderllon. All we *know* about life is that it is an immensely strong binding force and that its source—proximate, I mean, of course, not its ultimate origin—is the living spores that are drifting about in open space."

"Wait a minute," DuQuesne said. "We had a theory like that long ago. So did Tellus—a scientist named Arrhenius —but all such theories were finally held to be untenable. Wishful thinking."

"I know. Less than one year ago, however, after twenty years of search. I found one such spore. Its descendants have been living and evolving ever since."

DuQuesne's jaw dropped. "You don't say! *That* I want to see!"

Tammon nodded. "I have rigorous proof of authenticity. While it is entirely unlike any other form of life with which I am familiar, it is very interesting."

"It would be, but there's one other objection. What is the chance that on any two worlds humanity would have reached exactly the same stage of evolution at any given time?"

"Ah! That is the crux of my theory, which I hope some day to prove; that when man's brain becomes large enough and complex enough to employ his hands efficiently enough, the optimum form of life for that environment has been reached and evolution stops. Thenceforth all mutants and sports are unable to compete with *Homo Sapiens* and do not survive."

DuQuesne thought for a long minute. Norlamin was very decidedly *not* a Tellus-type planet. "Some Xylmnians have it, 'Man is the ultimate creation of God.' On Tellus it's 'God created man in his own image.' And of course the fact that I've never believed it—and I still think it's unjustifiable racial self-glorification—does not invalidate it."

"Of course it doesn't. But to revert to the main topic, would you be willing to cooperate in an *in vivo* experiment?"

DuQuesne smiled at that, then chuckled deeply. "I certainly would, sir; and not for purely scientific reasons, either."

"Oh, *that* would be no problem. Nor is your present quest—it will take only a short time to install the various mechanisms in your vessel and to instruct you in their use. If my snap judgment is sound, however, this other may very well become of paramount importance and require a few days of time." He touched a button on an intercom and said, "Senny."

"Yes?" came in a deep contralto from the speaker.

"Will you come in here, please? It concerns the *in vivo* experiment we have been discussing."

"Oh? Right away, Tamm," and in about half a minute a young woman came striding in.

DuQuesne stared, for she was a living shield-maiden—a veritable Valkyrie of flesh and blood. If she had had wings and if her pale blonde hair had been flying loose instead of being piled high on her head in thick, heavy braids, DuQuesne thought, she could have stepped right out of Wagenhorst's immortal painting *Ragnarok*.

Tammon introduced them. "Seeker Sevance of Xylmny,

Savant Sennlloy of Allondax, you two are to become friends."

"I'm happy that we are to become friends," the girl said, in English, extending her hands. DuQuesne took them, bowed over them, and said, "May our friendship ripen and deepen."

She examined him minutely, from the top of his head down to his toenails, in silence; then, turning to Tammon, she uttered a long sentence of which DuQuesne could not understand a word.

"You should speak English, my dear," Tammon said. "It is inurbane to exclude a guest from a conversation concerning him."

"It is twice as inurbane," she countered in English, "to insult a guest, even by implication, who does not deserve it."

"That is true," Tammon agreed, "but I have studied him to some little depth and it is virtually certain that the matter lies in your province rather than mine. The decision is, of course, yours. Caps-on with him, please, and decide."

She donned a helmet and handed its mate to DuQuesne. Expecting a full-scale mental assault, he put up every block he had; but she did not think *at* him at all. Instead, she bored deep down into the most abysmal recesses of his flesh; down and down and down to depths where he— expert though he was at synthesizing perfectly any tangible article of matter—could not follow.

Eyes sparkling, she tossed both helmets onto a bench and seized both his hands in a grip very different from the casual clasp she had used a few minutes before. "I *am* glad—very, *very* glad, friend Seeker Sevance, that we are friends!"

Although DuQuesne was amazed at this remarkable change, he played up. He bowed over her hands and, this time, kissed each of them. "I think you, Lady Sennlloy. My pleasure is immeasurable." He smiled warmly and went on, "Since I am a stranger and thus ignorant of your conventions and in particular of your taboos, may I without offense request the pleasure of your company at dinner? And my friends call me Vance."

She returned his smile as warmly. Neither of them was paying any attention at all to anyone else in the room. "And I accept your invitation with joyous thanks. We go out that mine call me Senny. You may indeed, friend Vance, and archway there and turn left."

They walked slowly toward the indicated exit; side by side and so close together that hip touched hip at almost every step. In the corridor, however, Sennlloy put her hand on DuQuesne's arm and stopped. "But hold, friend Vance," she said. "We should, don't you think, make this, our first meal together, one of full formality?"

"I do indeed. I would not have suggested it but I'm very much in favor of it."

"Splendid! We'll go to my room first, then. This way," and she steered him into and along a corridor whose blankly featureless walls were opaque instead of transparent.

Was this his cue? DuQuesne wondered. No, he decided. She wasn't the type to rush things. She was civilized . . . more so than he was. If he didn't play it just about right with this girl, who was very evidently a big wheel, she could and very probably would queer his whole deal.

As they strolled along DuQuesne saw that the walls were not quite featureless. At about head height, every twenty-five feet or so, there was inset a disk of optical plastic perhaps an inch in diameter. Stopping, and turning to face one of these disks, Sennlloy pressed her right forefinger against it, explaining as she did so, "It opens to my finger-prints only."

There was an almost inaudible hiss of compressed air and a micrometrically fitted door—a good seven feet high and three feet wide—moved an inch out into the hall and slid smoothly aside upon tracks that certainly had not been there an instant before. DuQuesne never did find out how the thing worked. He was too busy staring into the room and watching and hearing what the girl was doing and saying.

She stepped back a half-step, bowed gracefully from the waist, and with a sweeping gesture of both hands invited him to precede her into the room. She started to say something in her own language—Allondaxian—but after a couple of words changed effortlessly to English. "Friend Seeker Sevance, it is in earnest of our friendship that I welcome you into the privacy of my home"—and her manner made it perfectly clear that, while the phraseology was conventionally formal, in this case it was really meant.

And DuQuesne felt it; felt it so strongly that he did not bluff or coin a responsive phrase. Instead: "Thank you, Lady Sennlloy. We of Xylmny do not have anything comparable, but I appreciate your welcome and thank you immensely."

Inside the room, DuQuesne stared. He had wondered what this girl's private quarters would be like. She was a master scientist, true. But she was warmly human, not bookishly aloof. And what would seventy thousand years of evolution do to feminine vanity? Especially to a vanity that apparently had never been afflicted by false modesty? Or by any sexual taboos?

The furniture—heavy, solid, plain, and built of what looked like golden oak—looked ordinary and utilitarian enough. Much of it was designed for, and was completely filled with and devoted to, the tools and equipment and tapes and scanners of the top-bracket biologist Sennlloy of Allondax in fact was. The floor was of mathematically figured, vari-colored, plastic tile. The ceiling was one vast sheet of softly glowing white light.

Three of the walls were ordinary enough. DuQuesne scarcely glanced at them because of the fourth, which was a single canvas eight feet high and over thirty feet long. One painting. What a painting! A painting of life itself; a painting that seemed actually to writhe and to crawl and to vibrate with the very essence of life itself!

One-celled life, striving fiercely upward in the primordial sea toward *the light*. Fiercely striving young fishes, walking determinedly ashore on their fins. Young about-to-become tion's tremendous ladder. Striving young mammals developing tails and climbing up into trees—losing tails, with the development of true thumbs, and coming down to earth again out of the trees—the ever-enlarging brain resulting in the appearance of true man. And finally, the development and the progress and the history of man himself.

And every being, from unicell to man, was striving with all its might upward; toward THE LIGHT. Upward! *Upward!!* UPWARD!!!

At almost the end of that heart-stopping painting there was a portrait of Sennlloy herself in the arms of a man; a yellow-haired, smooth-shaven Hercules so fantastically well-drawn, so incredibly alive-seeming, that DuQuesne stared in awe.

Beyond those two climactic figures the painting became a pure abstract of form and of line and color; an abstract, however, that was crammed full of invisible but very apparent question marks. It asked—more, it demanded and it yelled—*"What is coming next?"*

DuQuesne, who had been holding his breath, let it out and breathed deeply. "And you painted *that* yourself," he marveled. "Milady Sennlloy, if you never do anything else as long as you live, you will have achieved immortality."

She blushed to the breasts. "Thanks, friend Vance. I'm very glad you like it: I was sure you would."

"It's so terrific that words fail," he said, and meant. Then, nodding at the portrait, he went on, "Your husband?"

She shook her head. "Not yet. He has not the genes the Llurdi wish to propagate, so we could not marry and he had to stay on Allondax instead of becoming one of this group. But he and I love each other more than life. When we Jelmi aboard this *Mallidaxian* have taught those accursed Llurdi their lesson, we will marry and we'll never be parted again. But time presses, friend Vance; we must consider our formalities."

Walking around the foot of her bed—the satin coverlet of which bore, in red and gold, a motif that almost made even DuQuesne blush—she went to a bureau-like piece of furniture and began to pull open its bottom drawer. Then, changing her mind, she closed it sharply; but not before the man got a glimpse of its contents that made him catch his breath. That drawer contained at least two bushels of the most fantastic jewelry DuQuesne had ever seen!

Shaking her head, Sennlloy went on, "No. My formality should not influence yours. The fact that you appreciate and employ formality implies, does it not, that you do not materialize and dematerialize its material symbols, but cherish them?"

"Yes; you and I think very much alike on that," DuQuesne agreed. He was still feeling his way. This *hadn't* been a cue; that was now abundantly certain. In fact, with Sennlloy so deeply in love with one man, she probably wouldn't be in the business herself at all . . . or would she? Were these people advanced enough—if you could call it advancement—different enough, anyway—to regard sex-for-love and sex-for-improvement-of-race as two entirely different matters; so completely unrelated as not to affect each other? He simply didn't know. Data insufficient. However the thing was to go, he'd played along so far; he'd still play along. Wherefore, without any noticeable pause, he went on:

"I intended to comply with your conventions, but I'll be glad to use my own if you prefer. So I'll ask Tammon to flip me over to my own ship to put on my high-formal gear."

"Oh, no; I'll do it." Donning the helmet that had been lying on the beautifully grained oak-like top of the bureau, she took his left hand and compared his wristwatch briefly with the timepiece on the wall. "I'll bring you back here in . . . in how many of your minutes?"

"Ten minutes will be time enough."

"In exactly ten minutes from—" She waited until the sweep hand of his watch was exactly at the dot of twelve o'clock. "Mark," she said then, and DuQuesne found himself standing in his own private cabin aboard the *Capital D*.

He picked up shaving cream and brush; then, asking aloud, "How stupid can you get, fool?" he tossed them back onto the shelf, put on his helmet, and thought his whiskers off flush with the surface of his skin. Then, partly from habit but mostly by design—its richly masculine, heady scent was supposed to "wow the women"—he rubbed on a couple of squirts of after-shave lotion.

Opening closet doors, he looked at the just-nicely-broken-in trappings he had made such a short time before. How should he do it, jeweled or plain? She was going to be gussied up like a Christmas tree, so he'd better go plain. Showy, plenty; but no jewels. And, judging by that spectacular coverlet and other items in her room, she liked fire-engine red and gold. Okay.

Taking off his watch and donning one exactly like it except for the fact that it kept purely imaginary Xylmnian time—that had been a slip; if she'd noticed it, she'd have wondered why he was running on Tellurian time—he dressed himself in full panoply of Xylmnian finery and examined himself carefully in a full-length mirror.

He now wore a winged and crested headpiece of interlaced platinum strips; the front of the crest ridging up into a three-inch platinum disk emblazoned with an intricate heraldic design in deeply inlaid massive gold. A heavy collar, two armbands, and two wristlets, all made of woven and braided platinum strands, each bore the same symbolic disk. He wore a sleeveless shirt and legless shorts of gleaming, glaringly-red silk, with knee-length hose to match—and red-leather-lined buskins of solid-gold chain mail. And lastly, a crossed-strap belt, also of massive but supple gold link, with three platinum comets on each shoulder, supported a solid-platinum scabbard containing an extremely practical knife.

He drew the blade. Basket-hilted and with fifteen inches of heavy, wickedly curved, peculiarly shaped, razor-edged and needle-pointed stainless-steel blade, it was in fact an atrocious weapon indeed—and completely unlike any item of formal dress that DuQuesne had ever heard of.

All this had taken nine and one half minutes by his watch—by his Earth-watch, lying now upon his dresser. The time was now zero minus exactly twenty-eight seconds.

14 • SEEKER SEVANCE OF XYLMNY

PRECISELY on the tick of time DuQuesne stood again in Sennlloy's room. He glanced at her; then stood flat-footed and simply goggled. He had expected a display, but *this* was something that had to be seen to be believed—and then but barely. She was literally ablaze with every kind of gem he had ever seen and a dozen kinds completely new to him. Just as she stood, she could have supplied Tiffany and Cartier both for five years.

Yet she did *not* look barbaric. Blue-eyed, with an incredible cascade of pale blonde hair cut squarely across well below her hips, she looked both regal and virginal.

"Wow!" he exclaimed finally. "The English has—not a word for it, but a sound," and he executed a long-drawn-out wolf-whistle.

She laughed delightedly. "Oh? I did not hear that on Tellus; but it sounds . . . appreciative."

"It is, Milady. Very." He took her hands and bowed over them. "May I say, Lady Senny, that you are the most beautiful woman I have ever seen?"

" 'Milady.' 'Lady.' I have not told you how much I like those terms, friend Vance. I'm wonderfully pleased that you find me so. You're magnificently handsome yourself . . . and you smell nice, too." She came squarely up to him and sniffed approvingly. "But the . . . the blade of formality. May I look at it, please?"

She examined it closely, then went on, "Tell me, Vance,

how old is your recorded history? Just roughly, in Tellurian years?"

This could be a crucial question, DuQuesne realized; but, since he didn't know the score yet, he hadn't better lie too much. "Before I answer that; you're a biologist, aren't you, and in the top bracket?"

"Yes. In English it would have to be 'anthropological biologist' and yes, I know my specialty very well."

"Okay. For better or for worse, here it is. Xylmny's recorded history goes back a little over six thousand Tellurian years."

"Oh, wonderful!" she breathed. "Perfect! That's what I read, but I could scarcely believe it. A *young* race. Mature, but still possessing the fire and the power and the genius that those accursed Llurdi have been breeding out of all us Jelmi for many thousands of years. They want us to produce geniuses for them, but they kill or sterilize all our aggressive, combative, rebellious young men. A few of us women carry all the necessary female genes, but without their male complements, dominant in heredity, we all might exactly as well have none of them."

"I see . . . but how about Tammon?"

"He's sterile, since he was a genius before he became a rebel. And he kept on being a genius; one of the very few exceptions to the rule. But since the Llurdi are insanely logical, one exception to any rule invalidates that rule." She glanced at the clock. "It's time to go now."

Walking slowly along the corridor, DuQuesne said, " 'Insanely logical' is right. I knew that there was a lot more to this than just an experiment, but I had no idea it was to put new and younger blood into an entire race. But with mothers such as you have in mind—"

"Mothers?" She broke in. "You already know, then?"

"Of course. I am sufficiently familiar with your specialty to know what a top-bracket biologist can do and how you intend to do it. With mothers of your class some of our sons may make genius grade, but what's to keep them alive?"

"We will." Sennlloy's voice and mien became of a sudden grim. "This fourth-dimension device that Tammon is going to give you was developed only a few weeks ago, since we left Llurdiax. The Llurdi know nothing whatever of it. When we get back to our own galaxy with it, either the Llurdi will grant us our full freedom or we will kill every Llurdi alive. And being insanely logical, they'll grant it without a fight: without even an argument, Sancil burn their teeth, wings, and tails!"

DuQuesne did not tell the girl how interested he was in the Llurdi; especially in Llanzlan Klazmon the Fifteenth. Instead, "That makes a weird kind of sense, at that," he said. "Tell me more about these Llurdi," and she told him about them all the rest of the way to the dining hall.

They went through an archway, stepped aside, and looked around. Three or four hundred people were in the hall already, and more were streaming in from all sides. Some were eating, in couples or in groups of various numbers, at tables of various sizes. Dress varied from nothing at all up to several spectaculars as flamboyant as Sennlloy's own. Informal, semi-formal, and formal; and the people themselves were alike in only one respect—that of physical perfection. DuQuesne had never seen anything like it and said so; and Sennlloy explained, concluding:

"So, you see, we eight hundred are the very pick of two hundred forty-one planets; which makes this an ideal primary situation. The reason I wanted you to look around carefully is that perhaps I should not be the only Prime Operative." She paused: it was quite evident that she was not at all in favor of the idea.

"Why not?" DuQuesne wasn't in favor of it, either; even though he couldn't begin to understand either her attitude or her behavior. How could any woman possibly be as deeply in love with one man as Sennlloy very evidently was, and yet act as she was acting toward such a complete stranger as himself? It baffled him completely, but he'd *still* play along—especially since he was suffering no pain at all. "It won't make any difference in the long run, will it?"

"Of course not. I just thought maybe you would relish diversity," Sennlloy said.

"You can unthink it. I wouldn't. There's no tomcat blood in me—and remember what I said?"

"Do you think I don't? But you've seen some *really* beautiful women now. Much prettier than I am."

"You know what they call that technique in English? 'Fishing'," grinned DuQuesne. "Prettier or not, Milady, you top them all by a country mile."

"I know about fishing. I was fishing a little, perhaps." She laughed happily and hugged his arm against her firm breast. "But it did get you to say it again, and it means *ever* so much more, now that you've seen the competition."

She steered him to a table for two against a wall, where

he seated her meticulously—a gesture that, while evidently new to her, was evidently liked.

"You order," she said, handing him the helmet. "You invited me, you know."

"But I don't know what you like to eat."

"Oh, I like almost everything, really; and if there should be anything I don't like I won't eat it. Okay?"

"Okay," and DuQuesne proceeded to set the table with fine linen and translucent china and sterling silver and sparkling cut glass.

The first course was a thin, clear soup; which Sennlloy liked. She also liked the crisp lettuce with Roquefort dressing; the medium rare roast beef with mushroom sauce and the asparagus in butter and the baked Idaho potato stuffed with sour cream; and she especially enjoyed the fruits-and-nuts-filled Nesselrode ice cream. She did not, however, like his corrosively strong, black, unsweetened coffee at all. Wrinkling her nose, she sniffed at it, then took a tiny sip, which she let flow back into the cup.

"How can you possibly drink such vile stuff as that?" she demanded, and replaced it with a tall glass of fizzy, viscous concoction that looked like eggnog and reeked of something that was halfway between almond and lemon.

After dinner—DuQuesne wanted to smoke, but since no one else was doing anything of the kind he could and would get along without it as long as he was aboard the *Mallidaxian*—they milled about with the milling throng. She introduced him right and left and showed him off generally; especially to over a hundred stunning young women, with whom she discussed the "project" in American English with a completely uninhibited frankness that made DuQuesne blush more than once.

After something over an hour of this the crowd broke up; and as the two left the hall Sennlloy said, "Ha! We're free now, my Vance, to go about our business!"

Arms tightly around each other, savoring each contact and each motion, they walked slowly and in silence to Sennlloy's room.

Three Mallidaxian days later, DuQuesne took his leave. Of Sennlloy last, of course. She put her arms around him and rubbed her cheek against his. "Good-by, friend Vance. I have enjoyed our association tremendously. Scarcely ever before has work been such pleasure. So much so that I feel guilty of selfishness."

DuQuesne's Assassins / 107

"You needn't, Milady. That was exactly the way I wanted it, remember?"

"I remember with joy; and I have wondered why."

"Because you are the only one of your class aboard this ship," DuQuesne said.

"You said that, but still—well, I *am* the only Allondaxian aboard, which may account for our great compatibility. And there should be, as there has been, something more than the purely physical involved."

DuQuesne was very glad she had said that; it gave him one last chance to explore. "Definitely," he agreed. "Liking, respect, appreciation, admiration—you're a tremendous lot of woman, Milady Sennlloy. But not love. Naturally."

"Of course not. I have my love and my work and my planet; you have yours; it would be terrible for either of us or any of ours to be hurt.

"Our rememberings of each other should be and will be most pleasant. Good-by, friend Vance; may All Powerful Llenderllon guard you and aid you as you Seek."

15 • *DU QUESNE'S ASSASSINS*

NOT even Marc DuQuesne was able—quite!—to put his rather astonishing, and totally pleasurable, experiences with the Jelmi—and with one Jelm in particular!—out of his mind without a second's hesitation. In another man, his mood as he set a minimum-time course and began to speed back to Earth, might have been called nostalgic . . . even sentimental.

But as the parsecs fled by his thoughts hardened. And just in time; for some very hard things indeed had to be done.

First and foremost, his deal with Seaton was utterly, irrevocably and permanently *off*. He no longer needed it. With the information he had received from the Jelmi, he had no further reason to worry about Seaton's offensive capabilities.

Of course, there was no reason for Seaton to know that. Or not until it was entirely too late to do Seaton any good. Let Seaton go on dawdling toward this Galaxy DW-427-LU. Seaton would be traveling at only normal max; DuQuesne would have time to make his arrangements, transact his business and *act* while Seaton was still on the way.

He did not intend to go to Earth, only to within working distance of it. Even so, he had a certain amount of time to spend. He spent it, all of it, in studying and operating the new device, which was called by the Jelm a name which Sennlloy had told him corresponded roughly to "quad."

And immediately he ran headlong into trouble.

To DuQuesne's keen disappointment, the confounded thing was both more and less useful than he had hoped. More: Its range was enormous, much more than he had expected. Less:—well, it simply didn't do *any* of the normal things that *any* machine could be made to do. And he could not tell why. He had received too much knowledge too fast; it took time to nail down all the details.

He could send himself anywhere, but he could not bring himself back. He *had* to be at the controls. Remote control wouldn't work and he couldn't find out why not. The thing —in its present state of development, at least—couldn't handle a working projection; and he couldn't explain that fact, either. There was no way at all, apparently, of coupling the two transmitters together or of automating the controls—which was absurd on the face of it. There were job lots of things it couldn't do; and in no case at all could he understand why not.

That condition was, however, perfectly natural. In fact, it was inevitable. For, as has been pointed out, the laws of the fourth-dimensional region are completely inexplicable in three-dimensional terms. Obvious impossibilities become commonplace events; many things that are inevitable in our ordinary continuum become starkly impossible there.

Tammon had told DuQuesne just that; Seaton had told him the same, and much more strongly for having been there in person; but DuQuesne could not help but boggle at such information. Of the three men, he was far and away the least able to accept an obvious impossibility as a fact and go on from there.

So Blackie DuQuesne, his face like a steel-black thundercloud, methodically and untiringly worked with his new device until he was quite sure that of all the things he could make it do, he could make it do all of them very well.

And that would be enough. Never mind the things it wouldn't do. What it would do would be plenty to get rid of Richard Ballinger Seaton once and for all.

Within range of Earth at last, DuQuesne set about the first step in that program.

The simplest and crudest methods would work—backed by the weird fourth-dimensional powers of the quad. And DuQuesne knew exactly how to go about recruiting the assistance he needed in those methods.

He launched a working projection of himself to the Safe Deposit Department of the First National Bank. He signed a name and counted out a sheaf of currency from a box. He then took a taxi to the World Steel Building and an elevator up to the office of the president.

Brushing aside private secretaries, vice presidents, and other small fry, he strode through a succession of private offices into the *sanctum sanctorum* of President Brookings himself.

The tycoon was, as usual, alone. If he was surprised at the intrusion he did not show it. He took the big cigar from his mouth, little-fingered half an inch of ash from the end of it into a bronze tray, put it back between his teeth, and waited.

"Still thinking your usual devious, petty-larceny, half-vest thoughts, eh, Brookings?" DuQuesne sneered.

"Still thinking your usual devious, petty-larceny, half-vast sublime gall to show up around here again," Brookings said, evenly. "Even via projection, after the raw stuff you pulled and the ungodly flop you made of everything. Especially after the way your pal Seaton dragged you out of here with your tail between your legs. Incidentally, it took everything you had coming to repair the damage you did to the building on your way out."

"Stupid as ever, I see. And the galaxy's tightest penny-pincher. But back pay and the law of contracts and so forth are of no importance at the moment. What I'm here about is: with all these Norlaminian so-called 'observers' looking down the back of your neck all the time, Perkins' successor and his goon squads must be eating mighty low on the hog."

"We haven't any—" At DuQuesne's sardonically contemptuous smile Brookings changed instantly the sense of what he had been going to say—"work for them, to speak of, at that. Why?"

"So six of your best and fastest gunnies would be interested in ten grand apiece for a month's loaf and a minute's work."

"Don't say mine, Doctor. Please! You know very well that I never have anything to do with anything like that."

"No? But you know who took over the Perkins Cafe and the top-mobster job after I killed Perkins. So I want six off the top downstairs in the lobby at sixteen hours Eastern Daylight time today."

"You know I *never* handle—"

"Shut up! I'm not asking you—I'm telling you. You'll handle this, or else."

Brookings shrugged his shoulders and sighed. He knew DuQuesne. "If you want good men they'll have to know what the job is."

"Naturally. Dick and Dorothy Seaton, Martin and Margaret Crane, and their Jap Shiro and his wife—Apple Blossom or whatever her name is. Seaton's fast, for an amateur, but he's no pro. Crane is slow—he thinks and aims. And the others don't count. I'll guarantee complete surprise enough for one clear shot at Seaton. Anybody who is apt to need two shots I don't want. So—no problem."

"I'll see what I can do."

Since DuQuesne knew that was as close as Brookings ever came to saying "yes", he accepted it. "In advance, of course." Brookings held out his hand.

"Naturally." DuQuesne took a rubber-banded sheaf of thousand-dollar bills out of his inside coat pocket and tossed it across the desk. "Count 'em."

"Naturally." Brookings picked the sheaf up and riffled through it. "Correct. Good-by, Doctor."

"Good-by," DuQuesne said, and the projection vanished.

At four o'clock that afternoon DuQuesne picked up his goons—through the fourth dimension, which surprised them tremendously and scared them no little, although none of them would admit that fact—and headed for the galaxy toward which the *Skylark of Valeron* had been flying so long. The *Capital D* was of course much faster than the gigantic planetoid; and the actual difference in speed between the two intergalactic flyers was much greater than the rated one because DuQuesne was driving with all his engines at absolute max—risking burn-out, tear-out, and unavoidable collision at or near the frightful velocity of turnover—which Seaton of course was not doing. He didn't want to endanger the *Valeron*.

In the target galaxy—Galaxy DW-427-LU, according to Klazmon's chart—there was only one solar system showing really intense sixth-order activity. Almost all of that activity would be occurring on one planet; a planet whose inhabitants were highly inimical to (probably) all other forms of intelligent life.

Klazmon's side-bands of thought had been very informative on those points.

Thus it was by neither accident nor coincidence that DuQuesne came up to within long working range of the *Skylark of Valeron* well before that flying worldlet came within what DuQuesne thought was extreme range of a planet that DuQuesne *knew* to be a very dangerous planet indeed.

He had wanted it that way; he had risked his ship and his life to make it come out that way. When the *Valeron* came within range of the target planet she would be DuQuesne's not Seaton's. And DuQuesne was calmly confident that he and a *Valeron* re-tuned to his own mind could cope with any possible situation.

As a matter of fact, they couldn't. It was not, however, DuQuesne's error or fault that made it so; it was merely the way Fate's mop flopped. Neither he nor Seaton had any idea whatever of the appalling magnitude of the forces so soon to be hurled against Seaton's supposedly invulnerable flying fortress, the *Skylark of Valeron*.

Operating strictly according to plan, then, DuQuesne called his goons to attention. "You've been briefed and you've had plenty of practise, but I'll recap the essential points.

"Guns in hands. They'll be eating dinner, with their legs under the table. Sitting ducks for one shot. But for one shot only. Especially Seaton—for an amateur he's fast. So work fast—land and shoot. I'll give you the usual three-second countdown, beginning, now—Seconds! Three! Two! One! Mark!" and the six men vanished.

And in the dining room of the Seatons' home in the *Skylark of Valeron* six forty-five-caliber automatics barked viciously, practically as one.

16 • *THE CHLORANS*

WHILE much work had been done on a personal gravity control, to provide for the comfort of such visitors as Dunark and Sitar, it was still in the design stage when the *Skylark of Valeron* neared Galaxy DW-427-LU. Wherefore, when the Skylarkers sat down to dinner that evening in the Seatons' dining room that room was almost forty per cent undergrav. And wherefore, when DuQuesne's six hired killers fired practically as one, all six bullets went harmlessly high.

For, at low gravity, two facts of marksmanship—unknown to or not considered by either DuQuesne or any of his men—became dominant. First, a pistol expert compensates automatically for the weight of his weapon. Second, the more expert the marksman, the more automatic this compensation is.

And one shot each was all those would-be killers had. Dunark and Sitar as has been said, went armed even to bed; and Osnomian reflexes were and are the fastest possessed by any known race of man. Each of their machine pistols clicked twice and four American hoodlums died, liquescent brains and comminuted skulls spattering abroad, before they could do anything more than begin to bring their guns back down into line for their second shots.

The other two gangsters also died; if not as quickly or as messily, just as dead. For Shiro and his bride were, for Earthmen, very fast indeed. Their chairs, too, flew away from the table the merest instant after the invaders appeared and both took off in low, flat dives.

Lotus struck her man with her left shoulder; and, using flawlessly the momentum of her mass and speed, swung him around and put her small but very hard knee exactly where it would do the most good. Then, as he doubled over in agony, she put her left arm around his head, seized her left wrist with her right hand, and twisted with all the strength of arms, shoulders, torso and legs—and the man's neck broke with a snap audible throughout the room.

And Shiro took care of his man with equal dexterity, precision, and speed; and of the invaders, then there were none.

Seaton was a microsecond slower than either the Osnomians or the two Japanese; but he was fast enough to see what was happening, take in the fact that the forces already engaged were enough to handle the six hoodlums and, in mid-flight, divert his leap toward the remote-control headset. He was blindingly certain of one thing: It was Marc DuQuesne who had unleashed these killers on them. And he was equally certain of that fact's consequence: The truce was off. DuQuesne was to be destroyed.

Wherefore what happened next astonished him even more than if it had occurred at another time.

A strident roar of klaxons filled the room. It was the loudest sound any human had ever heard—without permanent damage; it was calculated to come right up to the threshold of destruction. There was to be *no* chance that anyone would fail to hear this particular signal.

His hand on the headset, Seaton paused. The bodies of the six gunmen had not yet all reached the floor, but the other Skylarkers were staring too. They had never expected to hear that sound except in test.

It was the dire warning that they were under attack—*massive* attack—attack on a scale and of a persistence that they had never expected to encounter in real combat, with whatever forces.

For that klaxon warning meant that under the fierce impact of the enemy weapons now so suddenly and mercilessly beating down on them the life of the *Valeron's* defensive screens was to be measured only in seconds—and very few of them!

"Yipe!" he yelled then. "Control-room *fast!*" His voice of course went unheard in the clamor of the horns; but his yelling had been purely reflexive, anyway. While uttering the first syllable he was energizing beams of force that hurtled all eight of the party through ultra-high-speed locks that snapped open in front of them and crashed shut behind them—down into the neutral-gray chamber at the base of the giant Brain.

Seaton rammed his head into his master controller and began furiously but accurately to think . . . and as he sat there, face harsh and white and strained, a vast structure of inoson, interlaced with the heaviest fields of force generable by the *Valeron's* mighty engines, came into being around the Brain and the other absolutely vital components of the worldlet's core.

After a few minutes of fantastic effort Seaton sighed gustily and tried to grin. "We're holding 'em and we're getting away," he said. "But I had to let 'em whittle us down to just about a nub before I could spare power enough to grab a lunch off of them while they were getting a square meal off of us."

He spoke the exact truth. The attack had been so incredibly violent that in order to counter it he had had to apply the full power of the *Valeron,* designed to protect a surface of over three million square kilometers, to an area of less than thirty thousand.

"But what *was* it, Dick?" Dorothy shrieked. "What *could* it have been—possibly?"

"I don't know. But you realize, don't you, that it was two separate, unrelated attacks? Not one?"

"Why, I . . . I don't think I realize *anything* yet."

"Those guns were Colts," Seaton said, flatly. "Forty-fives. Made in the U.S.A. So that part of it was DuQuesne's doing. He wanted—still wants—the *Valeron*. Bad. But those super-energy super-weapons were definitely something else —as sure as God made apples. No possible ship could put that much stuff out, let alone DuQuesne's *Capital D*. So the question rises and asks itself—"

"Just a minute, Dick!" Crane broke in. "Even granting so extraordinary a coincidence as two separate attacks—"

"Coincidence, hell!" Seaton snarled. "There *is* no such thing. And why postulate an impossibility when you've got Blackie DuQuesne? He sucked me in, as sure as hell's a mantrap—you can bet your case buck on that. And he outfoxed himself doing it, for all the tea in China!"

"What do you mean, Dick?" Dorothy demanded. "How could he have?"

"Plain as the nose on . . . plainer! He got it from somewhere, the son of a—" Seaton bit the noun savagely off— "probably from Klazmon, that Galaxy DW-427-LU up ahead there that we were heading for is full of bad Indians. So he honeyed up to the Jelmi, got that fourth-dimensional gadget off of them and tried to kill us with it. And he would have succeeded, except for the pure luck of our having lowered our gravity so drastically on account of Dunark and Sitar."

"I see," Crane said. "And the Indians jumped us when he pulled the trigger—perhaps attracted by his use of the 'gadget'."

"That's my guess, anyway," Seaton admitted. "DuQuesne thought he was allowing plenty of leeway in both time and space for his operation. But he wasn't. He had no more idea than we did, Mart, that any such forces as *those* could possibly be delivered at such extreme range. And one simple, easy lie—the coordinates of the Llurdan galaxy—was all he had to tell me and defend against my probe."

DuQuesne's attention was wrenched from his timer by a glare of light from a visiplate. He glanced at it, his jaw dropping in surprise; then his hands flashed to the controls of his fourth-dimensional transmitter and his six men appeared—four of them gruesomely headless. For a moment all six stood stiffly upright; then, as the supporting forces vanished, all six bodies slumped bonelessly to the floor.

DuQuesne, after making quickly sure that the two were in fact as dead as were the four, shrugged his shoulders and flipped the bodies out into deep space. Then, donning practically opaque goggles, he studied the incandescently glaring plate—to see that the *Skylark of Valeron* now looked like a minor sun.

Involuntarily he caught his breath. The *Valeron's* screens were failing—failing fast. Course after course, including her mighty zones of force, her every defensive layer was flaring into and through the violet and going black.

DuQuesne clenched his fists; set his teeth so hard that his jaw-muscles stood out in bands and lumps. Anything to put out that much of that kind of stuff would have to be vast indeed. Incredibly vast. Nothing could *be* that big—nothing even pertaining, as far as DuQuesne knew, to any civilization or culture of the known universe.

Relaxing a little, he assembled a working projection, but before sending it out he paused in thought.

Seaton hadn't attacked; he wasn't the type to. He wouldn't have, even if he could have done so at that range. So the strangers, whoever or whatever they might be, were the aggressors, with a capital "A." Guilty of unprovoked and reasonless aggression; aggression in the first degree. So what Tammon had told him about that galaxy being dominated by "inimical life-forms" was the understatement of the year. And he, DuQuesne himself, had triggered the attack; the fact that it had followed his own attack so nearly instantly made that a certainty. How had he triggered it? Almost certainly by the use of the fourth-dimensional transmitter . . .

But *how?* He didn't know and he couldn't guess . . . and at the moment it didn't make a lick of difference. He hadn't used any sixth-order stuff since then and he sure wouldn't use any now for a good while. If he did anything at all, he'd pussyfoot it, but good. He didn't want any part of anything that could manhandle the *Skylark of Valeron* like that. His *Capital D* was small enough and far enough back—he hoped!—to avoid detection. No he wouldn't do a single damn thing except look on.

Fascinated, DuQuesne stared into the brilliance of his plate. All the *Valeron's* screens were down now. Even the ultra-powerful innermost zone—the wall shield itself, the last line of defense of the bare synthetic of the worldlet's outer skin—was going fast. Huge black areas appeared, but they were black only momentarily. Such was the power of that incredible assault that thousands of tons of inoson flared in an instant into ragingly incandescent vapor; literally exploding; exploding with such inconceivable violence as to blast huge masses of solid inoson out of the *Valeron's* thick skin and hurl them at frightful speed out into space.

And the *Valeron* was not fighting back. She couldn't.

This fact, more than anything else, rocked DuQuesne to the core and gave him the measure of the power at the disposal of the "inimical" entities of that galaxy. For he, knowing the *Valeron's* strength, now knew starkly that she was being attacked by forces of a magnitude never even approximated by the wildest imaginings of man.

Scowling in concentration, he kept on watching the disaster. Watched while those utterly unbelievable forces peeled the *Valeron* down like an onion, layer after kilometer-thick layer. Watched until that for which he had almost ceased to hope finally took place. The *Valeron,* down now to the merest fraction of her original size—burned and blasted down to the veriest core—struck back. And that counterstroke was *no* love-tap. The ether and all the subethers seethed and roiled under the vehemence of that devastating bolt of energy.

The *Skylark of Valeron* vanished from DuQuesne's plate; that plate went black; and DuQuesne stood up and stretched the kinks out of his muscles. Seaton could of course flit away on the sixth; but he, DuQuesne, couldn't. Not without being detected and getting burned to a crisp. Against the forces that he had just seen in action against the *Skylark of*

Valeron, DuQuesne's own *Capital D* didn't stand the proverbial chance of the nitrocellulose dog chasing the asbestos
cat in hell.

If the *Skylark of Valeron* had been hurt, half-demolished
and reduced to an irreducible core of fighting muscle before
it could mount one successful counter-blow against this new
and unexpected enemy, then the *Capital D* would be reduced to its primitive gases. DuQuesne rapidly, soberly and
accurately came to the conclusion that he simply did not
own ship enough to play in this league. Not yet . . .

Wherefore he pussyfooted it away from there at an
acceleration of only a few lights; and he put many parsecs
of distance between himself and the scene of recent hostilities before he cut in his space-annihilating sixth-order
drive and began really to travel. He did not know whether
Seaton and his party were surviving; he did not care. He
did not know the identity of the race which had hurt them
so badly, so fast.

What DuQuesne knew was that, as a bare minimum, he
needed something as big as the *Valeron,* plus the fourth-
dimensional tricks he had learned from the Jelmi, plus a
highly developed element of caution based on the scene he
had just witnessed. And he knew what to do about it, and
where to go to do it; wherefore his course was laid for the
First Galaxy and Earth.

Hundreds of thousands of parsecs away from the scene
of disaster, Seaton cut his drive and began gingerly to relax
the terrific power of his defensive screens.

No young turtle, tentatively poking his head out of his
shell to see if the marauding gulls had left, was more
careful than Seaton. He had been caught off base twice. He
did not propose to let it happen again.

Another man might have raged and sworn at DuQuesne
for his treachery; or panicked at the fear inspired by the
fourth-dimensional transmitter DuQuesne had come up
with, or the massive blow that had fallen from nowhere.
Seaton did not. The possibility—no, the virtual certainty—
of treachery from DuQuesne he had accepted and discounted in the first second of receiving DuQuesne's distress
call. He had accepted the risks, and grimly calculated that
in any encounter, however treacherous, DuQuesne would
fail; and he had been right. The sudden attack from out of
nowhere, however, was something else again. What made
it worse was not that Seaton had no idea of its source or
reason. The thing that caused his eyes to narrow, his face

to wear a hard, thoughtful scowl was that he in fact had a very good idea indeed—and he didn't like it.

But for the moment they were free. Seaton checked and double-checked every gauge and warning device and nodded at last.

"Good," he said then, "I was more than half expecting a kick in the pants, even way out here. The next item on our agenda is a council of war; so cluster 'round, everybody, and get comfortable." He turned control over to the Brain, sat down beside Dorothy, stoked his pipe, and went on:

"Point one; DuQuesne. He got stuff somewhere—virtually certainly from the Jelmi—at least the fourth-dimensional transmitter and we don't know what else, that he didn't put out anything about. Naturally. And he sucked me in like Mary's little lamb. Also naturally. At hindsight I'm a blinding flash and a deafening report. I've got a few glimmerings, but you're the brain, Mart; so give out with analysis and synthesis."

Crane did so; covering the essential points and concluding: "Since the plug-chart was accurate, the course was accurate. Therefore, besides holding back vital information, DuQuesne lied about one or both of two things: the point at which the signal was received and the direction from which it came."

"Well, you can find out about that easily enough," Dorothy said. "You know, that dingus you catch light-waves with, so as to see exactly what went on years and years ago. Or wouldn't it work, this far away?"

Seaton nodded. "Worth a try. Dunark?"

"I say go after DuQuesne!" the Osnomian said viciously. "Catch him and blow him and his *Captial D* to hellangone up!"

Seaton shook his head. "I can't buy that—at the moment. Now that he's flopped again at murder, I don't think he's of first importance any more. You see, I haven't mentioned Point Two yet, which is a datum I didn't put into the pot because I wanted to thrash Point One out first. It's about who the enemy really are. When I finally got organized to slug them a good one back, I followed the shot. They knew they'd been nudged, believe me. So much so that in the confusion I got quite a lot of information. They're Chlorans. Or, if not exactly like the Chlorans of Chlora, that we had all the trouble with, as nearly identical as makes no difference."

"*Chlorans!*" Dorothy and Margaret shrieked as one, and

five minds dwelt briefly upon that hideous and ultimately terrible race of amoeboid monstrosities who, living in an atmosphere of gaseous chlorine, made it a point to enslave or to destroy all the humanity of all the planets they could reach.

All five remembered, very vividly, the starkly unalloyed ferocity with which one race of Chlorans had attacked the planet Valeron; near which the *Skylark of Valeron* had been built and after which she had been named. They remembered the horrifyingly narrow margin by which those Chlorans had been defeated. They also remembered that the Chlorans had not even then been slaughtered. The Skylarkers had merely enclosed the planet Chlora in a stasis of time and sent it back—on a trip that would last, for everyone and everything outside that stasis, some four hundred years—to its own native solar system, from which it had been torn by a near-collision of suns in the long-gone past. The Skylarkers should have blown Chlora into impalpable and invisible debris, and the men of the party had wanted to do just that, but Dorothy and Margaret and the essentially gentle Valeronians had been dead set against genocide.

Dorothy broke the short silence. "But how *could* they be, Dick?" she asked. " 'Way out here? But of course, if we human beings could do it—" She paused.

"But of course," Seaton agreed sourly. "Why not? Why shouldn't they be as widespread as humanity is? Or even more so, if they have killed enough of us off? And why shouldn't they be smarter than those others were? Look at how much we've learned in just months, not millennia, of time."

Another and longer silence fell; which was broken by Seaton. "Well, two things are certain. They're rabidly anti-social and they've got—at the moment—a lot more stuff than we have. They've got it to sell, like farmers have hay. It's also a dead-sure cinch that we can't do a thing—not *anything*—without a lot more data than we have now. It'll take all the science of Norlamin and maybe a nickel's worth besides to design and build what we'll have to have. And they can't go it blind. Nobody can. And we all know enough about Chlorans to know that we won't get one iota or one of Peg's smidgeons of information out of them by remote control. At the first touch of any kind of a high-order feeler they'll bat our ears down . . . to a fare-thee-well. However, other means are available."

And he glanced at a monitor where for some minutes a display had shown a planet of the galaxy from which their recent attacker had come.

During this fairly long—for Seaton—speech, and during the silence that had preceded it, two things had been happening.

First the controlling Brain of the ship had been carrying out a program of Seaton's. Star by star, system by system, it had been scanning the components of the nearest galaxy to the scene of their encounter. It had in fact verified Seaton's conclusions: the galaxy was dominated by Chlorans. Their works were everywhere. But it had also supported a—not a conclusion; a hope, more accurately—that Seaton had hardly dared put in words. Although the Chlorans ruled this galaxy, there were oxygen-breathing, warm-blooded races in it too—serfs of the Chlorans of course, but nevertheless occupying their own planets—and it was one such planet that the Brain had finally selected and was now displaying on its monitor.

The other thing was that the auburn-haired beauty who was Mrs. Richard Ballinger Seaton had been eyeing her husband steadily. At first she had merely looked at him thoughtfully. Then look and mien had become heavily tinged, first with surprise and then with doubt and then with wonder; a wonder that turned into an incredulity that became more and more incredulous. Until finally, unable to hold herself in any longer, she broke in on him.

"Dick!" she cried. "You *wouldn't!* You *know* you wouldn't!"

"I wouldn't? If not, who . . . ?" Changing his mind between two words, Seaton cut the rest of the sentence sharply off; shrugged his shoulders; and grinned, somewhat shamefacedly, back at her.

At this point Crane, who had been looking first at one of them and then at the other, put in: "I realize, Dorothy, that you and Dick don't need either language or headsets to communicate with each other, but how about the rest of us? What, exactly, is it that you're not as sure as you'd like to be that he wouldn't do?"

Dorothy opened her mouth to reply, but Seaton beat her to it. "What I would do—and will because I'll have to; because it's my oyster and nobody else's—is, after we sneak up as close as we can without touching off any alarms, take a landing craft and go get the data we absolutely have to have in absolutely the only way it can be gotten."

"And that's what I most emphatically do *not* like!" Dorothy blazed. "Dick Seaton, you are *not* going to land on an enslaved planet, alone and unarmed and afoot, as an investigating Committee of One! For one thing, we simply don't have the time! Do we? I mean, poor old *Valeron* is simply a wreck! We've got to go somewhere and—"

But Seaton was shaking his head. "The Brain can handle that by itself," he said. "All it needs is time. As a matter of fact, you've put your finger on a first-rate reason for my going in, alone. There's simply not much else we can do until the *Valeron* is back in shape again."

"Not *your* going in." Dorothy blazed. "Flatly, positively *no*."

Again Seaton shrugged his shoulders. "I can't say I'm madly in love with the idea myself, but who's any better qualified? Or as well? Because I know that you, Dottie, aren't the type to advocate us sitting on our hands and letting them have all the races of humanity, wherever situate. So who?"

"Me," Shiro said, promptly if ungrammatically. "Not as good, but good enough. You can tell me what data you want and I can and will get it, just as well as . . ."

"Bounce back, both of you, you've struck a rubber fence!" Dunark snapped. "That job's for Sitar and me." The green-skinned princess waved her pistol in the air and nodded her head enthusiastically and her warlord went on, "You and I being brain-brothers, Dick, I'd know exactly what you want. And she and I would blast—"

"Yeah, that's what I know damn well you'd do." Seaton broke in, only to be interrupted in turn by Crane—who was not in the habit of interrupting anyone even once, to say nothing of twice.

"Excuse me, everyone," he said, "but you're all wrong, I think. My thought at the moment, Dick, is that your life is altogether too important to the project as a whole to be risked as you propose risking it. As to you others, with all due respect for your abilities, I do not believe that either of you is as well qualified for this kind of an investigation as I am—"

Margaret leaped to her feet in protest, but Crane went quietly on: "—in either experience or training. However, we should not decide that point yet—or at all, for that matter. We are all too biased. I therefore suggest, Dick, that we feed the Brain everything we have and keep on feeding it everything pertinent we can get hold of, until it has enough data to make that decision for us."

"*That* makes sense," Seaton said, and both Dorothy and Margaret nodded—but both with very evident reservations. "The first time anything has made sense today!"

17 • KY-EL MOKAK THE WILDER

THE first thing Seaton and Crane had to do, of course, was to figure out how to get back somewhere near Galaxy DW-427-LU, within fourth-order range of that one particular extremely powerful Chloran system, without using enough sixth-order stuff to touch off any alarms—but still enough to make the trip in days instead of in months. Some sixth-order emanations could be neutralized by properly phased and properly placed counter-generators; the big question being, how much?

The answer turned out to be, according to Crane, "Not enough"—but, according to Seaton, "Satisfactory". At least, it did make the trip not only possible, but feasible. And during the days of that trip each Skylarker worked—with the Brain or with a computer or with pencil and paper or with paint or India ink and a brush, each according to his bent—on the problem of what could be done about the Chlorans.

They made little headway, if any at all. They did not have enough data. Inescapably, the attitude of each was very strongly affected by what he or she knew about the Chlorans they had already encountered. They were all smart enough to know that this was as indefensible as it was inevitable.

Thus, while each of them developed a picture completely unlike anyone else's as to what the truth probably was, none of them was convinced enough of the validity of his theory to defend it vigorously. Thus it was discussion, not argument, that went on throughout the cautious approach to the forbidden territory and the ultra-cautious investigation of the Tellus-type planet the Brain had selected through powerful optical telescopes and by means of third- and fourth-order apparatus. Then they fell silent, appalled; for that world was inhabited by highly intelligent human beings and what had been done to it was shocking indeed.

They had seen what had been done to the planet Valeron. This was worse; much worse. On Valeron the ruins had been recognizable as having once been cities. Even those that had been blown up or slagged down by nuclear energies had shown traces of what they had once been. There had been remnants and fragments of structural members, unfused portions of the largest buildings, recognizable outlines and traces of thoroughfares and so on. But here, where all of the big cities and three-fourths or more of the medium-sized ones had been, there were now only huge sheets of glass.

Sheets of glass ranging in area from ten or fifteen square miles up to several thousands of square miles, and variously from dozens up to hundreds of feet thick: level sheets of cracked and shattered, almost transparent, vari-colored glass. The people of the remaining cities and towns and villages were human. In fact, they were white Caucasians—as white and as Caucasian as the citizens of Tampa or of Chicago or of Portland, Oregon or of Portland, Maine. Neither Seaton nor Shiro, search as they would, could find any evidence that any Oriental types then lived or ever had lived on that world—to Shiro's lasting regret. He, at least, was eliminated as a spy.

"Well, Dottie?" Seaton asked.

She gnawed her lip. "Well . . . I suppose we'll have to do *something*—but hey!" she exclaimed, voice and expression changing markedly. "How come you think you have to go down there at all to find out what the score is? You've snatched people right and left all over the place with ordinary beams and things, *long* before anybody ever heard of that sixth-order, fourth-dimensional gizmo."

Seaton actually blushed. "That's right, my pet," he admitted. "Once again you've got a point. I'll pick one out that's so far away from everybody else that he won't be missed for a while. Maybe two'd be better."

Since it was an easy matter to find isolated specimens of the humanity of that world, it was less than an hour later that two men—one from a town, one found wandering alone in the mountains—were being examined by the Brain.

And *what* an examination! Everything in their minds— literally everything, down to the last-least-tiniest coded "bit" of every long-chain proteinoid molecule of every convolution of their brains—everything was being transferred to the *Valeron's* Great Brain; was being filed away in its practically unfillable memory banks.

When the transfer was complete, Sitar drew her pistol, very evidently intending to do away with the natives then and there. But Dorothy of course would not stand for that. Instead, she herself put them back into a shell of force and ran them through the *Valeron's* locks and down into a mountain cave, which she then half-filled with food. "I'd advise you two," she told them then, in their own language, "to stay put here for a few days and keep out of trouble. If you really *want* to get yourselves killed, though, that's all right with me. Go ahead any time."

When Dorothy brought her attention back into the control room, the Brain had finished its analysis of the data it had just secured from the natives, had correlated it with all their pertinent data it had in its banks, and was beginning to put out its synthesized report.

That report came in thought; in diamond-sharp, diamond-clear thought that was not only super-intelligible and super-audible, but also was more starkly visible than any possible tri-di. It gave, as no possible other form of report could give, the entire history of the race to which those two men belonged. It described in detail and at length the Chlorans and the relationship between the two races, and went on to give, in equal detail, the most probable course of near-term events. It told Seaton that he should investigate this planet Ray-See-Nee in person. It told him in fine detail what to wear, where to go, and practically every move to make for the ensuing twenty-four hours.

At that point the report stopped, and when Seaton demanded more information, the Brain balked. "Data insufficient," it thought, and everyone there would have sworn that the Great Brain actually had a consciousness of self as it went on, "This construct—" it actually meant "I"—"is not built to guess, but deals only in virtual certainties; that is, with probabilities that approximate unity to twelve or more nines. With additional data, this matter can be explored to a depth quite strictly proportional to the sufficiency of the data. That is all."

"That's the package, Dottie," Seaton said then. "If we

want to reach the Chlorans without them reaching us first, there's how. That makes it a force, wouldn't you say?"

Dorothy wasn't sure. "For twenty-four hours, I guess," she agreed, dubiously. "After which time I think I'll be screaming for you to come back here and feed that monster some more data. So be mighty darn sure to get some."

"I'll try to, that's for sure. But the really smart thing to do might be to take this wreckage half a dozen galaxies away and put the Brain to work rebuilding her while I'm down there investigating."

"D'you think I'll sit still for *that?*" Dorothy blazed. "If you do, you're completely out of your mind!"

And even Crane did not subscribe to the idea. "Why?" he asked, "Just to tear her down again after you've found out what we'll have to have?"

"That's so, too." Seaton thought for a moment, gray eyes narrowed and focused on infinity, translating the imperatives of the Brain into practical measures. Then he nodded. "All right. I admit I'll feel better about the deal with you people and the Brain standing by."

And Seaton, now lean and hard and deeply tanned, sat down in his master controller and began to manufacture the various items he would need; exactly as the Brain told him to make them.

And next morning, as the sun began to peer over the crest of the high mountain ridge directly below the *Skylark of Valeron*, Seaton came to ground, hid his tiny landing-craft in a cave at the eighteen-thousand-foot level, and hiked the fifteen miles down-mountain to the nearest town.

He now looked very little indeed like the Doctor Richard B. Seaton of the Rare Metals Laboratory. He was almost gaunt. His skin was burned to a shade consistent with years of exposure to wind and weather. His hair had very evidently been cut—occasionally—with shears by his own hand; his beard had been mowed—eqaully occasionally— with those same shears.

He wore crudely made, heavy, hobnailed, high-laced boots; a pair of baggy, unsymmetrical breeches of untanned deerskin; and a shapeless, poor-grade-leather coat that had been patched crudely and repeatedly at elbows and shoulders and across the back. He also wore what was left of a hard hat.

As he strode into the town and along its main street, more than one pair of eyes looked at him and then looked again, for the people of that town were not used to seeing anyone walk purposefully. Nor was the sloppily uniformed guard at the entrance to City Hall. This wight—who couldn't have been a day over fifteen—opened his eyes, almost straightened up and said:

"Halt, you. Who'a you? Whatcha want?"

"Business," Seaton said, briskly. "To see the mayor, Ree-Toe Prenk."

"Awri'; g'wan in," and the youth relapsed into semi-stuporous leaning on his ratty-looking rusty rifle.

It was easy enough to find His Honor's office, since it was the only one in the building doing any business at all. Seaton paused just inside the doorway and looked around. Everything was shabby and neglected. The wall-to-wall carpet was stained and dirty, worn through to the floor, in several places. The divider-rail leaned drunkenly, forward here, backward there. The vacant receptionist's desk was as battered and scarred as though it had been through a war. The place hadn't been cleaned for months, and not very thoroughly then.

And the people in that office were in perfect sync with their surroundings. Half a dozen melancholy-looking people, men and women, sat listlessly on hard, straight-backed chairs; staring glumly, fixedly at nothing; completely disinterested, apparently, in whether they were ever called into the inner office or not.

And the secretary! She was dressed in what looked like a gunny-sack. She was scrawny. Her unkempt, straight, lank hair was dirty-mouse brown in color. She didn't look very bright. She was, however, the only secretary in sight, so Seaton strode up to her desk.

"Miss What's-your-name!" he snapped. "Can you, without rupturing a blood-vessel, come to life long enough to do half a minute's work?"

The girl jumped, started to rise to her feet at her desk, and blushed. "Why, yes . . . yes, sir, I mean. What can we do for you, Mister—?"

"I'm Ky-El Mokak. I want to talk to Hizzonner about turning myself in."

That brought her to life fast. "About *what?*" she cried, and her half-scream was followed instantly by a deeper, louder voice from the intercom.

His Honor had not been asleep after all. "You *what?* All right, Fy-Ly, send him in; but be sure he hasn't got a gun first."

"Gun? What would I be doing with a gun?" Seaton

patted his pockets, shucked off his dilapidated coat, and made a full turn to show that he was clean. Then, seeing no coat-rack or hangers, he pitched the coat and hat into a corner and strode into the inner office.

It was, if possible, in even worse shape than the outer one. The man behind the desk was fifty-odd years old; lean and bald. He looked worried, dyspeptic and nervous. He held a hand-weapon—which was not the least bit rusty—in workmanlike fashion in a competent-looking right hand. It was not pointed directly at Seaton's midsection. It evidently did not have to be.

"What I'd ought to do right now," the man said quietly, "is blow your brains out without letting you say a word. You're another damn rat. A fink—a spy—maybe a revver or an undergrounder, even. You don't look like any wilder I ever saw brought in."

The Brain had not dumped Seaton on a strange and dangerous new planet without providing him with a full "knowledge" of its history, its mores and even its dialects. Through the educators Seaton had received enough of Ray-See-Nee's cultural patterns to be able to carry off his role. He knew what His Honor was thinking about; he knew, even, very accurately just how far the man could be pushed, where his real sympathies lay, and what he could be counted upon to do about it.

Wherefore Seaton said easily: "Of course I don't. I've got a brain. Those lard-headed chasseurs couldn't catch me in a thousand years. None of 'em can detect a smell on a skunk. And you won't shoot me, not with the bind you're in. You aren't a damn enough fool to. You wouldn't shoot a crippled kid on crutches, let alone a full-grown, able-bodied man."

Prenk shivered a little, but that was all. "Who says I'm in a bind? What kind of a bind?"

"I say so," Seaton said, flatly. "You're hitting bottom right now. You're using half-grown kids: girls, even. How many weeks is it going to be before you don't make quota and your town and everything and everybody in it get turned into a lake of lava?"

Prenk trembled visibly and his face turned white. "You win," he said unsteadily, and put his pistol back into the top right-hand drawer of his desk. "Whoever you are, you know the score and aren't afraid to talk about it. You'd have no papers, of course—on you, at least . . . Let's see your arm."

"No number." Seaton rolled up his left sleeve and held his forearm out for examination. "Look close. Scars left by good surgery are fine, but they can't be made invisible."

"I know they can't." His Honor looked very closely indeed, then drew a tremendously deep breath of relief. "You *are* a wilder! You mean to say you've been up in the hills ever since the Conquest without getting caught?"

"That's right. I told you I'm smart, and the brains of a whole platoon of chasseurs, all concentrated down into one, wouldn't equip a half-witted duck."

"But they've got *dogs!*"

"Yeah, but they aren't smart, either. Not very much smarter than the chasseurs are. Hell, I've been living on those dogs half the time. Pretty tough, fried or roasted, but boiled long enough they make mighty tasty stew."

"Mi-Ko-Ta's beard! Who *are* you, really, and what were you, before?"

"I told you, I'm Ky-El Mokak. I am—was, rather—a Class Twelve Fellow of the Institute of Mining Engineers. Recognize the ring?" Seaton went to the desk and placed his left hand flat on its surface.

Prenk studied the massive ornament. It had been fabricated, in strict external accord with the Brain's visualization of what it should have been, from synthesized meteoric metal—metal that had actually never been in open space, to say nothing of ever having been anywhere near the gray-lichened walls of the revered Institute that Seaton had never seen.

Having examined the ring minutely, Prenk looked up and nodded; his whole manner changed. "I recognize the ring and I can read the symbols. A *Twelve!* It's a shame to register and brand you. If you say so I'll let it drop."

"I'll say so. I'm not committing myself that deep yet."

"All right, but why did you come in? Or is it true that whatever undergrounds spring up are smashed flat in a week?"

"I don't know. I couldn't find any. Not one, and I searched every square mile for a thousand miles north, east, south, and west of here. And I didn't find anybody who wasn't too dangerous to travel with, and I'm gregarious. Also, I don't like caves and I don't like camp cooking and I don't like living off the land—and I do like music and books and art and educated people and so on—in other words, I found out that I can't revert to savagery. And, not least, I like women and there aren't any out there. What few ever make it up there die fast."

"I'm beginning to believe you." A little of the worry and harassment left His Honor's face. "One more question. Why, knowing the jam we're in, did you come here instead of going somewhere where you'd be safe?"

"Because, on the basis of stuff I picked up here and there, you and I together can make it safe here. I can fix your mining machinery easily enough so you can make quota every week with no sweat; so the town won't get slagged down; not right away, anyway. You aren't a quisling, and my best guess is that most of the spies and stormtroopers have sneaked out or have been pulled out because of what's supposed to be about to happen here," Seaton said.

Prenk stared thoughtfully at Seaton. "You don't appear to be the suicidal type. But you know as well as I do that just making quota won't be enough for very long. What have you really got in mind, Ky-El Mokak?"

Seaton thought for a moment. Then, shrugging his shoulders, he dug down into his baggy breeches and brought out two closely folded headsets.

"Put one of these on. It isn't a player or a recorder; just a kind of super-telephone. A fast way of exchanging information."

Prenk wore it for a couple of minutes, then took it off, staring suspiciously in turn at it and at Seaton. "Why didn't I ever hear of anything like *that* before?" he demanded. Seaton didn't answer the question and Prenk went on, "Oh; secret. Okay. But what makes you think you can set up an underground right out here in the open?"

"There's no reason in the world why we can't," Seaton declared. "Especially since we'd just be reviving one that everybody, including the Premier and you yourself, thinks is smashed flat and is about to be liquidated."

This was the second really severe test Seaton had made of the Brain's visualizations, and it too stood solidly up. All Prenk said was, "You're doing the talking; keep it up," but his hands, clenching tightly into fists, showed that Seaton's shot had struck the mark.

"I've talked enough," Seaton said then. "From here on I'd be just guessing. It's your turn to talk."

"All right. It's too late now, I'm afraid, for anything to make any difference. Yes, I was the leader of a faction that believed in decent, humane, civilized government, but we weren't here then, we were in the capital. Our coup failed. And those of us who were caught were exiled here and arrangments were made for us to be the next wipe-out."

"Some of your party survived, then. Could you interest them again, do you think?"

"Without arms and equipment, no. That was why we failed."

"Equipment would be no problem."

"It wouldn't?" Prenk's eyes began to light up.

"No." Seaton did not elaborate, but went on, "The problem is people and morale. I can't supply people and we have to start here, not over in the capital. Self-preservation. We've got to make quota. Your people have been hammered down so flat that they don't give a whoop whether they live or die. As I said, I can fix the machinery, but that of itself won't be enough. We'll have to give 'em a shot in the arm of hope."

"Okay, and thanks."

And no one in the outer office, not even the secretary, so much as looked up as the two men, talking busily, walked out.

DuQuesne, en route to Earth, knew just what a madhouse Earth was, and in just what respects. He knew just how nearly impossible it was to buy machine tools of any kind. He also knew just what an immense job it was going to be to build a duplicate of the *Skylark of Valeron*. Or, rather, to build the tools that would build the machines that would in turn build the planetoid. With his high-order constructors he *could* build most of those primary machine tools himself; perhaps all of them in time; but time was exactly what he did not have. Time was decidedly of the essence.

DuQuesne's ex-employer, The World Steel Corporation, had billions of dollars' worth of exactly the kind of tooling he had to have. They not only used it, they manufactured it and sold it. And what of it they did not manufacture they could buy.

How they could buy! As a result of many years of intensive, highly organized, and well directed snooping, Brookings of Steel had over a thousand very effective handles upon over a thousand very important men.

And he, DuQuesne, had a perfect handle on Brookings. He was much harder and more ruthless than Brookings was, and Brookings knew it. He could make Brookings buy his primary tooling for him—enough of it to stuff the *Capital D* to her outer skin. And he would do just that.

Wherefore, as soon as he got within working range of Earth, he launched his projection directly into Brookings' private office. This time, the tycoon was neither calm nor quiet. Standing behind his desk, chair lying on its side behind him, he was leaning forward with his left hand flat on the top of his desk. He was clutching a half-smoked, half-chewed cigar in his right hand and brandishing it furiously in the air. He was yelling at his terrified secretary; who, partly standing in front of her chair and partly crouching into it, was trying to muster up courage to run.

When DuQuesne's projection appeared Brookings fell silent for a moment and goggled. Then he screamed. "Get out of here, you!" at the girl, who scuttled frantically away. He hurled what was left of his cigar into his big bronze ashtray, where it disintegrated into a shower of sparks and a slathery mess of soggy, sticky brown leaves. And finally, exerting everything he had of self-control, he picked his chair up, sat down in it and glared at DuQuesne.

"Careful of your apoplexy, Fat," DuQuesne sneered then. "I've told you—you'll rupture your aorta some day and that will just about break my heart."

Brookings' reply to that was unprintable; after which he went on, even more bitterly, "This is all it lacks to make this a perfect day."

"Yeah," DuQuesne agreed, callously. "Some days you can't lay up a cent. I suppose you've been eager to know why I didn't return your goons to you."

"There's nothing in the world I'm less interested in."

"I'll tell you anyway, for the record." DuQuesne did not know what had actually happened, but Brookings was never to know that. "They each got one free shot, as I said they would. But they missed."

"Skip that, Doctor," Brookings said, brusquely. "You didn't come here for that. What do you want this time?"

DuQuesne reached over, took a ball-point out of Brookings' pocket, tore the top sheet off of the memorandum pad on Brookings' desk, and wrote out an order for one hundred twenty-five millon dollars, payable to the World Steel Corporation, on a numbered account in a Swiss bank. He slid the order across the glass top of the desk and said:

"You needn't worry about whether it's good or not. It is. I want machine tools and fast deliveries."

Brookings glanced at the paper, but did not touch it. His every muscle tensed, but he did not quite blow up again. "Machine tools," he grated. "You know damn well money's no good on them."

"Money alone, no," DuQuesne agreed equably. "That's why I'm having you apply pressure. You'll get the details—orders, specs, times and places of delivery, and so forth—by registered mail tomorrow morning. Shall I spell out the 'or else' for you?"

Brookings was quivering with rage, but there wasn't a thing in the world he could do about the situation and he knew it. "Not for me," he managed finally, "but I'd better record it for certain people who will have to know."

"Okay. Any mistake in any detail of the transaction or one second more than twenty-four hours' delay in any specified time of delivery will mean a one-hundred-kiloton superatomic on North Africa Number Eleven. Good-by."

And DuQuesne cut his projection. To Brookings, he seemed to vanish; to DuQuesne himself, he simply was back in his own *Capital D*, far out in space; and DuQuesne allowed himself to smile.

Things were going rather well, he thought. Seaton was tangled up with whoever the new enemy had turned out to be; might well be dead; at any rate, was not a factor he, DuQuesne, needed currently to take into his calculations. By the time Seaton was back in circulation DuQuesne should have his new ship and be ready to handle him. And from then on . . .

From then on, thought DuQuesne, it was only a short step to his rightful, inevitable destiny: *His* universe. No one able to contest his mastery.—So thought DuQuesne, who at that point in time knew nearly every factor that bore upon his plans, and had carefully and correctly evaluated them all. He knew about the Llurdi and the Jelmi; he knew that Seaton and the Chlorans were, from his point of view, keeping each other neutralized; he knew that the Norlaminians, even, were unlikely to cause him any trouble. DuQuesne really knew all the relevant facts but one—or, you might say, two. These two facts were a very long distance away. One was a young girl. The other was her mother.

Two individuals out of a universe! Why, even if DuQuesne had known of their existence, he might have discounted their imporance completely. In which he would have been—completely—wrong.

18 • HUMANITY TRIUMPHANT, NOT INC

SINCE Seaton as Ky-El Mokak was not the least bit fussy, he accepted the first house that Prenk showed him. His honor offered also—with a more than somewhat suggestive expression—to send him a housekeeper, but Seaton declined the offer with thanks; explaining that that could wait until he got himself organized and could do a little looking around for himself.

Prenk gave Seaton a handful of currency and a ground-car—one of Prenk's own, this; a beautifully streamlined, beautifully kept little three-wheeled jewel of a ground-car —told him where the shopping-centers were, and went back to City Hall.

Seaton bought a haircut and a shave, a couple of outfits of clothing, and some household supplies, which he took out to his new home and stowed away.

By that time it was the local equivalent of half-past three, and the shifts changed at four o'clock; wherefore he drove his spectacular little speedster six miles up-canyon to the uraninite mine that was the sole reason for the town's existence. Since he did not want to be shot out of hand, he did not dare to be late or to do anything unusual, either during the five-mile train-ride along the main tunnel or during the skip-ride down to the eighty-four-hundred-foot level where he was to work.

Once in the stope itself, however, he stopped—exactly thirteen feet short of the stiffly erect young overseer—and stood still while his shiftmates picked up their tools and started for the hanging wall—the something-more-than-vertical face of the cavernous stope—to begin their day's work.

The overseer was a well-fed young man, and the second native Seaton had seen who looked more than half alive. His jacket, breeches and boots were as glossily black as his crash-helmet was glossily white. He was a very proud young

133

man, and arrogant. His side-arm hung proudly at his hip. His bull-whip coiled arrogantly ready for instant use.

This wight stared haughtily at Seaton for a moment, and began to swell up like a pouter pigeon. Then, as Seaton made an unmistakeable gesture at him, he went into smoothly violent action.

"Oh, you're the wilder!" he snarled, and swung the heavy blacksnake with practised ease.

But Seaton had known exactly what to expect and he was ready for it. He ducked and sidestepped with the speed and control of the trained gymnast that he was; he handled the short, thick club that had been in his sleeve as though it were the wand of the highly skilled prestidigitator that he was. Thus, in the instant that the end of the lash curled savagely around the hickory he swung it like a home-run hitter swings a bat—and caught the blacksnake's heavy, shot-loaded butt on the fly in his right hand.

The minion went for his gun, of course, but Seaton's right arm was already swinging around and back, and as gun cleared holster the bull-whip's vicious tip snapped around both gun and hand with a pistol-sharp report. The trooper stared, for an instant stunned, at the blood spurting from his paralyzed right hand; and that instant was enough. Seaton stepped up to him and put his left fist deep into his midsection. Then, as the half-conscious man began to double over, he sent his right fist against its preselected target. Not the jaw—he didn't want to break his hand—the throat. Nor did he hit him hard; he didn't want to kill the guy, or even damage him permanently.

As the man fell to the hard-rock floor—writhing in agony, groaning, strangling and gasping horribly for breath —the men and women and teen-agers looking on burst as one into clamor. "Stomp 'im!" they shrieked and yelled. "Give 'im the boots! Stomp 'im! Kill 'im! Stomp 'is head clean off! Stomp 'im right down into the rock!"

"Hold it!" Seaton rasped, and the miners fell silent; but they did not relapse into their former apathy.

Seaton stood by, waiting coldly for his victim to be able to draw a breath. He picked the overseer's pistol-like weapon up and looked it over. He had never seen anything like it before, and casual inspection didn't tell him much about how it worked, but that could wait. He didn't intend to use it. In fact, he wasn't really interested in it at all.

When the overseer had partially recovered his senses, Seaton jammed a headset onto his head and thought viciously at him; as much to give him a taste of real punishment as to find out what he knew and to impress upon his mind exactly what he had to do if he hoped to keep on living. Then Seaton made what was for him a speech. First, to the now completely deflated officer:

"You—you slimy traitor, you *quisling!* Know now that a new regime has taken over. Maybe I'll let you live and maybe I'll turn you over to these boys and girls here—you know what they'd do to you. That depends on how *exactly* you stick to what I just told you. One thought of a squeal —if you ever get one milli-meter out of line, and you'll be under surveillance every second of every day—you'll die a long, slow, tough death. And I mean *tough!*"

He turned to the miners; studied them narrowly. His "shot in the arm" had done them a lot of good. Excitement was still high; none of them had relapsed into the apathy that had affected them all such a short time before. In fact, one close-clustered group of men was eyeing Seaton and the overseer in a fashion that made it perfectly clear that, had it not been for Seaton's mien and the gun and the whip, there would have been a lynching then and there.

"Take it easy, people," Seaton told them. "I know you all want to tear this ape apart, but what good would it do? None. Not a bit. So I won't let you do it, if I have to use the whip and even the gun to keep you from it. But I don't intend to use either whip or gun and I don't think I'll have to, because this is the first bite of a fresh kettle of fish for every civilized human being of this world. I won't go into much detail, but I represent a group of human beings, as human as yourselves, called HUMANITY TRIUMPHANT. I'm a fore-runner. I'm here to bring you a message; to tell you that humanity has never been conquered permanently and never will be so conquered. Humanity has triumphed and will continue to triumph over all the vermin infesting all the planets of all the solar systems of all the galaxies of all surveyed space.

"HUMANITY TRIUMPHANT's plans have been made in full and are being put out into effect. Humanity will win here, and in not too long a time. Every Chloran in every solar system in this region of space will die. That's a promise.

"Nor do we need your help. All we ask is that you produce the full quota of ore every week, so that no Chloran warship will come here too soon. And that production will be no problem very shortly, since I can repair your machinery and will have it all back in working order by one week from today. So in a very few weeks you women can go back to keeping house for your families; you youngsters can go back to school; and half of you men will be able to make quota in half a shift and spend the other half of it playing penny-ante. And you, Brother Rat—" he turned back to the deposed overseer—"you can peel that pretty uniform. You're going to work, right now. You and I are going to be partners—and if you so much as begin to drag your feet I'll slap your face clear around onto the back of your neck. Let's go!"

They went. They picked up a drill—which weighed all of three hundred pounds—and lugged it across the rough rock floor to the foot of the face; which, translated from the vernacular, means the lower edge of the expanse of high-grade ore that was being worked.

It was a beautiful thing, that face; a startlingly high and wide expanse of the glossly, lustrous, submetallic pitch black of uraninite; slashed and spattered and shot through at random with the characteristic violent yellows of autunite and carnotite and the variant greens of torbernite.

But Seaton was not particularly interested in beauty at the moment. What he *hoped* was that he could keep from giving away the fact that this was the first time he had ever handled a mining machine of any kind or type. He thought he could, however, and he did.

For, after all, there are only so many ways in which holes can be made in solid rock. Second, since the hard-rock men who operate the machinery to make those holes are never the greatest intellects of any world, such machinery must be essentially simple. And third, the Brain's visualizations had been very complete and Richard Seaton was, as he had admitted to Prenk, an exceptionally smart man.

Wherefore, although Seaton unobtrusively let the ex-overseer take the lead, the two men worked very well together and the native did not once drag his feet. They set up the heavy drill and locked it in place against the face. They slipped the shortest "twelve-inch" steel into the chuck and rammed it home. They turned on the air and put their shoulders to the stabilizing pads—and that monstrous machine, bellowing and thundering under the terrific urge of two hundred pounds to the square inch of compressed air, drove that heavy bit resistlessly into the ore.

And the rest of the miners, fired by Seaton's example as well as by his "shot in the arm," worked as they had not worked in months; to such good purpose that when the shift ended at midnight the crew had sent out almost twice as much high-grade ore as they had delivered the night before.

It need hardly be mentioned, perhaps, that Seaton was enjoying himself very much. Although he was not, in truth, the "big, muscle-bound ape—especially between the ears" he was wont to describe himself as, there was certainly a pleasure in being up against the sort of problem that muscle and skill could settle. For a time he was concerned about the fact that events elsewhere might be proceeding at a pace he could not control; but there was not a minute spent on the surface of this planet that was not a net gain in terms of the automatic repair of the *Valeron*. That great ship had been *hurt*. Since there was at the moment very little that Seaton could do effectively about DuQuesne, or directly about the Chlorans, or the Fenachrone—and was a great deal he could do here on the surface of Ray-See-Nee —he put the other matters out of his mind and did what had to be done.

And enjoyed it enormously!

Seaton went "home" to the empty and solitary house that was his temporary residence and raised the oversize ring to his lips. "Dottie," he said.

"Oh, Dick!" a tiny scream came from the ring. "I *wish* you wouldn't take such horrible chances! I thought I'd *die!* Won't you, tomorrow morning, just shoot the louse out of hand? *Please?*"

"I wasn't taking any chances, Dot; a man with half my training could have done it. I *had* to do something spectacular to snap these people out of it; they're dead from the belt-buckle up, down, and back. But I've done enough, I think, so I won't have any more trouble at all. It'll get around—and *how!*—and strictly on the Q and T. All those other apes will need is a mere touch of fist."

"You hope. Me, too, for that matter. Just a sec, here's Martin. He wants to talk to you about that machinery business," and Crane's voice replaced Dorothy's.

"I certainly do, Dick. You say you want two-hundred-fifty-pound Sullivan Sluggers, complete with variable-height mounts and inch-and-a-quarter—that's English, remember —bits. You want Ingersoll-Rand compressors and Westinghouse generators and Wilfley tables and so on, each item by name and no item resembling any of their own machinery in any particular. Since you are supposed to be repairing their own machinery, wouldn't it be better to have the Brain do just that, while you look on, make wise motions, and learn?"

"It might be better, at that," Seaton admitted, after a moment's thought. "My thought was that since nobody now working in the mine knows anything much about either mining or machinery it wouldn't make any difference, as long as the stuff was good and rusty on the outside, and I know how our stuff works. But I can learn theirs and it will save a lot of handling and we'll have the time. They're working only two shifts in only one stope, you know. Lack of people. But nine-tenths of their equipment is as dead as King Tut and the rest of it starts falling apart every time anybody gives any of it a stern look—I was scared spitless all shift that we'd be running out of air or power, or both, any minute. So we'll have to do one generator and at least one compressor tonight; so you might as well start getting the stuff ready for me."

"It's ready. I'll send it down as soon as it gets good and dark. In the meantime, how about Brother Rat? Have you anyone watching him?"

"No, I didn't think it was necessary. But it might be, at that. From up there, would you say?"

"Definitely. And Shiro and Lotus haven't much to do at the moment. I'll make arrangements."

"Do that, guy, and so long 'till dark."

"Just a sec, Dick," Dorothy said then. "I'm not done with you yet. You remembered the no-neighbors bit, I think?"

"I sure did, Honey-Chile. No neighbors within half a mile, So, any dark of the moon, slip down here in one of the fifteen-footers and all will be well."

"You big, nice man," Dorothy purred. "Comes dark, comes me! an' you can lay to that."

Countless parsecs away, DuQuesne made proper entry into the Solar System, put his *Capital D* into a parking orbit around Earth, and began to pick up his tremendous order of machine tools and supplies. It went well; Brookings had done his job. There was, however, one job Du-Quesne had to do for himself. During the loading, accordingly, he went in person to Washington, D.C., to the Rare Metals Laboratory, and to Room 1631.

That room's door was open. He tapped lightly on it as he entered the room. He closed the door gently behind him.

"Park it," a well-remembered contralto voice said. "Be with you in a moment."

"No rush." DuQuesne sat down, crossed his legs, lighted a cigarette, and gazed at the woman seated at her electronics panel. Both her eyes were buried in the light-shield of a binocular eyepiece; both her hands were manipulating vernier knobs in tiny arcs.

"Oh! Hi, Blackie! Be with you in half a moment."

"No sweat, Hunkie. Finish your obs."

"Natch." Her attention had not wavered for an instant from her instruments; it did not waver then.

In a minute or so she pressed a button, her panel went dark, and she rose to her feet. "It's been a long time, Blackie," she said, stepping toward him and extending her hand.

"It has indeed." He took her hand and began an encircling action with his left—a maneuver which she countered, neatly but still smilingly, by grasping his left hand and holding it firmly.

"Tsk, tsk," she tsked. "The merchandise is on display, Blackie, but it is not to be handled. Remember?"

"I remember. Still untouchable," he said.

"That's right. You're a hard-nosed, possessive brute, Blackie—any man to interest me very much would have to be, I suppose—but no man born is ever going to tell me what I can or can't do. Selah. But let's skip that." She released his hands, waved him to a chair, sat down, crossed her legs, accepted the lighted cigarette he handed her, and went on, "Thanks. The gossip was that you were all washed up and had, as Ferdy put it, 'taken it on the lam.' I didn't believe it then and I don't believe it now. I've been wanting to tell you; you're a good enough man so that whatever you're really after, you'll get."

This woman could reach DuQuesne as no other woman ever had. "Thanks, Hunkie," he said; and, reaching out, he pressed her right hand hard then dropped it. "What I came up here for—have you a date for Thursday evening that you can't or won't break?"

Her smile widened; her two lovely dimples deepened. "Don't tell me; let me guess. Louisa Vinciughi in *Lucia*."

"Nothing else but. You like?"

"I love. With the usual stipulation—we 'Dutch' it."

"Listen, Hunkie!" he protested. "Aren't you ever going to get off of that 'Dutch' thing? Don't you think a man can take a girl out without having monkey-business primarily in mind?"

She considered the question thoughtfully, then nodded,

"As stated, yes. Eliding the one word 'primarily', no. I've heard you called a lot of things, my friend, but 'stupid' was never one of them. Not even once."

"I know." DuQuesne smiled, a trifle wryly. "You are not going to be obligated by any jot or iota or tittle to any man living or yet to be born."

Her head went up a little and her smile became a little less warm. "That's precisely right, Marc. But I've never made any secret of the fact that I enjoy your company a lot. So, on that basis, okay and thanks."

"On that basis, then, if that's the way it has to be, and thanks to you, too," DuQuesne said, and took his leave.

And Thursday evening came; and all during that long and thoroughly pleasant evening the man was, to the girl's highly sensitive perception . . . well, different, although very subtly so. He was not quite, by some very small fraction, his usual completely poised and urbane self. Even Vinciughi's wonderful soprano voice did not bring him entirely back from wherever it was he was. Wherefore, just before saying goodnight at the door of her apartment, she said:

"You have something big on your mind, Blackie. Tremendously big. Would it help to come in and talk a while?" This was the first time in all their long acquaintance that she had ever invited him into her apartment. "Or wouldn't it?"

He thought for a moment. "No," he decided. "There are so many maybes and ifs and buts in the way that talking would be even more futile than thinking. But I'd like to ask you this: how much longer will you be here in Washington, do you think?"

She caught her breath. "The Observer says it'll take me a year and a half to get what I should have."

"That's fine," DuQuesne said. His thoughts were racing, but none of them showed. What were those observers doing? And why? He knew the kind of mind Stephanie de Marigny had—they were feeding with a teaspoon a mind fully capable of gulping it down by the truckload . . . why? *Why?* So as not to play favorites, probably—that was the only reason he could think of. DuQuesne was playing for very high stakes; he could not afford to overlook any possibility, however remote. Had his interest in Hunkie de Marigny been deduced by the Norlaminians? Was it, in fact, possible—even likely—that he was under observation even now? Was their strange slowdown in her training meaningful? He could not answer; but he decided on caution. He went on with scarcely a noticeable pause, "I'll see you well before that—if I may?"

"Why, of course you may! I'd get an acute attack of the high dudgeons if you *ever* came to Washington without seeing me!"

He took his leave then, and she went into her apartment and closed the door . . . and stood there, motionless, listening to his receding footsteps with a far-away, brooding look in her deep brown eyes.

19 · THE COUP

As the days had passed, more and more of the Skylarkers had come to ground in Seaton's temporary home on the planet Ray-See-Nee; until many of them, especially Dorothy, were spending most of their nights there. On this particular evening they were all there.

Since the personal gravity-controls had been perfected long since, Dunark and Sitar were comfortable enough as far as gravity was concerned. The engineers, however, had not yet succeeded in incorporating really good ambient-atmosphere temperature-controllers into them; wherefore he was swathed in wool and she wore her fabulous mink coat. They each wore two Osnomian machine pistols instead of one, and they sat a couple of feet apart—in instant readiness for any action that might become necessary.

Lotus and Shiro, a little closer together than the two Osnomians but not enough so to get into each other's way, sat cross-legged on the floor. He was listening intently, while she wasn't. Almost everything that was being said was going completely over her head.

Dorothy, Margaret, and Crane sat around a small table, fingering tall glasses in which ice-cubes tinkled faintly.

Seaton paced the floor, with his right hand in his breeches pocket and his left holding his pipe, which he brandished occasionally in the air to emphasize a point.

"Considering that we can't do anything at all on un-muffled high-order stuff except when an ore-scow is here, masking our emanations," Seaton was saying, "we haven't done too bad. However, I wouldn't wonder if we'd just about run out of time and we're right between the devil and the deep blue sea. Mart, what's your synthesis?"

Crane sipped his drink and cleared his throat. "You're probably right in one respect, Dick. They apparently make a spectacle of these destructions of cities; not for the Chlorans' amusement—I doubt very much if they enjoy or abhor anything, as we understand the term—but to keep the rest of the population of this world in line. Whether or not the quisling dictator of this world arranged for this city to be the next sacrifice, it is certain that we have interfered with the expected course of events to such an extent that the powers-that-be will at least investigate. But I can't quite see the dilemma."

"I can," Dorothy said. "They *have* to have a grisly example, once every so often; and since this one didn't develop on schedule maybe they'll go crying to mama instead of trying to handle us themselves. You see, they may know more about us than we think they do."

"That's true, of course—" Crane began, but Seaton broke in.

"So I say it's time to let Ree-Toe Prenk in on the whole deal and add him to our Council of War," he declared, and talk went on.

They were still discussing the situation twenty minutes later, when someone tapped gently on the front door.

The Osnomians leaped to their feet, pistols in all four hands. The two Japanese leaped to their feet and stood poised, knees and elbows slightly flexed, ready for action. Forty-five-caliber automatics appeared in the hands of the three at the table, and Crane flipped his remote control helmet onto his head. Seaton, magnum in hand, snapped on the outside lights and peered out through the recently installed one-way glass of the door.

"Speak of the devil," he said in relief. "It's Hizzoner." He opened the door wide and went on, "Come in, Your Honor. We were just talking about you."

Prenk came in, his eyes bulging slightly at the sight of the arsenal of armament now being put back into holsters. They bulged still more as he looked at the Japanese, and he gulped as he stared fascinatedly at the green-skinned Osnomians.

"I knew, of course, within a couple of days," Prenk said then, quietly, "that you who call yourself Ky-El Mokak were not confining your statements to the exact truth. No wilder could possibly have done what you were doing; but by that time I knew that you, whoever you were, were really on our side. I had no suspicion until this moment, however, that you were actually from another world. I thought that your speech to the miners was what you said it was going to be, 'a shot in the arm of hope'. It now seems more than slightly possible that you were talking about the very matters I came here tonight to see you about. Certain supplies, you will remember."

"I remember. I lied to you, yes. Wholesale and retail. But how else could I have made the approach, the mood you were in, without blowing everything higher than up?"

"Your technique was probably the best possible, I admit."

"Okay. Yes, we're from a galaxy so far away from here that you could barely find it with the biggest telescope this world ever had. Our business at the moment is to wipe out every Chloran in this region of space, but we can't do it without—among other things—a lot more data than we now have. And we'll need weeks of time, mostly elsewhere, for preparation.

"But before we go too deeply into that you must meet my associates. People, this is His Honor Ree-Toe Prenk; what you might call the Mayor of the City of Ty-Ko-Ma of the Planet Ray-See-Nee. You know all about him. Ree-Toe, this is Hi-Fi Mokak, my wife—Lo-Test and Hi-Test Crane, husband and wife—" and he went on with two more pairs of coined names.

"Hi-Fi indeed!" Dorothy snorted, under her breath, in English. "Just you wait 'til I get you alone tonight, you egregious clown!"

"Wha'd'ya mean 'clown'?" he retorted. "Try *your* hand sometime at inventing seven names on the spur of the moment!"

Seaton then put on a headset, slipped one over Prenk's head, and said in thought: "This is what is left—the resi-you might say—of our mobile base the *Skylark of Valeron*," and went on to show him and to describe to him the Great Brain, the immense tank-chart of the entire First Universe, the tremendous driving engines and even more tremendous engines of offense and of defense.

Prenk was held spellbound and speechless, for this "residue," hundreds of kilometers in diameter and hundreds of millions of tons in weight, was so utterly beyond any artificial structure Prenk had ever imagined that he simply could not grasp its magnitude at all. And when Seaton went on to show him a full mental picture of what that base had been before the battle with the Chlorans and what it would have to be before they could begin to move against the Chlorans—the one-thousand kilometer control-circles, the thousands of cubic kilometers of solidly packed offensive and defensive gear, the scores of fantastically braced and buttressed layers of inoson that composed the worldlet's outer skin—he was so strongly affected as to be speechless in fact.

"I . . . I see. That is . . . a little, maybe . . ." he stammered, then subsided into silence.

"Yes, it *is* a bit big to get used to all at once," Seaton agreed. "It needs a lot of work. Some we're doing; some of it can't be done anywhere near here; but we don't want to leave without being reasonably sure that you and your people will be alive when we get back. So we want a lot of information from you."

"I'll be glad to tell you everything I know or can find out."

"Thanks. Ideas, first. How much do you think the quisling Big Shots actually know? What do you think they'll do about it? What do you think His Magnificence the Dictator will do? And what should we do about what he thinks he's going to do? In a few days we'll want all the information you can get—facts, names, dates, places, times, and personnel. Also one sample copy of each and every item of equipment desired; with numbers wanted and times and places of delivery. Brother Prenk, you have the floor."

"One advantage of a small town and a group like ours," Prenk said, slowly, "is that everybody knows everybody else's business. Thus, we all knew who the spies were, but the people were all so low in their minds that they simply did not care whether they lived or died. We had done our best and had failed; most of us had given up hope completely. Now, however, the few remaining spies have been locked up and are under control. They and the overseers are still reporting, but—" he smiled wolfishly—"they are saying precisely and only what I tell them to say. This condition can't last very long; but, after what you just showed me, I'm pretty sure I can make it last long enough. We have organized a really efficient force of guerrilla fighters and our plans for the capital are . . ."

A couple of weeks later, then, three hundred fifty-eight highly trained men and one highly trained woman set out.

A woman? Yes. Dorothy had protested vigorously.

"But Sitar! *You* aren't going, surely? *Surely* you're staying home?"

"Staying *home!*" the green girl had blazed. "The First Wife of a prince of Osnome goes with her prince wherever he goes. She fights beside him, at need she dies beside him. Would you have him die fighting and me live an hour? I'd blow myself to bits!"

"My God!" Dorothy had gasped, and had stared, appalled.

"That's right," Seaton had told her. "Their ethics, mores and customs differ more than somewhat from ours, you know." And nothing more had been said about Sitar being a member of the Expeditionary Force.

Prenk's guerrillas had infiltrated the capital city by ones and twos; no group ever larger than two. Each one wore the costume of an easily recognizable class of citizen. They were apparently artisans and workmen, soldiers, sailors, clerks, businessmen, tycoons of industry. Nor were the watches they all wore on their wrists any more alike than were their costumes—except in one respect. They all told the same time, to the tenth of a split second, and they all were kept in sync by pulses from a tiny power-pack that had been hidden in a tree in the outskirts of the city.

At time zero minus thirty minutes, three hundred fifty-nine persons began to enter into and to distribute themselves throughout an immense building that resembled a palace or a cathedral much more than the capitol building even of a world.

At time zero minus four seconds all those persons, who had in the meantime been doing inconspicuous this and innocuous that, changed direction toward or began to walk toward or kept on walking toward their objectives.

At time zero on the tick, three hundred fifty-nine knives came out of concealment and that exact number of persons fell.

Some of the guerrillas remained on guard where their victims lay. Others went into various offices on various businesses. On the top-most floor four innocent-looking visitors blasted open the steel door of Communications and shot the four operators then on duty. The leader of the four invaders stepped up to the master-control desk, shoved a body aside, flipped three or four switches, and said:

"Your attention, please! These programs have been interrupted to announce that former Premier Da-Bay Saien and his sycophants have been executed for high treason. Premier Ree-Toe Prenk and his loyalists are now the government. Business is to go on as usual; no new orders will be issued except as they become necessary. That is all. Scheduled programs will now be resumed."

It was not as easy everywhere, however, as that announcement indicated. By the very nature of things, the information secured by the counterspies was incomplete and sometimes, especially in fine detail, was wrong. Thus, when Seaton took his post on the fifteenth floor, standing before and admiring a heroic-size bronze statue of a woman strangling a boa constrictor whose coils enveloped half her height, he saw that there were four guards, instead of the two he had expected to find, at the door of the office that was his objective. But he couldn't—wouldn't—call for help. They hadn't had man-power enough to carry spares. He'd trip the S O S if necessary, but not until it became absolutely necessary—but that office *had* to be put out of business by time zero plus fifteen seconds. He'd just have to act twice as fast, was all.

Cursing silently the fact that his magnum was not to be used during the first few silent seconds of the engagement, he watched the four men constantly out of the corners of his eyes, planning every detail of his campaign, altering those details constantly as the guards changed ever so slightly their positions and postures. He could get three of them, he was sure, before any one of them could fire; but he'd have to be lucky as well as fast to get the fourth in time—and if the ape had time to take any kind of aim at all it would be very ungood.

On the tick of zero time Seaton shed his businessman's cloak and took off. Literally. His knife swept through the throat of the nearest guard before that luckless wight had moved a muscle. He kicked the second, who was bending over at the moment, on and through the temple with the steel-lined toe of one highly special sure-grip fighting shoe. He stabbed the third, whose throat was protected at that instant by an upflung left arm, through the left side of the rib-cage, twisting his blade as he pulled it out.

Ultra-fast as Seaton had been, the fourth guard had had time to lift his weapon, but he had not had time to aim it, or even to point it properly. He fired in panic, before his gun was pointed even waist-high. If Seaton had stayed upright the bullet would have missed him completely. But he didn't. He ducked and sidestepped and twisted—and the heavy slug tore a long and savage wound across the left side of his back.

One shot was all the fellow got, of course. Seaton kicked the door open and leaped into the room, magnum high and ready. The noise of that one shot might have torn it, but good.

"*Freeze*, everybody!" he rasped, and everyone in the big room froze. "One move of any finger toward any button and I blast. This office is closed temporarily. Leave the building, all of you; right now and fast. Just as you are. Come back in here after lunch for business as usual. Scram!"

The office force—some nonchalantly, some wonderingly, some staring at Seaton in surprise—"scrammed" obediently. All, that is, except one girl who came last; the girl who had been sitting at an executive-type desk beside the door of the inner office. She was a fairly tall girl; with hazel eyes and with dark brown hair arranged in up-to-the-second "sunburst" style. Her close-fitting white nylon upper garment and her even tighter fire-engine-red tights displayed a figure that could not be described as being merely adequate.

Instead of passing him as the others had done she stopped, held out both hands in indication of having nothing except peaceable intentions, and peered around his left side. Then, bringing her eyes back to his, she said, "You're bleeding terribly, sir. It doesn't seem to be very deep— entrance and exit holes in your shirt are only four or five inches apart—but you're losing an awful lot of blood. Won't you let me give you first aid? I'm a quite competent nurse, sir."

"*What?*" Seaton demanded, but whatever he had intended to add to that one word was forestalled by a bellow of wrath from behind the just-opening door of the inner office.

"Kay-Lee! You shirking slut! How much more of this do you think you can get away with? When I buzz you you *jump* or I'll cut your bloody—" The man broke off sharply and goggled at what he saw. He was a pasty-faced, paunchy man of forty; very evidently self-indulgent and as evidently completely at a loss at the moment.

"Come in, Bay-Lay Boyn," Seaton said. "Slowly, if you don't want your brains to decorate the ceiling. Did you ever see a man shot in the head with a magnum pistol?"

The man gulped and licked his lips. The girl broke the

very short silence. "Whatever you do to that poisonous slob, sir, I hope it's nothing trivial. I'd love to see his brains spattered all over the ceiling and I'd never let them be washed off. I'd look up at them week after week and gloat."

"Kay-Lee dear, you don't mean that! You *can't* mean it!" the man implored. "Do something! *Please* do something! I'll double your salary—I'll make you a First—I'll give you a diamond necklace—I'll—"

"You'll shut your filthy lying mouth, *Your Exalted*," she said—quietly, but with an icily venomous contempt that made Seaton stare. "I've taken all the raps for you I'm ever going to." She turned to Seaton. "Please believe, sir, that no matter who your people are or what you do, any possible change will be for the better. And I remind you—if you don't want to fall flat on your face from weakness you'll let me dress that wound."

"I wouldn't wonder," Seaton admitted. "Blood's running down into my shoes already and it's beginning to hurt like the devil. So get your kit. But before you start on me we'll use some three-inch bandage to lash that ape's hands around that pillar there."

That done, Seaton peeled to the waist and the girl went expertly to work. She sprayed the nasty-looking wound, which was almost but not quite a deep but open groove, with antiseptic and with coagulant. She cross-taped its ragged edges together with blood-proof adhesive tape. She sponged most of the liquid blood off of his back. She sprinkled half a can of curative-antiseptic powder; she taped on thick pads of sterile gauze. She wrapped—and taped into place—roll after roll of three-inch bandage around his body and up over his shoulder and around his neck. Then she stood back and examined her handiwork, eyes narrowed in concentration.

"That'll do it for a while," she decided. "I suppose you'll be too busy to take any time today, but you'll *have* to get that sewed up not later than tomorrow forenoon."

"I'll do that. Thanks a million, lady; it feels a lot better already," and Seaton bent over to pick up his shirt and undershirt.

"But you *can't* wear those bloody rags!" she protested, then went on, "But I don't know of anything else around here that you *can* wear, at that."

Seaton grinned. "No quandary—I'll go the way I am. Costume or the lack of it isn't imporant at the moment."

He glanced at his watch and was surprised to see how very few minutes had elapsed.

"Shall I go now, sir?"

"Not yet." Seaton was used to making fast decisions, and they were usually right. He made one now. "I take it you were that ape's confidential secretary."

"Yes, sir, I was."

"So you know more about the actual workings of the department than he does and can run it as well. To make a snap judgment, can run it better than he has been running it."

"Much better, sir," she said, flatly. "I've covered up for his drunken blunderings twice in the last two months. He passed the buck to me and I took it. A few lashes are much better than what he revels in doing to people; especially since he can't touch me now. He knows that after taking his floggings I'd go under hypnosis and tell everything I know about him if he tried to lay a finger on me."

"Lashes? Floggings? I see." Seaton's face hardened. "Okay, you're it." He took a badge out of his pocket, slid its slip out of its holder, and handed the slip to Kay-Lee. "Type on this your name and his rating and title and turn your recorder on."

She did so. He glanced at the slip, replaced it in its holder, and pinned the badge in place just above the girl's boldly outstanding left breast. "I, Ky-El Mokak, acting for and with the authority of Premier Ree-Toe Prenk, hereby make you, Kay-Lee Barlo, an Exalted of the Twenty-Sixth and appoint you Head of the Department of Public Works. I hereby charge you, Your Exalted, to so operate your department as to prevent, not to cause, the destruction of persons and of property by those enemies of all mankind the Chlorans." He stepped to the desk; cut the recorder off.

For the first time, the girl's taut self-control was broken. "Do you mean I can actually clean this pig-sty up?" she demanded, tears welling into her eyes. "That you actually *want* me to clean it up?"

"Just that. You'll be briefed at a meeting of the new department heads late this afternoon. In the meantime start your house-cleaning as soon as you like after your people get back from lunch; and I don't have to tell you how to act. Have you got or can you get a good hand-gun?"

"Yes, *sir;* there's a very good one—his—in his desk. I was trying to get up nerve enough to ask for it."

"It's yours as of now. Can you use it? That's probably a foolish question."

"I'll say I can use it! I made Pistol Expert One when I was eleven and I've been improving ever since."

"Fine!" He glanced again at his watch. "Go get it, be sure it's loaded, buckle it on and wear it. Show your badge, play the recording and lay down the law. If there's any argument, shoot to kill. We aren't fooling." He glanced at the prisoner. "He'll be out of your way. I'm taking him downstairs pretty soon to answer some questions."

"I—I thank you, sir. I can't tell you how much. But you —I mean . . . well, I—" the girl was a study in mixed emotions. Her nostrils flared and her whole body was tense with the beyond-imagining thrill of what had just occurred; but at the same time she was so acutely embarrassed that she could scarcely talk. "I want to tell you, sir, that I *wasn't* trying to curry . . ." She broke off in confusion and gulped twice.

"Curry? I know you weren't. You aren't the toadying type. That's one reason you got it—but just a second."

He looked again at his watch and did not put it down; but in a few seconds raised the ring to his lips and asked, "Are you there, Ree-Toe?"

"Here, Ky-El," the tiny ring-voice said.

"Mission accomplished, including selection and installation of department head."

"Splendid! Are you hurt?"

"Not badly. Scratch across my back. How're we doing?"

"Better even than expected. The Premier is dead, I don't know yet exactly how. All your people are all right except for some not-too-serious wounds. Ours, only ten dead reported so far. The army came over to a man. You have earned a world's thanks this day, Ky-El, and its eternal gratitude."

Seaton blushed. "Skip it, chief. Any change in schedule?"

"None."

"Okay. Off." Seaton, lowering his hand to his side, turned to Kay-Lee.

She, who had not quite been able to believe all along that all this was actually happening to *her*, was staring at him in wide-eyed awe. "You *are* a biggie!" she gasped. "A great *big* biggie, Your Exalted, to talk to the Premier himself like that! So this unbelievable appointment will stick!"

"It will stick. Definitely. So chin high and don't spare the horses, Your Exalted; and I'll see you at the meeting. Until then, so-long."

Seaton cut his prisoner loose and half-led, half-dragged him, gibbering and begging, out of the room. Almost Seaton regretted it was over; the work on Ray-See-Nee had been pleasurable, as well as useful.

But—now he had his base of operations, unknown to the Chlorans, on a planet they thought safely their own. Now he could go on with his campaign against them. Seaton was well aware that the universe held other enemies than the Chlorans, but his motto was one thing at a time.

However, it is instructive now to see just what two of those inimical forces were up to at this one—one which knew it was in trouble . . . and one which did not!

20 · DU QUESNE AND FENACHRONE

BEFORE the world of the Fenachrone was destroyed by Civilization's superatomic bombs it was a larger world than Earth, and a denser, and with a surface gravity very much higher. It was a world of steaming jungle; of warm and reeking fog; of tepid, sullenly steaming water; of fantastically lush vegetation unknown to Earthly botany. Wind there was none, nor sunshine. Very seldom was the sun of that reeking world visible at all through the omnipresent fog, and then only as a pale, wan disk; and what of its atmosphere was not fog was hot and humid and sulphurously stinking air.

And as varied the worlds, so varied the people. The Fenachrone, while basically humanoid, were repulsively and monstrously short, wide and thick. They were immensely strong physically, and their mentalities were as monstrous as their civilization was many thousands of years older than that of Earth; their science was equal to ours in most respects and ahead of it in some.

Most monstrous of all the facets of Fenachrone existence, however, was their basic philosophy of life. Might was right. Power was not only the greatest good; it was the only good. The Fenachrone were the MASTER RACE, whose unquestionable destiny it was to be the unquestionable masters of the entire space-time continuum—of the summated totality of the Cosmic All.

For many thousands of years nothing had happened to shake any Fenachrone's rock-solid conviction of the destiny of their race. Progress along the Master-Race line had been uninterrupted. In fact, it had never been successfully opposed. The Fenachrone had already wiped out, without really extending themselves, all the other civilizations within a hundred parsecs or so of their solar system. But up to the time of Emperor Fenor no ruler of the Fenachrone had become convinced that the time had come to set the Day of Conquest—the day upon which the Big Push was to begin.

But rash, headstrong, egomaniacal Fenor insisted upon setting The Day in his own reign—which was why First Scientist Fleet Admiral Sleemet had set up his underground so long before. He was just as patriotic as any other member of his race; just as thoroughly sold on the idea of the inevitable ultimate supremacy over all created thing wherever situated; but his computations did not indicate that success was as yet quite certain.

How right Sleemet was!

He knew that he was right after hearing the first few words of Sacner Carfon's ultimatum to Emperor Fenor: that was why he had pushed the panic button for the eighty-five-thousand-odd members of his faction to flee the planet right then.

He knew it still better when, after Fenor's foolhardly defiance of Sacner Carfon, of the Overlord, and of the Forces of Universal Peace, his native planet became a minor sun behind his flying fleet.

Even then, however, Sleemet had not learned very much —at least, nowhere nearly enough.

At first glance it might seem incredible that, after such an experience, Sleemet could have so lightly destroyed two such highly industrialized worlds about which he knew so little. It might seem as though it must have been impressed upon his mind that the Fenachrone were not the ablest, strongest, wisest, smartest, most highly advanced and most powerful form of life ever created. Deeper study will show, however, that with his heredity and conditioning he could not possibly have done anything else.

Sleemet probably did not begin really to realize the truth until the Llurd Klazmon so effortlessly—apparently—wiped out sixteen of his seventeen superdreadnoughts, then crippled his flagship beyond resistance or repair and sent it hurtling through space toward some completely unknown destination.

His first impulse, like that of all his fellows, was to storm and to rage and to hurl things and to fight. But there was no one to fight; and storming and raging and hurling and smashing things did not do any good. In fact, nothing they could do elicited any attention at all from their captors.

Wherefore, as days stretched out endlesly and monotonously into endless and monotonous weeks, all those five-thousand-odd Fenachrone—males and females, adults and teen-agers and children and babies—were forced inexorably into a deep and very un-Fenachronian apathy.

And when the hulk of the flagship arrived at the Llanzlanate on far Llurdiax, things went immediately from bad to worse. The volume of space into which the Fenachrone were moved had a climate exactly like that of their native city on their native world. All its artifacts—its buildings, and its offices and its shops and its foods and its drinks and its everything else—were precisely what they should have been.

Ostensibly, they were encouraged to live lives even more normal than ever before (if such an expression is allowable); to breed and to develop and to evolve; and especially to perform breakthroughs in science.

Actually, however, it was practically impossible for them to do anything of their own volition; because they were being studied and analyzed and tested every minute of every day. Studied coldly and logically and minutely; with an utterly callous ferocity unknown to even such a ferocious race as the Fenachrone themselves were.

Hundreds upon hundreds of the completely helpless captives died—died without affecting in any smallest respect the treatment received by the survivors—and as their utter helplessness struck in deeper and deeper, the Fenachrone grew steadily weaker, both physically and mentally.

This was no surprise to their captors, the Llurdi. Nor was it in any sense a disappointment. To them the Fenachrone were tools; and they were being tempered and shaped to their task . . .

On Earth, leaving Stephanie de Marigny's apartment, DuQuesne went back to the *Capital D* and took off on course one hundred seventy-five Universal—that is, five degrees east of Universal South. He went that way because in that direction lay the most completely unexplored sector of the First Universe and he did not want company. Earth and the First Galaxy lay on the edge of the First Quadrant. Llurdiax and its Realm lay in the Second. So did the Empire of the Chlorans and his own imaginary planet Xylmny. The second galaxy along that false line, which might also attract Seaton, lay in the Third. He didn't want any part of Richard Ballinger Seaton—yet—and this course was mathematically the best one to take to get out of and keep out of Seaton's way. Therefore he would follow it clear out to the Fourth Quadrant rim of the First Universe.

As the *Capital D* bored a hole through the protesting ether DuQuesne took time out from his thinkings to consider women. First, he considered Stephanie de Marigny; with a new and not at all unpleasant thrill as he did so. He considered Sennlloy and Luloy and some unattached women of the Jelmi. They all left him completely cold; and he was intellectually honest enough to know why and to state that "why" to himself. The Jelmi were so much older than the humanity of Earth that they were out of his class. He could stand equality—definitely; in fact, that was what he wanted—but he could not live with and would not try to live with any woman so demonstrably his superior.

But Hunkie—ah, *there* was a man's woman! His equal; his perfect equal in every respect; with a brain to match one of the finest bodies ever built. She didn't *play* hard to get, she *was* hard to get; but once got she'd stay got. She'd stand at a man's back 'till his belly caved in.

Slowed to a crawl, as Universal speed goes, the *Capital D* entered the outermost galaxy of the Rim of the Universe and DuQuesne energized his highest-powered projector. He studied the Tellus-type planets of hundreds of solar systems. Many of these planets were inhabited, but he did not reveal himself to the humanity of any of them.

He landed on an uninhabited planet and went methodically to work. He bulldozed out an Area of Work. He set up his batteries of machine tools; coupling an automatic operator of pure force to each tool as it was set up. Then he started work on the Brain; which took longer than all the rest of the construction put together. It was an exact duplicate of that of the *Skylark of Valeron;* one cubic mile of tightly packed ultra-miniaturized components; the most tremendous and most tremendously capable super-computer known to man.

While the structure of the two brains was identical, their fillings were not. As has been said, there were certain volumes—blocks of cells—in the *Valeron's* brain that Du-Quesne had not been able to understand. These blocks he left inoperative—for the time being. Conversely, DuQuesne either had or wanted powers and qualities and abilities that Seaton neither had nor wanted; hence certain blocks that were as yet inoperative in Seaton's vast fabrication were fully operative in DuQuesne's.

It is a well-known fact that white-collar men, who sit at desks and whose fellowship with machines is limited to week-end drives in automobiles, scoff heartily at the idea that any two machines of the same make and model do or can act differently from each other except by reason of wear. With increasing knowledge of an acquaintance with machines, however—especially with mechanisms of the more complex and sophisticated sorts—this attitude changes markedly. The men and women who operate such machines swear unanimously that those machines do unquestionably have personalities; each its unique and peculiar own.

Thus, while the fact can not be explained in logical or "common" sense terms, those two giants brains were as different in personality as were the two men who built them.

Nor was DuQuesne's worldlet, which he named the *DQ*, very much like the *Skylark of Valeron* except in shape. It was bigger. Its skin was much thicker and much denser and much more heavily armed. The individual mechanisms were no larger—the *Valeron's* were the biggest and most powerful that DuQuesne knew how to build—but there were so many of them that he was pretty sure of being safe from anyone. Even from whoever it was that had mauled the *Valeron* so unmercifully—whom he, DuQuesne, did not intend to approach. Ever.

It was, in fact, his prayerful hope that both mauler and maulee—Seaton himself—would ultimately emerge from that scuffle whittled down to a size where he would not have to consider them again.

He did not, in fact, consider them; nor did he consider the captive Fenachrone in the pens of Llurdiax; nor the Jelmi; nor—and this, perhaps, was his greatest mistake— did he consider, because he did not know about, a mother and daughter of whose existence neither he nor any other Tellus-type human being had yet heard.

He simply built himself the most powerspace vessel he could imagine, armed it, launched it . . . and set out to recapture the Universe Seaton had once taken away from him.

The revolution on the planet Ray-See-Nee was over and Richard Seaton, disguised under the identity of Ky-El Mokak, was ready to take the one tactical move for which all the effort and struggle on the planet had been only the preliminaries. But first he needed to know what had happened to his shipmates and friends; he had been busy enough fighting his own fights and taking his own prisoners to have temporarily lost sight of them.

Wherefore, in Ray-See-Nee's palatial Capitol Building, in the Room of State—which, except for the absence of an actual throne, was in effect a throne-room—Seaton turned his prisoner over to a guard and rounded up his own crew, so that they could look each other over and compare notes.

Sitar, limping badly but with fur coat still glossily immaculate, proudly displayed a left leg bandaged from the knee all the way up. "A slash from here, clear down to there." The Osnomian princess ran a fore-finger along a line six or seven inches long. "And a bullet right through there. That was the *gaudiest* fight I was ever in in my whole life!"

Dunark, whose right arm was in a sling, spoke up. "She got that slash saving my life. I'd just taken this one through the shoulder—" he pointed—"and was paralyzed for a second. So she kicked her leg up in the way—while she was flipping a gun around to blow this guy apart, you know—so his knife went into her leg instead of my neck."

"Yes, but go on and tell them about how many times you—" Sitar began.

"Sh-h-h-h," Dunark said, and she subsided. "Maybe some day we'll write a book. How about you, Mart? I notice you've been standing up all the time."

"I'll be standing up or lying on my face for a while, I guess."

"But that wouldn't account for the cane," Seaton objected. "Come clean, guy."

"One through the hip—thigh, rather, low down—no bones broken."

Shiro, who had a broken arm, would not talk at first, but they finally got the story out of him. His last opponent had been just too big and too strong and too well trained to be easy meat, but Shiro had finally got him with a leg-lock around the neck. "But how about you, Dick?" Shiro asked. "Whoever wrapped you up must get hospital supplies at wholesale."

Seaton grinned. "She had only one patient." He told his own story, then went on, "Since we can all walk, let's go over and see what they're finding out."

Ree-Toe Prenk had said that he wanted all thirty-one of the department heads taken alive if possible; but he had known that it would not be possible. He was surprised and highly pleased, in fact, that only six of the High Exalteds had been killed or had taken their own lives.

There is no need to go into the details of that questioning. Seaton took no part in any of it; nor did any of his group. He did not offer to help and Prenk did not ask him.

Nor is it necessary to describe the operation outside the palace. The rebels had learned much from their previous failure, and they now had all the arms, ammunition and supplies they needed. Thus, before sunset that day every known quisling had been shot and every suspect was under surveillance. Premier Ree-Toe Prenk sat firmly in the Capitol City's saddle; and whoever controlled that city always controlled the world.

Hours before control was assured, however, Prenk called Seaton. "About the daily report to Chloran headquarters that is due in half an hour," the new Premier said. "I am wondering if you have any ideas. Our ordinary reports are not dangerous to make, since they are made to underlings whose only interest in the human race is to encode and file our reports properly. But, since their automatic instruments have recorded much of this change of government, it will have to be reported in detail. And a Great One, or even a Greater Great One, may become interested, in which case the reporter's mind may be searched." Prenk looked gloss it over. In an event like this the Greatest Great One himself will very probably become interested and the reporter will die on the spot. In any case, even with an ordinary Great One, his mind will be shattered for life."

"I see," Seaton said. "I didn't think of it, but I'm not surprised. We've tangled with Chlorans before. But cheer up; I've got news for you. I locked eyes with their Supreme Great One . . ."

"You didn't!" Prenk broke in, in amazement. "You actually did?"

"I actually did, and I knocked him—it?—loose from his

teeth." Regretfully Seaton added, "But we can't make a battle out of this." He scowled in concentration for a minute, then went on, "Okay, there's more than one way to stuff a goose. I'll make the report. Let's go."

Wherefore, twenty-five minutes later, Seaton sat at an ultra-communicator panel in Communications, ready to flip a switch.

The reporter whose shift it was stood off to one side, out of the cone of vision of the screen. Crane sat—gingerly, sidewise, and on a soft pillow—well within the cone of visibility of the screen, at what looked like an ordinary communications panel, but was in fact a battery of all the analytical instruments known to the science of Norlamin.

"But, Your Exalted," said the highly nervous reporter. "I'm very glad indeed that you're doing this instead of me, but won't they notice that it isn't me? And probably do something about it?"

"I'm sure they won't." Seaton had already considered the point. "I doubt very much, in view of their contempt for other races, if they ever bother to differentiate between any one human being and any other one. Like us and beetles."

The reporter breathed relief. "They probably don't, sir, at that. They *don't* seem to pay any attention to us as individuals."

Seaton braced himself and, exactly on the tick of time, flipped the switch. Knowing that the amoeboids could assume any physical form they pleased and as a matter of course assumed the form most suitable for the job, he was not surprised to see that the filing clerk looked like an overgrown centipede with a hundred or so long, flexible tentacles ending in three-fingered "hands"—a dozen or so of which were manipulating the gadgetry of a weirdly complex instrument-panel. He was somewhat surprised, however, in spite of what he had been told, that the thing did not develop an eye and look at him; did not even direct a thought at him. Instead:

"I am ready, slave," a deep bass voice rolled from the speaker, in the language of Prenk's planet Ray-See-Nee. "Start the tape."

Seaton pressed a button; the tape began to travel through the sender. For perhaps five minutes nothing happened. Then the sender stopped and a deeper, heavier voice came from the speaker: a voice directed at the filing clerk, but using Rayseenese . . .

Why? Seaton wondered to himself. *Oh, I see. Soften 'em up. Scare the pants off of 'em, then put on the screws.*

"Yield, clerk," the new voice said.

"I yield with pleasure, O Great One," the clerk replied, and went rigidly motionless; not moving a finger or a foot.

"It pleases me to study this matter myself," the giant voice went on as though the clerk had not spoken. "While slight, the possibility does exist that some of these verminous creatures have dared to plot against the Race Supreme. If this is merely another squabble among themselves for place it is of no interest; but if there is any trace of non-submission, vermin and city will cease to exist. I shall learn the deepest truth. They can make lying tapes, but no entity of this or of any other galaxy can lie to a Great One mind to mind."

While the Great One talked, the picture on the screen began to change. The clerk began to fade out and something else began to thicken in. And Seaton, knowing what was coming, set himself in earnest and brought into play that part of his multi-compartmented mind that was the contribution of Drasnik, the First of Psychology of Norlamin.

This coming interview, he knew, must be vastly different from his meeting with the Supreme Great One of Chlora One. That had been a wide-open, hammer-and-tongs battle; a battle of sheer power of mind. Here it would have to be a matter of delicacy of control; of precision and of nicety and of skill as well as of power. He would have to play his mind as exactly and as subtly as Dorothy played her Stradivarius, for if the monster came to suspect any iota of the truth all hell would be out for noon with no pitch hot.

The screen cleared and Seaton saw what he had known he would see; a large, flatly ellipsoidal mass of something that was not quite a jelly not quite a solid; a monstrosity through whose transparent outer membrane there was visible, a large, intricately convoluted brain. As Seaton looked at the thing it developed an immense eye, from which there poured directly into Seaton's brain a beam of mental energy so incredibly powerful as to be almost tangible physically.

Braced as he was, every element of the man's mind quivered under the impact of that callously hard-driven probe; but by exerting all his tremendous mental might he took it. More, he was able to hold his Drasnik-taught defenses so tightly as to reveal only and precisely what the Great One expected to find—utter helplessness and abject submission.

That probe was not designed to kill. Or rather, the Great One did not care in the least whether it killed or not. It was intended to elicit the complete truth; and from any ordinary human mind it did.

"Can you lie to me, slave?" That tremendous voice resounded throughout every chamber of Seaton's mind. "Or withhold from me any iota of the truth?"

"I cannot lie to you, O Great One; nor withhold from you any iota, however small, of the truth." This took everything of camouflage and of defensive screen Seaton had; but he managed to reveal no sign at all of any of it.

"How much do you personally know, not of the details of the *coup d'etat* itself, but of the motivation underlying it?"

"Everything, O Great One, since I was Premier Ree-Toe Prenk's right-hand man," and Seaton reported the exact truth of Prenk's motivation and planning.

The Great One's probe vanished, the screen went dark, and the sender resumed its sending.

"Huh!" Seaton wiped his sweating face with his handkerchief. " 'This dope isn't of any interest, clerk old boy, so just file it away and forget it,' His Nibs says. It's a good thing he was after Prenk's motivation, not mine. If he'd really bored in after mine I don't know whether I could have kept things all nice and peaceful or not. I knew I'd been nudged, believe you me."

"I believe you," Crane said, looking into his friend's eyes. "Are you sure you're all right?" And:

The reporter goggled in awe: "And you can still talk intelligently, sir?"

"Yeah." Seaton answered both questions at once, but did not elaborate. "What did you get, Mart? Anything?"

"I learned where it is," said Crane. Nothing else.

Small reward for weeks of effort and risk of life . . . and yet it was for that the entire campaign on the planet Ray-See-Nee had been waged! The whole operation had been designed to get that one fact. A people had been given new hope; some hundreds had lost their lives; many thousands had received scars they would bear a long time; a regime had been deposed and a new one put in power.

But these were only by-products, only the small change

of a victory which justified all of Seaton's efforts . . and would have its consequences in every part of the Universe, for incalculable times to come!

21 · LLANZLAN MERGON

RAY-SEE-NEE'S new department heads, in their meeting with Premier Ree-Toe Prenk in the Room of State, were in unanimous agreement that everything was under control. Some quislings and recalcitrants had been shot and a few more would probably have to be. That was only to be expected. Yes, since all of the new incumbents had been jumped many grades in status and in authority and in salary, there was and would continue to be a certain amount of jealousy; but that was not of very much importance. The jealous ones would either accept the facts of life or be shot. Period.

After the meeting was over Kay-Lee Barlo came up to Seaton. She now bore herself as though she had been born an Exalted; her ex-boss' pistol swung jauntily at one very female hip as she walked. As she came up to him and took both his hands in hers, standing so close to him that her upstanding, outstanding hair-do almost tickled his nose, it became evident that her weapon had been fired quite recently. She wore no perfume, and the faint but unmistakable acrid odor of burned smokeless powder still clung to her hair.

"Oh, Ky-El!" she exclaimed, equal to equal now. "I'll simply *never* be able to thank you enough. Nor will all Ray-See-Nee. This world will be an entirely different place to live on hereafter."

"I sincerely hope so, Kay-Lee." Seaton smiled into the girl's eager, expressive face. "Ray-See-Nee is lucky to have had as strong, able and just a man as Ree-Toe Prenk to take over."

"As you said a while back, 'You can say *that* again.' He's all of that. What he's done already is marvelous. But everyone knows—he does, too, he's put you up on a pedestal a mile high—that it's you who put him in the saddle. That's what I wanted mostly to tell you. Also, I wanted to ask you—" she paused and flushed slightly—"you'll forget, won't you please, what I said about that louse's brains? I didn't mean that, really; I'm not the type to cherish a grudge like *that*. I was a little . . . well, I'd been a little put out with him, just before you came in." With which masterpiece of understatement she gave his hands another vigorous, friendly squeeze and, swinging around, walked hip-wiggling out of the room.

She thereupon took certain steps and performed certain actions which would have astonished Seaton very much, had he known about them. But he did not—until much later.

Prenk came up to the Skylarkers a few minutes later. He shook hands with each of the off-worlders; thanked them in rounded phrases. "I would like very much to have you stay here indefinitely, friends," he concluded, "but I know of course that that is impossible. If all the resources of the world could be devoted to the project and if all our technical men could work on it undetected for a year, we could not build anything able to withstand those Chlorans' beams."

"We can't either. Not here," Seaton said. "That's why we have to go; but we'll be back. I don't know when; but we'll be back some day."

"I'm sure you will: and may Great My-Ko-Ta ward you and cherish you as you build."

Back on what was left of their worldlet, now reconditioned to the extent that it was not likely to fall apart on the spot, and out in deep space once more, the Skylarkers began efficiently and expertly to put the pieces of their victory together.

They had located the Enemy. They even had an operating covert base in Chloran territory, to which they could return at any time. They had weapons which, in theory at least, could cope with anything the Chlorans were likely to own.

Yet Seaton fretted. The weapons were there, but his control was not adequate; the weapons had outgrown the control. Dealing with Chlorans was touchy business. You wanted all the space you could get between you and them. Yet, at any operating range which even Seaton, to say nothing of Crane and the others, considered safe, their striking power was simply too erratic to depend on.

"It's a bust," Seaton said gloomily. "Course, if worst came to worst I could go back to undercover methods. Smuggle in a bomb, maybe—just to throw their main centers off balance while the rest of you hit them with all we've got. I could stow away aboard one of those ore-scows taking the booty off Ray-See-Nee easily enough—"

"You talk like a man with a paper nose," Dorothy scoffed. "I have a picture of *that* expedition—of you in armor, with air-tanks strapped on your back and lugging an underwater camera or projector around. Un-noticed . . . I don't think."

And Dunark added, "And since you haven't got any idea of what to look for, you'd have to lug around a full anal-synth set-up. A couple of tons of stuff. Uh-uh."

Seaton grinned, unperturbed. "That's what I was coming to. Getting in would be easy, but doing anything wouldn't. And neither would getting out. But Mart, we've chopped one horn off of the dilemma, but we haven't even touched the other. We've got to master that fourth-dimension rig; and we're not even close. It's a matter of *kind,* not merely of degree."

"I can't see that. If so, we could not have warded off their attack at all."

"Oh, I didn't mean the energies themselves; it's the control of that much stuff. Synchronization, phasing in, combination, and so forth. Getting such stuff as that closely enough together. Look, Mart. This bit that we've got left of the *Valeron* is stuffed with machinery practically to the skin. She's so small, relatively, that you wouldn't think there'd be any trouble meshing in machines from various parts of her. But there is. Plenty. It never showed up before because we never had to use a fraction of our total power before, but it showed up plenty back there. My beam was loose as ashes, and I've figured out why.

"Sixth-order stuff moves as many times faster than light as light does faster than a snail—maybe more. But it still takes a little time to get from one machine to another, inside even as small a globe as this is. See?"

Crane frowned in thought. "I see. I also see what the difficulties would be in anything large enough and strong enough to attack the Chlorans. It would mean timing each generator and each element of each projector; and each with a permissible variation of an infinitesimal fraction of a microsecond. That, of course, means Rovol and Caslor."

"I suppose it does . . . unless we can figure out an easier, faster way . . . I don't know whether the Chlorans have got anything like that or not, but they've got *something*. There ought to be some way of snitching it off of them."

"Why must they have?" Dunark demanded. "It's probably just a matter of size. They have a whole planet to fortify. Dozens of 'em if they want to. So it doesn't have to be a matter of refinement at all. Just brutal, piled up, overwhelming power."

"Could be," Seaton agreed. "If so, we can't match it, since the *Valeron* was as big as she could be and still have a factor of safety of two point two." He paused in thought, then went on, "But with such refinement, we could take a planet, no matter how loaded it was . . . I think. So maybe we'd better take off for Norlamin, at that."

"One thing we should do first, perhaps," Dorothy suggested. "Find out what that DuQuesne really did. He has me worried."

"Maybe we should, at that," Seaton agreed. "I'd forgotten all about the big black ape."

It was easy enough to find the line along which DuQuesne had traveled; the plug-chart was proof that he had not lied about that. They reached without incident the neighborhood of the point DuQuesne had marked on the chart. Seaton sent out a working projection of the device that, by intercepting and amplifying light-waves traversing open space, enabled him actually to see events that had happened in the not-too distant past.

He found the scene he wanted. He studied it, analyzed and recorded it. Then:

"He lied to me almost a hundred and eighty degrees," Seaton said. "That beam came from that galaxy over there." He jerked a thumb. "The alien who bothered him was in that galaxy. That much I'll buy. But it doesn't make sense that he'd go there. That alien was nobody he wanted to monkey with, that's for dead sure. So where did he meet the Jelmi, if not in that galaxy?"

"On the moon, perhaps," Margaret said.

"Possibly. I'll compute it . . . no, the timing isn't right—" Seaton thought for a moment— "but there's no use guessing. That galaxy may be the first place to look for sign; but I'll bet my case buck it'll be a long, cold hunt. I'd like awfully well to have that gizmo—flip bombs past the Chlorans' screens and walls with it . . ."

"From a distance greater than *their* working range?" Crane asked.

"That's so, too . . . or maybeso, at that, chum. Who knows *what* you can do through the fourth? But it looks as though our best bet is to beat it to Norlamin, rebuild this wreck, and tear into that business of refinement of synchronization. So say you all?"

So said they all and Seaton, flipping on full-power sixth-order drive, set course for Norlamin.

As the student will be aware, the events in this climactic struggle between the arch-enemies, Seaton and DuQuesne, were at this point reaching an area of maximum tension. It is curious to reflect that the outer symptom of this internal disruptive stress was, in the case of nearly every major component of the events to come, a psychological state of either satisfied achievement, or contented decision, or calm resignation. It is as though each of the major operatives were suffering from a universe-wide sense of false tranquility. On Ray-See-Nee, the new government felt its problems were behind it and only a period of solid, rewarding rebuilding lay ahead. (Although Kay-Lee Barlo had taken certain prudent precautions against this hope being illusory —as we shall see.) The Chlorans, proud and scornful in their absolute supremacy, had no hint that Seaton or anyone else was making or even proposed to make any effective moves against them. The Fenachrone, such few weary survivors as remained of them, had given themselves over to—not despair, no; but a proud acceptance of the fact that they were doomed.

There was in fact no tranquility in store for any of them! But they had not yet found that out.

Meanwhile the Jelmi, for example, were just beginning to feel the first itch of new challenges. In their big new spacerover, the *Mallidaxian*, Savant Tammon was as nearly perfectly happy as it is possible for a human or humanoid to be. He had made the greatest breakthrough of his career; perhaps the greatest breakthrough of all history. Exploring its many ramifications and determining its many as yet unsuspected possibilities would keep him busy for the rest of his life. Wherefore he was working fourteen or fifteen hours every day and reveling in every minute of it. He hummed happily to himself; occasionally he burst into song —in a voice that was decidedly not of grand-operatic quality.

He had enlarged his private laboratory by tearing out

four storerooms adjoining it; and the whole immense room was stacked to the ceiling with new apparatus and equipment. He was standing on a narrow catwalk, rubbing his bristly chin with the back of his hand as he wondered where he could put another two-ton tool, when Mergon and Luloy came swinging in; hand in hand as usual. Vastly different from Tammon, Mergon was not at all happy about the *status quo*.

"Listen, Tamm!" he burst out. "I've been yapping at you for a week and a half for a decision and your time is up as of right *now*. If you don't pull your head out of the fourth dimension and make it right now I'll do it myself and to hell with you and your authority as Captain-Commander."

"Huh? What? Time? Decision? What decision?" It was plain that the old savant had no idea at all of what his first assistant was so wrought up about.

"You set course for Mallidax and said we were going back to Mallidax. That's sheer idiocy and you know it. Of all places in the charted universe we should *not* go to, Mallidax is top and prime. We're too close for comfort already. Even though Klazmon must have lost us back there in Sol's system, he certainly picked us up again long ago and he'd give both wings and all his teeth for half the stuff you have here," and Mergon waved both arms indicatively around the jam-packed room.

"Oh?" Tammon gazed owlishly at the pair. "There was some talk . . . but why should I care where we go? This is the merest trifle, Mergon. Do not bother me with trivia any more," and Tammon cut communications with them as definitely as though he had thrown a switch.

Mergon shrugged his shoulders and Luloy giggled. "You're it, boy. That's what you get for sticking your neck out. All hail our new Captain-Commander!"

"Well, *somebody* had to. All our necks would have been in slings in another week. So pass the word, will you, and I'll skip up to the control room and change course."

Luloy spread the word; which was received with acclaim. Practically everybody aboard who was anybody agreed with Sennlloy when she said, "It's high time *somebody* took over and Merg's undoubtedly the best man for the job. Tammy's a nice old dear, but ever since he got bitten by that fourth-dimension germ he hasn't known what month it is or which way is up or within forty million parsecs of where he is in space."

"You see, Merg?" Luloy crowed, when it became evident that the shift in command was heartily approved. "I wouldn't even dream of ever saying 'I told you so', but I said at the first meeting that you should be Captain-Commander, and now everybody thinks so, almost."

"Yeah, almost," he agreed; not at all enthusiastically. "Everybody except the half-wits. Pass the buck. Let George do it. Nobody with a brain firing on three barrels wants the job."

"Why, that isn't so, Merg. You *know* it isn't!" she protested, indignantly.

"Well, *I* don't want it," he broke in, "but since Tamm wished it onto me I'll take a crack at it."

The *Mallidaxian,* swinging wide and braking down, hard, skirted the outermost edge of the Realm; the edge farthest away from Llurdiax. Mergon did not approach or signal to any planet of the Jelmi. Instead, he picked out an uninhabited Tellus-type planet four solar systems away from the Border and landed on it. And there, under cover of the superdreadnaught's mighty defensive screens and with Captain-Commander Mergon tensely on watch, the engineers and scientists disembarked, set up their high-order projectors, and went furiously to work building an enormous and enormously powerful dome.

The work went on uninterruptedly, day after day; for so many days that both Mergon and Luloy became concerned —the girl very highly so. "Do you suppose we've figured wrong?" she asked.

Mergon frowned. "I can't be sure, of course, but I don't think so. Pure logic, remember. Everything we've done has been designed to keep Klazmon guessing. Off balance. He's fortified Llurdiax, that's sure, but we don't know how heavily and we can't find out." He paused.

"Without using the gizmo, which of course is out," said Luloy.

"Check. We haven't sent any spy-rays or anything else. They wouldn't have got us anything. But he certainly expected us to try. He'll think we don't care . . . which as a matter of fact, we don't . . . too much. It's almost a mathematical certainty that we can handle anything he can throw at us as of now. But if we give him time enough to build more really big stuff it'll be just too bad."

"And the horrible old monster is probably doing just exactly that," Luloy said.

"I wouldn't wonder. But we can finish the dome before

he can build enough stuff, and he can't let that happen. Especially since we're not interfering with his prying and spying, but are treating him with the same contempt he used to treat us. That'll bother him no end. Burn him up! Also . . . remember that stuff in the dome that no Llurd can possibly understand."

Luloy laughed. "Because it isn't anything whatever, really, except Llurd-bait? I'm scared that maybe they will understand it yet—even though I'm sure they won't."

"They can't. Their minds won't stretch that far in that direction," Mergon said postively. "They knew we made a breakthrough, so they'll know that what they see is only a fraction of what the thing really is; and that'll scare 'em. As much as Llurdi can be scared, that is. Which isn't very much. So Klazmon will do something before our dome is finished. As I read the tea-leaves, he'll have to."

"But just suppose he doesn't take the bait?"

"Then we'll have to take the initiative. I don't want to—it'd weaken our bargaining position tremendously—but I will if I have to."

He did not have to. His analysis of the Llurdan mentality and temperament had been accurate.

Four full days before the scheduled date of completion of the dome, Klazmon's full working projection appeared in the *Mallidaxian's* control room. Mergon had detected its coming, but had done nothing to interfere with it. The Llurd quite obviously intended parley, not violence.

"Hail, brother llanzlan, Klazmon of the Llurdi," Mergon greeted his visitor quietly, but in the phraseology of one ruler greeting another on the basis of unquestionable equality. "Is there perhaps some service that I, Llanzlan Mergon of the Realm of the Jelmi, may perform for you and thus place you in my debt?"

This, to a human dictator, would have been effrontery intolerable; but Mergon had been pretty sure that it would have little or no effect, emotionally, upon Klazmon. Nor did it; to all seeming it had no effect at all. The Llurd merely said, "You wish me to believe that you Jelmi have made a breakthrough sufficiently important to justify the establishment of an independent but coexistent Realm of the Jelmi."

This was in no sense a question; it was a flat statement. Mergon had been eminently correct in his assumption that he would not have to draw the Llurd a blueprint. Mergon quirked an eyebrow at Luloy, who pressed the button that signaled all the savants in the dome to drop their tools and dash back into the ship.

"That is correct," Mergon said.

Klazmon's projection remained motionless and silent; both Jelmi could almost perceive the Llurd's thoughts. And Mergon, who had tracked the Llurd's thoughts so unerringly so far, was practically certain that he was still on track.

Klazmon did not actually know whether the Jelmi had made a breakthrough or not. The Jelmi intended to make him believe that they had, and that breakthrough was something that made them either invulnerable or invincible, or both. Any of those matters or assumptions could be either true or false. One of them, the question of invulnerability, could be and should be tested without delay. If they were in fact invulnerable, no possible attack could harm them. If they were not invulnerable they were bluffing and lying and should therefore be eliminated.

Wherefore Mergon was not surprised when Klazmon's projection vanished without having said another word—nor when, an instant after that vanishment, the *Mallidaxian's* mighty defensive screens flared white.

They did not even pause at the yellow or the yellow-white, but went directly to the blinding white; to the degree of radiance at which the vessel's spare began automatically to cut in—spare after spare after spare.

After staring in silence for two long minutes, Mergon said, "We figured their most probable maximum offense and applied a factor of safety of three—and look at 'em!"

White-faced, Luloy licked her lips. "Mighty Llenderllon!" she cried. "How can they *possibly* deliver such an attack 'way out here?"

Then Mergon picked up his microphone and said, "Our screens are still holding and they're protecting the dome; but we're going to need a lot more defense. So go back out there, please, and give me everything you can."

He then sat back and stared tight-jawed at the ever-climbing needles of his meters and at the unchanging blinding-white brilliance of his vessel's screens.

22 • THE GEAS

As the Llurd's attack mounted to higher and ever higher plateaus of fury, Mergon slid along his bench to his fourth-dimensional controls and there appeared on the floor beside him a lithium-hydride fusion bomb, armed and ready.

He stared at it, his jaw-muscles tightening into lumps. Luloy stared at the thing, too, and her face became even paler than it had been.

"But could you, Merg?" she asked, through stiff lips. "I . . . I mean, you couldn't possibly . . . could you?"

"I don't know," he said harshly, scarcely separating locked teeth. "I may have to whether I can or not. We had a factor of safety of three. Two point nine of them are in now and the last tenth is starting up. The dome can't put out more than that."

"I know! But if we blow the llanzlanate up, won't they kill all the Jelmi of all our worlds and start breeding a more tractable race of slaves?"

"That's the way I read it. In that case we eight hundred could get away clean and start a better civilization somewhere out of range."

She shuddered. "In that case would life be worth living?"

"It's a tough decision to make . . . since the alternative could be for us to kill all the Llurdi."

"Oh, no!" she cried. "But don't you think, Merg, that he'll cooperate? They're absolutely logical, you know."

"Maybe. In one way I think so, but I simply can't see any absolute ruler making such an abject surrender. However, we've got to decide right now and we'll have to stick to our decision—we both know that he can't be bluffed. If it comes right down to it we can do one of three things. First, commit suicide for our whole eight hundred by not touching the bomb off. Second, wipe them out. Third, let them wipe out all Jelmi except us. What's your vote?"

"Llenderllon help me! Put that way, there's—*oh, look!*" she screamed, in a miraculously changed tone of voice.

"The master-meter! It's slowing down! *It's going to stop!*" She uttered an ear-splitting shriek of pure joy and hurled herself into her husband's arms.

"It's stabilized, for a fact," Mergon said, after their emotions had subsided to something approaching normal. "He's throwing everything he's got at us. We're holding him, but just barely, so the question is——"

"One thing first," she broke in. "My vote. I hate to say it, but we *can't* let them kill our race."

He put his arm around her and squeezed. "That's what I was sure you'd say. The question now is, how long do we let him stew in his own juice before we skip over there and talk peace terms?"

"*Not* long enough to let him build more generators than we can to fry us with," she replied, promptly if a bit unclearly. "One day? Half a day? A quarter?"

"But long enough to let him know he's licked," Mergon said. "I'd say one full day would be just about right. So let's go get us some sleep."

"*Sleep!* Llenderllon's eyeballs! Can you even *think* of such a thing as *sleep* after all *this?*"

"Certainly I can. So can you—you're all frazzled out. Come on girl, we're hitting the sheets."

"Why, I won't be able to sleep a *wink* until this is all over!"

But she was wrong; in ten minutes they were both sleeping the sleep of exhaustion.

Twelve hours later she came suddenly awake, rolled over toward him, and shook him vigorously by the shoulder. "Wake up, you!"

He grumbled something and tried to pull away from her grip.

She shook him again. "Wake up, you great big oaf! Suppose that beast Klazmon has got more generators built and our screens are all failing?"

He opened one eye. "If they fail, sweet, we won't know a thing about it." He opened the other eye and, three-quarters awake now, went on, "Do you think I'm running this ship single-handed? What do you think the other officers are for?"

"But they aren't *you*," she declared, with completely feminine illogic where her husband was concerned. "So hurry up and get up and we'll go see for ourselves."

"Okay, but not 'til after breakfast, if I have to smack you down. So punch us up a gallon of coffee, huh? And a couple slabs of ham and six or eight eggs? Then we'll go see."

They ate and went and saw. The screens still flared at the same blinding white, but there were no signs of overloading or of failure. They could, the Third Officer bragged, keep it up for years. Everything was under control.

"You hope," Mergon said—but not to the officer. He said that under his breath as he and Luloy turned away toward their own station.

Much to Mergon's relief, nothing happened during the rest of the day, and at the end of the twenty-fourth hour he sent the actual bomb and working projections of himself and Luloy into the llanzlanate. Into the llanzlan's private study, where Klazmon was hard at work.

It was an immense room, and one in which a good anthropologist could have worked delightedly for weeks. The floor was bare, hard, smooth-polished; fantastically inlaid in metal and colored quartz and turquoise and jade. The pictures—framed mostly in extruded stainless steel—portrayed scenes (?) and things (?) and events (?) never perceived by any Earthly sense and starkly incomprehensible to any Earthly mind. The furniture was . . . "weird" is the only possible one-word description. Every detail of the room proclaimed that here was the private retreat of a highly talented and very eminent member of a culture that was old, wide and high.

"Hail, Llanzlan Klazmon," Mergon said quietly, conversationally. "You will examine this bomb, please, to make sure that, unlike us two, it is actual and practical."

The Llurd's eyes had bulged a little and the tip of his tail had twitched slightly at the apparition. That was all. He picked up an instrument with a binocular eyepiece, peered through it for a couple of seconds, and put it down. "It is actual and practical," he agreed.

Whatever emotions may have been surging through the llanzlan's mind, his control was superb. He did not ask them how they had done it, or why, or any other question. After the event he knew much and could guess more—and he was perhaps the starkest realist of the most starkly realistic race of intelligent beings yet known to live.

"You realize, of course, that we do not intend to fire it except as the ultimately last resort."

"I do now."

"Ah, yes. Our conduct throughout has surprised you; especially that we did not counterattack."

"If not exactly surprised, at least did not anticipate that Jelmi would or could act with practically Llurdan logic," the Llurd conceded.

"We can. And when we think it best, we do. We suggest that you cut off your attack. We will then put on air-suits and return here in person, to discuss recent developments as reasoning and logical entities should."

The Llurd was fast on the uptake. He knew that, given time, he could crush this threat; but he knew that he would not have the time. He could see ahead as well as Mergon could to the total destruction of two hundred forty more planets. Wherefore he barked a couple of syllables at a com and the furiously incandescent screens of the *Mallidaxian* went cold and dark.

Jelmi and bomb disappeared. Mergon and Luloy donned gas-tight, self-contained, plastic-helmeted coveralls and reappeared in the Llanzlan's study. Klazmon seated them courteously in two Jelman easy-chairs—which looked atrociously out of place in that room—and the peace conference, which was to last for days, began.

"First," the llanzlan said, "this breakthrough that you have accomplished. At what stage in the negotiations do you propose to give me the complete technical specifications of it?"

"Now," Mergon said, and a yard-high stack of tapes appeared on the floor beside the Llurd's desk. It was the entire specs and description of the fourth-dimensional translator. Nothing was omitted or obscured.

"Oh? I see. There is, then, much work yet to be done on it. Work that only you Jelmi can do."

"That is true, as you will learn from those tapes. Now," said Mergon, settling down to the bargaining session, "first, we have shown you that Jelmi capable of doing genius-type work cannot be coerced into doing it. Second, the fact is that it is psychologically impossible for us to do such work under coercion. Third, we believe firmly that free and independent Jelmi can coexist with the Llurdi. Fourth, we believe equally firmly that for the best good of both races they should so coexist . . ."

And at that first day's end, after supper, Luloy said, "Merg, I simply would not have believed it. Ever. I'm not sure I really believe it now. But you know I almost like— I actually *admire* that horrible monster in some ways!"

Seaton called Rovol of Rays, on Norlamin, as soon as he could reach him. He told him the story of what he had done on Ray-See-Nee, and what he hoped to gain by it, in detail, then went on to ask his help on the control of the fourth-dimensional translator. "You see, Rovol, at perfect sync it would—theoretically—take zero power. I don't expect the unattainable ideal, of course—" he winked at Dorothy—"just close enough so we can pack enough stuff into the *Valeron* to handle everything they can throw at us and still have enough left over to fight back with."

"Ah, youth, a fascinating problem indeed. I will begin work on it at once, and will call in certain others in whose provinces some aspects of it lie. By the time you arrive here we will perhaps have determined whether or not any solution is at present possible."

"What?" Seaton yelped. "Why—I thought—surely—" he almost stuttered. "I thought you'd have it done by then— maybe be sending it out to meet us, even."

The old Norlaminian's paternally forbearing sigh was highly expressive. "Still the heedless, thoughtless youth, in spite of all our teachings. You have not studied the problem yourself at all."

"Well, not very much, I admit."

"I advise you to do so. If you devote to it every period of labor between now and your arrival here you may perhaps be able to talk about it intelligently," and Rovol cut com.

Dorothy whistled. She didn't whistle very often, but she could do it very expressively.

"Yeah," Seaton said, ruefully. "And the old boy wasn't kidding, either."

"Not having a sense of humor, he can't kid. He really slapped you on the wrist, friend. But why would it be such a horrible job to sync a few generators in?"

"I don't know, but I'll find out." He went, worked for four solid hours with the Brain, and came back wearing a sheepish grin. "It's true," he reported. "I knew it'd be tricky, but I had no idea. You have to work intelligently, manipulably and reproducibly in time units of three times ten to the minus twenty-eighth of a second—the time it takes light to travel a billionth of a billionth of a centi- meter."

"Hush. You don't expect me to understand that, do you?"

"I'll say I don't. I don't expect to even really understand it myself."

Seaton did not work on the problem every day until

arrival, but he worked on it for over a hundred hours—enough so that he began to realize how difficult it was.

The *Skylark of Valeron* entered the Green System, approached Norlamin, and went into orbit around it. The travelers boarded a shuttle, which thereupon began to slide down a landing-beam toward Rovol's private dock.

The little craft settled gently into a neoprene-lined cup. The visitors disembarked and walked down a short flight of metallic steps, at the foot of which the ancient, white-bearded sage was waiting for them. He greeted them warmly—for a Norlaminian—and led them through the "garden" toward the metal-and-quartz palace that was his home.

"Oh, Dick, isn't it *wonderful!*" Dorothy pressed his arm against her side. "It's so much like Orlon's and yet so different . . . "

And it was both. The acreage of velvet-short, springy grass was about the same as that upon which they had landed so long before. The imperishable-metal statuary was similar. Here also were the beds of spectacular flowers and the hedges and sculptured masses of gorgeously vari-colored plant life. The tapestry wall, however—composed of millions upon millions of independently moving, flashing, self-luminous jewels of all the colors of the rainbow—ran for a good three hundred yards beside the walk. It was evident that the women of the Rovol had been working on it for hundreds of centuries instead of for mere hundreds of years. Instead of being only form and color, as was the wall of the Orlon, it was well along toward portraying the entire history of the Family Rovol.

Rovol wanted to entertain his guests instead of work, but Seaton objected. "Shame on you, Rovol. The Period of Labor is just starting, and remember how you fellows used to bat my ears down about there being definite and non-interchangeable times for work and for play and so forth?"

"That is of course true, youth," Rovol agreed, equably enough. "I should not have entertained the idea for a moment. My companion will welcome the ladies and show them to your apartments. We will proceed at once to the Area of Experiment," and he called an aircar by fingering a stud at his belt.

"I've been studying, as you suggested," Seaton said then. "Can the thing be solved? The more I worked on it the more dubious I got."

"Yes, but the application of its solution will be neither

easy nor simple." The aircar settled gently to the walk a few yards ahead of the party and Rovol and Seaton boarded it; Rovol still talking. "But you will be delighted to know that, thanks to your gift of the metal of power, what would have been a work of lifetimes can very probably be accomplished in a few mere years."

Seaton was not delighted. Knowing what Rovol could mean by the word "few," he was appalled; but there was nothing whatever he could do to speed things up.

He spent a couple of weeks rebuilding the *Skylark of Valeron*—with batteries of offensive and defensive weaponry where single machines had been—then stood around and watched the Norlaminians work. And as day followed day without anything being accomplished he became more and more tense and impatient. He concealed his feelings perfectly, he thought; but he should have known that he could hide nothing from the extremely percipient mind of the girl who was in every respect his other half.

"Dick, you've been jittering like a witch," she said one evening, "about something I can't see any reason for. But you have a reason, or you wouldn't be doing it. So break down and tell me."

"I can't, confound it. I know I'm always in a rush to get a thing done, but not like this. I'm all of a twitter inside. I can't sleep . . ."

Dorothy snickered. "You can't? If what you were doing last night wasn't sleeping it was the most reasonable facsimile thereof I've ever seen. Or heard."

"Not like I ought to, I mean. Nightmares. Devils all the time sticking me with pitchforks. Do you believe in hunches?"

"No," she said, promptly. "I never had any. Not a one."

"I never did, either, and if this is one I never want to have another. But it could be a hunch that we ought to be investigating that alien galaxy of DuQuesne's. Whatever it is, I want to go somewhere and I haven't the faintest idea where."

"Oh? Listen!" Dorothy's eyes widened. "I'll bet you're getting an answer to that message we sent out!"

He shook his head. "Uh-uh. Can't be. Telepathy has got to be something you can understand."

"Who besides you ever said it would have to be telepathy? And who knows what telepathy would have to be like? Come on, let's go tell Martin and Peggy!"

"Huh?" he yelped. "Tell M. Reynolds Crane, the hardest-boiled skeptic that event went unhung, that I want to go skyshooting to hellangone off into the wild blue yonder just because I've got an itch that I can't scratch?"

"Why not?" She looked him steadily in the eye. "We're exploring *terra incognita*, Dick. How much do you really know about that mind of yours, the way it is now?"

"Okay. Maybe they'll buy it; you did. Let's go."

They went; and, a little to Seaton's surprise, Crane agreed with Dorothy. So did Margaret. Hence three hours later, the big sky-rover was on her way.

Four days out, however, Seaton said, "This isn't the answer, I don't think. The itch is still there. So what?"

There was silence for a couple of minutes, then Dorothy chuckled suddenly. Sobering quickly, she said, with a perfectly straight face, "I'll bet it's that new department head girl-friend of yours, Dick; the pistol-packing mama with the wiggle. She wants to see the big, bold, handsome Earthman again. And if it is, I'll scratch . . ."

Seaton jumped almost out of his chair. "You're not kidding half as much as you think you are, pet. That crack took a good scratch at exactly where it itches." He put on his remote-control helmet and changed course. "And that helps still more." He thought for minutes, then shrugged his shoulders and said, "I'm not getting a thing . . . not anything more at all. How many of you remember either Ree-Toe Prenk or the girl well enough to picture either of them accurately in your minds?"

They all remembered one or both of the Rayseenians.

"Okay. This'll sound silly. It *is* silly, for all the tea in China, but let's try something. All join hands, picture either or both of them, and think at them as hard as we can. The thought is simply 'we're coming.' Okay?"

More than half sheepishly, they tried it—and it worked. At least Seaton said, "Well, it worked, I guess. Anyway, for the first time in weeks, it's gone. But I didn't get a thing. Nothing whatever. Not even a hint either that we were being paged or that our reply was being received. Did any of you?"

None of them had.

"Huh!" Seaton snorted. "If this is telepathy they can keep it—I'll take Morse's original telegraph!"

A week or so after the *Skylark of Valeron* left the neighborhood of Ray-See-Nee, that planet's new government began to have trouble. Ree-Toe Prenk had said and had believed that whoever controlled the capital controlled the world, but that was not true in his case. It had always been true previously because the incoming powers had always been of the same corrupt-to-the-core stripe as those who were ousted—and when corruption has been the way of life for generations it is deep-rooted indeed.

There were, of course, other factors behind the unrest. But neither Prenk nor any other human knew about them —then.

All the district bosses had always gone along with the Big Boss as a matter of course. Not one of them cared a whit who ran the world, as long as his own privileges and perquisites and powers and takes were not affected. Prenk, however, was strictly honest and strictly just. If he should succeed in taking over Ray-See-Nee's government in full, every crook and boodler on the planet would lose everything he had; possibly even his life. Thus, while the new Premier held the capital—in a rapidly deteriorating grip— his influence outside that city's limits varied inversely as about the fourth power of the distance.

This resistance, while actual enough, was in no sense overt. Every order was ostensibly obeyed to the letter; but everything deteriorated at an accelerating rate and Prenk could do nothing whatever about it. Whenever and wherever Prenk was not looking, business went on as usual— gambling, drugs, prostitution, crime and protection—but he could not prove any of it. Neither uniformed police nor detectives could find anything much amiss. They made arrests, but no suspect was ever convicted. The prosecution's cases were weak. The juries brought in verdicts of "innocent", usually without leaving the box.

Even when, in desperation, Prenk went—supposedly topsecretly—to an outlying city, fully prepared to stage a questioning that would have made Torquemada blush, he did nothing and he learned nothing. Every person on his list had vanished tracelessly and every present incumbent had abundant proof of innocence. Nor did any of them know why they had been promoted so suddenly. They were just lucky, they guessed.

It was indeed baffling. It would have been less so if Prenk had had any notion of the universe-wide stir of mighty events just beginning to bubble—if he had been able, as we are now able, to fit together all these patchwork stories into one nearly Norlaminian fabric of universal history.

But he wasn't—and, for his peace of mind, perhaps that was just as well!

Premier Ree-Toe Prenk sat at his desk in the Room of State. Kay-Lee Barlo, shapely legs crossed and pistol at hip, sat at his left. Sy-By Takeel, the new Captain-General of the Guard, stood at ease at his right.

"Whoever is doing this is a smooth, shrewd operator," Prenk said. "So much so that you two are the only people I can trust. And I don't suppose either of you will ever be approached. Probably neither of you would be bought even if you offered yourselves ever so deftly for sale."

"I wouldn't be, certainly," Takeel said. "Captains-General of mercenaries don't sell out. I wouldn't answer for any of my lieutenants, though, if there's loot to be had. There is here, I take it?"

"Unlimited quantities, apparently. So you, too, are subject to assassination?"

The soldier shrugged. "Oh, yes, it's an occupational hazard. How about you, Exalted Barlo? No chance either, I'd say?"

"None at all. My stand is too well known. Half my people would stab me in the back if they dared to and they all look me in the eye and lie in their Mi-Ko-Ta-cursed teeth. I wish Ky-El Mokak and his people would get back here quick," Kay-Lee said wistfully.

"So do I," Prenk said, glumly. "But even if we had a sixth-order tightbeamer and could use it, we haven't the slightest idea of where he came from or where he went to."

"That's true." She nibbled at her lip. "But listen. I'm a psychic. It runs in the women of some families, you know, being . . . well, what most people call witches, kind of. My talent isn't fully developed yet, but mother and I together could witch-wish at him to come back here as fast as he can and I'm sure he would."

The soldier's face showed quite plainly what he thought of the idea, but Prenk nodded—if more than somewhat dubiously. "I've heard of that 'witch-wishing' business, and that it sometimes works. So go home right now and get at it, Kay-Lee, and give it everything you and your mother both can put out."

Kay-Lee went home forthwith and went into executive session with her mother; a handsome, black-haired woman of forty-odd. "And I have positive identification," the girl concluded. "His blood was all over the place—positively *quarts* of it—and I saved some just in case." And, of course, she had—prudently, wisely and, as it turned out, luckily for all concerned!

The older woman's face cleared. "That's good. Without a positive, I'm afraid it would be hopeless at what the distance probably is by this time. Run and get the witch-holly, dear, while I fix the incense."

They each ate seven ritually preserved witch-holly berries and inhaled seven deep drafts of aromatic smoke. While they were waiting for the powerful drugs to take effect, Kay-Lee asked, "How much of this rigamarole is chemistry, do you suppose, mother, and how much is just hocus-pocus?"

"No one knows. Some day, whatever it is that we have will be recognized as having existence and will be really studied. Until then, all we can do is follow the ancient ritual."

"I think I'll talk to Ky-El about it. But listen. Witches with any claim at all to decency simply don't put geases on people. But what if he's so far away that we can't reach him any other way?"

The older woman frowned, then said, "In that case, my dear, we'll never, *never* tell anyone a thing about it."

23 • RE-SETTING OF THE PREMIER

As the *Skylark of Valeron* approached Galaxy DW-427-LU, Dorothy said, "Dick, I suppose it's occurred to you more than once that I'm not much of a woman."

"You aren't? I'd say you'd do until the real thing showed up." Seaton, who had been thinking of the problem of synchronization instead of his wife, changed voice instantly when he really looked at her and saw what a black mood she was in. "You're the universe's best, is all, ace. I knew you were feeling a little low in your mind, but not . . . listen, sweetheart. What could possiby make you think you aren't the absolute top?"

She did not answer the question. Instead, "What do you think you're going to get into this time?"

"Nothing much, I'm sure. Prenk's probably running out

of ammunition. We can make more in five minutes than he can in five years."

"I'm sure that isn't it. You're going into personal danger again and I'll be expected to sit up here in the *Skylark* eating my heart out wondering if you're alive or dead. You don't see Sitar going through that with Dunark."

"Wait up, sweetheart. Mores and customs, remember?"

"Mores and customs be damned! Do you remember exactly what Sitar said and exactly how she said it? Did it sound like mores and customs to you? Was there any element whatever of suttee in it?"

"But listen, Dottie——" He took her gently in his arms.

"You listen!" she rushed on. "If he dies she doesn't want to keep on living and she won't. And she doesn't care who knows it. Maybe it started that way—society's sanction—but that was her personal profession of faith. And I feel the same way. If you die I don't want to keep on living and won't. So next time I'm going with you."

Being an American male, he could not accept that without an argument. "But there's Dickie," he said.

"There are also her three children on Osnome. I learned something from her about what the basic, rock-bottom attitude of a woman toward her man ought to be. Even from little Lotus. She's no bigger than a minute and a half, but what did *she* do? So while we're having this moment of truth let's be rock-bottom honest with each other for the first time in our lives instead of mouthing the platitudes of our society. I'm not a story-book mother, Dick. If it ever comes right down to a choice, you know how I'll decide—and how long it will take!"

Seaton could not get in touch with Ree-Toe Prenk, of course, until the *Valeron* was actually inside Galaxy DW-427-LU; but as soon as communication could be established Kay-Lee Barlo asked eagerly, "You *did* get our thought, then, Ky-El? Mother's and mine? We didn't feel that we were quite reaching you."

"Not exactly," Seaton replied. "I didn't get any real thought at all; just a feeling that I ought to be going *somewhere* that bothered me no end until I headed this way. But since it was you people calling, I'm mighty glad I got what little I did."

The *Skylark* went into orbit around Ray-See-Nee and the Skylarkers climbed into a landing-craft that Seaton had designed and built specifically for the occasion. It was a miniature battleship—one of the deadliest fighting ships of its size and heft ever built. And this time the whole party was heavily armed. Dunark and Sitar were in full Osnomian panoply of war. Dorothy wore a pair of her long-barrelled .38 target pistols in leg-holsters under her bouffant skirt. Even little Lotus wore two .25 automatics. "I don't know whether I can hit anybody with one of these or not," she had said while Dorothy was rigging her. "I'd much rather work hand to hand. But if they're too far away to get at I can at least make a lot of noise and *look* like I'm doing something."

They were met at the spaceport by two platoons of the Premier's Guard, led by Captain-General Sy-By Takeel himself. They were guarded like visiting royalty from the spaceport to the Capitol Building and up into the Room of State, where they were greeted with informal cordiality by Prenk and by Kay-Lee, who was now an Exalted of the Thirty-Fifth, besides being First Deputy Premier.

Prenk seated his guests, not on stools in front of and below his throne-like desk, but at a long conference table with Seaton as its head. The two lieutenants posted guards outside the two immense doors at the far end of the vast room and stationed the rest of their men in position to cover both entrances. Takeel, with velvet slippers over his field-boots, stood on Prenk's desk, commanding the entire room, with a machine-gun-like weapon cradled expertly and accustomedly in the crook of his left arm.

"Are things this bad?" Seaton asked. "I knew it was tough when you told us to come loaded for bear—but *this?*"

"They're exactly this bad. These two—" Prenk jerked a thumb at Kay-Lee and at Takeel—"are the only two people on this whole world that I know I can trust. Until quite recently I was sure I held the city—but now I'm not at all sure of holding even this building. I can only hope that you're not too late. I'll tell you what the situation is; then you will tell me, please, if there is anything you can do about it."

He talked for twelve minutes. Then:

"P-s-s-s-st!" Kay-Lee hissed. "Danger! Coming—nearing us—fast! I can feel it—taste it—smell it! Get ready quick!" She sprang to her feet, drew her pistol, and arranged a dozen clips of cartridges meticulously on the table in front of her.

The Osnomians' chairs crashed backward, their heavy coats flew off, and they stood tensely ready, machine pistols in all four hands. And, seconds later, the other Skylarkers were on their feet and ready too. The Captain-General had not heard the low-voiced warning, but he had seen the action and that was enough. Trigger-nerved Dunark's chair had no sooner struck the floor on its first bounce than Takeel was going into his shooting stance, with his weapon flipping around into firing position as though it were sliding in a greased groove; the while glaring ferociously at his senior lieutenant—who thereupon began to have an acute attack of the jitters.

It was the commander's savage motion, actually, that ruined the attackers' split-second schedule. For, at a certain second, the two lieutenants were to shoot their captain; then to shoot Prenk and Kay-Lee Barlo; and then, as the attack proper was launched, they were to kill as many of their own men as they could. Thus, knowing what a savage performer the Captain-General was with his atrocious weapon, their hands were forced; they had to act a couple of seconds too soon. They tried—but with two short bursts so close together as to be practically one, Takeel cut them down. Cut them both almost literally in two.

Thus, when the two great doors were blasted simultaneously down and the attackers stormed in with guns ablaze, they did not find a half-dead and completely demoralized Guard and a group of surprised visitors. Instead:

The mercenaries were neither dead nor demoralized. They knew exactly what to do and were doing it. Dunark and Sitar had the fire-power of half a company of trained troops and were using it to the fullest full. The Captain-General, from his coign of vantage atop the desk, was spraying both entrances with bullets like a gardener watering two flower-beds with a hose. Kay-Lee was throwing lead almost as fast as Takeel was; changing magazines with such fluent speed and precision as to miss scarcely a shot. Dorothy, nostrils flaring and violet eyes blazing, was shooting as steadily and as accurately as though she were out on the range marking up another possible. Even tiny Lotus, with one of her .25's clutched in both hands, was shooting as fast as she could pull the trigger.

It was Seaton, however, who ended the battle. He waited long enough to be absolutely sure of what was going on, then fired twice with his left-hand magnum—through the doorways, high over the heads of the attackers, far down the corridors.

There were two terrific explosions; followed by one long rumbling crash as that whole section of the building either went somewhere else or collapsed into rubble. Falling and flying masonry and steel and razor-edged shards of structural glass killed almost everyone outside the heavily re-enforced wall of the Room of State. The shock-waves of the blasts, raging through the doorways, killed half of the enemy massed there and blew the others half the length of the room. And, continuing on with rapidly decreasing force, knocked most of the Skylarkers flat and blew the Captain-General off of the desk and clear back against the wall.

"Sangram's head!" that worthy yelled, scrambling to his feet with machine-gun again—or still? He had not for an instant lost control of *that!*—at the ready. "What in Japnonk's rankest hell was that?"

"X-plosive shell," Seaton said, his voice as hard as his eyes. "This time I came loaded for bear. Now we'll mop up and find out what's been going on. I gather, sir, that your two platoon leaders were in on it?"

"Yes. It's a shame I had to kill 'em without asking 'em a few questions." He did not explain that he had had neither the time in which nor the weapon with which merely to wound them seriously enough so that neither of them could fight back with any sort of weapon. There was no need.

"That won't make too much difference." Seaton looked around; first at his own crew and then at the guards, half of whom were down. Medics and first-aid men were rushing in to work on them. He looked again, more closely, at his people and at Prenk and Kay-Lee. Not one of them, apparently, had even been scratched.

That, however, was logical. The mercenaries were hard-trained fighting men, shooting was their business. Hence the attackers' orders had been to shoot the guards first, and there had been no time to evaluate the actual situation and to change the plan of attack. Hence, as far as anyone knew, not a single bullet had been aimed at the far end of the room.

Seaton took a pair of headsets out of his pocket and applied one of them, first to one of the two lieutenants' heads, then to the other.

"Uh-huh," he grunted then. "That ape didn't know too much, but this one was going to be the new captain-general. I suppose you've got a recorder, Ree-Toe?"

"I'll get it, sir!" Kay-Lee exclaimed; and Prenk, eyes bulging, gasped:

"Don't tell me you can read a *dead* brain, sir!"

"Oh, yes. They keep their charges, sometimes for days."

Kay-Lee handed Seaton a microphone then, and he spoke into it for ten minutes—the while three Rayseenian faces went through gamuts of emotion; each culminating in the same expression of joyous satisfaction.

When Seaton paused for breath Prenk said in awe, "That machine is certainly a something . . . I don't suppose . . ." He stopped.

"I do suppose, yes. I'll give you a few sets, with blueprints, and show you how they work," and Seaton went on with his reading.

A few minutes later he cut off the mike and said, "That ape over there," he pointed, "is one of the Big Wheels. Have someone latch onto him, Ree-Toe; we'll read him next. He's one you'll be really interested in, so I'll hook you up in parallel with me so you can get everything he knows into your own brain." He took a third headset from his pocket and began to adjust its settings, going on, "It takes a different set-up . . . so . . . and goes on your head so."

"That ape" was a fattish, sallow-faced man of fifty, who had been directing operations from outside the room and had intended to stay outside it until everything was secure within. He had been blown into the room and halfway along its length by the force of the blasts. He was pretty badly smashed up, but he was beginning to regain consciousness and was weakly trying to get to his feet.

This unlucky wight was a mine of information indeed, but Prenk stopped the mining operation after only a couple of minutes of digging.

"Sy-By," he said. "Two more of your officers you can shoot." He gave two names. "Then come back here with some men you think you can trust and we'll test 'em to make sure. By that time I'll have a list of people for you to round up and bring in for examination."

There is no need to follow any farther the Premier's progress in cleaning up his planet. In fact, only one more incident that occurred there is of interest here—one that occurred while Seaton and Dorothy were getting ready for bed in one of the suites of honor. She put both arms around him suddenly; he pressed her close.

"Dick, I belonged there. Beside you. Every fiber of my being belonged there. That was *exactly* where I belonged."

"I know you did, sweet. I'll have to admit it. But . . ."

She put her hand over his mouth. "But nothing, my dearest. No buts. I've killed rats and rattlesnakes, and that wasn't any different. Not a bit different in any way."

Of the more than five thousand Fenachrone who had left their noisome home planet in Sleemet's flagship, almost seven hundred had died and more were dying.

It was not that the Llurdi were physically cruel to them or abused them in any way. They didn't. Nor were they kind; they were conspicuously and insultingly neutral and indifferent to them. Conspicuous and insulting, that is, to the hypersensitive minds of the captives. In their own minds, the Llurdi were acting strictly according to logic. Every item of the subjects' environment duplicated precisely its twin on the subjects' home world. What more could logically be done? Nothing.

The Llurdi observed the mental anguish of the Fenachrone, of course, and recorded their emotions quite accurately, but with no emotional reactions whatever of their own. Practically all emotions were either illogical or unsane, or both.

To the illogical and unsane Fenachrone, however—physically, mentally, intellectually and psychologically—the situation was intolerable; one that simply could not be endured.

They were proud, haughty, intolerant; their race had always been so. Since time immemorial it had been bred into their innermost consciousnesses that they were the RACE SUPREME—destined unquestionably to be the absolute rulers of all things living or yet to live throughout all the transfinite reaches of the Cosmic All.

Holding this belief with every fiber of their beings, they had been plunged instantly into a condition of complete, utter helplessness.

Their vessel could not fight. While it was intact except for its tail-section and its power-pods, its every offensive projector was burned out; useless. Nor could they fight personally, either physically or mentally. Their physical strength, enormous as it was, was of no avail against the completely logical, completely matter-of-fact minds of the Llurdi.

Most galling condition of all, the Fenachrone were not treated as enemies; nor as menaces or threats; nor even as intelligent entities whose knowledges and abilities might be worthy of notice. These things were observed and recorded, to be sure, but only as component parts of a newly discovered class of objects, the Fenachrone; a class of objects that happened to be alive. The Fenachrone were neither more nor less noteworthy than were birds or barnacles.

Sleemet, no longer young and perhaps the proudest and most intractable and most intransigent of the lot, could not endure that treatment very long; but he did not bend. The old adage "Where there's life there's hope," simply is not true where such as the Llurdi and the Fenachrone are concerned. Sleemet lost all hope and broke; broke almost completely down.

He stopped eating. That did not bother the Llurdi in any way. Why should it? They were neither squeamish nor humane, any more than they were cruel or vindictive. The fact that certain of these creatures stopped taking nourishment under certain conditions was merely a datum to be observed and recorded.

But since Sleemet was big and strong, even for a Fenachrone, and had previously eaten very well indeed, it took him a long time to die. And as he weakened—as the bindings between flesh and spirit loosened more and ever more —he regressed more and ever more back into the youth of his race. Back and back. Still farther back; back into its very childhood; back to a time when his remote ancestors ate their meat alive and communicated with each other, sometimes by grunts and gestures, but more often by means of a purely mental faculty that was later to evolve into the power of ocular hypnosis.

Half conscious or less of his surroundings but knowing well that death was very near, Sleemet half-consciously sent out his race's ages-old mental message-in-extremity of the dying.

Marc C. DuQuesne knew vastly more about the Fenachrone than did any other man alive, not excluding Richard Seaton. He and Seaton were, as far as is known, the only two men ever to meet Fenachrone mind to mind and live through the experience; but DuQuesne had been in thought-helmet contact with a Fenachrone much longer and much more intimately and very much more interestedly than Seaton ever had—because of the tremendous intrinsic differences between the personalities of the two men.

Seaton, after having crippled a war-vessel of the Fenachrone, had pinned its captain against a wall with so many beams of force that he could not move his head and could scarcely move any other part of his monstrous body. Then, by means of a pair of thought-helmets, he had taken what of that captain's knowledge he wanted. He had, however, handled that horribly unhuman brain very gingerly. He had merely read certain parts of it, as one reads an encyclopedia; at no time had his mind become *en rapport* with that of the monster. In fact, he had said to Crane:

"I'd hate to have much of that brain in my own skull—afraid I'd bite myself. I'm just going to look . . . and when I see something I want I'll grab it and put it into my own brain."

DuQuesne, however, in examining a navigating engineer of that monstrous race, had felt no such· revulsion, contrariwise—although possibly not quite consciously—he had admired certain traits of Fenachrone character so much that he had gone *en rapport* with that engineer's mind practically cell to cell; with the result that he had emerged from that mental union as nearly a Fenachrone himself as a human being could very well become.

Wherefore, as DuQuesne in his flying-planetoid-base approached the point of its course nearest to the planet Llurdiax, he began to feel the thinnest possible tendril of thought trying to make contact with one of the deepest chambers of his mind. He stiffened; shutting it off by using automatically an ability that he had not known consciously that he had. He relaxed; and, all interest now, tuned his mind to that feeler of thought, began to pull it in, and stopped—and the contact released a flood of Fenachrone knowledge completely new to him.

A Fenachrone, dying somewhere, wanted . . . wanted what? Not help, exactly. Notice? Attention? To *give* something? DuQuesne was not enough of a Fenachrone to translate that one thought even approximately, and he was not interested enough to waste any time on it. It had something to do with the good of the race; that was close enough.

DuQuesne, frowning a little, sat back in his bucket seat and thought. He had supposed that the Fenachrone were all dead . . . but it made sense that Seaton couldn't have killed *all* of a space-faring race, at that. But so what? He didn't care how many Fenachrone died. But a lot of their stuff was really good, and he certainly hadn't got it all yet, by any means; it might be smart to listen to what the dying monster had to say—especially since he, DuQuesne, was getting pretty close to the home grounds of Klazmon the Llurd.

Wherefore DuQuesne opened his mental shield: and, since his mind was still tuned precisely to the questing wave and since the *DQ* was now practically as close to Llurdiax as it would get on course 255U, he received a burst of thought that jarred him to the very teeth.

It is amazing how much information can be carried by a Fenachrone-compressed burst of thought. It was fortunate for DuQuesne that he had the purely Fenachrone abilities to decompress it, to spread it out and analyze it, and later, to absorb it fully.

The salient points, however, were pellucidly clear. The dying monster was First Scientist Fleet Admiral Sleemet; and he and more than four thousand other Fenachrone were helpless captives of and were being studied to death by Llurdan scientists under the personal direction of Llanzlan Klazmon.

Realizing instantly what that meant—Klazmon would be out here in seconds with a probe, if nothing stronger—DuQuesne slammed on full-coverage screens at full power, thus sealing his entire worldlet bottle-tight against any and every spy-ray, beam, probe, band, zone of force and/or order of force that he knew anything about. Since this included everything he had known before this trip began, plus everything he had learned from Freemind One and from the Jelmi and from Klazmon himself, he was grimly certain that he was just as safe as though he were in God's hip pocket from any possible form of three-dimensional observation or attack.

Cutting in his fourth-dimensional gizmo—how glad he was that he had studied it so long and so intensively that he knew more about it than its inventors did!—he flipped what he called its "eye" into the Fenachrone Reservation on distant Llurdiax. He seized Sleemet, bed and all, in a wrapping of force and deposited the bundle gently on the floor of the *DQ's* control room, practically at his, DuQuesne's feet. Fenachrone could breathe Earth air for hours without appreciable damage—they had proved that often enough—and if he decided to keep any of them alive he'd make them some air they liked better.

Second, he brought over a doctor, complete with kit and instruments and supplies; and third, the Fenachrone equivalent of a registered nurse.

"You, doctor!" DuQuesne snapped, in Fenachronian. "I don't know whether this spineless weakling is too far gone to save or not. Or whether he is worth saving or not. But since he was actually in charge of your expedition-to-preserve-the-race I will listen to what he has to say instead of blasting him out of hand. So give him a shot of the strongest stuff you have—or is he in greater need of food than of stimulant?"

DuQuesne did not know whether the doctor would co-operate with a human being or not. But he did—whether from lack of spirit of his own or from desire to save his chief, DuQuesne did not care enough to ask.

"Both," the doctor said, "but nourishment first, by all means. Intravenous, nurse, please," and doctor and nurse went to work with the skill and precision of their highly trained crafts.

And, somewhat to DuQuesne's surprise, Sleemet began immediately to rally; and in three-quarters of an hour he had regained full consciousness.

"You spineless worm!" DuQuesne shot at the erstwhile invalid, in true Fenachrone tone and spirit. "You gutless wonder! You pusillanimous weakling, you sniveling coward! Is it the act of a noble of the Fenachrone to give up, to yield supinely, to surrender ignominiously to a fate however malign while a spark of life endures?"

Sleemet was scarcely stirred by this vicious castigation. He raised dull eyes—eyes shockingly lifeless to anyone who had ever seen the ruby-lighted, flame-shot wells of vibrant force that normal Fenachrone eyes were—and said lifelessly, "There is a point, the certainty of death, at which struggle becomes negative instead of positive. It merely prolongs the agony. Having passed that point, I die."

"There is no such point, idiot, while life lasts! Do I look like Klazmon of Llurdiax?"

"No, but death is no less certain at your hands than at his."

"Why should it be, stupid?" and DuQuesne's sneer was extra-high-voltage stuff, even for Doctor Marc C. DuQuesne.

Now was the crucial moment. IF he could take all those Fenachrone over, and IF he could control them after they got back to normal, *what* a crew they would make! He stared contemptuously at the ex-admiral and went on:

"Whether or not you and your four thousand die in the near future is up to you. While I do not have to have a crew, I can use one efficiently for a few weeks. If you choose to work with me I will, at the end of that time, give you a duplicate of your original spaceship and will see to it that you are allowed to resume your journey wherever you wish."

"Sir, the Fenachrone do not . . ." the doctor began stiffly.

"Shut up, you poor, dumb clown!" DuQuesne snapped.

"Haven't you learned *anything?* That instead of being the strongest race in space you are one of the weakest? You have one choice merely—cooperate or die. And that is not yours, but Sleemet's. Sleemet?"

"But how do I know that if . . ."

"If you have any part of a brain, fool, use it! What matters it to me whether Fenachrone live or die? I'm not asking you anything; I'm telling you under what conditions I will save your lives. If you want to argue the matter I'll put you three—and the bed—back where you were and be on my way. Which do you prefer?"

Sleemet had learned something. He had been beaten down flat enough so that he could learn something—and he realized that he had much to learn from any race who could do what his rescuer had just done.

"We will work with you," Sleemet said. "You will, I trust, instruct us concerning how you liberated us three and propose to liberate the others?"

"I can't. It was fourth-dimensional translation." DuQuesne lied blandly. "Did you ever try to explain the color 'blue' to a man born blind? No scientist of your race will be able to understand either the theory or the mechanics of fourth dimensional translation for something like eleven hundred thousand of your years."

24 • DU QUESNE AND SLEEMET

EN route to the galaxy in which DuQuesne's aliens supposedly lived, Dorothy said, "Say Dick. I forgot to ask you something. What did you ever find out about that thought business of Kay-Lee's?"

"Huh?" Seaton was surprised. "What was there to find out? How are you going to explain the mechanism of thought—by unscrewing the inscrutable? She said, and I quote, 'We didn't feel that we were quite reaching you,' unquote. So it was she and Ree-Toe Prenk. Obviously. Holding hands or something—across a Ouija board or some other focusing device, probably. Staring into each other's eyes to link minds and direct the thought."

"But they *did* hit you with something," she insisted, "and it bothers me. They can do it and we can't."

"No sweat, pet. That isn't a circumstance to what you do every time you think at a controller to order up a meal or whatever. How do you do that? Different people, different abilities, is all. Anyway, Earth mediums have done that kind of thing for ages. If you're really interested, you can take some time off and learn it, next time we're on Ray-See-Nee. But for right now, my red-headed beauty, we've got something besides that kind of monkey-business to worry about."

"That's right, we have," and Dorothy forgot the minor matter in thinking of the major. "Those aliens. Have you and Martin figured out a *modus operandi?*"

"More or less. Go in openly, like tourists, but with everything we've got not only on the trips but hyped up to as nearly absolutely instantaneous reactivity as the Brain can possibly get it."

Both DuQuesne's *DQ* and Seaton's *Skylark of Valeron* were within range of Llurdiax. DuQuesne, however, as has been said, was covering up as tightly as he could. Everything that could be muzzled or muffled was muzzled or muffled, and he was traveling comparatively slowly, so as to put out the minimum of detectable high-order emanation. Furthermore, his screens were shoved out to such a tremendous distance, and were being varied so rapidly and so radically in shape, that no real pattern existed to be read. The *DQ* was not indetectable, of course, but it would have taken a great deal of highly specialized observation and analysis to find her.

The *Skylark of Valeron,* on the other hand, was coming in wide open: "Like a tourist," as Seaton had told Dorothy the plan was to do.

In the llanzlanate on Llurdiax, therefore, an observer alerted Klazmon, who flew immediately to his master-control panel. He checked the figures the observer had given him, and was as nearly appalled as a Llurd could become. An artificial structure of that size and mass—it was certainly not a natural planetoid—had never even been thought of by any builder of record. He measured its acceleration—the *Valeron* was still braking down at max—

and his eyes bulged. That thing, tremendous as it was, had the power-to-mass ratio of a speedster! In spite of its immense size it was actually an intergalactic flyer!

He launched a probe, as he had done so many times before—but with entirely unexpected results.

The stranger's guardian screens were a hundred times as reactive as any known to Llurdan science. He was not allowed time for even the briefest of mental contacts or for any real observation at all. So infinitesimal had been the instant usable time that only one fact was clear. The entities in that mobile monstrosity were—positively—Jelmoids.

Not true Jelmi, certainly. He knew all about the Jelmi. Those tapes bore unmistakable internal evidence of being true and complete records and there was no hint anywhere in them of anything like this. If not the Jelmi, who? Ah, yes, the Fenachrone, whose fleet . . . no, Sleemet knew nothing of such a construction . . . and he was not exactly of the same race . . . ah, yes, that one much larger ship that had escaped. The probability was high that its one occupant belonged to precisely the same Jelmoid race as did the personnel of this planetoid. The escaped one had reported Klazmon's cursory investigation as an attack. It was a virtual certainty, therefore, that this was a battleship of that race, heading for Llurdiax to . . . to what? To investigate merely? No.

Nor merely to parley. They had made no attempt whatever to communicate. (It did not occur to Klazmon, then or ever, that his own fiercely driven probe could not possibly have been taken for an attempt at communication. He had fully intended to communicate, as soon as he had seized the mind of whoever was in command of the strange spacecraft.) And now, with the stranger's incredible full-coverage screen in operation, communication was and would remain impossible.

But he had data sufficient for action. These Jelmoids, like all others he knew, were rabidly anti-social, illogical, unreasoning, unsane and insane. They were—definitely—surplus population.

So thinking, Llanzlan Klazmon launched his attack.

As the *Skylark* entered that enigmatic galaxy, Seaton was not in his home, with only a remote-control helmet with which to work. He was in the control room itself, at the base of the Brain, with the tremendously complex-master-control itself surrounding his head. Thus he was attuned to and in instantaneous contact with every activated cell of that gigantic Brain. It was ready to receive and to act upon with the transfinite speed of thought any order that Seaton would think. Nor would any such action interfere in any way with the automatics that Seaton had already set up.

"I'm going to stay here all day," Seaton said, "and all night tonight, too, if necessary."

But he did not have to stay there even all day. In less than four hours the Ilanzlan drove his probe and Seaton probed practically instantaneously back. And since Seaton's hyped-up screens were a hundred times faster than the Llurd's, Seaton "saw" a hundred times as much as Klazmon did. He saw the city Llurdias in all its seat-of-empire pride and glory. He perceived its miles-wide girdle of fortresses. He perceived the llanzlanate; understood its functions and purposes. He entered the Hall of Computation and examined minutely the beings and the machines at work there.

How could all this be? Because the speed of thought, if not absolutely infinite, is at least transfinite; immeasurable to man. And the *Valeron's* inorganic brain and Seaton's organic one were, absolutely and super-intimately, the two component parts of one incredibly able, efficient and proficient whole.

Thus, when the alien's attack was launched in all its fury and almost all of the *Valeron's* mighty defensive engines went simultaneously into automatic action, the coded chirpings that the Brain employed to summon human help did not sound: that Brain's builder, fellow, boss, and perfect complement was already on the job.

And thus, since no warning had been given, the other Skylarkers were surprised when Seaton called them all down into the control room.

They were even more surprised when they saw how white and strained his face was.

"This may become ver*ee* unfunny," he said. " 'Tsa good thing I muscled her up or we'd be losing some skin and some of our defense. As it is, we're holding 'em and we've got a few megas in reserve. Not enough to be really happy about, but some. And we're building more, of course. *However*, that ape down there has undoubtedly got a lot of stuff otherwheres on the planet that he can hook in pretty fast, so whatever we're going to do we'd better do right now."

"They didn't try to communicate at all?" Crane asked. "Strange for a race of such obviously high attainments."

"Not a lick," Seaton said, flatly. "Just a probe; the hard-

est and sharpest probe I ever saw. When I blocked it—
Whammo!"

"You probed, too, of course," Dorothy said. "What did
you find out? Are they really monstrous, as DuQuesne said,
out purely to kill?"

"Just that. He wasn't lying a nickel's worth on that. His
Nibs down there had already decided that we were surplus
population and should be eliminated, and he set right out
to do it. So, unless some of you have some mighty valid
reasons not to, I'm going to try my damndest to eliminate
him, right now."

"We *could* run, I suppose," Margaret suggested—but not
at all enthusiastically.

"I doubt it. Not without letting him burn us down to
basketball size, like the Chlorans did. He undoubtedly let
us get this close on purpose so we couldn't."

Since no one else said anything, Seaton energized everything of offense he had. He tuned it as precisely as he possibly could. He assembled it into the tightest, solidest, hardest beam he could possibly build. Then, involuntarily tens-
ing his muscles and hunching his back, he drove the whole
gigantic thing squarely at where he knew the llanzlanate
was.

The Llurd's outer screen scarcely flickered as it went
black in nothing flat of time. The intermediate screen held
for eighty-three hundredths of a second. Then the practically irresistible force of that beam met the practically
immovable object that was Klazmon's last line of defense.
And as it clawed and bit and tore and smashed in ultra-
pyrotechnic ferocity, solar-like flares of raw energy erupted
from the area of contact and the very ether writhed and
seethed and warped under the intolerable stresses of the
utterly incomprehensible forces there at grips.

This went on . . . and on . . . and on.

Even to Seaton, who knew only that he was up against
an enemy nearly as potent as the Chlorans, the full import
of the enormous struggle of energies then being waged was
far from clear. We can wonder now, and ask ourselves what
the fate of the universe might have been if the *Skylark's*
Norlaminian designers had skimped on a course of screens,
or overlooked a detail of defense. Surely its consequences
would have been cataclysmic! Not only to Seaton and his
Skylarker, watching grim-faced as their gauges revealed the
enormous flow of destructive forces battling each other to
annihilation for countless parsecs in every direction. Not

only to the Jelmi, or the Rey-See-Neese, or the Norlaminians, or Earth itself . . . but to countless generations yet unborn, on planets not yet discovered . . .

But they held.

And after ten endless minutes of such terrible gouts and blasts of destruction as no planet could endure for a moment, Seaton heard a voice speak to him.

He had never heard it before, but it said in good American English: "Good morning, my friends. Or perhaps, by your clocks, it is good afternoon? I am the Llanzlan Mergon of Jelm, and I perceive that you are under attack by our old acquaintances, the Llurdi. You, I am sure, are the Seatons and the Cranes, about whom we heard so much on Earth, but whom we were not able to find."

Even though the Llurdi had been absolute rulers of all the planets of the Jelmi for many thousands of years, it was easy for them to accept, and to adopt themselves to, the new condition of coexistence with the Realm of the Jelmi on terms of equality. That was the way they were built.

The llanzlan fed the new data into Computer Prime and issued its findings as a directive. Since this directive was the product of pure logic, that was all there was to it.

With the Jelmi, however, even with a much simpler and easier agenda, things were distinctly otherwise. Everyone knows how difficult it is to change the political thinking of even a part of any human world. How, then, of the two hundred forty whole planets of the Jelmi? The conservatives did not want any change at all. Not even to independence. The radicals wanted everything changed; but each faction wanted each item changed in a different fashion. And the moderates, as usual, did not agree with either extreme wing on anything.

And, also as usual, no one faction would play ball with any other. Each would have its own way in setting up the Realm or there would be no Realm—it would pick up its marbles and go home.

Fortunately, however, the eight hundred best brains of the entire Jelman race were together in one place—in the fully operative base that the *Mallidaxian's* dome had now become. Their numbers included the most capable and most highly trained specialists in every field of Jelman endeavor and they all had been living together and working together for many months.

They knew better than to go off half cocked. They would have to develop a master-plan upon which they could all agree. Unanimously. Nothing less would do. Having developed such a plan they would put it into effect, each person or planetary group upon his or her or their home world. The constitution thus fabricated would be put into effect by reason if possible, by force if necessary. It was not to be amended except by process contained within itself.

Thus the Constitutional Committee of Eight Hundred was still living in the base and was still hard at work when the Officer of the Day called Mergon—who, after glancing at plates and instruments, called Luloy.

The ether was showing strains of a magnitude not observed since the Battle for Independence. A Llurd ship was putting out everything he had; fighting full-out against a—*something*—whose battle-screen covered such an immensity of space that Mergon could scarcely believe his instruments.

Luloy quirked an eyebrow. "Well, what are we waiting for?"

"Nothing," and Mergon, who could now handle projections through the fourth dimension, launched them. "I'll keep us invisible while we see what that thing is and how big it really is."

They went and saw—and the more they studied the immensity that was the *Skylark of Valeron* the more they marveled. Finally, in the *Valeron's* control room and still invisible, they studied the worldlet's personnel; the while talking to each other in the flesh at the *Mallidaxian's* main panel.

"Except for the green-skinned couple they *are* Tellurians," the girl insisted. "Everything about that—that ship, if you can call it a ship—is Tellurian. Just *look* at those clothes. You never saw anything like that anywhere except on Tellus and you never will."

"We never heard anything about anything like that mobile fortress on Tellus, either," he objected, "and we certainly would have if they'd known anything about it. How could they hide it?"

"Maybe it's so new that not too many people know about it yet. Anyway, whatever the truth about that, we heard a lot about Seaton and Crane. Especially Seaton. According to the lore, he's their principal god's right-hand man. He can do *anything.*"

"Or a devil's, depending on who you talked to. But we wrote that off as just that—lore. If not propaganda."

"We'll have to write it back on again. Those two *have* to be Seaton and Crane—there, the Jelm-sized one with his head in the controller, and that other bean-pole type standing there smoking a . . . a cigarette, they call it. And that smoking business clinches it. *Nobody* but Tellurians burn their lungs out with smoke."

"Okay." Mergon thickened their projections up to full visibility and spoke:

"You must be the Seatons and the Cranes, about whom we heard so much on Earth but whom we were not able to find."

Crane the Imperturbable was startled out of his imperturbability when Mergon and Luloy appeared in the *Valeron's* control room and Mergon spoke to him in English. But he did not show it—very much!—and realized in a moment what the truth was.

"We are," Crane said, stepping forward and holding out his hand. These people would understand the gesture. "I'm M. Reynolds Crane; Doctor Seaton is occupied at the moment. You are of course the people who had the spaceship on the moon. We have come all the way out here in the hope of finding you somewhere in this galaxy."

"Oh? Oh, you want the fourth-dimensional device."

"Exactly." Crane then introduced the others, and finally Seaton; who, having assured himself that the Brain could handle the stalemate without him, had disengaged himself from the master controller and had joined the party.

"That's right," Seaton said. "Since nothing like it is known to any science with which we are familiar, we hope to learn about it from you. But that . . . those monsters . . . they aren't, by any chance, friends of yours, are they?"

Luloy laughed. "No. Not exactly . . . or maybe they are, after a fashion, now. But the Llurdi were our unquestioned masters for so many thousands of years that they haven't yet decided to treat us or anyone who looks like us with the courtesy reserved for equals. You see, the llanzlan would have communicated with you in thought after he had investigated you a little."

"Yeah." Seaton's smile was grim. "With the stiffest, hardest probe he could build? And I'm supposed to sit still for that kind of manhandling?"

"No." Mergon took over. "No one but a Llurd could have expected you to. This situation is somewhat unfortunate. Until very recently they have always had overwhelmingly superior power. They never had any effective opposition until we wore them down a little, just recently." Mergon explained the situation in as few words as possible, concluding, "So this battle, while not due exactly to mis-understanding, is unfortunate. What I propose is that Luloy and I visit Klazmon via projection, as we are now visiting you, and explain matters to him as we have explained them to you. I take it you will cease fire if he does?"

"Of course. We didn't come here to start a war, or to bother him in any way; just to see you. So I'll do better than that; I'll cut my offense right now."

He thought at the Brain and the raging inferno above the llanzlanate went suddenly calm and still. "That beam is *no* pencil of force, believe me. If it should get through it would volatilize his palace and half the city, and that would be unfortunate—hey! He's quit slugging, too!"

"Of course," Mergon said. "As I told you, he is—all Llurdi are—completely and perfectly logical. With their own brand of logic, of course. Insanely logical, to our way of thinking . . . or perhaps *un*sanely may be the better word. On the basis of the data he then had it was logical for him to attack you. Your cease-fire was a new datum, one that he cannot as yet evaluate. He has deduced the fact that we Jelmi caused it, but he does not know why you stopped. Hence he has restored the *status quo ante,* pending our explanation. He wants additional data. If our explanation is satisfactory—data sufficient—he'll probably just let the whole matter drop. If not—if it's data insufficient—I wouldn't know. He'll do whatever he decides is the logical thing to do—which is 'way beyond my guess-point. He might even resume the attack exactly where he left off; although I think he'll be able to deduce a reason not to."

Seaton whistled through his teeth. "Holy . . . cat!" he said. "If that's pure logic I'll take vanilla. But how will you make the approach?"

"Very easily. If two of you will permit us to bring you over here we will send four working projections into the Llanzlan Klazmon's study, where I'm sure he's expecting us. You, Doctor Seaton, and your Dorothy, perhaps?"

"Not I!" Dorothy declared, shaking her head vigorously. "Uh-uh. Into battle, yes; this, no. If I never see a monster like that it'll be twenty minutes too soon. You're it, Martin."

"One more thing," Mergon went on, as Seaton and Crane appeared in the flesh beside him. "Since the Llurdi refuse to learn any language except their own, I must teach you Llurdan," and he held out two Jelman thought-caps.

"I prefer my own," Seaton said, after a very short trial.

"So will you, I think," and he sent back for four of the *Skylark's* latest models.

The two Jelmi put two of them on. "Oh, I do indeed!" Luloy exclaimed, and Mergon added, "As was to have been expected, we have much to learn from you, friends."

"But listen," Seaton said. "You gave the ape all the dope on that fourth-dimensional thing. Isn't he apt to toss a superatomic into our Brain with it?"

"There's no possibility whatever of that, either soon or later. Not soon because, since they work slowly and thoroughly, it will be months yet before they have a full-scale machine. Nor later, because the mutual destruction of four hundred eighty-two populated planets—excuse me, four hundred eighty, now—is not logical in any system of logic, however cockeyed that system may be."

It took Seaton a fraction of a second to get it, but when he did, it rocked him. "Oh! I hadn't figured on you coming all the way in. But does he know you will?"

"He certainly does know it!" Luloy broke in. "Beyond a doubt; or what you call peradventure."

"Oh," Seaton said again. "And that's why he isn't going to resume hostilities wih ordinary weapons, either? Thanks, you two, a million. We appreciate it. Okay; we're ready, I guess."

The four projections appeared in front of the llanzlan's desk. He was expecting them. "Well?" he asked.

Mergon began to explain, but Seaton cut him off. Mergon could not possibly feel equal to Klazmon in a face-to-face; Seaton could and did.

"I can explain us better than you can, friend Mergon," he said. Then, to the Llurd, "We came here to visit the human beings whom you call the Jelmi. We did not have, have not now, and do not expect to have any interest whatever in you Llurdi or in anything Llurdan. Our purpose is to promote intergalactic commerce and interhuman friendship. The various human races have different abilities and different artifacts and different knowledges—many of each of which are of benefit to other human races.

"You made an unprovoked attack on us. Know now, Llanzlan Klazmon, that I do not permit invasion, either mental or physical, by any entity—man, beast, god, devil or Llurd—of this or of any other galaxy. Although I can imagine few subjects upon which you and I could converse profitably, if you wish to talk to me as one intelligent and logical entity to another I will so converse. But I repeat—I will not permit invasion.

"If you wish to resume battle on that account that is your right and your privilege. You will note, however, that our attack was metered precisely to a point just below your maximum capability of resistance. Know now that if you force us to destroy your city and perhaps your world it will not have been the first city or the first world we have been forced to destroy; nor, with a probability of point nine nine nine, will it have been the last. Do you want peace with us or war?"

"Peace. Data sufficient," Klazmon said immediately. "I have recorded the fact that there is at least one Jelmoid race other than the Jelmi themselves of which some representatives are both able and willing to employ almost Llurdan logic," and he switched his attention from the projections to the tape he had been studying—cutting communications as effectively as though he had removed himself to another world.

Back in the *Mallidaxian*, while Luloy stared at Seaton almost in awe, Mergon said, "That was a beautiful job, Doctor Seaton. Perfect! Much better than I could have done. You used flawless Llurdan logic."

"Thanks to the ace in the hole you gave me with your briefing, I could do it. I'd hate to have to run a bluff on *that* ape. What's next on the agenda, Savant Mergon?"

"Make it 'Merg', please, and I'll call you 'Dick'. Now that this is settled, why don't you put your fortress-planetoid on automatic and let us bring you all here, so that our peoples may become friends in person and may begin work upon tasks of mutual interest?"

"That's a thought, friend; that really is a thought," Seaton said, and it was done forthwith.

Aboard the *Mallidaxian*, Seaton cut the social amenities as short as he courteously could; then went with inseparable Mergon and Luloy to Tammon's laboratory. That fourth-dimensional gizmo was what he was interested in. With his single-mindedness that was all he was interested in, at the moment, of the entire Jelman culture. All four donned Skylark thought-helmets and Seaton set out to learn everything there was to be known about that eight million cubic feet of esoteric apparatus. And Mergon, who didn't know much of anything about recent developments, was eager to catch up.

Seaton did not learn all about the fourth-dimensional

device in one day, nor in one week; but when he had it all filed away in the Brain he asked, "Is that all you have of it?" He did not mean to be insulting; he was only greatly surprised.

The old savant bristled and Seaton apologized hastily. "I didn't mean to belittle your achievement in any sense, sir. It's probably the greatest breakthrough ever made. But it doesn't seem to be complete."

"Of course it isn't complete!" Tammon snapped. "I've been working on it only—"

"Oh, I didn't mean that," Seaton broke in. "The *concept* is incomplete. In several ways. For instance, if fourth-dimensional translation is used as a weapon, you have no defense against it."

"Of course there's no defense against it!" Tammon defended his brain-child like a tigress defending her young. "By the very nature of things there *can't* be any defense against it!"

At that, politeness went by the board. "You're wrong," Seaton said, flatly. "By the very nature of things there has to be. All nature is built on a system of checks and balances. Doing a job so terrifically big and so brand new, I doubt if anybody could get the whole thing at once. Let's go over the theory again, together, with a microscope, to see if we can't add something to it somewhere?"

Tammon agreed, but reluctantly. Deep down in his own mind he did not believe that any other mind could improve upon any particular of his work. As the review progressed, however, he became more and more enthusiastic. As well he might; for the mathematics section of Richard Seaton's multi-compartmented mind contained, indexed and cross-indexed, all the work done by countless grand masters of the subject during half a million years.

Luloy started to pull her helmet off, but Mergon stopped her with a direct thought. "I'm lost, too, sweet, but keep on listening. We can get bits here and there—and we'll probably never have the chance again to watch two such minds at work."

"Hold it!" Seaton snapped, half an hour later. "Back up —there! This integral here. Limits zero to pi over two. You're limiting the thing to a large but definitely limited volume of your generalized N-dimensional space. I think it should be between zero and infinity—and while we're at it let's scrap half of the third determinant in that no-space-no-time complex. Let's see what happens if we substitute the gamma function here and the chi there and the xi there and the omicron down there in the corner."

"But *why?*" the old savant protested. "I don't see any possible reason for any of it."

Seaton grinned. "There isn't any—any more than there was for your original brainstorm. If there had been the Norlaminian would have worked this whole shebang out a hundred thousand years ago. It's nothing but a hunch, but it's strong enough so I want to follow it up—okay? Fine then, integrating that, we get . . ."

Five hours later, Tammon took his helmet off and stared at Seaton with wonder in his eyes. "Do you realize just what you've done, young man? You have made a breakthough at least equal to my own. Opened up a whole vast new field—a field parallel to my own, perhaps, but in no sense the same."

"I wouldn't say that. Merely an enlargement. All I did was follow a hunch."

"An intuition," Tammon corrected him. "What else, pray, makes breakthroughs?"

And Luloy, on the way out of the laboratory hand in hand with Mergon, said, "I had no idea that Tellus ever did or ever could produce anybody like *him*. He *is* their god's fair-haired child, for a fact. Sennlloy will have to know about this, Merg."

"She will indeed—I was sure you'd think of that."

And as soon as Dorothy could get Seaton alone that evening she stared at him with a variety of emotions playing over her face. As though she had never seen him before; or as though she were getting acquainted with him all over again. "I've been talking to Sennlloy," she announced. "Or, rather, she's been talking to me. She didn't lose much time, did she?"

Seaton blushed to the roots of his hair. "I'll say she didn't. Not any. She knocked me for a block-long row of ash cans."

"Uh-huh. Me, too—*and how!* She told me you said I'd blow my red top and I just about did, until she explained. She's *quite* a gal, isn't she? And *what* a shape! You know, I'm awfully glad I'm not too bad in that shape department myself, or I'd die of mortification looking at them? But Dick—don't you suppose there are any people in this whole cockeyed universe except us and the Rayseenians who don't run around naked all the time?"

"I wouldn't know; but what has all that got to do with the price of hasheesh c.i.f. Istanbul?"

"It ties in. She must have thought I was some kind of an idiot child, but she didn't show it. She couldn't really understand my taboos, she said, since they were not in her own heredity, but she could accept them as facts in mine and work within their limitations." Dorothy blushed, but went on, "I'd be the only Prime Operator—and so forth. You know about the 'and so forth'. Anyway, before she got done she actually made me feel ashamed of myself! They really *need* your genes, Dick. You didn't let on, did you, that DuQuesne's a Tellurian, too?"

"I'll say I didn't! The less they think that ape and I came from the same world, the better I'll like it."

"You and me both. Well, she didn't actually *say* so, but when she found out what kind of genes *you* have she decided to pour every one of DuQuesne's right down the drain."

"Could be." Seaton didn't agree with that conclusion at all, but he was too smart to argue the point.

At breakfast the following morning Seaton said, "You chirped it, birdie, about their thinking us some kind of idiot children. Besides, the First Principle and Prime Tenet of all diplomacy has always been, 'When in Rome be a Roman candle'. So I think we'd all better peel to the raw as of now. You and I had better, whether the rest do or not. Check?"

"Check—but I think they will. We're horribly conspicuous, dressed. People look at us as though we were things that had escaped from a zoo. And all the Green System people have always thought we were more than somewhat loco in the coco for covering up so much. We'll get used to it easily enough—look at the nudists. So lead on, my bold and valiant—I follow thee to the bitter end of all my raiment."

"I knew you would, ace. Let's go spread the gospel."

When they approached the Cranes and the Japanese on the subject, Margaret threw back her black-thatched head and laughed. "We must be psychic—we were going to spring the same thing on you. And after all, actually, how much do our bathing suits hide? Yours or mine either one? And we have it to show, too—so here goes! The last one undressed is Stinker of the Day!" She began to unzip, then paused and looked at Lotus.

The Nisei girl shrugged. "We all should, of course, I

won't like it and I positively know I'll never get used to it, but if you two do I will too if it kills me."

" 'At-a-girl, Lambie!" Margaret put her arm around the beautifully formed little body and squeezed. "But you just wait—you'll have it really made. None of them ever saw anything like *you* before, you gorgeous little doll, you. With your size and build you'll be the absolute Queen of the May!"

25 • ROMAN CANDLES

COUNTLESS parsecs away, Marc C. DuQuesne was carrying out his own plans—plans which would have been a most unpleasant surprise for the Skylarkers had they known about them.

DuQuesne moved the surviving Fenachrone into his *DQ* easily enough and without incident. Housing was no problem. How could it be, with millions upon millions of cubic kilometers of space available and with automatic high-order constructors to do the work? Nor was atmosphere, nor food nor any other necessity or desideratum of Fenachronian life and/or well-being a problem.

Fenachrone engineers did it all—by operating special keyboards and by thinking into carefully limited headsets—but none of them had any idea whatever of what it was that did any given task or how it did it. None of this knowledge, of either practice or theory, was in their science; and DuQuesne took great pains to be sure that none of them got any chance to learn any iota of it. He taught them, and they learned, purely by rote.

Like high-school girls learning to drive automobiles. They can become excellent drivers; but with only that type of instruction none of them will ever become able to design a hypoid gear or to understand in detail the operation of an automatic clutch.

The Fenachrone did not like such treatment. Sleemet in

particular, when he began to recover some of the normal pugnaciously prideful spirit of his race, did not like it at all and said so; but DuQuesne did not care a particle whether he liked it or not.

DuQuesne's snapping black eyes stared, contemptuously unaffected, into the furiously hypnotic, red-lighted black eyes of the Fenachrone. "You megalomaniacal cretin," he sneered. "How can you possibly figure that it makes any difference whatever to me, what you like or don't like? If you have any fraction of a brain you'd better start using it. If you haven't or can't or won't, I'll build you a duplicate of your original ship and turn you all loose today."

"You will? In that case—" Sleemet got that far and stopped cold in mid-sentence.

"Yeah." DuQuesne's tone cut like a knife. "Exactly. We're still within Klazmon's range; we will be for quite a while yet. Do you want to be turned loose here?"

"Well, no." If the thought occurred to him that DuQuesne was lying, he didn't show it. That was just as well for Sleemet and for the Fenachrone race. DuQuesne wasn't.

"Maybe you have a brain of sorts, at that. But if you don't forget this Master Race flapdoodle, all of it and fast, you'll last quick. Remember how easily that self-styled Overlord wiped out your navy and then volatilized your whole stinking world? And how easily Klazmon of Llurdiax smacked your whole fleet down? And what a fool I made and am still making of Klazmon? And I know of one race that is as much ahead of mine as I am ahead of you; and of another race that may be somewhat ahead of us Xylmnians in some ways. As I said, you're about eleven hundred thousand years behind. Have you got brains enough to realize that instead of being top dog you're just low man on the totem pole?"

"If you're so high and we're so low," Sleemet snarled, "why did you take us away from the Llurd? Of what possible use can we be to you?"

"You have certain mental and physical qualities that may perhaps be of use in a project I have in mind. You are not only able and willing to fight, you really *like* to fight. These qualities should, theoretically, make you better in some respects than automatics in operating the offensive weapons of a base as large as this one is." DuQuesne studied the Fenachrone appraisingly. "I do not really need you, but I am willing to make the experiment on the terms I have stated. I will allow you two Xylmnian minutes in which to decide whether or not to cooperate with me in such an experiment."

"We will cooperate," Sleemet said in less than one minute; whereupon DuQuesne told him in broad terms what he had in mind.

And for many days thereafter the two, so unlike physically but so similar in so many respects mentally, devoted themselves wholeheartedly to the finer and ever finer refinement of the placing and tuning of mechanisms and of the training of already hard-trained personnel.

But DuQuesne knew that, given the slightest opportunity, the Fenachrone would take high delight in killing him and taking the *DQ*. Wherefore he did not at any time trust any one of them as far as he could spit.

Moreover, DuQuesne was not quite as sure of his own victory as he had given the Fenachrone to understand.

DuQuesne was not easy in his mind about Galaxy DW-427-LU. He hadn't been, not since some superpowered enemy in that galaxy had attacked Seaton's *Skylark of Valeron* without warning and had burned her down to a core before she could get out of range. And she hadn't been able to fight back. That one blast back at them couldn't have done any damage.

It had been that uneasiness that had been responsible for the *DQ's* terrific armament and for DuQuesne's wanting the Fenachrone for a crew. Wherefore, as soon as the Fenachrone were settled in their new quarters and before they had recovered enough of their normal combativeness to become completely unmanageable, DuQuesne got "on the com" with Sleemet.

". . . I don't give a damn what happens to Earth or to Norlamin. I'm no longer interested in either," he said in part. "But I don't want it to happen to me and you don't want it to happen to you. You agree with me, I'm sure, that a good strategist does not leave an enemy behind him without knowing, at very least, who that enemy is and what he can do."

"That is one of the basics, yes."

"All right. Somebody in this galaxy here has more muscle than I like." DuQuesne pointed out Galaxy DW-427-LU in his tank and told Sleemet what had happened to the *Skylark of Valeron,* then went on, "On theoretical grounds, the degree of synchronization could make all the difference." He had reached by theory the same point that Seaton had arrived at by experience. "Hence, the greater the number of operators—of equal skill, of course—the tighter the output. The efficiency will vary directly as the cube of the number of operators."

"I see." Sleemet did see, and for the first time became really interested. "That will be to our advantage as well as yours. You will have to teach us much."

"I'll teach you everything you have to know. Nothing else."

"That is assumed . . . But I see no possibility of assurance that you will keep your bargain . . . or will you go mind to mind that you will release us and build us a ship after this one expedition as your crew?"

"Yes. Without reservation."

"In that case we will cooperate fully."

And they did—and so it was that the *DQ* became the most fantastically armed and powered and defended fortress that had ever moved its own mass through space.

As the *DQ* approached Galaxy DW-427-LU, with everything she had either wide open or on the trips, DuQuesne braked her down and swung into what he called "the curve of fastest getaway"—and as he did so, in the instant, the mighty vessel's every defense went blinding-white.

And in that same instant two thousand nine hundred seventy-seven Fenachrone, males and females but superlatively expert technicians all, pressed activating switches and took command, each of a tightly clustered battery of micrometrically synchronized generators.

And one black-browed, hard-eyed Tellurian, sat with his head buried in the *DQ's* master-control helmet.

While he had not expected to find any significant fraction of what he actually found, he was not too appalled to go viciously and pin-point-accurately to work. Working through the fourth dimension, with the transfinite speed of thought, he hurled bomb after bomb after multi-billion-kiloton superatomic bomb: and the target world of each one of those bombs became a sun.

And the *DQ* got away. She was by no means intact; but, since her skin had been very much thicker than the *Valeron's* to start with, there was still some of it left when she got out of range.

Thereupon DuQuesne put on the headset of the *DQ's* Brain and began to think. He had tried direct attack on the galaxy of Chlorans; it had failed. His next step, obviously, was—to decide what his next step should be.

The flesh-and-blood brain that was thinking into the

energy-and-metal Brain of the *DQ* was no whit less logical, no iota less unsentimental in its judgments than the great computer itself. Man-brain and machine-brain together considered the evidence. *Datum:* The *DQ* was not up to handling Galaxy DW-427-LU. *Datum:* Not even the added muscle conferred by the willing cooperation of the Fenachrone was enough to make it so. *Datum:* No discoverable increase of its armaments or its crew would give it even a fighting chance against the energies that had just come so close to destroying it.

Wherefore—

Finally, an hour later, DuQuesne raised the microphone of a repeating sixth-order broadcasting transmitter to his lips and said—dispassionately, unemotionally and with no more expression than if he had been ordering up his lunch:

"DuQuesne calling Seaton reply as before stop."

26 • THE TALENT

SEATON had thought that the visit to the Jelmi would be a short one, just long enough to get the "gizmo", but his own breakthrough put an end to such thinking. It took days to explored area of knowledge, to be fitted somehow into the *Skylark of Valeron* the gigantic installations Seaton wanted.

The very enormity of the breakthrough changed all plans, dislocated all schedules. To the Jelmi the fourth-dimensional translator had been a phenomenon—a weapon—in itself. It had extremely valuable applications, and each of them offered a long career of study. That was enough for them. But to Seaton and Crane and the Norlaminians it was something more than that; it was an effect, a new and unexplored area of knowledge, o be fitted somehow into the known and computed structure of sixth-order—perhaps of other-order—effects; and to be used and considered in conjunction with them. It was a theorist's dream—and an engineer's nightmare.

Meanwhile, as the male Skylarkers, their Jelm colleagues

and the Norlaminians were busily getting done the impossible task of exploring a whole new field of knowledge and transmuting it into actual structures and gigantic machines, the women of the party were exploring the life of an alien race . . . and having the time of their respective lives doing it. Sitar, of course, was in her element. Bare skin and jewelry she liked. She liked to look at and to feel her mink coat, she said, but she hated to have to wear it; and as for that horrible, scratchy underwear—augh! Hence, now that the personal gravity controls were personal heaters as well, she was really enjoying herself.

Dorothy and Margaret, of course, took to it as though to the manner born. In three days neither of them was any more conscious of nudity than was Sennlloy herself. Even Lotus got used to it. While she could never become an enthusiastic nudist, she said, she did stop blushing. In fact, she almost stopped feeling like blushing.

"Dick," Dorothy said one evening, "I've finally made contact with them on music."

"Music!" he snorted. "Huh! It sounds to me like a gaggle of tomcats yowling on a back fence."

She laughed. "It's unworldly, of course, but a lot of it is beautiful, in a weird sort of way, and they have some magnificent techniques. I've been trying everything on them, you know, and they've just been sitting on their hands. I'll give you three guesses as to what I finally hit them with."

"Strauss waltzes? Jazz? *Don't* tell me it was rock-'n'-roll."

She laughed. "Old-fashioned ragtime. Not what they call rag these days, but real syncopation. And polkas. Specifically, three old, old recordings—with improved sound, of course. Pee Wee Hunt's *Twelfth Street Rag,* Plehal Brothers' *Beer Barrel Polka,* and—of all things!—Glahe Musette's *Hot Pretzels*. They simply grabbed the ball and ran all over the place with it. What they came up with is neither rag nor polka—in fact, it's like nothing ever heard before on any world—but it's really toe-tingling stuff. Comes the dance tomorrow evening I'll show you some steps and leaps and bounds that will knock your eyes right out of their sockets."

"I believe that, if what the gals have been teaching me is any criterion. You have to be a mind-reader, an adagio dancer and a ground-and-lofty tumbler, and have an eidetic memory. But I *hope* I won't smash any of the girls' arches down or kick any of their faces in."

"Don't fish, darling. I *know* how good you are. Ain't I been practicing with you for lo, these many periods?"

At the dance it became clear that Seaton's statement was (as, it must be admitted, some of his statements were!) somewhat exaggerated. There was a great deal of acrobatics —Seaton and Sennlloy took advantage of every clear space to perform handspring-and-flip routines in unison. But everything was strictly according to what each person could do and wished to do. Thus, men and women alike danced with the Osnomians as though they were afraid of breaking them in two—which they were. And thus Lotus was, as Margaret had foretold that she would be, the belle of the ball. Hard-trained gymnast and acrobat that she was, her feet were off the floor most of the time; and before the dance was an hour old she was being tossed delightedly by her partner of the moment over the heads of half a dozen couples to some other man who was signalling for a free catch.

Three days before the *Skylark's* departure, Mergon announced that there would be a full-formal farewell party on the evening before the takeoff.

"What are you going to wear, Dick?" Crane asked.

Seaton grinned. "Urvan of Urvania's royal regalia. All of it. You?"

"I'm going as Tarnan, the Karbix of Osnome; with guns, knives, bracelets and legbands complete. And a pair of forty-fives besides."

"Nice! And I'll wear my three-fifty-sevens, then, too. If I can find a place to hang them on anywhere."

And Dorothy and Margaret each wore about eleven quarts of gems.

As the eight guests entered the dining hall—last, as protocol dictated—and the eight hundred Jelmi rose to their feet as one, the spectacle was something that not one of the six Tellurians would ever forget. DuQuesne had seen a few Jelmi in full formal panoply; but here were eight hundred of them!

After the sumptuous meal the tables vanished; music—a spine-tingling, not-too-fast march—swelled into being; and dancing began.

Dancing, if dancing it could be called, that bore no relationship whatever to the boisterous sport of which there had been so much. Each step and motion and genuflection and posture was stately, graceful, poised and studied. The whole was very evidently the finished product of centuries of refinement and perfection of technique. And at its close each of the eight honored guests was amazed to find that their movements had been so artfully yet inconspicuously guided that each of them had grasped hands once with every Jelm on the floor.

And on the way to their quarters Dorothy, her eyes brimming with unshed tears, pressed Seaton's arm against her side. "Oh, Dick, wasn't that simply *wonderful?* I could cry. Only once in my life before has anything ever hit me as hard as that did."

Well on the way back to Galaxy DW-427-LU, Seaton was humming happily to himself. He had gone through everything for the umpteenth time and for the umpteenth time had found everything good.

"Mart," he said. "We have now got exactly what it takes to make big medicine on those Chloran apes. The only question is, do we wipe 'em completely out now or do we let 'em suffer a while longer? Suffer in durance vile?"

If he had waited a few hours longer to speak so, he would have kept his mouth shut; for that same afternoon the *Skylark's* screens again went instantaneously into full-powered incandescent defense. The Brain took evasive action at once; but it was five long hours before they got far enough away from the source of that incredible flood of energy so that it became ineffective and was cut off. During that five hours Seaton and Crane observed and computed and analyzed and thought. When it was over, Seaton scanned the *Skylark's* reserve supply of power uranium; and his face was grim and hard when he called the others into conference.

"I wouldn't have believed it possible," he said flatly. "I can hardly believe it now, after watching it happen. Either they've been building stuff twenty-four hours a day ever since we left . . ." He paused.

"Or they've got myriads of myria-watts," Dunark said into that pause, "that they couldn't sync in then, but can now."

"Could be," Seaton agreed. "Let's see if we can find anything out. We're too far away to hold anything, even a planet. But with all of us looking we should be able to see something—and the gizmo can handle eight projections as easily as one. Has anybody got any better ideas?"

Since no one had, they tried it. "Riding the beam" is a weird sensation; a sense of duality of personality that must be experienced to be either appreciated or understood. The physical body is here; its duplicate in patterns of pure force is there: the two separate entities see and hear and smell and taste and feel two entirely different environments at the same time. It is a thing that takes some getting used to; but all the Skylarkers except Lotus were used to it. And she, as has been intimated, was a quick study.

Seaton could not hold the projections anywhere near any planet; could not hold them even inside a solar system. Even with the vernier controls locked and Seaton's hands resolutely off, the point of view jumped erratically about in fantastic leaps of hundreds of billions of miles. Not even the huge—and reinforced—mass of the *Skylark of Valeron* could hold them steady. They swept dizzily into the chromospheres of suns, out into the cold dark of interstellar vacuum, through tenuous gas clouds and past orbiting planets. In theory—if theory meant anything in this un-explored area—the fourth-dimensional "gizmo" should have been able to lock steadily on a target. In practice, they could hardly find a target to lock onto. All eight of the Skylarkers were synced in at once to the master controls, but their best efforts could not keep them even inside a solar system, much less give them the rock-steady fix that would have permitted them to spy on enemy activity.

And the magnitude of error grew. In a minute they were swinging in huge arcs of a parsec or more. In another min-ute the swings had become so enormous and so random that they could not measure them. Their speed was im-mense; they swung dizzyingly toward a cepheid variable and it winked at them like a traffic blinker, spun past a flare star and watched its great gouts of flame leap out and fall back.

Five minutes of this insane cavorting made half the party seasick, and they pulled out of projection and returned, gasping and staggering, to the welcome stability of the *Skylark*. Seaton stuck it out for half an hour. Then he pushed the "cancel" button.

"That's what I was afraid of," he growled. "Every time we wiggle a finger or a fly lights on a table it changes the shape of the whole ship. Oh, for something really *rigid* to build with!" (The eternal complaint of the precise worker in any field!) "But we each saw *something*. We'll report in turn."

Seaton gave a brief description of his own observations. He had seen something, no more than a flicker, but clearly big and Chloran-made. Dunark had spotted what sounded like the same planet-sized mass, but in the system of a G-3 star, as nearly as he could tell; Seaton's had been an F.

The others had seen nothing. Seaton nodded. "Okay. There are at least two solar systems having fortified Chloran planets, with one more probable. Ideas, anybody?"

Crane broke the ensuing silence. "I can't come up with anything constructive. Just the opposite. There's something basically wrong here, Dick. As I understand the Tammon-Seaton Theory, the operators involved here are all in the no-space-no-time field, so that distance does not enter. Hence it is possible in theory, and should be in practice, to place a bomb anywhere in all total space as accurately and as easily as you can touch the end of your nose with the tip of your finger."

Dorothy whistled, Dunark looked shocked, and the others looked blank. Seaton scowled and said, "Yeah . . . But with all points in total space coexistent—Gunther's Universe—how are you going to pick any given one out? What kind of an operator would it take? There's a hole, Mart, in either the theory or in the reduction . . ." He paused, frowning in thought.

"Or both," Crane said.

"Or both," Seaton agreed. "Okay, let's skip down and find it."

They went down and worked with the Brain all the rest of the day; but they did not find the hole. Nor did they find it the next day, or the next. Then Seaton began to pace the floor.

"So, in all probability, another breakthrough is required," Crane said. "And I can't help you on that; I'm not the genius type."

"Neither am I!" Seaton snorted. "In my book one flash-in-the-pan hunch does *not* make a genius . . . But here's another angle, fella. If this thing *can* be worked out it'll be so much better than that synchronization idea that it isn't funny. Also, it might not take the years to work out. Don't you think it'll be worth while, Mart, to spend a few days seeing if we can set it up as a problem? See if we can take it out of the pure brainstorm category before we spring it on Rovol?"

"I do indeed," and Seaton and Crane both went down to the control room and got into their master controllers.

However, before that task was finished there was a surprise for Richard Seaton.

27 • CO-BELLIGERENTS

"DuQuesne calling Seaton reply . . ."

Since Seaton's head was inside his master controller, no speaker sounded. Since everything pertaining to DuQuesne was on file in the Brain's memory banks, there was no delay whatever in making the proper connections: Seaton cut in before the first send of the message; short as it was, was completed.

"What the *hell*, DuQuesne!" his thought blazed out. "I didn't think even you would have the sublime guts to call on me again!"

"Save it, Seaton. This is important. Do you know how many solar systems of Chlorans there are in that galaxy where your *Skylark of Valeron* got burned out?"

Seaton paused for one microsecond. Then, cautiously:

"No idea. Hundred, maybe. Or, in view of this—thousands?"

"You aren't even warm. My apparatus put one hundred forty-nine million three hundred nineteen thousand two hundred ninety-seven of them into my tank before my scanners went out. And they hadn't covered a quarter of the galaxy yet."

"Je . . ." Seaton began, but shut himself up. Dorothy was listening in. "But to be able to use a sixth-order analsynth *that* long you must have had a little more . . . okay, gimme the dope."

DuQuesne told his story, including his superpowered *DQ* and his Fenachrone crew, concluding, "We knocked out over fifteen thousand of them before I had to run. But of course that wasn't a drop in the proverbial bucket. Worse, I doubt like the devil if any mobile base possible to build can ever get that close to them again. Apparently they sync in just enough stuff—no matter how much it takes—to cope with the maximum observed threat."

"Could be. But how come *you* are interested? I know damn well what *you* want."

"Not any more you don't," snapped DuQuesne's thought.

"With every two-bit Tom, Dick, and Harry of a race in all space having atomic energy already, what's the chance of a monopoly? So what good is Earth or anything else in the First Galaxy? I've changed my plans—you and Crane can both live forever, as far as I'm concerned."

Seaton absorbed and filed that statement—guardedly. He only said:

"So what? Why should you give a whoop about the Chlorans? Don't tell me you're altruistic all of a sudden."

"You apparently don't see the point. Listen—the Fenachrone *talked* about mastering the cosmos. That race of Chlorans is quietly and unobtrusively doing it. It may be too late to stop them; and I didn't help matters a bit by making them double or quadruple their synchronized output. You and I are, as far as we know, humanity's ablest operators. Each of us has stuff the other lacks. If you and I together can't stop them it can't—as of now—be done. What do you say?"

Seaton pondered. What was DuQuesne's angle this time? Or was the ape actually on the up and up? It did make sense, though—even though he was a louse and a heel and a case-hardened egomaniac, if it came down to a choice of which was going to be wiped out, those monsters or humanity . . . sure he would . . .

"Okay, Blackie. You give your word?"

"I give my word to act as one of your party until this Chloran thing is settled, one way or the other."

A few days later, the ultra-fast speedster that Seaton had left on Ray-See-Nee hailed the *Valeron,* matched velocities with her, and was drawn aboard. Three women disembarked; one of whom was Kay-Lee Barlo. She introduced her black-haired mother, Madame Barlo; who, with the added poise and maturity of her extra twenty-odd years, was even better-looking than her daughter. She in turn introduced her mother, Grand Dame Barlo, who did not have a single white hair in her thick brown thatch and who did not look more than half as old as she must in reality have been.

"But, listen," Seaton said. "You couldn't use any sixthorder stuff at first, so you must have been on the way for weeks. What happened? Trouble with the Chlorans?"

He had been talking to Kay-Lee, but her mother, who was very evidently the head of the party, answered him.

"Oh, no. That is, they've tripled the quotas—" Seaton shot a glance at Crane. *That* tied in!—"but with the new machinery that did not bother us at all. No. We learned many weeks ago that you would have need of us, so we came."

"Huh?" Seaton demanded, inelegantly. "What need?"

"We do not surely know. All we know is that it is written upon the Scroll that a time of need will come, and soon. All Ray-See-Nee is enormously and eternally in your debt: we are here to repay a tiny portion of that debt."

"Can't you tell me more about it than that?"

"A little; not much. We received your original message, but at that time there was nothing to connect it with you as Ky-El Mokak. In studying it we encountered something unknown upon Ray-See-Nee that increased a hundredfold our range and scope and strength: three *male* poles of power of tremendous magnitude, men who, we found out later, you already know. They are Drasnik and Fodan of the planet Norlamin and Sacner Carfon of Dasor. With three such pairs of poles of power—three is the one perfect number, you know—it was a simple matter to locate those interested in your message, to develop the powers that had been latent in such people as yourself—"

"What?" Seaton yelped. That was all he could get out.

"—and Dr. DuQuesne and others, yes," Madame Barlo went on smoothly. "You were, of course, not aware you possessed them."

"That's putting it mildly, ace," said Seaton. "You mean *I* am . . . I hate to use the word . . . well, 'psychic'?"

"The word is of no importance," said the woman impatiently. "Use any word you like. The fact is that you do have this power; we have developed it . . . and we now propose to put it to use."

Seaton's reply to that has not been recorded for posterity. Perhaps it is as well. Let it only be said that even twenty-four hours later he was no more than half-convinced . . . but it was the half of him that was convinced that was governing his actions.

One of the data that helped convince him was the fact that Madame Barlo and her daughter had not merely located these "poles of power"—they had summoned them to the *Skylark!* They had not waited for Seaton's concurrence; before Seaton even knew what they were up to, all the named individuals from three galaxies and a dozen planets were on the way.

A shipload of Norlaminians and Dasorians—including the three pre-eminent "male poles of power"—was the contingent first to arrive. Then came Tammon and Sennlloy and Mergon and Luloy and half a hundred other Jelmi; bringing with them three Tellurians: Madlyn Mannis, the red-haired stripper; Doctor Stephanie de Marigny of the Rare Metals Laboratory; and Charles K. van der Gleiss, Petrochemical Engineer T-8. And last, but by less than an hour, came Marc C. DuQuesne in person.

"Hi, Hunkie," he said, shaking hands cordially. "A little out of your regular orbit? Like me?"

"More than a little, Blackie—like you." She showed two deep dimples in a wide and friendly smile. "And if you have any idea of what I'm here for I'd be delighted to have you tell me what it is."

"I scarcely know what I'm here for myself," and Du-Quesne turned to the others; nodding at them as though he had left them only minutes before. He was no whit embarrassed or ill at ease; nor conscious of any resentment or ill-will directed at him. He was actually as unconcerned as, and bore himself very much like, a world-renowned specialist called into consultation on an unusually difficult case.

Before the situation could become strained, the three Rayseenian women came into the big conference room and approached the conference table—a table forty feet long and three feet wide.

Their faces were white; their eyes were wide and staring. All three were doped to the ears. "Doctor Seaton," Madam Barlo said, "you will cover the top of this table with one large sheet of paper, please?"

Seaton donned his helmet and a sheet of drafting paper covered exactly the table's top, adhering to it as though glued down.

"You mean to say, Doc, you're going along with this magic flummery?" one of the Jelmi asked.

"I certainly am," Seaton said. "You will leave the room until this test is over. So will everyone else with a mind closed to what these women are trying to do." The scoffer and two other Jelmi walked toward the door and Seaton quirked an eyebrow at DuQuesne.

"I'm staying," that worthy said. "I can't say that I'm a hundred per cent sold; but I'm interested enough to give it a solid try."

The two older women stationed themselves, one at each end of the table; Kay-Lee stood at her mother's right, holding in her hand a red-ink ballpoint at least a foot long.

Majestic Fodan, the Chief of the Five of Norlamin, stood

behind Madame Barlo, but did not touch her; Drasnik and Sacner Carfon stood similarly behind Grand Dame Barlo and Kay-Lee. Each of the three women rubbed a drop of something (it was actually Seaton's citrated blood) between thumb and forefinger and Madame Barlo said:

"You will all look fixedly at any one of the six of us and think of our success with everything that in you lies. Help us with all your might to succeed; give us your total mental strength. Kay-Lee, daughter, the time is . . . now!"

Reaching across the end of the table, Kay-Lee began to write a column eighteen inches wide; the height of which was to be the thirty-six-inch width of the table. When she got to the middle of the fourth line, however, a man gasped in astonishment and the pen's point stopped. This Jelm, a mathematician, had let his eyes slip from the operator to the paper—and what he saw was high—*very* high!—math! Mathematics of a complexity that none of those women, by any possible stretch of the imagination, could know anything about!

"Quit peeking!" Seaton snarled, "You're lousing up the whole deal! Concentrate! Think, dammit, THINK!"

Everyone resumed thinking and Kay-Lee resumed writing. She wrote smoothly and effortlessly, with the precision and with almost the speed of the operating point of a geometric lathe.

She wrote the first column and the second and the third and the fourth—six feet by three feet of tightly packed equations and other mathematical shorthand. Then came twelve feet of exquisitely detailed "wiring" diagram. Then, covering all the rest of the paper, came working drawings of and meticulously detailed specifications for machines that no one there had ever heard of.

Then all three women collapsed. As well they might; they had worked without a letup for three hours.

Men and women sprang to their aid with restoratives, and they began to recover.

"Mister Fodan," Madlyn Mannis said then, coming up to the Chief of the Five arm-in-arm with Stephanie de Marigny. Her usually vivid face was strangely pale. "I can understand Hunkie here having a place in a brawl like this, she's got half the letters in the alphabet after her name, but what good could I do? Possibly? I only went to school one day in my life and that day it rained and the teacher didn't come."

"Formal education does not matter, child; it is what you

intrinsically are that counts. You and your friend Charles are two perfectly matched male and female poles of tremendous power. You felt your paired power at work, I'm sure."

"Wel-l-l, I felt *something*." Madlyn looked up at her Charley, her eyes full of question marks. "My whole brain was full of . . . well, it was all kind of spizzly, like champagne tastes." And:

"That's it exactly," van der Gleiss agreed.

Kay-Lee, fully recovered now, looked in surprise at some of the equations she had written, then turned to Sacner Carfon. "Did it come out all right?" she asked hopefully. "Oh, I *hope* it did!"

"I think so," the porpoise-man replied. "At least, all of it I can understand makes sense."

The T-8 engineer stared at Kay-Lee. "But didn't you *know* what you were doing?"

"Of course she didn't." Again Madame Barlo did the talking. "None of us did, consciously. We are not masters of The Power, but Its servants. We are merely Its tools; the agents through which It does Its work."

And, off to one side, Dorothy was saying, "Dick, those women actually *are* witches! I *liked* Kay-Lee, too . . . but real, live, practicing *witches!* I got goose bumps as big as peas. I don't *believe* in witchcraft, darn it!"

"I don't either. That is, I never did before . . . but what else are you going to call it now?"

28 · PROJECT RHO

THE mathematicians and physical scientists began at once to study the wealth of new data. Drasnik, the First of Psychology, after conferring with Fodan, with Sacner Carfon and with each of the three witches in turn, actually rushed over to the group of Tellurians. It was the first time Seaton had ever seen an excited Norlaminian.

"Ah, youths of Tellus, I think you!" he enthused. "I thank you immensely for the inestimable privilege of meeting the ladies Barlo! They possess a talent that is indubitably of the most tremendous—"

"Talent?" Dorothy snorted. "Do you call *witchcraft* a talent? Why, the very idea of it makes me . . ." She paused.

"Uh-huh, me too," Madlyn agreed fervently. "If I have to believe in practicing witches I'll go not-so-slowly nuts."

"Witchcraft, my children? Bosh and fiddle-faddle! It is a *talent*. Extremely rare and lamentably rudimentary in our part of the universe, yet these women have it in astoundingly full measure. Unfortunately, you have no name for it except 'witchcraft', which term has deplorable connotations. It is the ability to . . . but the English has no words for that, either. But no matter, you have seen it in fine, full action. Fodan and Sacner and I each have a very little of it . . ."

"But those women couldn't *possibly* have known anything about that kind of stuff!" Madlyn protested.

"Of course they didn't. Richard here and Tammon and Doctor DuQuesne were the principal sources of information. But all three of them together lacked a great deal of having full knowledge, and the rest of us had very little indeed. While the comparison is lamentably loose, consider a large, finely cut jigsaw puzzle. Seaton and DuQuesne and Tammon could each assemble an area. But no two of the three areas were contiguous, while none of the rest of us could fit more than a very few pieces together. But the ladies Barlo—particularly Grand Dame Barlo, who is a veritable powerhouse of strength—with some little help from the rest of us, exerted and directed The Power. The Power that, by tapping the reservoir of infinite knowledge, enabled the scribe Kay-Lee to fill in the missing parts of the puzzle."

"But why . . ." Seaton began, but changed his mind. "I see. You didn't tell me anything about it because at that time it was both insignificant and inapplicable."

"That is correct. As I was saying, our Fodan, who has more of it than any other entity previously known, had perhaps the thousandth of what Kay-Lee, the weakest by far of the three, has. That is why he is Chief of the Five. And they tell me that there are other women of their race who also have this talent. Remarkable!" At this thought Drasnik, who had quieted down, became excited all over again. "When this is all over I shall go at once to Ray-See-Nee and study. Marvelous! They did not know even that it is a talent or that, when they learn, there will be no need to drug themselves into half-unconsciousness to employ it successfully. Thank you again, young friends, for this wonderful opportunity. Marvelous!" and Drasnik scurried away.

The Seatons and Madlyn and van der Gleiss stared after the Norlaminian until he was out of sight. They turned and stared at each other.

"Well . . . I'll . . . be . . . a . . . dirty . . . name," Madlyn said.

Seaton was pacing the floor, talking to Dorothy, emitting a cloud of smoke from his battered and reeking briar. "I like to do my thinking with you, ace."

She chuckled. "At me, you mean, don't you? That stuff is over my head like a beach umbrella."

"Don't fish, sweetie. You not only have a body and some hair, but also a brain. One that fires on all sixteen barrels all the time."

She laughed delightedly. "Thank you so much. You know that isn't true, but you also know how I lap it up and purr. But to proceed, Dunark wants to smash them all with planets, the way he was going to smash Urvania. Martin and Peggy, after talking the way they did, crawfished and are now talking about enclosing the whole galaxy in a stasis of time . . ."

"Huh? That's news to me. How's he figuring on doing it—did he say?"

"Uh-uh. I didn't talk to him. Peggy says he isn't going to say anything about it until he can present the package."

"He should live so long. But 'scue, please; go ahead."

"Only one more. Fodan, the simple-minded old darling, wants to *work* with them. *Convert* them!"

"Yeah. Make Christians of 'em. I've got a life-sized picture in technicolor of anybody ever accomplishing *that* feat. The trouble is, everybody wants to do something different and none of their ideas are any good at all."

"Oh? I noticed that you haven't been enthusiastic about any of them. Pretty grim, in fact. Why not?"

"Because none of 'em will come even close to getting 'em all and this has got to be a one hundred point zero zero zero per cent cleanup. You know how they operate on a cancer. They cut deep enough and wide enough to get it all. Every cell. If they don't get it all it spreads all over the body and the patient dies. This is a cancer. It's already eaten just about all of that galaxy by Chlora-typing planets wherever they go—or rather, enslaved humans are doing it for them—and it's spreading fast. And when that galaxy begins to get crowded they won't just jump to one other; they'll go for hundreds or thousands of galaxies and there goes the ball game. So that cancer has got to be operated on before it spreads any farther."

Dorothy's face began to pale. "By that analogy you mean destroy the whole galaxy! How can such a thing be possible? It can't *possibly* be possible!"

He told her how the operation could be performed. That apparatus that the Barlo women had dredged up out of nowhere had a lot of capabilities that did not appear on the surface. Blackie DuQuesne had perceived one set of those possibilities, and he and Blackie had been working on the hardware. They were calling it Project Rho.

Her face, already pale, turned white as he talked; and when he had finished:

"Project . . . Rho," she breathed. "How utterly horrible! And yet . . . I never dreamed . . . have you talked to Martin yet?"

"No. You first. I don't want to even think about pushing that kind of a button without being sure you're standing at my back."

"I'll do better than that, Dick," She looked him steadily in the eye. "I'll take half of it. My finger will be right beside yours on that button."

"You are an ace, ace. As maybe I've said once before."

"Uh-huh, at least once—but we're one, remember?"

After a moment she went on, "But we can't possibly sell the Norlaminians any such bill of goods as that."

"I'll say we can't. They'd cry their eyes out all over the place. Or wait. When they find out that they can't stop it, they'll help save the human planets, which will be all to the good; the witches can use the help. But basically, the grand slam will be up to DuQuesne and his Fenachrone and the witches and Mart and me. Even Mart will need some persuasion, I'm afraid; and you'll have to really work on Peg. She'll simply have a litter of kittens."

"Why, Dick; *what* a way to talk!" She smiled in spite of herself, but sobered quickly. "She'll come around, I'm sure; she'll have to. But Dick, is it actually physically possible? It's so *huge!*"

"Definitely. You see, we'll be operating in a Gunther universe, so that mass as such won't enter and power will be no problem. All we have to do is build an apparatus to alter the properties of space around and throughout the object to be moved—altering those properties in such a way as to make its three-dimensional attributes incompatible with those of its . . ."

She stopped him with an upraised hand. "Hold it! Wait up, please. We'll dispense with the high math, if you don't mind. It's the sheer *size* of the thing that scares me witless."

Seaton did grin then. "Well, you've always known that making things bigger and better is the fondest thing I am of. But we know exactly how to do it, and I think we can get it done before the Norlaminians finish theirs. But DuQuesne should be about ready to take off. I'll flip myself over there and see."

He did so and said, "How're you doing, Blackie?"

"A few minutes yet to finish final checking. I've been thinking. What kind of a celestial object will that galaxy be when we get done with it? Not a quasi-stellar, certainly; that's only a star with the energy of a hundred thousand million stars. This will be a galaxy with the energy of a hundred thousand million galaxies—the energy of an entire universe."

"Yeah. Something new, I'd say. It'll give some astronomers a thrill, some day. But what I can't compute is, whether or not it will sterilize the interstellar space of that galaxy," Seaton said.

"Well, if it doesn't, you might put the Osnomians and Urvanians on it. Keep 'em from thinking about fighting each other."

"You know, Blackie, I'd thought of doing exactly that? 'Great minds' and so forth. 'Bye now; be seein' ya," and Seaton flipped himself back home.

En route to his destination—barren planet in a starcluster on the opposite side of the galaxy from the *Skylark of Valeron*—DuQuesne again went into a huddle with Sleemet.

"So far, you've done a job," he began. "What I told you to do—what I knew how to do—and done it well. But nothing else. Now I want something more than that. Something you can do, if you will, that I can't. As you know, I've made arrangements so that in case of my death this whole planetoid goes up in an atomic blast. That was to keep you from killing me and making off with it. The same thing will happen, though, if those Chlorans kill me in the fracas that's coming. It would seem as though that fact would be enough to make you make an honest-to-God effort to be sure that they *don't* kill me by doing your damnedest to help me kill them. Mentally. Both you and the Chlorans know more about one phase of that than I do—as yet. So, as added inducement to really top effort, if you'll really tear into it on this Project Rho I'll teach you everything I know that you can take. And I'll help you build any kind of spacecraft you want before you leave; one even as big as this one. What do you say?"

Sleemet's strange eyes glowed. "If you will go mind to mind with me on that I can now assure you of such co-operation as no member of my race has ever given to any non-Fenachrone form of life," he declared; and DuQuesne handed him a headset.

It wasn't easy, not even for such an accomplished liar as Marc C. DuQuesne was, to make the four-dim gizmo very much more incomprehensible than it actually was; but he accomplished the feat—and he actually did give Sleemet practically everything else.

The *DQ* went into a one-day orbit above one point of an immense plain of the barren planet that was its goal. A plain some ten thousand square miles of which became forthwith an Area of Work. Enormous mechanisms sprang into being, by means of which DuQuesne and several hundred top-bracket Fenachrone engineers sent gigantic beams of force hurtling across the galaxy to the *Skylark of Valeron* and to hundreds of thousands of other micrometrically determined points.

But not Sleemet. That wight, knowing now almost everything that DuQuesne knew, was working in his own private laboratory—working with all the power of his tremendous mind on the various mental aspects of the battle of giants to come.

Hour after hour, Crane worked in his master control at the base of the Brain, with Madame Barlo and Drasnik and Margaret, each wearing an extra-complex headset, sitting close to him. They were mapping and modeling three galaxies, on such a large scale that the vast "tank" of the *Skylark of Valeron* was millions of times too small. They were using a discus-shaped volume of open space some ten light-years in diameter and three light-years thick.

Galaxy DW-427-LU was already meticulously in place; its every celestial body being represented by a characteristically colored light. "Above" Galaxy DW-427-LU and "below" it (the terms are used in the explanatory sense only; "on one side of" and "on the other side of" could be used just as well) as close to it as possible, two other galaxies were being modeled; each as nearly like DW-427-LU in size and shape as could be found in that part of the First Universe. They were so close together that in many places the three models actually interpenetrated.

Now in the space-time continuum of the strictly material —the plenum in which we ungifted human beings live and which our friends the semanticists would have us believe is the only one having any reality—the map is not the territory. That is taken as being axiomatic. In the demesne of The Talent, however, known to some scholars as psionics and to scoffers as magic or witchcraft, the map is—and *definitely!*—the territory.

Thus, as Madame Barlo and Drasnik, those two matched poles of tremendous power; and Crane, the superlatively able coordinator and his matching pole Margaret; and that immense Brain—as these five labored together, the "map" (in this case the meticulously accurate space-chart) became filled with tendrils and filaments of psionic force, connecting models of suns with models of suns and those of planets with those of planets. And as those joinings occurred in the map, the same joinings occurred in the actual galaxies out in deep space.

Those joinings were invisible, it is true, and intangible, and indetectable to any physical instrument. But they were nevertheless as real as was the almost infinite power from which they sprang.

The other pairs of psiontists were also hard at work. Fodan and Grand Dame Barlo, Sacner Carfon and Kay-Lee, Charles van der Gleiss and Madlyn Mannis, Mergon and his Luloy, Tammon and Sennlloy—all were shooting heavy charges fast and flawlessly straight. And as all those matched pairs labored, and as the automatics of pure psionic force they produced reproduced themselves in geometric ratio, the intergalactic couplings increased at a rate that was that ratio squared.

Seaton was fantastically busy, too. He was deep in his controller, with Dorothy and Stephanie de Marigny, both helmeted, one on each side of him. Dorothy, was, of course, his matched pole of power; Stephanie was his link to Du-Quesne. He, too, was operating a ten-thousand-square-mile Area of Work with the speed of thought and he was not making any mistakes. It is true that the *Skylark of Valeron* was the biggest thing he had ever built before, and that the members with which he was working now were parsecs instead of inches long. Nevertheless each one fitted perfectly into place and every one that was supposed to connect with anything of DuQuesne's connected perfectly therewith.

After many hours of this furiously grinding work, a myriad of hells began to break out, at the rate of hundreds of thousands per second. Of hells, that is, infinitely hotter than anything imaginable by man. Of super-novae, no less.

In one galaxy, A, a large hot sun vanished.

It reappeared instantaneously—with no lapse of time whatever—close beside the sun of a Chloran-dominated solar system in Galaxy DW-427-LU.

And in that same no-time the Tellus-type planet in the Chloran system vanished therefrom and reappeared in a precisely similar orbit around a Type G dwarf sun in Galaxy B, the third galaxy in the psiontists' tremendous working model.

And those two suns in the Chloran solar system in Galaxy DW-427-LU, with photospheres in contact and with intrinsic velocities not only diametrically opposed but increased horribly by their mutual force of gravitation, crashed together in direct central impact and splashed with tremendous force.

Except for the heat, the collision might have lasted for a long time. But heat was the all-important factor—the starkly incomprehensible heat of hundreds of millions of Centigrade degrees.

Each of those suns was already an atomic furnace in precise equilibrium; generating and radiating the energy of some five million tons per second of matter being converted completely into energy. Thus there was no place for the added energy of billions of tons of matter to go. It could not be absorbed and it could not be radiated. Therefore the whole enormous mass of super-hot, super-dense material began to go into the long series of ultra-atomic explosions that is the formation of a supersuper-nova—the most utterly, the most fantastically violent display of pure, raw energy known to or possible in the universe of man.

Flares and prominences of this insanely detonating material were hurled upward and outward for millions upon millions of miles. Shock-wave after shock-wave, so hellishly hot as to be invisible for days, raged and raved spherically outward; converting instantaneously all the flotsam in their paths into their own unknown composition or atomic and subatomic debris. Planets lasted a little longer. Oceans and mountain ranges boiled briefly; after which each world evaporated comparatively slowly, as does a drop of water riding a cushion of its own steam on a hot steel plate.

And the sphere of annihilation, ravening outward with unabated ferocity, reached and passed the outermost limits of the Chloran solar system and kept on going . . .

On and on . . .

And on . . .

Until there came to pass an event which not even Seaton, not even Madame Barlo herself had foreseen . . . and an event which nearly canceled all their efforts and their lives as well; for the Chlorans were not left without resources even in the destruction of their galaxy . . .

29 • DU QUESNE TO THE RESCUE

As has been said, the Chlorans of Galaxy DW-427-LU as a race were more conversant with the Talent than were any of the human or near-human races of the First Galaxy: that is, with the phases or facets of it that had to do with the remarkable hypnotic qualities of their minds. Thus their mathematicians were more or less familiar with no-space-no-time theory, and some of the Greater Great Ones had played with it a little more or less for fun, in practice. Since they had never had any real use for it as a weapon, however, it had never been fully developed.

Thus there were no detectors or feeling for that type of attack. "It was not sixth-order, but no-space-no-time, which is no-order." Thus millions upon millions of Chloran planets were destroyed without any intelligent entity either giving or receiving warning that an attack was being made.

And that was the way Richard Seaton wanted it. This was not a game; not a chivalric tournament. This was a matter of life and death, in which the forces of human civilization, outnumbered untold billions to one, needed all the advantage they could get.

Unfortunately for Seaton's desires and expectations, the Chlorans had a Galactic Institute for Advanced Study.

In common with all such institutions everywhere, its halls harbored at least one devotee of any nameable subject, however recondite or arcane that subject might be. So there was one old professor of advanced optical hypnosis who, as a hobby, had been delving into no-space-no-time for a couple of hundred years. He did not feel the light preliminary surveying tendrils of the human witches; but when the big Gunther beams began to come in he became interested fast and got busy fast.

He called his first assistant and his most advanced student —the latter a Greater Great One who was also interested in and a possessor of the Talent and thus familiar with the mysterious power of the number three—and, synchronizing their three minds, they traced those beams to the *Skylark of Valeron* and the *DQ*, and to Seaton and to Crane and to DuQuesne.

"First," the professor told his two weaker fellows, "we will attune our Union of Three to theirs and break it apart with blasts of psionic force. Then, each of us having tuned to one of the separated strands, we will kill the three murderers forthwith."

And the Chlorans proceeded to do their best to bring this event about—and their best was very potent indeed.

If things did not quite work out the way they had planned it, it was no fault of the individual Chlorans. Their minds were fully capable of killing three "murderers" at a distance. The first enormous surge of mental energy they thrust into the Tellurian union of minds destroyed its fabric. The coupling of "poles of power" was wrenched asunder. The individual minds of the operators were left alone against the Chloran thrust . . . and each of the three Chlorans selected one of the three mightiest intellects of their enemies and commanded it to die.

In that moment, Seaton, Crane and DuQuesne were seized and pinned. The minds that thundered destruction at them were not merely of great intrinsic power, carefully trained: they were backed up by all the million-year evolution of Chloran science, aided by the impact of total surprise.

The three helpless Tellurians were helpless before they knew what hit them.

But they did not die. What saved them was DuQuesne's bargain with the Fenachrone. Sleemet had had a few microseconds' warning by that Fenachrone ferocity, and the backing of every last member of his feral race.

His primary purpose was, of course, the defense of DuQuesne's life—not for the sake of DuQuesne, to be sure, but for the protection of the Fenachrone. He succeeded. DuQuesne's rigidity melted and he was back in control of himself, his own great intellect reinforcing Sleemet's counterblows. The two of them had enough psionic power left over to help Seaton and Crane . . . but not enough. The blow had been too powerful and too sudden.

Both Seaton and Crane slumped bonelessly to the floor of the control room, leaving their controllers empty and idle.

In that moment the one great pole of strength left to humankind was—Dr. Marc C. DuQuesne.

To Dorothy Seaton, that moment was pure horror. It was every terrible fear she had ever thought of, all come to pass at once: Seaton disabled, perhaps dying; DuQuesne in control of all the mighty resources of the *Skylark*. Dorothy shrieked and leaped from her chair—

And was stopped in her tracks by DuQuesne's shout, crackling out of a speaker to emphasize his hard-driven thoughts:

"Dorothy! Margaret! Quit it! Pick up your loads and *carry* 'em. Pole to me!"

And Dorothy hesitated, irresolute, torn between her love for Seaton and her urgent duty to help against the Chlorans, while the whole vast net of human mental energies wavered and hung in the balance.

"Now!" snarled DuQuesne, the thought like a lash. "Move! To hell with the dead—" Dorothy screamed again —*"you're* still alive! But you won't be long if you goof off!" Rapidly he scanned the quavering net. "You Barlo women and your poles! Drop what you're doing and locate this interference for me—*fast!* All of you—find it for me so I can slug it! Hunkie? Yeah—good girl! Stay with it just as you are!"

"But DuQuesne," Dorothy protested, "I've *got* to . . ."

"Oh, *hell!*" DuQuesne wrenched out, every nuance of his tone showing the tremendous strain under which he was laboring. "Savant Sennlloy! You can't be spared from there, but have you got a couple of girls who can tune themselves to me?"

"Yes, Doctor DuQuesne." Neither she or any other Jelm aboard understood why Seeker Sevance of Xylmny had been masquerading as Doctor Marc C. DuQuesne of Tellus when he received his Call. They all knew, however, that it had to do with his Seeking; hence none of them did anything to interfere with it. "We have many very good mentalists in our party."

"Fine! Have two of 'em relieve these two weak sisters here—and fast!"

"Here we are, sir," two thoughts came in, in unison. And two powerful female Jelman minds—the minds of two girls with whom he was already very well acquainted—fitted themselves snugglingly to his and picked up the loads that the two Earthwomen had been unable to carry.

It was not that either of those Earthwomen was weak. Both were tremendously strong; mentally and psychically. Both disliked DuQuesne so intensely, however, that it was psychologically impossible for either of them to work with him. Of course, he regarded that fact itself as an extreme weakness. Sentiment was as bad as sentimentality, he held, and both bored him to tears.

"Ah, that's better." DuQuesne's thought was a sigh of relief. "That makes it at least possible."

And it did. DuQuesne and his two new assistants did not do much to keep the wave of destruction sweeping through Galaxy DW-427-LU, but he and they, with a lot of very high-powered Fenachrone help, did hold the Chloran attackers at bay until the three witches and the three warlocks found the planet upon which the Chloran Galactic Institute of Advanced Study was located. Then, with locked teeth and hard-set muscles and sweating face, he made the superhuman effort required to drive that three-man beam single-handed and keep those three rabid Chloran attackers at bay besides.

By a miracle of coordination and timing he did it—and practically collapsed when all attack and all necessity of resistance ceased. The Chloran Institute simply ceased to be. Its members died. DuQuesne recovered so quickly that no one else except the two Jelman girls knew that he had been affected at all.

"Dorothy! Margaret! Break it up!" he snapped. Doctors had been working on Seaton and Crane for minutes. Both were beginning to recover consciousness. Neither, apparently, had been permanently damaged; and both their wives were making enthusiastically joyful noises. "Come on, come on, take them home to do your slobbering over them. The rest of us have work to do—or do you expect us to hold this demolition job up until they organize another threesome to go to the mat with us?"

Stretchermen carried Seaton and Crane away; Dorothy and Margaret went along. The Chloran blow at the lives of the two Skylarkers had been deadly and fast, but it had not succeeded—quite.

And the "demolition job" went on.

In the great light-years-thick "tank" that was the psiontists' working model of the three galaxies they were manipulating, lights were winking out and reappearing as stars and planets were hurled through four-dimensional curves to new orbits and positions. Already Galaxy A—the "raw-material" source that was being used for a supply of suns—was visibly dimmer, visibly poorer in stars. Tens of millions of them had already been stolen away and tossed through four-space into Chloran suns in Galaxy DW-427-LU. And when they reappeared, in a head-on collision course with those Chloran suns, and struck, and destroyed themselves in the titanic outflow of energies that produced super-nova blasts, the model of Galaxy DW-427-LU showed another tiny but blindingly bright flare—and another—and another—

There were more than fifty thousand million suns to move, in all. As the first targets had been the strongest and most dangerous Chloran systems, resistance soon ceased to matter; the task became monotonous, exhausting and mind-deadening.

To the Chlorans, of course, it was something else again. They died in uncounted trillions. The greeny-yellow soup that served them for air boiled away. Their halogenous flesh was charred, baked and desiccated in the split-second of the passing of the wave front from each exploding double star, moments before their planets themselves began to seethe and boil. Many died unaware. Most died fighting. Some died in terrible, frantic efforts to escape . . .

But they all died.

And for each sun that DuQuesne's remorseless net located and flung into the Chloran galaxy, an oxygen-bearing, human-populated planet was snatched out of the teeth of the resulting explosion and carried through four-space into the safety of Galaxy B, there to slip quietly into orbit around a pre-selected, hospital sun. No human world was destroyed in all of Galaxy DW-427-LU.

It went on and on . . .

And then it was over.

Marc DuQuesne rose, stretched and yawned. "That's all. Everybody dismissed," he said, and at once the vast psiontic net ceased to be. He was alone for the first time in many hours.

His face was lined, his eyes deeper and darker than ever. Apart from that there was no sign of the great extermination he had just conducted. He was simply Marc DuQuesne. The man who slew a galaxy looked no different after the deed than he had before.

He allowed his sense of perception to roam for a moment about the "working model". In Galaxy A, where billions of suns had gone through the stellar cycle of evolution for billions of years, there was scarcely a corporal's guard of primaries left. It was a strange, almost a frightening sight. For with the loss of the suns the composition of the galaxy had changed to something never before seen in all the plenum of universes. Nearly every sun had had planets; nearly every planet remained behind when its sun was stolen. Now they roamed at random—uncontrolled, barren, uninhabited—lacking not only the light and heat of their primaries, but freed from their gravitational reins as well.

Galaxy B, on the other hand, looked quite normal—in "working model". The planets it had acquired, both from the "working model". The planets it had acquired, both from the exploded Chloran suns and from the looted solar systems of Galaxy A, were not even visible. Galactically speaking, it was essentially unchanged; the additional mass of a few billion planets did not matter, and each of the new planets was already in orbit around a friendly sun. There would be readjustments, of course. It would be necessary to keep a watch on the developments of each affected solar system, over a period of years. But that was no problem of Marc DuQuesne's.

But the Chloran galaxy! What *was* it?

In the "working model" it was rapidly becoming a single, light-years-thick concentration of living flame. In the reality it was even huger, even more deadly. A name would be invented for it some day—quasi-stellar? Or something greater still?

But that, too, was no longer a concern for Marc Du-Quesne. He dropped from his mind, without a qualm, the memory of the trillions of lives he had taken, the billions of worlds he had dislocated. He ignored the question of Richard Ballinger Seaton, now stirring back to consciousness, to worry—and ultimately, to reassurance—somewhere on the *Valeron*. He had more pressing business to take care of. Personal business. And to DuQuesne that was the most pressing of all.

Shrugging his shoulders, he sent Stephanie de Marigny a tight-beamed thought:

"Hunkie—some time before you go back to Washington, can I flip you over to the *DQ* for a private conference that we know will be private?"

Her beautifully dimpled smile flashed on. "I should say not! You know I'm not *that* kind of a . . ." she began; then, as she perceived how much in earnest he was, she changed tone instantly and went on, "Of course, Blackie. Any time. Just give me time to pack a toothbrush and my pajamas. Top Secret, or can you give me a hint to allay my 'satiable curiosity?"

"Hint; large economy size. Every time I think of what those damned observers are doing to you—feeding a mind like *yours* with an eye-dropper instead of a seventy-two-inch pipeline—it makes me madder and madder. I can give you everything that Seaton, I, Crane and half the Norlaminians know, and give it to you in five hours."

"You can *what?*" The thought was a mental scream. She licked her lips, gulped twice, and said, "In that case we needn't wait for either toothbrush or pajamas. Do it now."

He laughed deeply. "I wasn't sure that would be your attitude, but I'm glad it is. But I can't do it this minute. I have to help Sleemet finish building his planetoid, watch him very carefully for a while on course and do a couple of other crash-pri chores. Three or four days, probably. Say Saturday, seventeen hours?"

"That'll be fine, Blackie, and thanks. I'll be here with my ears pinned back and my teeth filed down to needle points."

30 · EMPEROR

THE Fenachrone had taken off and DuQuesne had watched them go, taking extreme precautions—none of which, it turned out, had been necessary—that they did not eliminate

either him or the rest of the party as soon as it became safe
for them to do so. He had taken Stephanie de Marigny and
all her belongings aboard, saying that he was going close
enough to Tellus so that it would be no trouble at all to
drop her off there. And lastly, when Seaton and Crane had
insisted upon thanking him for what he had done:

"Save it," he had sneered. "Remember, that time on X-
World, what I told you to do with that kind of crap! That
still goes," and he had taken off at full touring drive on
course one seven five Universal. This course, which would
give the First Galaxy a near miss, was the most direct route
to a galaxy that was distant indeed; the galaxy lying on the
extreme southern rim of the First Universe; the galaxy in
which the *DQ* had been built; the galaxy that DuQuesne
had surveyed so thoroughly and which he intended to rule.

DuQuesne and Stephanie were in the *DQ's* control room,
which was an exact duplicate of the *Skylark of Valeron's.*
He placed her in the seat that on the *Valeron* was Crane's,
showed her how to elevate herself into his own station.

"Oh," she said. "You're going to give me the whole
gigantic Brain?"

"That's the best and easiest way to do it. I boiled down
about ten thousand lifetimes of knowledge and experience
into ten half-hour sessions. The ten tapes on that player
there are coded instructions for the Brain—what to give
you and how. There are minds who could take the whole
jolt in seconds, but yours and mine aren't that type—yet.
But you'll get it all in five hours. Every detail. It'll shock
you all hell's worth and it'll scare you right out of your
panties, but it won't hurt you and it won't damage your
brain. Yours is one of the very few human brains that *can*
take it. I'll start it and in five hours I'll be back. Ready?"

"As much so as I ever will be, I guess. Go."

He started the player; and, after waiting a few minutes
to be sure that everything was going as programmed, he
left the room . . .

He came back in just as the machine clicked off, lowered
her "chair," and lifted her to her feet.

"Good—God—In—Heaven!" she gasped. Her skin, normally so dark, was a yellowish white; so pale that her scat-
tered freckles stood out sharply, each one in bold relief.
"I don't . . . I can't . . . I simply can't *grasp* it! I know
that I know it, but . . ." She paused.

He shook his head in sympathy. Which, for Marc C.
DuQuesne, was a rare gesture indeed. "I know. I couldn't

tell you what it would be like—no possible warning can be enough. But that's the bare minimum you'll have to start with, and it won't take you very long to assimilate it all. Ready for some talk?"

"Not only ready, I'm eager. First, though, I want to give you a vote of full confidence. I'm sure that you'll succeed in everything you try from now on; even to becoming Emperor Marc the First of some empire."

"Huh? Where did you get *that?*"

"By reading between the lines. Do you think I'm stupid, is that why you gave me all this?"

"Okay. You've always known, as an empirical, non-germane fact, that the Earth and all it carries isn't even a fly-speck in a galaxy, to say nothing of a universe; but now you know and really understand just how little it actually does amount to."

She shuddered. "Yes. It's . . . it's appalling."

"Not when viewed in the proper perspective. I set out to rule Earth, yes; but after I began to learn something I lost that idea in a hurry. For a long time now I haven't wanted Earth or any part of it. Its medical science is dedicated whole-heartedly to the deterioration of the human race by devoting its every effort to the preservation of the lives of the unfit. In Earth's wars its best men—its best breeding stock—are killed. Earth simply is not worth saving even if it could be saved; which I doubt. Neither is Norlamin. Not because its conquest is at present impossible, but because the Norlaminians aren't worth anything, either. All they do —all they *can* do—is think. They haven't done anything constructive in their entire history and they never will. They're such bred-in-the-bone pacifists—look at the way the damned sissies acted in this Chloran thing—that it is psychologically impossible for any one of them to pull a trigger. No; Sleemet had the right idea. And Ravindau— you have him in mind?"

"Vividly. Preserve the race—in *his* way and on *his* terms.*"

"You're a precisionist; that's my idea exactly. To pick out a few hundred people—we won't need many, as there are billions already where we're going—as much as possible like us, and build a civilization that will be what a civilization ought to be."

The girl gasped, but her eyes began to sparkle. " 'In a distant galaxy', as Ravindau said?"

"Very distant. Clear out on the rim of this universe. The

last galaxy out on the rim, in fact; five degrees east of Universal south."

"And you'll be Emperor Marc the First after all. But you won't live long enough to rule very much."

"You're wrong, Steff. The ordinary people are already there, and it's ridiculous for a sound and healthy body to deteriorate and die at a hundred. We'll live ten or fifteen times that long, what with what I already know and the advances our medical science will make. Especially with the elimination of the unfit."

"Sterilization, you mean?"

"No; death. Don't go soft on me, girl. There will be no second-class citizens, at least in the upper stratum. Testing for that stratum will be by super-computer. Upper-stratum families will be fairly large."

"Families?" she broke in. "You've come to realize, then, that the family is the *sine qua non* of civilization?"

"I've always known that." Forestalling another interruption with a wave of his hand, he went on, "I know. I've never been a family man. On Earth or in our present cultures I would never become one. But skipping that for the moment, it's your turn now."

"I like it." She thought in silence for a couple of minutes, then went on, "It must be an autocracy, of course, and you're the man to make it work. The only flaw I can see is that even absolute authority can not make a dictated marriage either tolerable or productive. It automatically isn't, on both counts."

"Who said anything about dictated marriage? Free choice within the upper stratum and by test from the lower. With everybody good breeding stock, what difference will it make who marries whom?"

"Oh. I see. That does it, of course. Contrary to all appearances, then, you actually do believe in love. The implication has been pellucidly clear all along that you expect . . ."

" 'Expect' is too strong a word. Make it that I'm 'exploring the possibility of'."

"I'll accept that. You are exploring the possibility of me becoming your empress. From all the given premises, the only valid conclusion is that you love me. Check?"

"The word 'love' has so many and such tricky meanings that it is actually meaningless. Thus, I don't know whether I love you or not, in your interpretation of the term. If it means to you that I will jump off of a cliff or blow my brains out if you refuse, I don't. Or that I'll pine away and not marry a second best, I don't. If, however, it means a lot of other things, I do. Whatever it means, will you marry me?"

"Of course I will, Blackie. I've loved you a long time."